RUN

with the

WIND

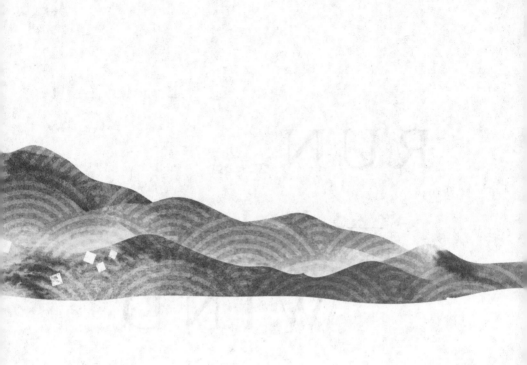

Shion Miura

Translated from the Japanese by Yui Kajita

RUN
with the
WIND

A Novel

HarperVia

An Imprint of HarperCollins*Publishers*

RUN WITH THE WIND. Copyright © 2006 by Shion Miura. English translation copyright © 2024 by Yui Kajita. All rights reserved. Printed in the United States of America. No part of this book may be used or reproduced in any manner whatsoever without written permission except in the case of brief quotations embodied in critical articles and reviews. For information, address HarperCollins Publishers, 195 Broadway, New York, NY 10007.

HarperCollins books may be purchased for educational, business, or sales promotional use. For information, please email the Special Markets Department at SPsales@harpercollins.com.

Originally published as *Kaze ga Tsuyoku Fuiteiru* in Japan in 2006 by SHINCHOSHA Publishing Co., Ltd. English-language rights arranged with SHINCHOSHA Publishing Co., Ltd through Emily Agency, Ltd.

FIRST HARPERVIA HARDCOVER PUBLISHED OCTOBER 2024

Designed by Janet Evans-Scanlon
Title page and chapter-opening art © marukopum/Shutterstock
Illustration on page viii reprinted with permission ©YAMAGUCHI Akira

Library of Congress Cataloging-in-Publication Data has been applied for.

ISBN 978-0-06-333089-4

24 25 26 27 28 LBC 5 4 3 2 1

The Eight Leagues of Hakone

Mount Hakone is the most savage in the world:

far more formidable than Hanguguan,

its peaks soaring to lofty heights, its ravines plunging deep.

Onwards, the steep hill towers over the wanderer;
    behind, the deep valley hinders.

A sea of clouds swirls around the ridges; fog obscures the valleys.

The thick forest of cedars darkens the day;

the winding paths are slippery with moss.

One guarding the pass will thwart an army of thousands.

The fearless warrior roams across the country,

a sword on his waist, shod in tall geta,

clacking over the ragged boulders across the weary road—

such was the bearing of the bygone warrior.

Words by Makoto Torii
Music by Rentaro Taki
First published in 1901 in *Chūgaku Shōka*
(Songbook for Students of Secondary School)

Contents

An illustration of Chikusei-so

AKIRA YAMAGUCHI

Prologue

Even in a place like this, only about a twenty-minute walk away from Kanpachi-dori, Tokyo Circular Route 8, in the opposite direction from the big city, the air cleared at night. On sunny days, warning alerts for photochemical smog were broadcast all day long, but at night, it felt like a different world. A hush fell over the residential neighborhood lined with rows of small houses, dotted by a few lonely streetlights.

As he traced the maze of narrow, one-way alleys, Haiji Kiyose looked up at the sky. It was no match for the starry night sky of his hometown in Shimane, but still, he could make out tiny specks of light here and there.

Wouldn't mind seeing a shooting star, he thought, but nothing stirred in the sky.

A breath of wind skimmed his neck. Though it was nearly April, the nights were still cold. The chimney at Tsuru no Yu, a bathhouse he frequented, rose above the low rooftops of the houses around him.

Kiyose stopped looking at the sky and, burying his chin in the padded collar of the dotera jacket he had flung on, quickened his pace toward Tsuru no Yu.

Bathhouses in Tokyo were too hot for him. Tonight, he dipped in the bath after washing himself in the shower as always, but the sheer heat of the water drove him out in no time. That made the local plasterer, another regular at the bathhouse, chuckle from his seat in the washing area.

"Your baths never last more than a second, Haiji."

If Kiyose left now, he wouldn't get his money's worth, so he sat down again on the plastic stool in front of the showers. He peered into the mirror and shaved with the razor he'd brought in with him. The plasterer sauntered past behind him and sunk into the bath with a deep, satisfied groan.

"You know us Edo kids, we've always said a proper bath's got to bite your ass. That's how steaming hot it should be."

The old man's voice echoed in the tiled room under the high ceiling. There was no sign of life from the women's bath next door. Over at the watch seat, the owner of the bathhouse looked bored; he'd started plucking out his nose hairs a short while ago. Apparently, his only customers for the night were Kiyose and the plasterer.

"Every time you say that, I think it's a good way to put it, but there's one thing I don't get," said Kiyose.

"What's that?"

"We're not in old downtown Tokyo. This is uptown Yamanote, so not exactly the place for Edo natives."

Kiyose finished shaving his face and approached the bathtub again. Eyeing his neighbor to keep him in check, Kiyose twisted the faucet and added cold water to the boiling hot bath. The cool liquid rippled through the bath, blending into the heat. Once he made sure it was mixed enough, he lowered himself into the tub. He hogged the space around the faucet and stretched out his legs in the water, now mellow enough not to scald him.

"If you can tell the difference between downtown and uptown round here, you're getting to be a local." The plasterer seemed to give up any claim on the faucet. He glided over to the other corner of the bathtub, away from the water that was growing tepid.

"Well, I've been living here for four years now," Kiyose responded.

"How're things going down at Chikusei-so? Does it look like all the rooms will be filled up this year?"

"There's only one room left, but we'll see."

"Hope you find someone."

"Me too," Kiyose agreed. And he really meant it. *It's my last year, and I'm finally getting my big chance. Just one more person to go.* He cupped some bathwater in his hands and rubbed his face. There was no way around it: he simply needed one more person.

The hot water nipped his cheeks—maybe it was razor burn.

Kiyose left the bathhouse with his neighbor. They strolled down the quiet street, the old man pulling his bicycle along. Thanks to the hot bath, Kiyose didn't feel the cold at all. Just as he was debating whether to take off his thick dotera, he heard pounding footsteps and angry shouts from behind.

He turned around and saw the shadows of two men in the distance, rushing pell-mell down the narrow path. One of them was running toward Kiyose, his arms and legs slicing the air in precise strokes as he left behind the other man, who was shouting something at him. As Kiyose and the plasterer watched, the runner rapidly approached them, and by the time Kiyose registered that he looked young, the man had already whizzed past them on the side of the alley. The second man wearing a convenience store apron was chasing after him, though he was lagging far behind.

The young man had been breathing steadily as he brushed past Kiyose's shoulder. Kiyose almost started to run after him, but the plasterer's disapproving grumble checked his impulse: "A shoplifter—what a shame."

At that, Kiyose realized that the salesclerk must have been yelling, "Stop him!" as the shoplifter ran past. But the clerk's voice had sounded like a jumble of meaningless sounds to Kiyose's ears. Kiyose had been too spellbound by the young man's stride, how his legs propelled his body forward like a well-oiled machine.

Kiyose grabbed the handles of the old man's bike. "Let me borrow this."

He pedaled as hard as he could without bothering to sit down, leaving his wide-eyed neighbor behind as he chased after the young man who had disappeared into the night.

He's the one. He's the one I've been looking for all this time.

This conviction flared up inside him like magma erupting from a dark crater. There was no way Kiyose could lose sight of the runner. A single trail of light gleamed through the narrow alleys in his wake. The streak of light guided Kiyose, like the Milky Way crossing the night sky, like the scent of a sweet flower luring an insect.

Wind filled his dotera, and it billowed out behind him. Finally, the bike lights caught the runner. Every time Kiyose pushed down on the pedals, the white circle of light swayed from side to side across the man's back.

Kiyose observed the man's run while struggling to contain his excitement. A balanced form. A single straight line went down the runner's spine like an axis. His legs stretched out free and easy below his knees. His shoulders weren't stiff with excessive tension, and his ankles looked flexible, absorbing the shock of each landing. Light and supple, yet powerful, too. Sensing Kiyose's presence, the runner cast him a sideways glance as they passed under a streetlight. When Kiyose saw the man's profile illuminated in the dark, he let out a murmur of surprise.

So it was you, he thought.

An indescribable feeling roiled inside Kiyose—whether it was delight or fear, he couldn't tell. Only one thing was clear: he was on the cusp of something about to begin.

He sped up and came abreast of the runner. Then, without meaning to—as if under the spell of some obscure presence or spurred on by a call from the deepest pit of his being—the question burst out of him: "Do you like to run?"

The runner stopped abruptly, turning to face Kiyose with an expression that hovered between troubled and angry. His glinting eyes, concealing a fierce passion in their boundless black depths, threw the question back at Kiyose: *And what about you? Can you answer a question like that?*

In that instant, Kiyose realized something. If happiness, or beauty, or goodness existed in this world, for him, they would take the form of this runner.

This flash of conviction would live on in Kiyose and continue to glow long afterward. Like the beacon cast by a lighthouse across a dark, raging ocean, the beam of light would unfailingly illuminate the path he was to take.

The light would remain with him always, unchanging.

I

THE RESIDENTS OF CHIKUSEI-SO

Who knew running could be so useful?

The rubber soles of Kakeru Kurahara's shoes pummeled the hard asphalt. He laughed silently, relishing the sensation of his feet striking the ground.

He softened the impact of each stride by letting it flow smoothly from the tip of his toes into every muscle in his entire body. Wind whistled by his ears. He was heating up just under his skin. Without any conscious thought on his part, Kakeru's heart pumped out blood throughout his frame, and his lungs drew in air in a steady rhythm. His body grew lighter and lighter. He could keep on running forever.

But the question was, to where? And for what?

The thought reminded him why he was running at the moment, and he slackened his pace a little. He listened intently for anyone who might be chasing after him. The angry shouts and footsteps were gone now. The bag of sweet pastry was rustling in his hand. As though to destroy the evidence, he opened it and wolfed down the bread as he ran. He wondered what to do with the empty bag for a moment before stuffing it into the pocket of his hoodie. He knew the bag itself would be concrete proof he'd stolen the pastry, but still, he couldn't bring himself to throw it away on the side of the road. *Funny how that works,* he thought.

Nobody cared what he did anymore, but Kakeru didn't miss a single day of training. It was an ingrained habit—just as he couldn't allow himself to litter the street. He'd been taught that it was a bad thing to do from when he was little.

Whenever someone taught him something, as long as he thought it was reasonable, he'd faithfully abide by it. Once he set a rule, he held himself to it with the utmost rigor.

Perhaps the pastry had made his blood sugar level spike. His legs started kicking against the ground at a regular pace again. Feeling his heartbeat, he focused on his own breathing. He fixed his gaze on his feet and the road slightly ahead of him, his eyelids half-closed. He looked only at the tips of his feet striding forward by turns and the single white line drawn on the black asphalt.

Kakeru ran, tracing the thin line.

Though he couldn't bring himself to litter, he didn't feel any guilt for stealing the bread. He only felt satisfied to soothe his sharp pangs of hunger.

I'm like an animal, he thought. Through daily training, Kakeru had built up a stable, resilient body. He'd stolen a bag of pastry from a convenience store because he'd been too famished to do anything else. In that sense, he was no different from a beast, going around on a set route in his territory and pouncing on his prey when the need arose.

Kakeru's world was simple and brittle. He ran. He ingested sources of energy in order to run. That was basically it. Everything else was just vague, undefinable things undulating inside him. But sometimes, he could hear someone howling from within the wavering haze.

As he ran swiftly through the night, Kakeru replayed a scene in his head, the same images that had been coming back to haunt him for the past year or so. Rage so violent that his vision turned bright red. The fist he'd swung as hard as he could.

Maybe this is what regret feels like. The howl he heard from deep within must be the sound of his own voice reproaching him.

He couldn't take it anymore. He let his eyes wander over the scene around him. Thin branches stretched out to form a mesh over the path. They would start budding soon, but he couldn't see any soft flecks of green yet. A single, glimmering star hung from the tip of a branch. The empty bag in his pocket rustled like footfalls on dead leaves.

Kakeru suddenly sensed a presence near him, and his spine tensed.

It was chasing him. Something was hunting him down. The creaking of rusty metal was drawing closer. Even if he clamped his hands over his ears, he would still have felt the sensation through his skin. He'd had a taste of it countless times at track meets. The rhythm of another organism shaking the ground. The sound of breathing. The moment when a different smell enters the wind.

A thrill ran through Kakeru's body and spirit—a rush he hadn't felt in a long time.

But he wasn't running on the track that drew an infinite oval in an athletic field. He turned abruptly onto a side street bordering an elementary school. His speed rose steadily. No one was going to catch him. He was determined to lose the pursuer.

All the roads in this neighborhood, whether private or public, were narrow paths crisscrossing in a complex network, which meant many of them led to cul-de-sacs. Kakeru proceeded deftly, careful not to be cornered in a dead end. He dashed past the elementary school windows, which were so dark they looked like they had been painted by the night. He hurtled on as he looked sideways at the campus of the private university that he was supposed to start attending this spring.

He came to a slightly wider road. He almost turned right in the direction of the Circular Route 8, but he decided to keep running straight through the residential neighborhood.

He crossed the street without stopping—the traffic light was on his side. His footsteps rang out in the quiet streets. But the pursuer seemed just as familiar with the lay of the land, and Kakeru could feel him drawing closer and closer.

Once again, Kakeru realized that he wasn't just running, but running away. A surge of frustration and regret clogged his throat. *I'm always running away.* Now he was even more desperate to keep moving. If he stopped here, it would mean admitting to himself that he was running away from something.

A faint white light lit up the ground around his feet. The source of the light, which swayed slightly from side to side, clung to him, unwilling to let him go.

When he finally realized that his pursuer was on a bike, Kakeru shook his head at himself. Though he'd surely heard that creaking, metallic sound, the thought hadn't even occurred to him that whoever it was could be riding a bike. But Kakeru should have known from experience that hardly anyone could keep up with his speed on foot.

Now the race felt ridiculous, and Kakeru glanced back. A young man was pedaling a typical mamachari, one of those casual city bikes with a front basket. It was too dark to make out the stranger's expression, but he wasn't from the convenience store. He didn't have an apron on, for one thing. This guy was wearing an old-fashioned padded jacket and plain massage sandals, the kind with acupressure bumps on the inner soles.

What the hell?

Just to see what his pursuer would do, Kakeru slowed down. Creaking like a rickety water mill, the bike drew up next to him like it was the most natural thing in the world.

Kakeru stole a sideways glance at the guy. He had a simple, open face, and his hair was wet; apparently, he'd just gotten out of a bath. For some reason, there were two plastic bath bowls in the basket. The stranger was looking at Kakeru, too—especially at his legs. Slightly creeped out, Kakeru hoped the man wasn't some kind of pervert.

The man was silent, pedaling next to Kakeru while keeping a slight distance between them. Kakeru also maintained a steady pace, watching for his next move. *Did that salesclerk ask him to chase after me, or is he a random dude passing by?* Just as Kakeru felt he might explode with anxiety and irritation, a serene voice washed over him like the sound of distant waves.

"Do you like to run?"

Kakeru stopped dead in surprise—as if the road in front of him had suddenly fallen away, and he was stuck, bewildered, on the edge of a precipice. He stood rooted to the spot in the middle of the dark, quiet street, his heart pounding in his ears. The bike screeched to a halt. Kakeru slowly turned around to face the stranger. The man, straddling the bike, was staring back intently. After a few beats, Kakeru registered that the question had come from this man in front of him.

"Don't stop so suddenly. Let's cool down a bit," the man said.

He started pedaling again at an easy pace. *Why should I follow you? I don't even know who you are*, Kakeru thought. But he still jogged after the man as if pulled by strings.

As he stared at the back of the stranger in the dotera, Kakeru felt something like rage and amazement welling up inside him. It had been a long time since someone had asked him whether he liked to run.

He could have said "I like it," as casually as if the question were about some dish served at a meal. Or he could have answered, "I don't like it," as indifferently as tossing out trash. Either way, it seemed impossible to Kakeru. *I can't just answer a question like that*, he thought. He simply found himself running, every single day, though there wasn't anywhere in particular he wanted to go. How could anyone like him find it in himself to declare outright whether he liked or disliked running?

The man on the bike gradually slowed down and came to a halt in front of a small, shuttered shop. Kakeru stopped, too, and, out of habit, he did some casual stretches to loosen his muscles. The guy bought two cans of cold tea from the vending machine, which emitted a dull glow, and threw one to Kakeru. They found themselves side by side, squatting in front of the shop. Kakeru felt the coolness of the can in his hand sucking the heat away from his body.

"You run well." After a few moments of silence, the man said, "'Scuse me," and slowly stretched out his hand toward Kakeru's calves.

Kakeru, feeling reckless, let him feel his legs over his jeans. *Whatever, who cares if this guy's a pervert?* He was parched, so he gulped down the entire can of tea.

The man checked Kakeru's muscles methodically, like a doctor inspecting a patient's legs for any tumors. Then he looked up and fixed his eyes straight on Kakeru.

"Why did you steal?"

After a beat, Kakeru said bluntly, "Who are you?" He threw his empty can into the garbage bin next to the machine.

"I'm Haiji Kiyose. Fourth-year at Kansei University, Faculty of Letters."

So he was at the university Kakeru was about to enter. Almost by reflex, he yielded and answered, "I'm . . . Kakeru Kurahara." Thanks to growing up in a militantly hierarchical community since junior high school, Kakeru found it hard to be rude to more senior students.

"Nice name, Kakeru," the man remarked, calling his first name as though they already knew each other. "You live around here?"

"I'll be starting at Kansei in April."

"Oh yeah?"

Kakeru couldn't help shrinking back as a peculiar gleam shot through Kiyose's eyes. After all, he was the kind of guy who'd come chasing down a stranger on a bike to grope his legs. The man couldn't be sane.

"Well, I'll be off now. Thank you for the tea." Kakeru tried to make a quick getaway, but Kiyose didn't let him. He pulled on the hem of Kakeru's shirt and tried to force him back down.

"What department?"

"Sociology . . ."

"Why did you steal?"

They'd come full circle. Like an astronaut who couldn't escape the binding force of the earth's gravity, Kakeru tottered down to his seat again.

"Seriously, what do you want from me? Are you gonna blackmail me?"

"No, I don't mean it like that. I just wondered if you're in a tight spot, maybe there's something I can do to help."

Kakeru grew even more wary. Kiyose must have some hidden agenda. There was no way he would say something like that out of sheer goodwill.

"Now that I know you're a fellow student, I can't turn my back on you. Is it . . . money?"

"Well, yeah."

Kakeru hoped Kiyose might lend him some, but apparently, all Kiyose had on him were two plastic bowls and a bit of change in his pocket. Without offering any cash, he merely went on asking questions.

"Don't your parents send you money?"

"They gave me money for a rental contract, but I used it all up on mahjong games. Basically I've got no choice but to sleep somewhere on campus till they send me money for next month."

"So you're homeless."

Seemingly lost in thought, Kiyose leaned forward, gazing at the air around Kakeru's legs. Kakeru, feeling awkward, wriggled his toes inside his sneakers.

After a while, Kiyose said earnestly, "That sounds tough. If you'd like, I can introduce you to the landlord of the apartment I live in. There's just one room that's available right now. It's called Chikusei-so, and it's close to here. Five-minute walk to campus, and the rent's thirty thousand yen per month."

"*Thirty thousand yen?*" Kakeru stammered. He had to wonder what was behind that unbeatable price. He pictured a closet with blood oozing out from under the sliding doors or a pale apparition wandering the gloomy hallways, and shivered. Things like ghosts and paranormal activity made him nervous. The phenomena that occupied the murky, in-between spaces of the world were incompatible with Kakeru's own world, where speed was everything, accurately measured in numerical values—a world where he could joyfully devote himself each day to building up the ideal body of a runner.

But Kiyose seemed oblivious to this inner turmoil in Kakeru, assuming his pained cry was that of a man who'd lost everything he had on mahjong. "It's all right. If we ask the landlord, he'll wait for your rent. At Chikusei-so, you don't have to pay a security deposit, key money, or anything like that."

Apparently, Kiyose had already made up his mind. Before Kakeru could say anything else, Kiyose had thrown out his empty can and straightened up, snapping up the bike's kickstand. Kakeru had nothing but serious misgivings about this apartment building, which housed such an eccentric character.

"Come on, let's go. I'll take you there," Kiyose urged him. "But before we do that, we better go pick up your stuff. Where've you been sleeping?"

Kakeru had found a spot on the side of the gym and had been huddled against the concrete wall to escape the wind and rain. All the belongings he'd brought from home fit into a single duffel bag. He figured if he needed anything else, he could ask for it to be sent over. He'd casually left home with no clue where his next address would be, hopped on the train, and come to Tokyo. On his very first night, he went to a mahjong parlor and squandered all his money.

Even so, he wasn't worried or scared at all. He didn't mind being alone in a place where no one would recognize him. In fact, he even felt liberated. Still, he did want to settle in somewhere before the semester started, and he was sick of having to scrape by, shoplifting at convenience stores on his jogging routes.

When Kakeru stood up obediently, Kiyose gave a satisfied nod. Instead of straddling the bike, he held it by the handles and pulled it along, the worn-out chain rattling noisily as he walked ahead. The frayed edges of his dotera looked white, lit up by the streetlights.

Oddly enough, despite his obvious interest in the way Kakeru ran, Kiyose didn't ask Kakeru anything about his experience in track. He didn't chide Kakeru for shoplifting either. Kakeru took a deep breath and called out to him. "Why are you being nice to me, Kiyose?"

Kiyose turned and smiled quietly, as though he'd just spotted a clump of fresh green grass sprouting through cracks in the asphalt. "You can call me Haiji."

Kakeru gave up interrogating Kiyose and walked alongside him. No matter how cheap the place was, no matter how peculiar the residents were, staying there had to be better than sleeping outside.

The apartment building was older than Kakeru had expected. "So . . . is this it, Haiji?"

"Yeah, this is Chikusei-so. We call it Aotake."

Kiyose proudly looked up at the building in front of them. Kakeru could only stand there and gape at it. Other than cultural heritage sites, it was the first time he'd seen such an old wooden building. The two-story structure had obviously been built on a low budget, and it looked as though it might collapse at any minute. Kakeru could hardly believe anyone lived there. But, alarmingly, some of the windows were glowing with a soft light.

Chikusei-so was about halfway between the university campus and the Tsuru no Yu bathhouse. Just beyond the alley, the neighborhood was a mix of vegetable patches that had been there for many years and new apartment buildings, which were growing in numbers. Nestled in this setting stood Chikusei-so, on a small plot of land bordered by dense, green hedges. There was a gap on one side of the hedge instead of a gate, where a visitor could peer into the premises.

There was a wide, graveled yard in front of the building, and a one-story house stood on the left, toward the back, where the landlord probably lived. Unlike the apartment building, this house appeared to have been recently reroofed with new tiles. The roof gave off a gentle sheen, reflecting the starlight. On its right was the infamous Chikusei-so.

"There are nine rooms in total. Thanks to you, Kakeru, every room is filled now."

The gravel crunched beneath Kiyose's feet as he guided Kakeru toward the entrance of the apartment building. The quaint sliding door was latticed and fitted with a thin sheet of glass. The light above it flickered fitfully, hooded by an oblong cover that had trapped a mass of tiny flies. Kakeru squinted at the wooden plate hanging next to the door, trying to make out the name on it in the sooty light. The kanji letters, handwritten in cursive with a valiant flourish, seemed to read "Chikusei-so": the lodging of green bamboo.

Kiyose parked the bike in a random spot in the yard and, carrying the plastic bowls stacked under his arm, put his hand on the front door. "I'll introduce you to the others later. We're all students at Kansei. There's a little trick to this," he added, as he hitched up the sliding door in its groove and tugged it open at the same time.

Inside the threshold, the genkan space consisted of a concrete floor for entering with shoes and a lidded shoe cupboard on one side, which evidently doubled as a mailbox. There were horizontal lines cut in the lid, and someone had scribbled each room number on a scrap of paper and stuck them on with tape. All the labels were browned from the sun. From a quick look at the row of numbers, Kakeru saw that there were four rooms on the first floor and five on the second.

The stairs to the second floor were on the right in front of the genkan entrance. Kakeru didn't even need to walk on it to see that the steps were uneven. He wondered how this building was still standing.

Kiyose took off his sandals on the concrete floor. "Come on in," he prompted Kakeru.

Kakeru did as he was told and put his shoes in the box labeled "103." Just then, he heard someone call, "Hey, Haiji!" The sound made him jump and look around, but no one was there. Kiyose frowned suspiciously.

"Up here," the voice said.

Kakeru and Kiyose looked up at the ceiling. For some reason Kakeru couldn't fathom, there was a fist-sized hole right above them. Whoever had spoken was pressing his face against the floor above. An eye with a mischievous gleam peered at them through the hole.

"Joji," Kiyose grumbled. "What's that hole doing there?"

"Put a foot through the floor."

"Wait there, I'm coming up."

Though he seemed disgruntled, Kiyose's bearing was calm as he started up the stairs. Kakeru hesitated, then decided to go after him. As soon as Kakeru put his foot down on a stair, it gave a high-pitched squeak like the nightingale floors in old castles and temples.

Kakeru climbed all the way up the dark, steep stairs and surveyed the second floor. The ceiling was higher than he'd expected. There were two doors next to the staircase, probably leading to a toilet and a sink, respectively, and two more rooms beyond that. Across the hallway, there were three rooms. The whole floor was quiet, but light fell through the crack of the door facing the staircase, labeled "201."

With firm steps, Kiyose approached room 201 and swung the door open without knocking. Kakeru hung back, peeking in through the doorway.

The room was roughly 160 square feet, fitting about ten tatami mats, with a low table in the middle and two futons laid out on either side. There seemed to be two people living here. Books and random junk were scattered around the futons, which looked as though they'd been left lying there for days. What stood out most of all were the tenants themselves. Two young men with the exact same face were looking at Kiyose beseechingly. Kakeru peered closely at the twins, but he could hardly spot a difference between the two.

"I told you to be careful. Which one of you made the hole?" Kiyose declared coldly, hands on his hips. The twins, who had been huddled together, started babbling at once.

"It was Jota."

"It was Joji."

"Hey, that's not fair. Don't blame me!"

"But you made the hole bigger."

"I just fell into the hole that *you* made."

Even their voices were the same. Kiyose silenced them by putting up his right hand. "Didn't I warn you that the floorboards above the genkan are getting weaker?"

Room 201 was covered with tatami mats, but one rectangle of the floor just above the entrance hall was bare wood. The twins nodded in sync at Kiyose's reproach.

"We did try to be careful."

"We were just walking over it as usual—it's not like we were stomping. It just snapped out of nowhere."

"You can't just walk over these floorboards like it's nothing—they'll break," Kiyose snorted. "From now on, be as careful as you can when you step on them. Got it?"

The twins nodded readily again. Kiyose cautiously knelt on the floor and inspected the hole.

"Umm, Haiji," one of the twins called hesitantly.

"What?"

"Who's that?"

The twins were looking at Kakeru, who was still hovering in the doorway.

"Ah." Kiyose glanced back as if he had just remembered his companion. "Kakeru Kurahara. He'll be going to Kansei starting this spring, like you two. He's moving in today."

Kakeru stepped into the room and stood next to the low table, giving a small nod.

The twins greeted him in unison.

"Hi there."

"Nice to meet you."

"Kakeru, meet the Jo twins. Taro Jo is the older brother, and Jiro Jo the younger."

The brothers each gave a slight bow as they were introduced. If they swapped places now, Kakeru wouldn't be able to tell them apart.

"Call me Joji. And he's Jota," Jiro said with an easygoing smile. "That's what everyone calls us."

"Wonder if we can use that hole for something. What do you think,

Kakeru?" Taro asked, as if they'd always known each other. Kakeru mumbled something vague, overwhelmed by the chatty twins.

"I guess we'll just have to cover it up with a magazine or something," Kiyose stood up and announced, looking down at the gap. "Did you hurt your legs when it happened?"

"Not at all." The twins shook their heads in sync, relieved to see that Kiyose's anger had abated.

If the twins are so afraid of him, Kakeru thought, *I guess Haiji's the one who calls all the shots at Chikusei-so.* Kakeru let out a heavy sigh, contemplating the communal life that awaited him in this old house. Wherever he went, it seemed impossible to escape cliques and hierarchy.

"I haven't even shown Kakeru his room yet. Just make sure you don't break anything else in Aotake, all right?" With that warning, Kiyose was gone. The twins saw Kakeru off at the door, talking in chorus.

"Too bad, it's only your first night, and you've already seen how the place is falling apart."

"The house is nice and quiet, though. You'll see."

Kakeru bade them good night and followed Kiyose, who was already heading downstairs.

The brothers were right. An air of stillness pervaded Chikusei-so. Despite all the noise the twins had made, there was no sign of the other residents, who might have been out. The only sounds Kakeru could hear were the rustling of the trees in the neighborhood and cars passing on some distant roads. Through the front door, which was left wide-open, a night breeze drifted in, warmer now that it was spring, carrying a soft scent of earth from the vegetable patches.

Kakeru picked up the duffel bag he'd left by the front door. The freshly made hole above was already covered up with a magazine, which had a woman in a bathing suit on the front cover. Now that the magazine blocked the light from the twins' bedroom, the entrance hall felt dim.

For the first time, Kakeru could take his time to look closely at the first floor of the building. The floor plan was more or less the same as the second, and the hallway extended in a straight line from the front door. On the left, the closest room to the entrance was the kitchen, followed by rooms 101 and 102. The twins' room, 201, was just above the entrance hall and the kitchen, which meant the second floor had one bedroom more than the first. Room 101, where Kiyose lived, was right under 202, 102 was under 203, and so on.

The right side of the first-floor hallway was exactly the same as the second floor. There were two doors for the toilet and the sink next to the staircase, then rooms 103 and 104 came after those, under rooms 204 and 205, respectively.

Kiyose offered to show him around, and Kakeru was about to walk farther down the hallway, but he stopped dead in his tracks. The deep end of the hall was hazy with thick, white smoke.

"Isn't that a fire, Haiji?"

But Kiyose merely muttered, "Oh, that," and was about to explain, when the door to room 102 in the far left corner banged open. Someone shot out from inside. Kakeru expected him to flee from the fire, but instead of running to the front door, he hammered on door 104.

"Hey! Come out, Nico-senpai!" He pounded on the door a dozen times, so hard that all the doors on the floor shook, until it finally opened.

"Quiet down, Yuki."

Kakeru thought he could make out a tall shadowy figure slowly emerging from the room, but the smoke was too dense. The two launched into a fierce argument, oblivious to Kakeru and Kiyose standing by the kitchen.

"Your cigarette smoke comes all the way into my room."

"Lucky you, you get to enjoy it without buying a single pack."

"But I don't smoke! Anyway, it's really annoying, so I'd appreciate it if you didn't." The resident of room 102 flailed his arm to fan away the smoke, muttering, "See? Look how thick it is." The toxic fumes coiled toward Kakeru and Kiyose. Now Kakeru could smell the tobacco. He was relieved it wasn't a fire, but the clash between the two was escalating.

"You know how much noise you make?" the smoker attacked.

"Playing crazy-ass music at max volume all night long. I can hear it going *boom-chicka boom-chicka womp womp womp*—it's gonna give me nightmares."

"I put on headphones when it's late."

"But it's still leaking, and those *boom-chickas* drive me up the wall!"

"It's an old building, you have to live with some noise."

"I wouldn't let my smoke out either if I could help it. It's 'cause the door doesn't fit properly—"

"All right, that's enough." Kiyose clapped to get their attention. "Right on time. I'll introduce you to our new resident."

When the fight quieted down, it was clear that heavy bass beats laced with electronic noise were flowing out of room 102, and dense, white smoke like dry ice was swirling out of room 104. Kakeru didn't feel like going anywhere near them, but Kiyose didn't seem to mind.

With the wind taken out of their sails, the two residents waited with their fists in the air and mouths hanging open for Kiyose and the newcomer to reach them.

"Senpai, Yuki, this is Kakeru Kurahara, who'll be living in 103 starting today. A first-year in sociology. Kakeru, this is Akihiro Hirata in 104, a longtime resident of Chikusei-so. Everyone calls him Nico-senpai."

"'Cause he's the Dark Lord of Nicotine," the one called Yuki sighed, his music booming in the background.

Kiyose pressed on, "Nico-senpai will be a third-year in science and engineering this spring. When I first arrived, he was my senpai, a year ahead of me, but we've swapped places since then."

Nico-senpai, big and burly like a bear, nodded to Kakeru without a hint of a smile. "So you'll be my next-door neighbor, huh. Good to meet ya."

Judging from his stubble and brazen attitude, Kakeru couldn't imagine Nico-senpai being an undergrad. Kakeru whispered to Kiyose, "Uh, how many years can you stay at university?"

"Eight years."

Nico added, "I'm still in my fifth."

Yuki, whose real name Kakeru still didn't know, snapped, "Plus you failed the entrance exams two years in a row."

Kakeru did a quick mental calculation; that meant Nico-senpai was twenty-five this year, but his self-possessed air made him seem older. He kept his cool despite Yuki's snide remarks. Kakeru wanted to steer clear of secondhand smoke, but Nico-senpai seemed like someone who'd be easy to get along with.

Finally, Kiyose got around to introducing the other resident. "Kakeru, this is Yukihiko Iwakura. He's in the Law Faculty and a fourth-year like me. We call him Yuki. He might not look like it, but he's already passed the bar exam."

"Hey," Yuki said bluntly. He was sickly pale—fitting for his name, which basically meant "snow boy." His spindly figure and glasses made him look rather neurotic. *I better try not to cross this guy*, Kakeru thought.

Nico pulled out a cigarette from his pocket and lit it, apparently indifferent to Yuki's icy stare. "By the way, Haiji. I heard a racket upstairs a little while ago—did something happen?"

"The twins, surprise surprise, knocked a hole in the floor."

"That didn't take long," Nico chuckled.

"Those two are idiots." Yuki frowned. "We let them have the biggest room in Aotake, but it's pointless if they can't use that corner anymore."

"That side was getting worn-out, so it was only a matter of time. We have to come up with a way to fortify it," Kiyose said.

Yuki narrowed his eyes. "If you ask me, it's Prince's fault."

As Kiyose and Yuki talked, Kakeru and Nico stood there like bystanders. With an incredible lung capacity, Nico soon turned the cigarette nearly into ash and stubbed the butt out on his own door.

"Hey, Kakeru." Nico also skipped formalities and went straight to a first-name basis, just as the twins had done. "I just made a shocking discovery."

"What is it?"

"All three of you have the same names as characters from a classic anime!"

"Oh . . ." Kakeru didn't know much about anime, so he could only give a lukewarm response. Nico pointed at each of them in turn with his second cigarette pinched between his fingers.

"He's Haiji, like *Heidi, Girl of the Alps*, right? Kakeru's last name is Kurahara, so he's Clara. Then there's Yuki, like 'Snowflake,' the little goat. See?"

"Don't turn me into a goat." Yuki shoved Nico back into 104.

"Feel free to call me Peter the goatherd—"

Ignoring Nico, Yuki banged the door shut in his face. He spun around and stormed back into his own room, slamming the door behind him. Only the lingering traces of smoke and music drifted in the dark hallway.

"Um . . ." Kakeru was at a loss for words. Kiyose responded with a shrug.

"Don't worry about it. They're always like that. But I'm glad they took a liking to you."

They liked me? Really? Kakeru was even more baffled, but he kept quiet as he watched Kiyose walk back to room 103 and open the door.

"So, this is your room. And here's the key." Kiyose pointed out the brass key with a round head hanging on the inner side of the door. "When you want to lock your room from inside, you have to insert this into the keyhole from your side, just like you'd lock it from outside. Most of the time, we can't be bothered, so we just keep our doors unlocked when we're in."

Kakeru took the dull golden key. It had an old-fashioned shape, like a key that might be used to open a magic door. The gilt was coming off in some places, and after being handled by generations of residents, the edges had rubbed away into a homely roundness.

Kiyose went in and opened the window, letting in fresh air. The six-mat room, about a hundred square feet, had a built-in oshiire closet with sliding doors. Kakeru slid open the door apprehensively, just in case. He was afraid he'd find bloodstains or something, but in spite of its age, the room was nice and clean.

"I'll show you a shop where you can borrow a futon tomorrow.

You'll have to make do with just my blanket for tonight—I'll bring it over later," Kiyose said.

"Thank you."

"There's a toilet and sink on each floor. We take turns cleaning it— the roster's put up in the kitchen at the start of each month. You've just moved in, so you're off the hook till April. I make breakfast and dinner for everyone."

"All by yourself?"

"Just something simple. For lunch, everyone gets their own food. When you don't need breakfast or dinner, let me know the day before."

Kiyose reeled off the house rules without a pause. "For baths, you could head to Tsuru no Yu over there, or you can also use the bath at the landlord's house. For the landlord's, the bath is available between eight and eleven p.m. No need to reserve it beforehand or wash the bathtub afterward. It's a hobby of the landlord's, washing the bath."

"Okay." Kakeru paid close attention to everything Kiyose said to commit it to memory.

"There's no curfew or anything like that. If you're unsure about something, just ask."

"What times are the meals?"

"It depends on everyone's schedule, so we just warm stuff up when- ever we want. I guess most people eat around eight thirty in the morning, and seven thirty at night."

"Got it." Kakeru nodded, then bowed more properly. "Thank you for everything."

Kiyose smiled again. Though Kakeru had suspected some hidden motive behind his invitation to Chikusei-so, now that he'd met half the residents, it was hard to remain skeptical. Everyone he'd met so far, including Kiyose, was a little eccentric, but they'd welcomed Kakeru with open arms. There wasn't anything pushy about Kiyose's expres- sion, either; it was a reserved smile, not overly friendly.

From the direction of the kitchen, Kakeru heard one *bong* from the wall clock.

"Ten thirty," Kiyose said, glancing at the plastic washing bowls that he'd left near the front door, as if he'd just remembered them. "You can still take a bath at the landlord's. If you're not too tired, do you want to go up to the main house? I'll introduce you."

They went out again, Kiyose offering a pair of sandals so Kakeru wouldn't have to take out his shoes every time. Apparently, the residents of Chikusei-so were a fan of massage sandals. Several pairs had been cast off around the genkan.

They crossed the garden on the gravel path toward the one-story wooden house where the landlord lived. It wasn't much of a garden, in fact: just some tall trees planted along the hedges, suitable for casting shade, which didn't seem particularly looked after. A white station wagon was parked nearby. It looked as though it was just left there on a whim, as indifferently as the garden had been designed, and the yard didn't seem to have a particular parking space. For a house in the metropolitan area, it was a rather extravagant way of using the land.

Now that he'd found a place to live, Kakeru felt a personal connection to this neighborhood for the first time. Before he came to Tokyo, he'd imagined it to be a grimy, restless city. He took a deep breath, filling his lungs with the night air. Surprisingly, it wasn't like that. In Tokyo, just like anywhere else, people were going about their ordinary lives. It was no different from the town where he was born and raised. He could sense the everyday lives of the residents, who tried to make a comfortable home by planting hedges or laying out a garden.

In the dark, Kakeru heard the huffing and puffing of some excitable creature that seemed to have detected their footsteps. When he strained his eyes, he could make out a brown mutt coming out from under the engawa veranda of the main house, wagging its tail furiously.

"I forgot about an important resident." Kiyose knelt down and stroked the dog's head. "This is Nira, the landlord's dog."

"That's a weird name. Nira, like garlic chives?" Kakeru squatted next to Kiyose and peered into the dog's wet, black eyes.

"An older student who used to live in Aotake brought him home,"

Kiyose explained, picking up Nira's droopy ears with his fingers and pointing them up. "In Okinawa, they call paradise Nira-something, apparently . . . can't remember what it was. Anyway, that's where the name comes from."

"Paradise, huh." The dog did look as though he didn't have a care in the world, and he had the kind of face that could win anyone over. The name was perfect.

"He's a silly dog who's friendly with everyone, but he's cute." Kiyose played with the dog, tugging at his ears and stroking out the curl in his tail, but Nira just looked at the two of them with an adoring expression. Kakeru patted the dog, too, as a greeting. Nira wore a bright red leather collar. "Looks good on you," Kakeru whispered to him.

The landlord was a hale and hearty old man named Gen'ichiro Tazaki.

When Kiyose explained Kakeru's situation—with a bit of drama-tizing here and there—and asked the landlord to wait awhile for the rent, he acquiesced without batting an eye. It was only when he heard Kakeru's name that there was a slight change in his expression.

"Kakeru Kurahara . . . You're not Kurahara from Sendai Jōsei Senior High School, are you?" Tazaki burst out and then nearly had a coughing fit, his face contorting as though he'd just gotten sprayed by seawater. It was impossible to tell whether he was irritated or excited. Kakeru's whole body tensed up, ready to face someone who might know of his past. His suspicions about Kiyose's motives for bringing him to Chikusei-so welled up again and made him feel sick. Kakeru had had enough of the kind of world he had come from: a world in which he was forced to run only for the sake of breaking records, at the mercy of his teammates' jealousy and rivalry. He never wanted to go back to that life if he could help it.

Kakeru stood rooted in place, his face downcast and stiff. Noticing the change in him, the landlord didn't press him any further.

"Well, hope you get along with everyone. Try not to wreck the apart-ment." That was all the old man said before promptly retiring to the living room, where the TV was on. Kakeru glanced at Kiyose, thinking about the fresh hole in the ceiling.

"Keep quiet about that," said Kiyose. "As long as we don't make the whole building collapse, he won't come to check."

The bathroom was at the back of the house, and there was also a large laundry machine in the changing room. A piece of paper bearing the words "Laundry before 10 p.m.—underwear should be prewashed" was pinned to the wall with a thumbtack. The notice was written with a calligraphy brush in a flowing, bold style, like a decorative scroll hanging in the tokonoma alcove at a traditional inn. Kakeru was distracted by the stark gap between the majestic calligraphy and the content of the note when the door to the dark bathroom suddenly opened from inside.

A Black man stepped out of the steam into the changing room. Kakeru sprang back and bumped into the laundry machine. The man looked at them in mild surprise.

"Good evening, Haiji," he said in a very natural accent as he dried himself with a towel. "And this is . . . ?"

"Kakeru Kurahara. He's a newcomer. Kakeru, this is Musa Kamala, an exchange student. He lives in 203, a second-year in science and engineering."

"Pleasure to meet you, Kakeru."

Still naked from head to toe, Musa held out his hand in a flawless gesture. Kakeru took it awkwardly, not used to shaking hands.

Musa was about the same height as Kakeru, and his eyes had a calm, thoughtful depth to them. Since the other residents had been on the rowdy side, Kakeru felt a little relieved to meet someone who looked like he might be a peaceful person with some common sense.

There was something that puzzled Kakeru, though. "Why were you bathing in the dark?" he asked.

Musa beamed. "To train myself," he said. "Going in the water when it's dark makes us feel great unease. But I do so deliberately in order to reflect on myself. Perhaps you could challenge yourself, too, Kakeru?"

Musa's refined Japanese sounded stiff for a casual conversation, which made it amusing in a peculiar way.

"I'll give it a try," Kakeru replied. *Yet another weirdo.*

Kiyose and Musa left the changing room, and Kakeru let out a sigh, alone at last. He took off his clothes, switched on the light in the bathroom, and scrubbed his body in the shower area. He hadn't been able to go to a bathhouse, so it was the first time in a while that he'd cleaned his body properly. When he was done washing, he decided to turn off the light.

Just as Musa had said, it felt somewhat unsettling to bathe in the dark. Besides, it was his first time in this house. Since he didn't have a feel for where things were, he knocked his shin against a step inside the tub, which had probably been installed for the elderly landlord. He groped around the tub and settled down, stretching out his legs. The water, starting to get lukewarm, felt heavy in the dark. Each movement of his body sent ripples through the water, and the darkness made the lapping feel louder than usual, too.

Kakeru closed his eyes. His thoughts about this new chapter in his life, his fears and misgivings, floated in the water around him. He saw the bitterly disappointed faces of his parents, who had dismissed him with a brusque "We'll send you enough for the living costs. Do what you like." He saw the oval track where he used to run every single day and the rows of houses nearby. He saw his teammates slamming their lockers shut as they threw him contemptuous looks. All this rushed into his head, and he sank until his nose was submerged underwater.

He was running out of air. But he didn't budge—instead, he started counting his own heartbeat out of habit. He was used to this feeling. Countless times while running, he'd felt like he was suffocating, much worse than the tightness in his chest that he felt now. Many times, his lungs had filled up with blood, and he could taste it at the back of his throat. Still, he kept running—but why? Was it because he felt pleasure when he ran? Or was it because he didn't want to admit defeat to anyone, least of all himself?

His heart was pounding so hard he could pinpoint exactly where it was inside him. He pressed his wet hands over his ears, but the booms resonated throughout his entire body until it felt overwhelming. At last, Kakeru rose above the water and breathed in deep, opening his eyes at the same time.

Through the window, he saw the shadowy shape of Chikusei-so next door. More windows were lit up now. Soft squares of light fell on the yard outside, which was engulfed in darkness. *Maybe Musa likes to look at this view from the bath,* Kakeru thought.

When he returned to his new room at Chikusei-so, he found that Kiyose had left him a blanket. He heard the creaks and groans of the old building in every corner of the room, especially from the ceiling. It sounded as if something was taking an endless supply of dry branches and snapping them into pieces.

This is going to be my home from now on. Kakeru lay down and pulled up the blanket. He caught a whiff of the grassy scent of the tatami mat. The house was still creaking, but compared to sleeping out in the open, he felt much more at ease.

When he closed his eyes, sleep came to him at once.

Musa Kamala parted from Kiyose as they entered Chikusei-so and went up the stairs to his own room.

Last spring, when Musa had just arrived, he couldn't bring himself to feel safe in a wooden house, and he had been nervous even just to walk down the hallway. He grew up in a Western, colonial-style house made of stone. Before he came here, he couldn't have imagined what it was like to live in a house where the walls were so thin he could hear voices from the next room, where the hallways were so narrow it was a struggle for two people to pass each other. But by now, Musa had grown very fond of Chikusei-so, both the building itself and his fellow residents.

Musa thought about Kakeru, the newcomer he had just met. He

hoped they'd get along, too. He recalled how nimble Kakeru was on his feet—he probably played some kind of sport—and the strong-willed eyes that looked at Musa with slight bewilderment. *I bet he'll fit in here in no time*, Musa thought.

Of the three rooms on the left side of the hallway, Musa's was the last one, and he noticed that the door of the middle room, 202, was slightly ajar. He popped his head in as he passed by. The occupant of 202, Yohei Sakaguchi, a fourth-year in sociology, was watching TV with Takashi Sugiyama, a third-year in business who lived across from Musa in room 205.

"Good evening," Musa said, since he felt like talking to someone. The two turned around and casually invited him in. They gave him a sweaty can of beer, and Musa sat up straight on the tatami, folding his legs underneath him.

"Are you watching a quiz show again, King?" Musa said, mildly astonished as the celebrities on the screen raced to push the buzzer button. Sakaguchi's hobby was to watch every single quiz show, even recording them on video when he couldn't catch them in real time. Everyone at Chikusei-so called him King, as in "Quiz King," to tease him just a bit.

"What else would I watch?" he replied, just as he thwacked a tissue box with his hand and shouted at the top of his voice, "The public baths of Caracalla!" The tissue box was his substitute for a buzzer.

"You'll never get bored if you watch quiz shows with King," Sugiyama laughed, inviting Musa to drink the beer. "He's so dramatic."

Sugiyama's nickname was Shindo. At first, Musa couldn't understand how someone so soft-spoken could be called shindo, which meant "a quake." When Shindo had first noticed Musa's confusion, he cleared things up right away.

"You see, I was born in a village deep in the mountains. It takes me two days to return home from Tokyo. Oh, do you know this word for *return*?"

"Yes. But does it really take two whole days? Even when I fly back to my home country, it only takes a little over a day."

"Hmm, so in terms of the time it takes, my hometown is even farther away than yours, Musa. That puts things in perspective—it really is a remote village. Oh, do you know *remote*?"

"I'm not sure. Do you mean it's in the countryside?"

"Yeah, exactly. And in my village, I used to be called a shindo—well, just a local one, anyway. Uh, *shindo* literally means a child of god, and it's what you call a child prodigy . . ."

Most residents of Chikusei-so used slang when they talked to Musa without pausing to check whether he understood. Though his Japanese was above the intermediate level, Musa was often at a loss when it came to colloquialisms. But Shindo was an exception: he always offered a thorough definition for any slang or difficult vocabulary that Musa might not be familiar with. It was thanks to him that Musa grew even more fluent in Japanese. Musa knew more slang words now, but he tried to avoid using them, emulating Shindo's courteous manner instead. Sometimes, Nico-senpai from downstairs would joke, "Hearing you talk makes my shoulders go stiff."

Musa looked on at the quiz show for a while, sipping his beer.

The only residents at Chikusei-so who owned a TV were King, the twins, and Nico. Nico's room was full of toxic fumes, so everyone else stayed away for the most part. King's TV was exclusively used for quiz shows. So, whenever there was a program they wanted to watch, everyone usually headed to the twins' room.

Musa could hear the TV in the twins' room next door, but no talking. The brothers seemed to be enjoying a quiet evening by themselves, left in peace by their raucous seniors.

King was shouting answers at the screen and smacking the tissue box as enthusiastically as ever. As soon as a commercial break started, he snatched up the remote and fast-forwarded. Musa realized they'd been watching a recording the whole time. King skipped over the commercials and resumed the show. This time, it wasn't a buzzer round. He finally pulled himself away from the TV a little.

"Hey, Musa. Shindo's been watching the quiz without uttering a single word. Can you believe it?"

Musa cocked his head, not quite following King's point. King swiveled around to face Musa and Shindo, who were sitting side by side.

"Come on, no one can help calling out the answers when you're watching a quiz show. Isn't it human nature? I mean, if you hear a question like 'What kanji character do you get when you put together the *fish* radical and the kanji for *blue*?,' you've *got* to answer 'mackerel'! But this guy, he just sits there. What's the fun in watching, right?"

"I noticed you like to call out the answers even when you're watching by yourself," said Musa, thinking back to all those nights he'd heard King through the wall, yelling random words.

"*Ob*-viously. That's the whole point of quiz shows. I just don't get why anyone would wanna sit through it like a statue."

I don't know about that, Musa thought.

"I don't know about that," Shindo countered out loud. "I think you're actually in the minority. In my view, I don't understand why you can get so fired up about it when you're not even a contestant."

"Why don't you apply to compete in one of these shows?" Musa added. They all knew how zealous King was about quiz questions, surfing around on quiz-related websites on a daily basis. King even dared to step into the hellhole of smoke that everyone shied away from just to research quizzes on Nico's computer. The residents regarded King's fervor for quizzes from a safe distance.

"A true connoisseur knows the best way to enjoy quizzes is to watch from the other side of the screen and answer more quickly, accurately, and copiously than any famed champion," King declared proudly.

As brash as he seemed, King was actually prone to stage fright, so it was unthinkable for him to go on TV. When Musa sensed the truth behind King's bravado, he didn't press the matter. Shindo nodded along and said good-naturedly, "I guess you're right."

King seemed slightly uncomfortable, so Musa changed the subject. "Have you heard we have a new resident here?"

"Since when?!"

"What's he like?"

King and Shindo jumped at the news. It clearly excited their curiosity—King even turned down the volume of the TV. A little startled by their eagerness, Musa told them about the encounter outside the bath. "I believe he arrived tonight. Haiji said he'll be starting in the Faculty of Sociology this spring. Haiji looked happy."

"I've got a bad feeling about this," King muttered.

"Why so? Kakeru looked like a nice, honest person," said Musa.

"It's not his personality that King's concerned about, Musa," Shindo explained. "You know how Haiji was so keen to fill room 103, don't you?"

"Yes. What about it?"

"That's the big question," King said. He propped his elbow on his knee and theatrically stroked his chin. "Musa, you must've heard Haiji muttering the same thing over and over these days—'One more, just one more . . .' He's like that ghost who obsesses over the tenth missing plate in *Bancho Sarayashiki*."

"What's *Bancho Sarayashiki*?" Musa asked.

"Let me explain—" Shindo began, but King cut him off.

"He's definitely up to something. A secret plot."

"I wonder . . . why is it so important for Haiji to have ten people in Aotake?" Shindo frowned.

With an air of gravity, King began to spin a hypothesis. "It's my fourth year living here, but we've never had ten tenants—pun unintended—"

"We know. Go on."

"We've never had ten tenants at the same time, since there are only nine rooms."

"Naturally."

"But this year, it's different. The twins moved into 201. And that was when Haiji started chanting that mantra like a ghost: *just one more*."

"It's true, Haiji did seem fixated on having ten people," Musa agreed.

Normally, Kiyose wasn't the expressive type. No matter what kind of commotion the others stirred up at Chikusei-so, Kiyose stayed calm and collected. But when it came to whether a new tenant would move into room 103, he seemed worried sick. It was almost bizarre how he made his concern so obvious. Musa had also wondered what could be on his mind.

"What on earth is going to happen when there's ten people in the house?" Musa said.

"No clue." King tossed the question out the window as quickly as he'd taken it up. "Maybe we'll see a ghost who counts plates."

"You're the one made a fuss about a 'secret plot'—the least you could do is put more thought into it," Shindo complained. But King had turned back to the TV and was already absorbed in the quiz, and they couldn't get anything more out of him except monosyllabic grunts. Shindo and Musa debated Haiji's true intentions for a little while longer, but eventually they left the matter unsettled.

Silence fell over room 202. Even the quiz show went quiet, a dramatic pause awaiting the contestant's answer.

"Whatever it is," King said, "if anything bad was gonna happen to us, I'm sure Haiji would tell us about it. I mean, he sure as hell won't get off your back if you 'forget' to clean the bathroom when it's your turn—but other than that, he's a pretty good guy."

He's right, Musa thought. Kiyose would never make them walk into a trap.

Musa couldn't imagine anything bad in store for them. Kiyose had looked too happy for that when Musa saw him earlier. Kiyose looked as excited as Musa had been last year when he'd seen a carpet of snow for the first time in his life.

II

THE SAVAGE MOUNTAIN

Every morning and every night, Kakeru jogged ten kilometers. This had been his routine since senior high school.

By the summer of his second year in senior high, when he'd already built up his body and was doing the most intense training, he achieved a record of 13:50.32 for running 5,000 meters at the big track meet. Not only was this an astonishing feat for a high schooler, but his speed was also on par with professional athletes representing Japan. What's more, Kakeru was still young; his natural talent was sure to flourish even more in the years to come, with the promise of a glowing performance even in the Olympics. He was inundated with offers of admission from numerous universities. Everyone seemed to want him—that is, until he got kicked off the track team for engaging in violence.

Kakeru had no regrets about leaving it all behind. He wasn't interested in running as a representative of some school or making his mark in international competitions. It was far more exciting for him to run free, feeling every swing of his body and the wind on his face. He was sick of being tied down by institutional expectations and ambitions, micromanaged like a guinea pig.

On the day he got his record for the 5,000-meter run, something was wrong with his stomach. A runner had no excuses for days like that; staying in good shape was part of running the race. But judging from how he'd felt that day, Kakeru had a hunch that he could run even faster. He was sure he could break through that wall, to finish 5,000 meters in less than thirteen minutes and forty seconds.

Even after he quit the track team, Kakeru kept up his training by himself, driven by the desire to reach that new horizon of speed he had yet to experience. When he ran, the world around him streamed by in a blur. Wind whistled past his ears. What would he see when he attained that level of speed, and how much would his blood seethe as heat rose in his body? Kakeru was ready to do whatever it took to experience the unknown.

Kakeru kept running, a watch equipped with a stopwatch function on his left wrist. He ran with unwavering resolve, even though he had no coach to guide him, nor teammates to compete with. The touch of wind on his skin told him what he needed to know. His own heart was screaming: *Keep running. Faster, faster.*

A few days had gone by since he moved into Chikusei-so, and now he had a pretty good grasp of everyone's names and faces. Perhaps settling in had loosened him up. On his morning jog, his feet struck the earth in smooth, fluid strokes.

The one-way road surrounded by greenery was still fairly empty at this hour. He passed only a handful of people: an elderly neighbor walking a dog, office workers heading to the bus stop for their early-morning commute, and so on. Kakeru traced his jogging course, which was starting to sink into his muscle memory, keeping his eyes on the white center line.

Chikusei-so stood in an old neighborhood between the Keio and Odakyu railway lines. The Kansei University campus was the only building nearby that qualified as "big." The closest train stations were Chitose-karasuyama on the Keio line, and Soshigaya-Okura and Seijogakuen-mae Stations on the Odakyu line, but all of them were a bit too far to be convenient. Since it took more than twenty minutes to go to any of the stations on foot, many residents of the neighborhood rode the bus or their bicycles to get there.

Kakeru, of course, always went on foot. It was faster for him to run, for one thing, and it gave him extra practice. He quickly became familiar with the neighborhood, thanks to his trips to the grocery store at the shotengai shopping arcade upon Kiyose's request and to the bookstore at Seijo, running alongside the twins as they rode double on their city bike.

Kakeru settled on several different jogging routes. For the most part, they were narrow paths with little traffic, along thickets and vegetable patches. He would rarely pay any attention to the view at track meets, but sometimes, on his daily jogs or during practice, he looked around absent-mindedly at his surroundings. He liked to observe the little things: a tricycle parked by a house or a bag of fertilizer left in the corner of a vegetable plot. On rainy days, the tricycle was moved under the eaves. There was less and less fertilizer in the bag until, eventually, it was replaced with a new one.

Somehow it tickled Kakeru to notice things like that, the traces of people going about their lives. Whoever owned these objects would never know that someone was jogging by on this path every morning and taking note of them. When he thought about it, it was funny, as though he were secretly peeking into a box of peaceful paradise.

It was 6:30 a.m. He decided to head back to Aotake for breakfast. Just as he was passing by a small park, he caught sight of something from the corner of his eye. Jogging in place, he stretched his neck to look into the park. Kiyose was sitting by himself on a bench.

Kakeru entered the park, walking on the gritty sand that dusted the ground. Kiyose sat with his head down, motionless. Kakeru paused a little way off next to the iron bars and watched him.

Kiyose was wearing a T-shirt and a worn-out navy tracksuit. Nira's red leash lay on the bench. Kiyose's right pant leg was rolled up, and he was massaging his calf. Kakeru saw a mark running down from his knee across the upper half of his shin, which seemed to be a scar from a surgery.

Kiyose was still unaware of Kakeru, but Nira, who was nosing around the shrubs, scampered over to him. A small plastic poop bag was tied to the dog's collar. Nira sniffed Kakeru's shoes with his wet nose and, finally convinced of the wearer's identity, wagged his tail with even more enthusiasm.

Crouching down, Kakeru took Nira's face in both hands and ruffled his fur. Nira, bubbling over with glee to see a friend on a walk, wheezed like an old man hacking up a higashi sweet stuck in his throat.

The sound made Kiyose look up. He seemed uneasy as he rolled down his pant leg.

"Morning," Kakeru said, trying to sound cheerful, and sat next to him. "Is it your job to walk Nira, too?"

"I run every day like you, so I might as well bring him along. This is the first time we've run into each other."

"I start getting bored, so I switch up my route a little each time."

Kakeru found himself attempting to close the distance between him and Kiyose. He wanted to be discreet, like someone transmitting ultrasonic waves into the sea to detect signs of fish through the reflected echoes.

"Do you . . . run to stay healthy?" As soon as Kakeru uttered the question, he regretted it. So much for ultrasonic waves—this was like firing a torpedo right at the target. What if it scared away the fish? The fish might dive into the depths of the sea, its back fin glimmering, keeping all its secrets hidden in its belly. Kakeru panicked inside, hating himself for once again failing to make conversation with any semblance of tact or subtlety.

But the question didn't seem to bother Kiyose. A perplexed, almost resigned smile crossed his face. Kakeru accepted the fact that he had zero talent for steering the conversation through well-worded questions and waited in silence for Kiyose to make his move. Kiyose brushed his hand over his right knee.

"I don't run for my health, and it's not a hobby either," he said firmly. "And I think the same goes for you, Kakeru."

Kakeru nodded. If somebody asked him "Then why *do* you run?," he wouldn't know what to say. And if he were to fill out a résumé form to apply for a part-time job, he could never bring himself to write "jogging" under "Hobbies."

"I got injured when I was in senior high," Kiyose said. He let go of his knee and called to Nira with a light whistle. Nira, who had been padding around the park, dashed back to Kiyose without missing a beat. Kiyose knelt down and hooked the leash onto the red collar. "But it's almost completely healed now. I can feel my speed and instinct coming back, so it's fun to run."

The moment he saw the scar, somehow it dawned on Kakeru that Kiyose was a runner: a serious runner with high aspirations, just like Kakeru himself. It became clear to him that Kiyose had pedaled so hard to catch up with him on the first night they met because his curiosity was piqued as a fellow runner.

Now that the leash was back on his collar, Nira kept tugging at it, eager to start walking again. As he held the dog back, Kiyose asked Kakeru, "What about you, are you heading home?"

Kakeru leaned back on the bench and didn't say anything. In the end, he decided to come out with it. "Did you invite me to live in Chikusei-so because you thought I used to be on a track team?"

"I went after you because the way you ran was really incredible," Kiyose replied. "But that's not why I brought you back to Aotake. I thought you looked so free when you ran. You were so into it, just living in the moment. It wiped out everything else—it didn't even matter that you were shoplifting. I really liked that."

"Let's go back."

Kakeru stood up from the bench. Kiyose's answer didn't bother him.

The bustle of the morning air pressed into the empty park as the neighborhood began to rouse itself. A car honking as it rolled down the main street. The creaking of a mailbox as someone pulled out the day's newspaper. The presence of people hurrying to their workplaces or schools.

Breathing in the air, filled with all that life, pumped a fresh wave of blood down to Kakeru's fingertips.

Kakeru left the park with Kiyose and started jogging again toward Chikusei-so. Nira had the rules of the game down pat; he ran straight ahead alongside them. Without having to talk about it, the light, rhythmical scratches of Nira's nails against the asphalt became a measure of their pace. For Kakeru, it was much slower than his usual speed. But he didn't mind at all. He observed Kiyose, who was running next to him, holding Nira's leash.

From the way Kiyose carried himself, Kakeru was certain that Kiyose had a thorough grasp of how every inch of his body moved. It was the kind of run that one could master only through constant training and tireless commitment.

"Hey, Haiji," Kakeru said, "why do you make Nira carry the poop bag?"

"I'm too lazy," Kiyose answered breezily. No matter what he said, he said it with confidence.

Kakeru felt sorry for Nira, though. A dog's sense of smell far surpassed a human's—wasn't it unbearable for Nira to have poop hanging right in front of his nose?

Not that Nira seemed to mind. He kept on trotting at a steady pace, his curly brown tail swishing from side to side, as if dancing to a rhythm.

In April, life suddenly got hectic for the residents of Chikusei-so.

They had to frequent the campus for orientation sessions and figure out which courses to register for. Like honeybees carried by the spring breeze, they flitted from one place to another without a moment's rest.

As soon as the entrance ceremony was over, Jota and Joji threw themselves into finding a club with cute girls. Nico-senpai, who was running out of time to graduate, was engrossed in *The Complete Guide to Scoring Easy Credits*, a pamphlet circulating in the student black market, and was racking his brain over which courses to take. Nightmarish moans about job hunting oozed from King's room and echoed throughout the building, while Yuki, who had already passed the bar last year, didn't even show up at his seminar group and went club-hopping every night, plunging into an endless flood of music. The diligent Musa and Shindo, who took things at their own pace, had quickly sorted out their course registrations without a fuss and were now on the lookout for new part-time jobs.

As for Kakeru, he managed to finish registering for classes, too, and he'd met a handful of people. Because he was out of cash, he sneaked into drinking parties that the clubs hosted to welcome in the freshies and helped himself to free booze. No one dug into what he used to do in the past or urged him to do anything in the future. It wasn't long till Kakeru felt at home amid the carefree vibes of the college, which seemed to attract people who didn't try to stick their noses too much in other people's business.

One day—when class registrations were finally complete and lectures were about to start the next day—Kakeru returned from his evening jog to find a note on a string hanging down from the hole in the twins' room. It read, "TODAY: Kakeru's welcome party. All residents come to the twins' room at 7 p.m."

My welcome party? Kakeru felt a little embarrassed. It had already been nearly two weeks since he moved in, and almost every night, he and the others had been drinking together or playing mahjong in someone's room on the slightest pretext. He thought it was well past the point for a welcome party, but it made him happy all the same.

"I'm back," he called, walking down the hallway. In the kitchen, Kiyose and the twins were cooking up a storm. Kiyose was stir-frying some minced onions and lumps of garlic in a giant wok. Kakeru was puzzled. *Why does it smell like olive oil when he's using a wok?* Kiyose, who had been keeping an intent eye on the wok, shouted, "Now!" Jota snapped open the can of whole tomatoes and poured them into the wok in one swift motion. Apparently, they were making pasta sauce.

Jota held the can in one hand, while maneuvering a frying pan in the other. A mass of takana mustard leaves and jako fish flew in the air, and this time, the roasted scent of sesame oil wafted through the kitchen.

"Stir-fried rice's on the menu." Jota grinned at Kakeru. "You like takana?"

Kakeru nodded. *Pasta and rice—lots of carbs.*

Joji was sitting at the dining table, making a bowl full of what looked like shiraae salad with mashed tofu and spinach. He was mixing it so strenuously that beads of sweat were starting to form on his brow. The mash was turning into a sort of light green paste. Kakeru, concerned about where the dish was going, offered to help, but he was shooed away. "Just sit back and relax, you're the guest of honor," Joji said. The house had already had a welcome party for the twins, the other first-years, before Kakeru came to Chikusei-so. Now, Jota and Joji took on the cooking with the stature of earlier residents.

With nothing to do, Kakeru went to the Tsuru no Yu bathhouse, came back refreshed, and waited in his own room for 7 p.m.

He must have dozed off while waiting. When he jerked awake, it was already five minutes to seven. He thought of heading to the twins' room, but he didn't want to show up early and look overeager. Instead, he opened his door a crack and listened. There was no one in the kitchen, and the first floor was silent. All the voices and footsteps were coming from the twins' room.

After another three minutes, Kakeru went upstairs.

Just as he opened the twins' door, Nico-senpai grabbed Musa in a headlock and demanded, "Just answer the roll call for me in this class, got it?!"

"Oh, Kakeru!" Jota squealed. "Hey, guys, Kakeru's here already."

For a moment, Kakeru worried that he'd come too early. As it turned out, they were planning to pull the party poppers as soon as he opened the door. Joji sulked that thanks to Nico-senpai kicking up a fuss, they'd missed the moment. Shindo stepped in between them and rescued Musa from Nico's grip.

The twins' room was packed. The low table in the middle was

crammed with dishes whipped up by Kiyose and the twins, along with snacks and sake that the others had brought. King, who'd already sneaked a bite, mumbled to Kakeru through a mouthful of food, "Hey, sit down."

Ignoring Kiyose's warnings, everyone decided they'd gather round the window and pull the party poppers out toward the landlord's house. A startled Nira scrambled out from under the veranda and barked at the moon.

"Right, time for a toast." Nico held up a beer can.

Kiyose looked around the room. "I feel like we're missing something."

"Prince isn't here!" piped the twins in unison.

"Who's that?" asked Kakeru.

"Akane Kashiwazaki in room 204," Yuki explained. "Second-year in the Faculty of Letters."

So there's still someone I haven't met, Kakeru thought. *Why's he called Prince?*

"I'll go get him." Kiyose stood up. "Come with me, Kakeru."

Kiyose walked over to room 204, which was closest to the staircase.

"Prince? I'm coming in."

Without waiting for a reply, Kiyose opened the door. When Kakeru saw what awaited them on the other side, he staggered in a spasm of vertigo.

In the small room, which had the same layout as Kakeru's, massive pillars of manga towered over them, nearly as high as the ceiling. Except for a narrow passageway between the stacks, books were all Kakeru could see. At the back of this slim aisle near the window lay a folded blanket. It appeared that the resident must wrap himself up in a blanket when he slept, since there was no space to spread out a futon. Though the light was on in the room, it seemed to be empty.

Kakeru stared at the bewildering mass of comics. Room 204 was right above Kakeru's room. Now he could see why the ceiling creaked so much at night. He lightly put his hand against one of the walls of manga.

"Watch it. Don't mess with them. They're sorted into categories."

The voice came from beyond the heaps of books on one side of the room. Startled, Kakeru glanced around to find the speaker and backed into a pile. Books slid down over his head.

"Ugh, I told you!" A man with a rather gorgeous face crawled out of the slit between the stacks and the ceiling, and made his way down to the floor. He blinked, fluttering heavy eyelashes befitting his nickname. "What do you want, Haiji? Is he new?"

"Kakeru's been here for about two weeks." Kiyose gathered up the scattered manga off the ground and handed them to Prince. "We're having a welcome party for him tonight. Didn't you see the note hanging by the front door?"

"Nope. I haven't gone out for the past several days."

"By all means, join us."

Prince grumbled about what a bother it was, but he slouched out of the room under Kiyose's piercing gaze.

"Um," Kakeru blurted out, "I can hear the house creaking like crazy in my room . . ."

"So what? It creaks everywhere." Lured by the smell of food, Prince tottered toward the twins' room.

"But I swear, it must be the worst in my room." Kakeru was desperate. He could be risking his life to live under so much weight. "Could we please swap rooms?"

Prince flatly refused. "No way I'm storing my precious manga downstairs, it's too damp," he said. "Kakeru, was it? Think of it as living right under Niagara Falls."

"What does that mean?"

"A thrilling life that never gets boring." Prince opened the twins' door and added, "Plus, everyone will think you're so lucky to live under such a treasure trove. My manga collection is definitely very valuable, no question about it."

Kakeru looked at Kiyose for help.

"I really feel for you," Kiyose sighed, "but it's no use."

At last, every resident of Chikusei-so was gathered in the twins' room. As soon as they raised their beer cans in a toast, the concentration of alcohol in the atmosphere started shooting up, and the room filled with bursts of laughter.

To take responsibility for hoarding so many comics, Prince was made to sit in the wood-floored corner of the room, where the danger of falling through was highest. Kakeru sat next to Kiyose, their backs to the window overlooking the garden. When they were all together, the relationships between each member of Chikusei-so were thrown into relief. Of course, living together in a cramped house, they all had to be on the same wavelength, but some of them were especially close. The twins and Prince were having a heated debate about manga while wolfing down packets of snacks. Musa and Shindo were lending their sympathetic ears to King's anxieties over job hunting.

"I don't even have money to buy a suit," King groaned.

"How about getting a part-time job?" Musa suggested.

"What about your high school uniform—was it a blazer jacket? You could wear that instead," Shindo added.

Nico and Yuki were engrossed in a discussion about computers that went right over Kakeru's head. As usual, they sounded like they were bickering, but Kakeru let them be—he'd learned that that was just the way they were. Even during their argument, Nico got up to lean out the window and take long drags on his cigarette.

Kakeru and Kiyose sat in comfortable silence, drinking and eating. They didn't talk about anything in particular, but they never felt awkward.

Though the two of them knew that the one thing that brought them together was running, they somehow stayed away from the topic. After all, Kiyose had the knee injury, and Kakeru hadn't processed what happened in high school enough to bring it up himself. He had the feeling that if they talked about running, they would end up commiserating with each other, and he didn't want that.

When they had drunk the last of the beer, they opened a bottle of local sake from Shindo's village that his family had sent him. It was an unknown brand and weirdly sweet, but none of them gave much thought to the taste. They brought up some cucumber, salt, and miso paste from the kitchen for a snack as they guzzled down more and more alcohol.

Then Kiyose made his announcement. "Listen up, everyone," he said, in a slow, calm tone. "There's something important I want to tell you."

Everyone stopped fooling around and turned to Kiyose. They naturally formed a circle around the sake bottle. Kakeru looked sideways at Kiyose, wondering what he could have in mind.

"I'm going to need your help over the next year."

"You taking the bar exam or something?" Nico asked casually.

"If you are, I can give you tips," Yuki said. They all assumed he was stepping down from cooking duties to focus on job hunting or something along those lines. But Kiyose shook his head.

"Let's aim for the top. All of us, together."

"The top . . . of what?" Yuki prompted dubiously. The twins drew closer together, as if cowering from what might come next.

"I knew you were plotting something, Haiji," King mumbled. Shindo and Musa exchanged looks.

"I'm talking about sports. We'll band together and conquer the summit," Kiyose proclaimed. "If all goes well, you'll be popular with girls, *and* it'll give you an edge in job hunting."

The twins pricked up their ears. "Is that really true?" They closed in on the circle little by little, sidling toward Kiyose.

"Of course it is. Everyone knows that girls love an athlete. And big companies can't get enough of them either."

The twins immediately put their heads together. "If it'll help me get a girlfriend, I'll do it. What about you, bro?"

"I say let's do it," Jota agreed, then turned to Kiyose. "But which sport are we talking about? There's ten of us—it's nine for a baseball team."

"And soccer's eleven."

"Is it kabaddi?" Nico cut in.

"No," said Kiyose.

Yuki shot Nico a withering look. "Do you seriously believe playing kabaddi in Japan today would make anyone so famous that it'd help them land a job?"

"Besides, a kabaddi team has seven players," King added, showing off the trivia he'd stored up from his quiz training. Nico and Prince raised their hands at once and announced, "All right then, I'm out."

Despite his snide remark, Yuki joined them and volunteered to step down, too. "It's up to the rest of you now—good luck."

Musa looked around the group and reported with a smile, "Now there's exactly seven of us."

"I said it's not kabaddi." Kiyose cleared his throat. "And let me remind you, Yuki, you have no right to back out of this. Remember how every New Year's, I made a feast of osechi and ozoni soup especially for you, just because you didn't want to go back to your family for the holidays?"

"Is that a threat, Haiji?" Yuki protested, but he already sounded utterly defeated.

Kiyose's face twisted into an ominous grin. "Why do you think I've cooked for the whole house every day and looked after your health all these years?"

What was Kiyose driving at? A hush fell over them as they sensed looming danger. Every one of them had been benefiting quite a bit from Kiyose's household prowess. Now that the captives had been fattened up just enough, it was time to devour them. They felt like siblings hauled out in front of the witch who awaited them, whetting her knife.

Kakeru turned over all the clues in his head. Kiyose, who had shown an interest in his running, used to be on a track team himself. Kiyose had made a point of gathering all the residents of Chikusei-so for tonight's party, even dragging Prince out by force. And finally, the sport he was talking about had to be one with a team of ten people.

Kakeru had a bad feeling about this. *He can't possibly mean . . .*

"You still don't get it? It's the challenge I've been dreaming of." Kiyose was clearly having the time of his life browbeating the residents. Every one of them shrank under his penetrating gaze, averting their eyes and shaking their heads, like timid mosquitoes flittering out uncertainly at the beginning of the season.

"It's a sport that everyone has seen at least once in their lives—on TV, while having ozoni over the New Year's holidays."

"Wait, you don't mean . . . !" Shindo gulped.

Still leaning on the window frame, Kiyose said in a leisurely manner, "That's right, the biggest relay marathon in the country. Our target is the Hakone Ekiden."

Roars of anger and confusion erupted in the room.

"No way."

"Have you lost your mind?"

"Why would we want to scramble up a mountain wearing shorts and a sash across our chest when we can be chilling at home for New Year's?"

"What's a hakone-ekiden?"

"Well, ekiden is a relay marathon, and the name comes from the ekiba tenma system, back in the days when couriers would swap post-horses at each station—"

"First of all, no one here's on a track team."

And so on.

Amid all the commotion, only Kakeru kept his mouth shut.

For track athletes, Hakone was one of the most meaningful races. Kakeru knew full well just how formidable a goal it was. What Kiyose had just announced was pure fantasy. Hakone wasn't the kind of thing a bunch of amateurs could strive for simply because they felt like it.

Kiyose sprang to his feet and, uncharacteristically, stomped down the stairs.

"Do you think we've upset him?" Joji murmured, a little worried.

"Well, I'm upset, too," Yuki said irritably and knocked back his sake. "What a joke."

Kakeru was observing their reactions, wondering where this was going, when Kiyose reappeared. He held the large doorplate that had been hanging next to the front door. Everyone instinctively recoiled like a turtle, expecting a blow on the head with the board. But Kiyose stood in the middle of the circle and scrubbed away the grime on the wood with his sleeve.

"Look at this."

Kiyose held out the clean board like a talisman. To make sure every single one of them had a good look, he turned around full circle.

"Uh . . . what the heck?!"

Shouts of alarm went up around the group. Kakeru leaned forward, too, digesting the letters on the board, vaguely aware that jaws actually do drop in real life.

On the plain wood, kanji characters in sumi ink spelled out "Chikusei-so." But that wasn't all. Though years of dirt had obscured them until now, there were two lines of smaller letters above those characters:

Kansei University
Track and Field Club Training Hall

It was undeniable. That really was what the board said.

"Since *when?*" Nico groaned, even though he'd been living there longer than any of them. The newbies, Jota and Joji, looked at each other, the color draining from their faces. It was finally starting to sink in: Kiyose wasn't pulling their leg at all. He was actually serious about taking on the Hakone Ekiden.

"Hang on . . . does our college even have a track team?" Shindo croaked, as pitifully as a feudal peasant begging his lord to bring down the yearly fee for his land.

"It's small and weak, but it does exist. I told you once that I competed in a track meet when I was in my first year, remember?" Kiyose answered.

"But I thought you were doing that on your own," Prince muttered. He had no idea how the world of track and field worked.

Kiyose was unfazed. Still holding up the sign, he dropped another bombshell. "Of course, all of us here are club members."

"How?!" This time, the uproar was even more vehement. Yuki shot up to his feet and demanded, "When did *that* happen?!"

"Since you moved in here," Kiyose answered coolly. "Didn't you think it was odd? Thirty thousand yen a month for room *and* board, in this day and age—there's bound to be a catch."

Heedless of everyone's protests, Kakeru glared at Kiyose quietly. "In other words, the moment we moved into Aotake, we were entered into the track team?"

"Exactly."

"Meaning, we were automatically registered in the Inter-University Athletic Union of Kanto?"

"Exactly."

"*Exactly?* You've got to be kidding me . . ." Kakeru sighed. "You did all that without our consent? Talk about a dirty trick. How many people are on the track team?"

"There's about a dozen short-distance runners. Though they're really third-rate. As for long distance, we have the ten of us here."

"But we never joined!" King tried to snatch the board from Kiyose.

Musa rushed to intervene. "I still don't understand. Let's stop for a moment and talk it over."

"Good idea. Let's calm down. Have a seat, everyone," Kiyose instructed, unperturbed.

Everyone had the same thought: *It's you who started this mess.* But at Chikusei-so, Kiyose's words always held absolute power. The group stifled their anger as much as they could and sat in a circle again. No one spoke. None of them knew what to say.

Yuki nudged Kakeru with his elbow. *Go for it*, he prompted with a look. Kakeru, at a loss, surveyed the group. The twins threw glances at him as if to say, *We're counting on you.* By now, they all knew that Kakeru went jogging twice every day. The only one who wasn't aware of this was Prince, who'd been shutting himself up in his room, burying his nose in manga.

Kakeru was used to hierarchy; to speak up before any of the older residents felt like crossing a line. But, lacking Kakeru's familiarity with the world of track and field, the others couldn't hope to persuade Kiyose to abandon his sudden proposal.

Kakeru sat up straight.

"Let me ask you just in case," he began. "Who's the coach? And what do they think of so-called members who don't even know they're part of the club?"

"That's nothing to worry about. Our head coach is the landlord, Mr. Gen'ichiro Tazaki."

"That's crazy!" Tragic cries shot up again from the circle. Joji was so shocked he started choking on his sake. "That tottering old man?" he spluttered. "How would he even coach anything? It's hopeless!"

"Don't be rude," Kiyose chided him. "Our landlord was once called the greatest treasure of Japanese athletics."

"Uh . . . when was that?" Jota asked tentatively, stroking his brother's back.

"Let's see. He was already well known as a legendary coach of Kansei University when Kokichi Tsuburaya died and left behind his suicide note about all the food he enjoyed."

"I have no idea what you're talking about," Musa said sadly. This time, both Shindo and the king of trivia were too preoccupied to explain. Kokichi Tsuburaya was a prominent runner who won a bronze medal at the 1964 Tokyo Olympics, but since he didn't want to stray into a whole other topic, Kakeru decided to ignore Musa's remark.

"Haiji, you said Hakone is our target. But frankly, that's flat-out impossible," said Kakeru.

Everyone except Kiyose seemed relieved to hear Kakeru being so assertive.

"How do you know without even trying?" Kiyose asked.

"It's obvious. Only a handful of varsity teams can compete in the Hakone. No one's guaranteed a place—not even those universities with powerful teams, who've been training hard every day for years."

Now Prince looked up after having been absorbed in his manga the entire time. "I don't mean to brag, but I've never even run properly in my whole life," he said. "Imagine how long it would take for someone like me to compete in the Hakone Ekiden. Probably longer than it takes for a slipper animalcule to evolve into a human being."

"Even you have to be a faster runner than a paramecium, Prince," King said, in a half-baked attempt at consolation.

"A paramecium is a paramecium. It would never evolve into a human," Yuki said curtly.

Ignoring the others, Kiyose looked straight at Kakeru. "I'm surprised you're turning tail right from the get-go. Practice is essential, but you know it's not just about blindly throwing yourself into intense training."

Kakeru didn't budge. "As an experienced runner, you must realize that these people are amateurs. What would you gain from dragging them into this? It's a pipe dream."

"True. If we don't rise up to the challenge, that's what it'll be—a pipe dream." Losing his usual composure, Kiyose raised his voice in exasperation. "But they have plenty of potential. Nico-senpai used to be on a track team. The twins and King played soccer in high school, and Yuki was in the kendo club. Shindo used to climb up and down a mountain to go to school—that's more than six miles there and back, every day. And who knows how much latent strength Musa's muscles might have?"

"It's just a stereotype that Black people are good at running," Musa said softly. "I'm not a particularly fast runner—just like there are Black people who hate hip-hop or can't dance."

"And it's been at least seven years since I quit track," Nico said with a rueful grin as he lit another cigarette.

"So I don't even count? Fine, I suck at sports," Prince moped as he idly flipped through his manga.

Kiyose kept his eyes on Kakeru. "And you came to Aotake, Kakeru," he said fervently. "We have ten people now. Mount Hakone isn't just some mirage. This isn't an unattainable dream. It's a real goal that we can work together to achieve!"

There was a smattering of listless clapping, but it stopped when Kiyose barked, "I'm dead serious!" Kakeru opened his mouth to argue back, but Kiyose cut him off and gave one last push by reciting the Hakone Ekiden's rules of participation by rote: "'Eligible participants must be registered in the varsity teams of participating universities and in the Inter-University Athletic Union of Kanto; furthermore, they must not have previously applied to compete in this race more than four times. Any participation in the preliminary competition is included in this count, regardless of the outcome.' Aotake's residents are members of the Kansei University Track and Field Club, and all the club members are automatically registered in the Union. None of us have ever participated in the Hakone Ekiden or the prelim. See? We meet all the requirements."

"The problem is the prelim," Kakeru said, finally managing to get a word in. "There's no way a team can just randomly pop in and pass through to the final round."

"Is that true? I didn't know that," murmured Shindo.

"Most people only see the final race at New Year's." Kakeru nodded. "Twenty university teams can participate in the Hakone Ekiden, but only the top ten get seed rights to participate in the following year. About thirty teams compete over the remaining ten spots at the prelim in October."

"Thirty teams from colleges in Kanto? That doesn't sound like a lot," Joji remarked.

"It's tougher than it sounds!" Kakeru said. "In Hakone, you run ten sections split between ten people, but each leg is more than twenty kilometers. So, the prelim is a twenty-kilometer race, and they add up each members' record to get the time for the whole team. But . . . from the get-go, the length of the race is a major obstacle."

Prompted by Kakeru's look, Kiyose added begrudgingly, "It's hard to line up ten people who can run at a decent pace for twenty kilometers. And the speed's been getting faster and faster in recent years. There's also a condition for competing in the prelim. You have to hold an official record of running 5,000 meters in under seventeen minutes, or 10,000 meters in under thirty-five minutes."

Hearing the daunting numbers, everyone fell silent.

"The university teams that end up competing at the Hakone Ekiden are the best of the best," said Kakeru. "If you average out the team members' records, most of them can run 5,000 meters in less than fourteen minutes and thirty seconds. Plus, those colleges round up the most promising athletes from all across the country. Hakone isn't the kind of race you can compete in just by telling each other the sky's the limit. There's no space for a tiny, pathetic track team at some random university that doesn't even take sports referrals for admissions."

"Umm . . ." Prince raised his hand hesitantly. "I don't really get what the big deal is about those numbers."

"Back in high school, didn't you ever do long-distance runs in phys ed?" Jota asked in a slightly hoarse voice.

"Nope." Prince shook his head. "I went to a high-ranked school, so we were all about studying. Our long-distance runs were just three kilometers."

"If you had to run five kilometers in under seventeen minutes, your pace would have to be faster than 3.5 minutes per kilometer," Yuki said calmly.

"Three and a half?! I probably took like fifteen minutes to run three kilometers," Prince said.

"That's . . . hopelessly slow," Nico groaned as he puffed away on his cigarette.

"Five kilometers in seventeen minutes is only the condition you have to meet to compete in the prelim," Kiyose explained, laying it on the line. "Realistically, we'd all have to be able to run it in around fourteen minutes to make it to Hakone."

"Well, that's obviously impossible in our case," Joji said brightly, already relieved to be off the hook.

But Kiyose didn't back down. "What you need to run a long-distance race is endurance and focus. Without that, training gets you nowhere. If we narrow down our target and tune our training to Hakone, and only Hakone, we'll make the impossible possible."

"Seriously, what makes you so confident?" Kakeru said in amazement.

"I already told you. Everyone at Aotake has hidden strength," Kiyose declared boldly. Even the residents who'd lived with him for several years had never noticed before how much passion lay dormant within him. "Let's talk numbers. Kakeru can run five kilometers in under fourteen minutes. It's a remarkable record, on par with only a select few people who would compete in Hakone. As for me, my official record was just over fourteen minutes, ten seconds at the last track meet before I got injured. But I can feel my leg getting better these days—I'll push hard to beat my record, even if that means my leg will be broken by the time I finish running Hakone."

"No thanks," Yuki muttered. He didn't like it when people got fanatical. "And while I'm at it, no thanks to dragging me into this either."

Kiyose ignored him. "And Musa could probably run in a little less than fourteen minutes, too. All the foreign athletes who compete in Hakone have records in the range of thirteen to fourteen minutes."

"Those people must have been invited to study at the university because of their athletic performance," Musa reasoned, glancing at Shindo for help. "Not like me. I'm just a science and engineering overseas student on a government scholarship. Besides, back home, I used to be driven to school by our driver."

Joji was puzzled. "If you're so rich, how did you end up in Aotake?"

"To learn more about society. I didn't expect it would turn into this . . ." Musa trailed off, wilting like a shriveled morning glory.

Kiyose bulldozed on into his closing argument. "Anyway, channel even a fraction of the passion you have for mahjong and nightlife into running, and I'm sure you'll see positive results. After all, if there's one thing you guys have in abundance, it's stamina."

Kiyose's enthusiasm was starting to catch on with a few people in the circle. Kakeru could feel a slight change in the air. *It's not that easy.* He grabbed the sake bottle angrily and poured some into his cup.

A bunch of amateurs trying to compete in the Hakone Ekiden. And there was only half a year to go until the prelim in October. If any serious athlete on a track team heard the story, they'd snort. It was laughably reckless. What did running really mean for Kiyose?

Did he invite me to Chikusei-so all because of this scheme? Maybe he's no different from those people in high school who just wanted me for my speed.

But Kakeru didn't storm out of the room. Even though he told himself, *Don't put up with this crazy talk, just go back to your own room,* his body didn't budge. Somewhere deep inside him, a voice whispered, *It could be fun. Are you going to keep running by yourself for the rest of your life, isolated from the world of athletics? You might as well team up with these people and stage a raid on Hakone. Just give it a try. Why not?*

The whispers kindled Kakeru into flame.

He remembered what Kiyose had told him: that Kakeru had looked so free when he ran, just living in the moment. Kiyose had said that was why he'd called out to Kakeru. No one in Kakeru's life had told him anything like that before.

Running doesn't need pleasure. Focus only on increasing your speed. Make that your priority before everything else—other things, like having fun, hanging out with friends, or finding a girlfriend should come later. Kakeru was sick and tired of hearing those commands from the supervisor, the coach, the upperclassmen. All they'd required of him was to run like a machine. The only value they'd seen in him was the numbers he achieved on a stopwatch. He wanted to leave those days behind for good.

The others were lost in thought, too. As the muddy swirl of his thoughts pressed down on him, Kakeru looked around the still room.

Eventually, Shindo looked up. "I wouldn't mind trying."

Everyone turned to him in surprise. No one had expected quiet, reliable Shindo to be the first to assent.

"Back in the country, I used to walk many kilometers in the mountains every day, so I'm confident about my endurance. Besides, if we manage to participate in the Hakone Ekiden, we'll be on TV. I think my parents would be excited about that."

"If Shindo is joining the challenge, I will as well," said Musa. "But I have to warn you, I'm really not a fast runner. Are you still okay with that?"

"It's all up to our practice, so that's nothing to worry about," said Kiyose in his gentlest voice.

Nico scowled and grumbled. Yuki ignored the room, staring out the window. Prince was edging toward the door. The rest of the group, who tended to go along with anything that sounded fun, perked up when Shindo and Musa stepped forward.

"Hey, Haiji," said one of the twins, "is it really true it'll help us get girls?"

"You promise?" said the other.

"And you're sure it'll help me secure a steady job?" King pressed.

"Of course," Kiyose assured the group.

Kakeru wanted to cry out, "He's duping you!" but he knew nothing he said would change anything. What King and the twins really wanted was just to escape for a little while from their harsh reality. And so they pounced on the bait that Kiyose dangled in front of them in the form of Hakone Ekiden, like horses lured on by sugary treats made of dreams.

"All right. Let's lend a hand to Haiji's ambition!" King proclaimed exuberantly.

Kiyose cast a razor-sharp look at each of the remaining residents who had yet to give their consent: Nico, Yuki, Prince, and Kakeru. "If this were a majority vote, the matter would be settled already. But I'm sure that wouldn't be enough to convince you."

Even his breathing shallowed as Kakeru braced himself for Kiyose's next attack.

"Therefore, I'm invoking state power. You have no right to veto," Kiyose said coolly.

"You tyrant!" Nico blurted out.

"You can't do that—this state is governed by laws," Yuki argued desperately.

Kiyose scoffed at their loud protests. "Nico-senpai. When you had an exam that you had to pass at all costs and begged me to help you, who was it that kicked you out of bed with the kindness and strictness of a mother, so you'd make it to the classroom on time? Who was it that helped you redo the wallpaper every year when your room got stained by tar? Who was it that fixed the floorboard in the hallway when you made a hole in it, so that you wouldn't get in trouble with the landlord?"

Nico fell silent, like a prisoner overcome with remorse for his past misdeeds right before his execution.

Kiyose's next target was Yuki. "You still remember those New Year's feasts I made just for you, don't you, Yuki? And don't tell me you've forgotten how I fed you lunch for the past year when you were too busy with the bar exam to work part-time and were low on cash . . ."

Yuki could only nod repeatedly like a broken wind-up toy. Riding on the momentum, Kiyose struck out at Prince, who was about to retreat out of the room.

"Prince. Thanks to your manga collection, Chikusei-so is on the brink of collapse. Which would you rather choose: throwing out your books, or training for Hakone Ekiden with us?"

Though he sank to the floor, Prince dared to put up a fight. "Neither! That's like telling me to die."

As this heartrending cry rang out in the room, Kiyose crossed his arms with a mild "hmm," then turned to Kakeru. Kakeru casually put up his hands in response.

"I know what you're going to say—'Who brought you to Chikusei-so? If you don't want to join, feel free to move out.' Right?"

"I can't threaten you like that when you've got nowhere else to go."

Kiyose unfolded his arms. "Fine. Kakeru and Prince, I'll give you a few days' grace to mull it over. Let me know when you change your mind."

Prince broke off his lamentation and sidled closer to Kiyose. "And if we don't?"

"Are you gonna declare a state of emergency next?" Yuki cut in sarcastically.

"Nope." Kiyose smiled pleasantly. "I'm going to be patient and keep demanding their surrender."

Kakeru and Prince each let out a heavy sigh.

A few days later, after class, Kakeru was running through campus toward the main gate, down a path lined with Himalayan cedars. Since the spring semester had just begun, the place was packed with chatty students hanging out in groups or strolling side by side. He zigzagged through the crowd.

He heard someone call his name. When he stopped and looked around, he noticed Prince sitting on a little chair at the edge of the path behind a long desk, presumably taken from a classroom. He gestured to Kakeru to come over.

"Looking for new club members?" Kakeru asked.

Prince held out a notebook to him with a big grin. "Can you put down your name and address in here?"

"My address? But we live in the same house."

Kakeru peered at the notebook. Apparently, recruitment wasn't going so well. Only Jota and Joji, with their Chikusei-so addresses, were on the list so far, as though they'd taken pity on Prince. After a pause, Kakeru asked tentatively, "What kind of group is it?"—though he knew the answer already.

"Manga Research Society!" Prince announced. "This year, I'm planning to do an experiment: piecing together lots of panels from different works by one manga artist to create a whole new story."

His eyes sparkled as he explained. Kakeru sat down on another chair next to him.

"Have you decided, Prince?"

"You mean, about *that*?" Prince murmured in a suggestive tone.

Kakeru simply nodded. "Yes, whether to go for the Hakone Ekiden."

Prince looked disappointed that he couldn't pretend to be a spy. "I'll do it. I have no choice," he said, closing the notebook. "You saw how big my collection is. I can't move anywhere else now with a load like that. I can't afford it."

"When Haiji told you to throw away your manga if you didn't want to join, wasn't that just an empty threat?"

"You think?"

On second thought, Kakeru wasn't so sure. He wouldn't put it past Kiyose to stick to his word and actually scrap Prince's precious collection. Kiyose's silent tactics to make them surrender were getting to Kakeru, too. These days, Kiyose kept including a vinegar-soaked salad in every dinner, and he never failed to give Kakeru a bigger serving than the rest. Only last night, Kakeru had grudgingly gulped down his bowl of sunomono, frowning at the sour slices of cucumber and seaweed. As long as he didn't give in to Kiyose's ploy, the sunomono sour attack was bound to continue.

"It just doesn't feel right when you're forced to run," Kakeru said.

"Sure." Prince shrugged. "But we're all living together at Aotake. We have to compromise to some extent."

This is going to be so much more than a little compromise, Kakeru thought. Prince was too far removed from sports to really grasp what was at stake. He didn't know what kind of torturous training awaited him on the road to the Hakone Ekiden. Kiyose was trying to lead them up a steep, grueling climb—a narrow, risky path along the edge of a precipice—without any guarantee of reaching the destination.

Oblivious to Kakeru's dark thoughts, Prince continued, "I heard Haiji used to compete in track meets when he was a first-year. He used to take practice really seriously."

"Why do you think he quit?" Kakeru pretended not to know about the scar on Kiyose's knee.

"Apparently, they push athletes too hard at some high schools. And the strain catches up on them later on, and they break down. Nico-senpai told me it's pretty common."

"Is it really true that Nico-senpai used to do track?" Kakeru asked. It was hard to believe that anyone athletic would smoke the way Nico did.

"Yup. From what I've heard, he was on the track team up to the end of high school." Prince picked up the notebook. Flipping through the blank pages, he stirred up a little wind. "You know, Kakeru. It's grown on me, life at Aotake. I think I can kind of understand how it feels for someone who wants to run but can't. When I imagine what it'd be like if I couldn't read manga anymore, I get it—which is why I'm starting to feel like maybe I wouldn't mind going along with Haiji's idea."

That night, the residents of Chikusei-so assembled in the twins' room again. When Kakeru and Prince both agreed to take on the Hakone Ekiden, the twins whooped in excitement.

"Yes! That makes ten of us!" Joji said.

"Practice starts tomorrow!" Jota chimed in.

Musa and Shindo skipped into the room, carrying Kiyose's creations from the kitchen. Freshly fried chicken karaage was heaped on a huge plate.

"Now that's settled, we have to build up our stamina," said Musa.

"Good job making up your minds, guys," Shindo added.

Kakeru didn't see anything sour on the menu and cast Kiyose a sideways glance. Kiyose feigned innocence, but he'd probably expected that Kakeru and Prince would reveal their decision that night. Kakeru was a little peeved that Kiyose had seen right through them.

"Come on, come on, take these." Joji was handing beer cans out around the room. "Let's make a toast."

Nico and Yuki couldn't hide their disappointment at the last stronghold crumbling. Reluctantly, they took the beer from Joji and grumbled at Kakeru under their breath.

"Why'd you give in?"

"Thought you had a bit more backbone, but you didn't last long," Yuki jabbed.

The group held up their cans and cheered. Half filled with hope for their new aspiration and half in reckless abandon, they shouted, "Mount Hakone is the most savage in the world!"

Soon, the twins' room hurtled into utter chaos. Prince sat by himself in the wooden corner, poring over a manga, as though to say that he'd done his part for the day. Figuring they wouldn't have a chance to play mahjong once the training started, Nico, Yuki, King, and Jota brought out a table and started a game, while Joji circled around them.

"You never hold back, do you, Yuki?" Nico said.

"You're making it too easy for me, Nico-senpai."

"Hey, Jota, I told you, you can't finish right after claiming a tile. Do you even know the rules?" King complained.

"Umm, not really."

"Joji, no cheating! Don't tell Jota what tiles we've got!"

Shindo and Musa were watching TV while waiting for their turn at the mahjong table.

"The ad says, 'Tune in for the late show on Monday!' but in reality, it's going to air at one a.m. on Tuesday. Isn't that odd, Shindo?" Musa asked.

"I suppose even after midnight they still see it as Monday, as long as you haven't gone to bed—but you're right, it's a confusing way to put it."

They soon stormed through all the cans of beer and switched to drinking sweet potato shochu. The room was buzzing with hope and excitement for their new endeavor. While none of them mentioned it, everyone felt a rush of adrenaline. They were too shy to show just how fired up they were, so they tried hard to hold it in and act the same way they always did. But the air was thrumming with energy.

Kakeru stayed away from the mahjong table and sat by the window. *It won't last*, he thought. *Maybe Kiyose's words got them pumped, but soon enough they'll get tired of practice and call it quits.* To run—to keep running—wasn't such an easy task. The Hakone Ekiden wasn't the kind of race you could enter based on sheer determination alone.

Sooner or later, the members would revolt or drop out, and Kiyose's scheme was bound to fail. *I might as well go along with it till then. I'll just keep up my own training as I've always done.*

Kiyose sat next to Kakeru, cracking peanuts. When he had extracted all the nuts from their shells and onto a plate, he looked satisfied. With a sigh of relief, he picked up a cup of shochu. "Help yourself," he said, sliding the plate toward Kakeru.

"Are you serious?" Kakeru asked in a low voice.

"Yeah. Go ahead."

"I don't mean the peanuts. You should know, Haiji. It's a stupid gamble."

Kiyose was silent for some time. Eventually, he held up his cup to the light as if the question he should ask was written there. "Do you like to run, Kakeru?" he said calmly.

It was the same question he'd asked the night they met. Kakeru was baffled.

"I want to find out. What it really means to run," Kiyose said, his eyes fixed on the cup.

This didn't answer Kakeru's question at all. Yet the earnest look in Kiyose's eyes in that moment would stay with Kakeru for a long time.

III

TRAINING BEGINS

"They're not getting up," Kiyose remarked.

"Looks like it," Kakeru agreed.

At the beginning of April, 5:30 a.m. was more night than day. A few early birds started chirping, a little out of tune. The light *vroom* of the newspaper delivery bike sounded from the road and faded away.

Kakeru and Kiyose stood in the yard outside Chikusei-so.

"What happened to the enthusiasm from last night? Was it all a dream, Kakeru? They were shouting they'll never give up, they'll offer themselves up to the wind, they'll devote their lives to reaching Mount Hakone! Didn't you all say that?"

"Not me. That was King getting all worked up."

Kakeru vaguely recalled Jota and Joji thrusting their fists in the air along with King, but the three of them probably wouldn't remember. *They were pretty hammered*, Kakeru thought, but he didn't say that out loud. He preferred not to provoke Kiyose.

Kiyose, who made no allowances for drunken behavior, ran out of patience. "I'll go wake them up," he said and disappeared into the house.

Kakeru did some stretches, watching the eastern sky gradually pale into pastel pink. He could hear Kiyose banging something hard on the back of a pot—probably a ladle. As though driven out by the noise, Nira trotted out from under the engawa and had a good stretch. Kakeru played tag with Nira around the yard. By the time Kakeru had thoroughly warmed up, the others had plodded out the front door, having been rounded up by Kiyose. They all looked groggy and had puffy faces.

"Okay. First, we have to meet the eligibility requirements for competing in the prelim. For that, we'll need to build up our speed and stamina."

Kiyose's enthusiastic announcement was met with a lukewarm response. Like strips of seaweed washed ashore, everyone stood limp, swaying a little on the spot. Jota's breath reeked of booze as he tottered, and Kakeru gently propped him up.

"This morning, we'll start off with a run up to the Tamagawa riverbank," Kiyose continued, ignoring this state of affairs. "I'll check everyone's current abilities and come up with a training plan."

"What about breakfast? I'm hungry," Joji said timidly.

"You can eat right after getting up? Ah, the joys of youth." Nico gave a tremendous yawn and scratched his tousled head. Next to him, Yuki was asleep on his feet.

Kiyose shrugged off the swirling mass of lethargy, appetite, and discontent in the air. "We'll eat after running. Come on, let's go."

"Isn't it at least five kilometers to the river?" Prince stammered, aghast. "You mean we're running ten kilometers there and back? At this ungodly hour?"

"You can go at your own pace. It's a breeze."

Kiyose marshaled the grumbling group out onto the road, like a watchful dog herding a flock of sheep. Musa and Shindo took the lead, following Kiyose's instructions. They tugged at King's arms, and he helplessly started running, too.

"Let's go," Kakeru called to the twins. "If you eat just before running, you'll get cramps. The best time to run is when you're feeling a bit hungry." He gave Joji's back an encouraging pat to get him moving.

By the time they reached the bus route, Prince was already wheezing. "Maybe I'll see you at the river in a couple of hours," he rasped, slogging at a pace that wasn't all that different from walking.

"Kakeru, you go ahead," said Kiyose. He seemed ready to monitor

Prince's progress without rushing him. "I'll bring up the rear. Can you make a note of everyone's finish times?"

"What does that mean, 'bring up the rear'?" Musa asked Shindo.

"It means he'll be the last person in the group." Shindo was jogging in light steps, with his usual composure.

Everyone had set off from Chikusei-so around the same time, but they soon spread out more and more according to their respective abilities. Kakeru slipped out of the line and started running at his own pace. The sounds of the others breathing and talking quickly faded away.

It had been a while since Kakeru had run with anyone else. But in the end, he always found himself alone. Speed and rhythm were things he couldn't share with anyone. They belonged to him, and him alone.

The sky grew steadily brighter. Most of the way to the riverbank passed through residential areas. He crossed two tributaries of Tamagawa called Sengawa and Nogawa, then a large, grassy field, and after that, he made his way through a posh neighborhood at the top of a small hill. The route had a lot of ups and downs.

Soon, the raised embankment of Tamagawa began to emerge beyond the rooftops. On a clear day, the ridges of the Tanzawa Mountains and Mount Fuji would have been visible in the distance, but it was a hazy morning.

Kakeru sprinted up the embankment and looked down at the river. Mist hung over it, drifting down with the current. Only a few people dotted the riverbank below: elderly people doing exercises and people walking their dogs. The Odakyu train rattled across the iron bridge. It was already crammed with people commuting to work or school.

The blades of grass on the bank shone with dewdrops catching the morning light. It wasn't good for his body to stop abruptly, so he jogged back and forth on the raised path along the river at a leisurely pace. His pace had been about three minutes, thirty seconds per kilometer. For a distance of just five kilometers, it was a much slower pace than what he was used to. But the other residents of Chikusei-so were still nowhere to be seen. As he cooled down, he glanced at his watch and the road in turns.

When the twins, Shindo, Musa, Yuki, and King finally arrived at the river, it was twenty-five minutes after they had left Chikusei-so. King looked spent, his breathing heavy, but the others seemed unruffled.

"You look like you could keep running," Kakeru remarked.

"I can't really tell," Jota replied, peering curiously at the features on Kakeru's watch. "I've never thought about the exact distance when I run, so I don't have a feel for how fast I can run for how long, you know? We ended up going along together at an easy pace."

"I'm starving." Joji crouched and started shredding the grass around him, ignoring the beauty of the morning dew. Yuki slumped down on the damp ground and closed his eyes in an attempt to snatch a bit more of his interrupted sleep. Shindo and Musa looked completely unfazed as they stroked King's back to comfort him.

Maybe, just maybe, these people might be cut out for running, Kakeru thought. They lacked the experience and the knack for it now, but at the very least they didn't seem to dislike the activity.

Had Kiyose seen their potential? Shindo and Musa seemed to have plenty of reserve in their fundamental physical strength. Both the twins and King used to play soccer. They must've done roadwork as part of their practice, and they should be no strangers to running. As for Yuki, he used to do kendo. He would've had a lot of intense running in his training, and he wouldn't have developed heavy muscles for it, so he could adapt well to distance running.

Though Kakeru had assumed the group would give up in no time, perhaps they'd put up a surprisingly good fight. Observing them after their run made him look at them in a different light. Of course, everything rested on their training to come, but he could see the promise in them, just as Kiyose had said. A new feeling crept into him: now he would have to get serious.

"When you finish a run, you have to loosen up your body," said Kakeru, shaking Yuki awake. "You should run back and forth here.

When your breathing gets regular again, do some stretches. After that, you can sit down and rest."

Since he didn't like standing around doing nothing—and still felt like he hadn't run enough—Kakeru taught them how to stretch properly, left his watch with Jota, and ran off to meet Nico and Prince, who hadn't yet made it to the river.

Straightaway, he bumped into Nico at the bottom of the embankment.

"Hey, Kakeru," Nico croaked. He was completely out of breath but doing his best to keep his legs moving. "My body's too heavy, my lungs are too tight—I'm just not feeling it." In the years away from track, his body had forgotten how to run. "Guess I gotta quit smoking and go on a diet."

Kakeru let Nico go on his way and ran farther up the path. When he came to the foot of the hill of houses, he found Prince collapsed by the side of the road. Kiyose was squatting next to him with a bottle of sports drink in his hand.

"Is everyone done?" Kiyose asked.

Kakeru nodded. "I just passed Nico-senpai on the way."

"That took a while."

"He said he's going to quit smoking and lose weight."

"Good attitude. And the rest?"

"They were going at a little less than five minutes per kilometer."

"What did you think of their run?"

"They looked like they could push more. Their form was pretty balanced for new runners."

Kiyose nodded, satisfied. But there was still a problem: Prince was sprawled out on the ground in front of them.

"Um, is Prince okay?" Kakeru asked.

"Do I look okay?" Prince retorted. "I don't even wanna stand up. Can you carry me back to Aotake, Kakeru?"

Kakeru could happily run vast distances, but he wasn't confident about lugging heavy loads with him. Before he could come up with an answer, Kiyose sternly shook his head. "Let's get to the river—if you can't run, you can walk. The important thing is to get a feel for going five kilometers on your own feet."

Kiyose's patience surprised Kakeru. Before the run, Kiyose had brandished his tyrannical authority over everyone at Chikusei-so—he'd invoked state power, put pressure on Kakeru by manipulating the dinner menu, and so on. But once they started running, Kiyose seemed to respect their individual paces as a matter of principle. He watched over them without interfering, waiting for them to reach the goal under their own power.

Haiji seems a bit different from the managers and coaches I've met before. Suddenly, Kakeru felt restless. Though he didn't realize this, the restlessness came from a spark of hope inside him. Because he had never met a mentor he had clicked with, he'd grown accustomed to stifling any expectations. He quickly dismissed this flicker of emotion.

"Can't I take the train back, at least?" Prince asked.

Kiyose rejected the suggestion with a mere look.

"Just keep walking, you'll feel like running again before long," Kakeru said. Ever since he was little, he couldn't stand the sluggish pace of walking. Wherever he went, his steps would go faster and faster until he found himself running. That way, he could reach his destination sooner, and it felt refreshing to feel the wind on his skin, the pounding of his heart.

"You do know there are people who hate sports?" Prince muttered, hauling himself up. "Oh hey, a butterfly."

They turned and followed Prince's gaze as a butterfly fluttered by, its wings like white petals. A soft beam of sunlight fell from the eaves of the house on the corner. The three of them watched the butterfly flit across this stream of light.

"Take your time. As long as you keep walking, you'll be able to run eventually," said Kiyose, as though to reassure himself as much as Prince.

As butterflies drift on the breeze, humans run on the ground. For Kakeru, running was as natural as breathing, but there were people in the world who saw it differently.

Interesting, he thought. Until now, almost everyone around him had been aspiring track athletes. Most of his waking hours were taken up by practice, and many of his friends and teachers were involved in athletics. So it came as a surprise to him that there were people in the world who hardly ever ran, who thought that even a bit of running was torture—and that, for one reason or another, there were people who couldn't run, even if they wanted to.

I've gone through my life without thinking about anything or feeling anything, he thought. He had been too preoccupied trying to survive in the track and field club, a narrow circle of people brought together just because they happened to be good at running long distances and shared a common goal.

It was only the first morning of the Chikusei-so team's foolhardy attempt to compete in the Hakone Ekiden. But Kakeru was already startled by everything he was discovering. There were people like the twins, who seemed to have the strength to run but hadn't shown any interest in the sport until now. There were Kiyose and Nico, who couldn't run the way they wanted to because of an injury or a long gap. And there was Prince, who seemed to hate running with a vengeance, even though it was, in a way, a basic activity for any animal with legs.

The world was far more complicated than Kakeru had imagined. But it wasn't the kind of complicated that made him uneasy or confused. Lost in thought, he watched the butterfly flutter toward the river.

When Kakeru got back from lectures that evening, the Chikusei-so residents were standing in a row in the yard. Apparently, Kiyose had ambushed them as they were coming home.

Now that he had all ten of them, Kiyose declared, "I made a basic training plan. I want to divide you into different levels, so we're going to run five kilometers at full speed."

Kakeru was impressed that Kiyose had already drawn up a plan, but naturally, the twins booed.

"But we just ran this morning! Do we have to run *again*?"

"I'm too exhausted. And my joints hurt around my groin."

"Does it hurt badly?" Kiyose said, acknowledging Joji's complaint.

"No, not that much."

"Wonder where it's coming from. Either your body's not used to running yet, your form is off, or your joints are vulnerable to begin with." With a worried frown, Kiyose knelt in front of Joji and gently pressed his thumb against his upper thigh.

Joji squirmed ticklishly. "Haiji! Come on, stop touching me there."

"It might be his shoes." Kakeru pointed out. "Aren't they for basketball?"

"You're right." Kiyose straightened up and examined everyone's feet. "Why are you all wearing basketball shoes and plain sneakers? Are you here to run or what?"

"But these are all we've got," Jota mumbled, hiding behind Prince. His shoes matched Joji's. As for Prince, he was wearing the sort of average sneakers you'd find at a big discount store.

"All of you, make sure you get running shoes," Kiyose ordered sternly.

"We did," said Musa and Shindo, holding up a bag from a sports store.

A moment later, Yuki held up a pair he'd been hiding behind his back, too. "It was pretty fun this morning, so."

"You're getting pretty hyped for a guy who was just griping about it," Nico teased.

"Good." Kiyose nodded. "As for the rest of you, pick up running shoes soon and find the right fit. If you can, get a wristwatch with a stopwatch function, too."

"I want the same one as Kakeru's," Jota said, staring at Kakeru's wrist. "Looks sharp. Nike, huh?"

Kakeru's watch was especially designed for runners, its plastic body round and streamlined. It was equipped with a range of functions and extremely light, too. Of all the watches he'd used before, this one was his favorite.

"They come in different colors. You can use it like a simple stopwatch, but you can also add up all the recorded times like this . . ." Kakeru explained, as the twins listened closely.

"I have to work more shifts now," Shindo said.

But Kiyose was quick to reject the idea. "From now on, part-time jobs—and mahjong—are forbidden for everyone at Aotake," he announced gravely. "This isn't the time for work. Focus on your training."

"Then how are we supposed to buy shoes and a watch?" King argued.

"Add running clothes to that list," Kiyose replied coolly. "Look at you, wearing tracksuits from high school and sweatpants—and even jeans, like Prince. You need something that wicks away your sweat and keeps you dry, or you'll get a chill. For training sessions, you should always come prepared with a towel and a change of clothes, and remember to get changed immediately after sweating."

"So how are we supposed to buy all that without part-time jobs?" King snapped again.

"No problem. If you're serious about practice, you won't have time for anything else. You'll rack up savings before you know it, even just from the money your family sends you."

"Whaaat?!" More cries of protest shot out.

"What's all this racket?" The door to the main house opened, and the landlord—who was meant to be the coach, at least officially—emerged. Nira had been stretched out on the ground with his eyes closed, but he perked up at his owner's appearance and thumped his tail.

"There's no need to worry about money," the landlord said, looking over the group. "Haiji told me everything. If you're really serious about Hakone, I'll ask the supporters' club and get all the equipment you need."

"Supporters' club? Does our school even have a group like that?" Yuki asked dubiously.

"Why, I'm going to make one," said the landlord.

"Hopeless," Nico murmured.

"Anyway, let's go to the track." Kiyose led the way, and they all followed, still wearing their ordinary outfits. Nira came along, too, hoping for a walk.

Kakeru assumed they were going to run at the university sports field to measure their times, but Kiyose kept going in the opposite direction. They seemed to be headed for the district's public sports ground on the other side of Sengawa.

"Why aren't we using the one on campus, Haiji?" he asked. "It's closer to Aotake, and it's in better condition."

"The campus field is used by a lot of sports teams and clubs. We'd have to wait about a million years if we wanted to use it."

"But we're the track team—don't we get priority to use the track?"

"Ranks matter in everything," Kiyose replied in an icy tone. In other words, their team was so small and weak that no one even recognized their existence. Kakeru kept his mouth shut after that. There was no point in stirring him up.

Though weeds sprouted here and there on the public sports field, it still had a proper track, with a single lap measuring four hundred meters.

Kiyose walked them through the basic steps for practice. Before and after every session, they were to spend about an hour on easy runs. In addition, they had to do stretches, massage one another, and so on.

"Does an 'easy run' mean jogging at a slow pace?" Musa asked.

"Yes, you run at a pace that doesn't put much burden on your body. If you start running without warming up first, or stop too abruptly, it could lead to injury."

"Imagine running a whole hour before practice. It'll knock me out before I even get started," Prince said, despairingly.

"You managed to run five kilometers this morning, remember? Don't worry, you'll get used to it soon enough," Kiyose assured him. "Stick to the training, and I promise you'll become a full-fledged runner."

Kiyose wasn't bluffing. To get through long-distance runs, you need different muscles from those of short-distance runners. Instead of instantaneous, explosive bursts of muscle power, long-distance runs are an endurance game of maintaining a steady level of energy to propel yourself forward over a long period of time. For short-distance athletes, their potential is almost completely decided by their innate muscle quality. For long-distance runners, it's possible to build up ability little by little through daily training.

On the flip side, this means that no one can achieve great success in distance running without engaging with their own body and persevering with their training every single day. Natural talent is deemed necessary in a variety of sports, but in almost no other sport are the scales between talent and hard work tipped more in favor of the latter.

On the empty sports field, they separated into two groups to measure their times. Some of them—namely, everyone except Kakeru and Kiyose—argued that they couldn't possibly jog for an hour before measuring the time, so they settled on diving straight in and running five kilometers as fast as they could. Kakeru and Kiyose were going to jog casually around the track with them, taking note of everyone's times. The idea was that by the time Prince finished his run, the two would've loosened up enough to launch into their own five kilometers at full throttle.

The pair had to pay close attention to keep an eye on the whole group while doing their own easy run. If they let their guard down, they would have messed up the lap counts.

"If only Nira could click on the stopwatch." Kiyose cast a regretful look at the dog, who was busy sniffing at the ground in a corner of the field.

Kakeru jogged next to him at a leisurely pace. "Hey, Haiji. Do you think Prince would ever reach the prelim level? Isn't that expecting a bit too much?" Even now, Prince was straggling far behind the rest. "He's definitely lagging by a lot more than a lap."

"Don't worry," Kiyose said.

"What makes you so sure?"

"Tell me, Kakeru, what kind of personality trait suits long-distance?"

"I don't know . . . It's probably a mix of things, but endurance, maybe?"

"I think it's tenacity. Did you see Prince's collection? How his head's full of manga all the time? It's abnormal. He doesn't go out at night, he doesn't splurge on anything. Instead, all his time and money go to manga. It's incredible how he never gets tired of it. He has it in him— that obsession and diligence to pursue a single thing over a long time. That tenacious passion is a sure sign that he's cut out for distance running."

Kakeru glanced sideways at Kiyose to check whether he was serious. He was. As far as Kakeru could tell, Kiyose was genuinely praising Prince.

When they were all done, Kakeru jotted down their times on a sheet of paper:

Kakeru	14:38.37
Haiji	14:58.54
Musa	15:01.36
Joji	16:38.08
Jota	16:39.10
Shindo	17:30.23
Yuki	17:45.11
King	18:15.03
Nico	18:55.06
Prince	33:13.13

Everyone gathered around the paper in a circle.

"Kakeru, you went easy, didn't you?" Kiyose asked.

"Of course not. I can't just run my personal best all the time. And maybe *you're* not in the best shape, Haiji?"

"I'm recovering. But look at Musa's time—I knew you'd be fast. At this rate, you can aim for under fourteen minutes."

"No, I'm already at the limit. I thought my heart would explode."

"Either way, these numbers aren't so bad for the first try." Kiyose looked around at the group. "Just as I'd expected, you guys have a lot of potential. If you can run this well right now, you'll go much further with practice."

The twins and Shindo high-fived each other, excited to receive Kiyose's stamp of approval. But Yuki wasn't quite satisfied by his own speed. As perceptive as ever, he was already analyzing his performance. "Over seventeen minutes . . . I should sharpen up my form."

"Ugh, knew I'd be slow," King sulked.

"Hey, your sweat stinks like nicotine," Yuki pointed out to Nico.

"Really?" Nico sniffed at his arms.

"As for King and Nico-senpai, it's only because you're not used to running yet. Your forms are fine, so you'll have no problem improving your time," Kiyose encouraged them attentively. "Right, let's head back to Aotake and have dinner."

Joji tugged at Kiyose's sleeve. "Uh, Haiji, you're forgetting someone."

Prince was sprawled face down on the side of the track. Nira anxiously nudged him with his snout, but there was no sign of life.

"What was Prince's time?" Kiyose asked.

"It was 33:13.13," Kakeru answered.

"Not sure what to say to that," Kiyose murmured, rubbing his temple. "But, well, it's commendable that even a manga otaku managed to run the whole distance. Let's not lose hope."

So you do think Prince is just an otaku, Kakeru thought, but he kept quiet.

"The real practice starts tomorrow," Kiyose said. "Running five kilometers might feel like the best you can do right now, but you'll definitely expand the distance you're capable of and shorten the time, too, so don't worry and follow my lead. All right, you're free to go!

"Oh," he added, "you all have to jog back to Aotake, of course."

Nico was groaning in agony in his room. He was barely making progress in his software programming gig. The deadline was fast approaching, but he was bone-tired from running. For Nico, who funded his own tuition and living costs, being tired wasn't an excuse to neglect his part-time work. He glared at the computer screen in frustration.

There was a knock at his door. It annoyed him a little. *Does King wanna borrow my PC again? I'm too frigging busy for that.* But he thought he needed a change, so he called out, "It's open."

It was the twins and Prince who peeked in the door. Joji crossed the threshold and looked all around the room. "Wooow! No smoke. I've never seen your room so clear."

"You really are quitting, then." Jota took a deep breath to feel the fresh air.

"Yeah, and I'm getting nowhere with my work, thanks to that," Nico grumbled as he finished twisting a piece of wire into another figurine about the length of his finger. Every time he wanted to reach for a cigarette, he made this little doll to distract himself. A throng of wire dolls were scattered around him on the tatami floor.

"Creepy. They look like they're cursed." Prince brushed aside the dolls and sat down. "Can I please borrow your computer?"

"If it's gonna be quick, feel free. What's up?"

"Prince wants to get a treadmill from an online auction," Jota explained. Prince was already focused on opening the website he wanted.

"What for?" Nico felt an urge to grab his tobacco pack again, so he picked up another piece of wire.

"I thought it might be a good idea to run in my room while reading manga . . . Nico-senpai, what *is* this?!" Prince exclaimed, noticing something next to the mouse.

"What do you mean, what? It's a pack of cigarettes."

The carton was wrapped round and round with wire.

"Rikiishi! You're Rikiishi, Nico-senpai!" Unfortunately, none of them had read *Ashita no Joe*, so Prince's outburst went unremarked. "You really are giving it your all." Prince dabbed at his eyes, nearly moved to tears.

Nico flinched as Prince's eyes misted over. "Same goes for you guys, right? I mean, you're even getting a treadmill."

"What else can we do? Haiji's dead serious," Joji sighed, toying with the wire dolls.

"We like living here, and we like Haiji." Jota nodded. "If he says we're gonna aim for Hakone, we just have to do the best we can."

Haiji's a lucky guy to have such loyal friends, Nico thought.

"But I wonder why it has to be Hakone Ekiden." Prince paused, looking puzzled. "If running is what he's after, he could easily run by himself. No need to drag me in, of all people."

"Well, you can't pass on that relay sash if you're the only one running," Nico said, trying to quash his craving for a cigarette.

"We get that Kakeru and Haiji are fast runners," Jota said. "But why doesn't he just look for other people who're faster than us?"

"There's ten of us at Aotake, so maybe he thought it was convenient," Nico replied.

Prince pouted at his answer. "So he's roping in whoever's around? Great."

"Whatever he really has in mind," Joji said in a carefree tone, "I think it's pretty fun, running." The twins started massaging each other's back and legs.

"Me too," Nico laughed and kneaded Prince's shoulders for him. On the day Kakeru moved into Chikusei-so, Nico already had a hunch. As a former track athlete, he could tell that the person Kiyose had been eagerly awaiting had finally arrived.

Driven by their all-consuming passion for running, the two of them would have a profound impact on each other: Kakeru, who seemed to have been born to run, and Kiyose, who knew the torment of not being able to run. They would soar to new, prodigious heights that most people would never even dream of glimpsing.

The rest of the members of Chikusei-so had to work together to make that happen. How much they could transform themselves in the six months leading up to the prelim, and whether they could secure their place at the Hakone Ekiden, were crucial factors that would shape Kakeru's and Haiji's futures. Nico almost reached for the cigarette pack, but he held himself back and clenched his fist.

There was another knock on the door. This time, it was Shindo. "There you are, Prince."

"What is it? If you're having a trivia night, could you tell King I can't come right now?"

"King and Musa were so tired, they went to sleep already." Shindo sat with his back straight in a corner of the room, as calm and quiet as usual. "You were saying you wanted a treadmill, weren't you? I just got off the phone with my parents, and they said they have one in our barn. It should still work, so I can ask them to send it over if you'd like—what do you think?"

"Big yes!" Prince closed the auction page immediately.

"Why do you even have a treadmill at home, though?" Joji asked.

"In the countryside, you can usually find a massage chair, a treadmill, and a power tower lying around the house, gathering dust," Shindo explained.

Nico was doubtful—*his* family's place didn't have anything like that—but the twins were genuinely impressed by how big Shindo's house must be.

"Could they send it by cash on delivery, please? Well, we've got an early start tomorrow, so I'm off to bed." Prince promptly left the room, showing his typical lack of concern for keeping step with others. He left the twins behind, but they didn't seem to mind one bit.

"We'll head out, too. Night ni-i-ight," they said, wrapping up their massage session. Just as they opened the door, Yuki stormed out of his room across the hallway.

"What's all the noise? I can't sleep!" he barked.

"Don't take it out on us just 'cause you got banned from nightclubs," Nico said, unfazed.

"There there, we have to run at six in the morning tomorrow. It's only going to wear you out if you quarrel," Shindo interrupted in an even tone. "By the way, Nico-senpai. Can I take some of these wire dolls?"

"Sure. What for?"

"I have an idea," he said, picking up a handful of the figurines and putting them in his pocket. He went upstairs along with the others. When their footsteps died down and their doors creaked shut, a hush once again fell over Chikusei-so.

"Are you really going to help Haiji?" Yuki murmured from the doorway.

"Got a problem with that? You're getting into it, too."

"I'm all right. I have enough credits, and I've passed the bar already. But you—if you drop this year again, it's game over."

All his life, Nico had taken the roundabout path, dabbling at just about anything that caught his interest, so he had plenty of things he could do to earn money. Even if he couldn't graduate from university, and even if he couldn't find a job at a normal company, he had the means to make his own way through life. But he could tell Yuki was worried for him, so he said, "Thanks, man."

Yuki shrugged sheepishly and turned away to leave.

"Hey, Yuki," Nico called. "Let's make it a good year, huh?"

It would be the last year they would spend together at Chikusei-so.

Without a reply, Yuki disappeared into his own room, and Nico turned to glare at the screen again, wrestling with the violent urge to light a cigarette. Naturally, he was getting nowhere with the coding. Only the heap of useless figurines kept growing bigger and bigger.

Kiyose's training regimen for April was divided into three levels. Kakeru and Kiyose had the toughest routine; Prince had the easiest; and the rest of them were somewhere in between.

At all levels, the most important point was to let their bodies get accustomed to running while gradually improving their speed and endurance. The plan included different courses to run, too, so that they wouldn't get bored. It was a perfect program, taking into account the runner's psychology as well as the different abilities of each member. Once again Kakeru thought, *Haiji is no ordinary guy.*

If Kiyose could construct such a solid training plan, he must be one hell of a runner himself. Kakeru wanted to know what kind of a runner he'd been before his knee injury. Kakeru couldn't remain indifferent to Kiyose; for the first time, he felt an urge to have a proper talk with Kiyose about track.

But the other residents of Chikusei-so were mostly new to track. Of course, they couldn't gauge Kiyose's own capability just from looking at the training plan. With puzzled looks on their faces, they merely scrutinized the schedule handed out to them.

"Hey, Haiji. What's 'CC'?" It was curious Joji who spearheaded the questioning.

"Short for *cross-country*. It means running in nature instead of a track or on city roads. We'll use an open field."

"You mean the field that's more than a mile away? We have to go all the way there to practice?"

"Running on soil puts less burden on your legs than asphalt. Plus, you get more ups and downs, so it'll be a nice change from the regular track."

"So, when it says 'CC 2.5k × 6,' it actually means . . . ?" Jota asked nervously.

"I measured some distances on the field and came up with a route that's 2.5 kilometers for one lap. I'll show you the course later. It means you'll be doing six laps there."

"You expect us to run *fifteen* kilometers in total?" Prince moaned.

"It's far too little, but we're only getting started." Kiyose was merciless. "Look at Kakeru, he's doing eight laps."

Musa raised his hand. "What's a 'pace training'?"

"You run at a fixed pace. I'll observe your physical condition and running ability, and give you specific instructions on the day." Kiyose looked up from the paper to check whether everyone was absorbing all the information.

"It's fine," Musa said with a smile. "So far, I understand everything."

"The main purpose of this plan is to build up your staying power—in other words, your stamina," Kiyose explained. "Don't push too hard. Just think about completing each run at a steady pace. Same goes for jogs before and after practice. If it starts getting painful, you're running too fast. Like I said, the point is to loosen up your body, keep running for long stretches of time, and slowly increase the distance you can run."

"So where it says 'JOG,' that's for jogging." Shindo was diligently noting down Kiyose's terminology.

"But if we're too sluggish, we can't improve our speed, so we'll do buildup training and interval training. For buildups, you gradually up your pace and finish with a sprint. For intervals, you alternate between fast and slow."

"I know what a sprint's like," King said. "It's like running in a fifty-meter, hundred-meter dash, right?"

"Correct. But as a rule, long-distance runners don't do short sprints much. They use different muscles for that." Kiyose looked down at the schedule again. "See where it says 'B-up 10K' for Kakeru's column in the latter half of April? That means 'buildup training': he'll gradually increase his pace while running ten kilometers. More specifically, I think it'll be effective for Kakeru if he starts by running at a pace of about three minutes, five seconds per kilometer, then picks up the speed till he's going at about two minutes, fifty seconds by the time he gets to the last kilometer."

"Sounds like torture," Joji commented, throwing an anxious glance at Kakeru.

"It won't be comfortable," Kakeru replied casually.

"The point of this method is to make your heart and lungs work extra hard—pain is a part of the game," Kiyose said with a smile. "When you can run ten kilometers at a certain pace, it means you can adapt to longer distances. To strike a good balance between speed and endurance, it's essential to strengthen your cardiorespiratory function. That's what speedwork is for."

"But you have to remember not to go too far, right?" Yuki asked, pushing up his glasses. Apparently, he'd been reading up on some theory. "Speedwork leaves you exhausted, and it's a significant load on your legs."

"Exactly. It defeats the whole purpose if you get injured." Kiyose nodded. "Buildups are too advanced for beginners. For now, you'll focus on building stamina most of all, but it's important to work on your speed. That's where interval training comes in."

Jota was scouring the schedule in vain, so Kakeru pointed it out for him. "You see the ones with the parentheses, like '200 (200) × 15'? Those are the intervals."

"What that means is," Kiyose went on, "you run two hundred meters at a fast pace, then go straight into running another two hundred meters at a slow pace and repeat the cycle fifteen times. That way, you can rest and recover when you're going at lower speed."

"Rest while running, huh. That's intense." Yuki turned to Kiyose again, his expression stiff. "And how fast is 'a fast pace'?"

"Ideally, I'd want you to run two hundred meters in about thirty to thirty-two seconds, but that's probably too much to ask right off the bat, so I'll see how things go and give you further instructions."

"Whoa, look at your interval sets, Kakeru," Joji exclaimed, half in awe and half in disbelief. "Some of them even go up to '400 (200) × 20'!"

"It's only April, so this is still on the lighter side," Kakeru said. "We'll have to run much harder from the summer onward."

"Harder than this?!" The group was gripped with anxiety for what awaited them. Prince had clammed up a while ago. Kakeru worried whether Prince felt hurt that he was the only one with a completely separate training plan. But he was just racking his brain for a way to weasel out of practice as much as possible.

"Um . . ." Prince began, trying to work out a compromise. "I was thinking of just focusing on self-training. What do you think?"

"Self-training? Like what?"

"I got a treadmill from Shindo. I can run while reading manga, and you know, I read manga pretty much all day, so I think we can expect bigger returns from this strategy."

"And at what speed would you set it?"

"Like . . . a slow walk?"

Kiyose raised an eyebrow, then cast his eyes over the whole group. "We'll use the track at the public sports ground except for cross-country. Make sure you look over the schedule carefully and go to the right meeting place." Prince's suggestion was completely ignored.

Kiyose was the cautious type, so he instructed everyone to keep a training log to record not just their times during the main practice sessions but also what kind of independent training they did each day along with their times and distances.

"Don't even think about putting down lies—I can get a rough idea of what you've been doing just by seeing how you run during the main training," he warned. "But if you have any complaints, or if there's anything physically wrong with you, it's important to write it down. Anything you want to say but can't say to my face, feel free to throw it in your notebook."

"I've already made a lot of complaints," Prince grumbled, "but you haven't listened to any of them."

"When I feel that you've reached your limits, I'll consider it," Kiyose assured him, then turned to everyone. "For those of you who want to run together, let's do our morning and evening jogs as a group. If anyone's concerned about waking up on time or keeping up with the distances, I'm here to help."

Since he preferred to run at his own pace, Kakeru decided to jog alone in the morning and evening, just as he had done before. Yuki and Nico also opted for jogging by themselves. Yuki was an individualist, and in order to regain his runner's instinct, Nico wanted to see his no-smoking and dieting commitment through to the end. It was settled that the rest of the group would start their independent practice all together under Kiyose's guidance.

Assiduously following the main training routines as well as his own,

Kakeru kept a close watch on the others. Their journey to Hakone took on such a gruesome aspect that anyone could have dropped out at any moment. After all, they were used to spending their days however they wanted, taking advantage of the undergrad life, which, if nothing else, left them with plenty of time on their hands. For most of them, it was quite an ordeal to adapt to a regular lifestyle.

They had to wake up early to go jogging, wolf down their breakfast, and head to lectures on campus. After classes, they assembled at either the open field or the public sports ground for their main practice, when they carried out whatever training was on the menu for the day. They had to juggle their other commitments in whatever time they had left before the evening jog.

Every morning, the sound of Kiyose banging on a pot rang throughout the house, and at night, some of the group passed out in bed without even taking a bath.

"It seems like there's a peculiar odor in the air at Aotake these days," Musa told Kakeru as they soaked in the bath in the landlord's house. They ran into each other in the changing room and decided to share the bathtub to save time. Following Musa's style, they kept the light in the bathroom switched off.

"Well, we've got ten scruffy men living together, and on top of that, some of them aren't even showering after their workout," Kakeru said.

"I don't want to name names, but it's the twins, King, and Prince."

"You've just named them, Musa."

Musa chuckled. "King and Prince are truly exhausted. But the twins are just being lazy."

"That's problematic indeed." Kakeru caught Musa's formal speech when he talked with him.

"I'm concerned. If they don't bathe, girls won't like them. You are coeval with the twins, aren't you, Kakeru? I think you had better drop them a hint sometime that it's not a good idea."

"Yes, I will," Kakeru answered. It was the first time he'd heard the word *coeval* in a normal conversation.

"Recently, something a bit interesting has been happening on our evening jogs," Musa said.

"What's that?"

"It occurs when we run through the shopping arcade. You might like to come see it sometime," Musa chuckled again.

They sat quietly in the dark, hugging their knees to their chests, facing each other. A round white light wavered in the water between them.

"Ah, Kakeru. I thought it was a street lamp, but it's the moon."

Musa was right. Beyond the open window, a hazy spring moon hung in the night.

"Look." Musa cupped his hands under the floating moon in the water and smiled. "I've caught it."

"Oh yeah," Kakeru laughed and grinned back. The tiny moon quivered like a soft, doughy shiratama inside Musa's hands.

They were one week into the training regimen, but not one of them had dropped out—even when practice left them so exhausted that they didn't even feel like having a bath at the end of the day. Kakeru hadn't expected that. *But why?* he wondered. Was it ego, making each of them loath to be the first one to give up? Was it peer pressure, with each one trying to be a team player and toe the line, especially because they were all living together? Or were they starting to get something out of running itself?

And what if everyone stuck to the training and kept going till the end? What if the Chikusei-so team really could run the Hakone Ekiden? In the bath, Kakeru drifted into a daydream.

The thing that surprised him most was the change in himself: that these thoughts came to him at all.

For as long as he remembered, he had always run alone. He was still running alone, even now.

But he seemed to be hoping for something. When he let out a small sigh, the moon in the water trembled a little. The hope stirred in him a hint of unease over potential disappointment, as well as a warmth he'd never felt before.

Kakeru and Musa got out of the bath and went back to Chikusei-so together. As they were slipping off their sandals in the entrance hall, they heard clattering and rattling above them. The door to room 101 slammed open, and Kiyose charged up the stairs. They could hear him bellowing in the twins' room. "I told you, mahjong is banned! I'm confiscating this!"

Maybe Hakone is just a pipe dream after all, Kakeru thought with a sigh.

A scorecard fluttered down through the hole in the ceiling, along with Joji's whisper. "We'll tally it up later. Can you keep it hidden from Haiji?"

"All right, all right," Musa laughed, picking up the paper.

A serious student long-distance athlete runs at least 600 kilometers in one month. Come prerace crunch time, it's common to run more than 1,000 kilometers in a month. Kakeru pushed himself to run more and more, his sights set on reaching those levels. While he was, of course, rooting for the others, that didn't mean he was going to lower his standards to go along with a group of beginners.

"You're running a bit too much," Kiyose told Kakeru after checking his training log. It was right after a main practice session on the open field, when everyone was cooling down, doing stretches, and changing into fresh clothes.

During the first two weeks of practice, the group plowed on despite suffering miserably from sore muscles, blood blisters, and shoe bites. But each of them had had potential as a runner. Now it seemed that their bodies were gradually adapting, and they were starting to get into running itself. Though they still struggled, they had progressed enough to handle the load of the training plan.

Kakeru was secretly impressed by everyone's adaptability, but still, they were only doing beginner-level practice. He was running on a completely different plane, striving for new heights. If no one stopped him, he would have kept running forever.

"You're still young, too. Your body's a work in progress—you shouldn't push yourself too hard," Kiyose said. "What would you do if you overdid it now and ended up with injuries later on?"

Kakeru felt lighter than ever these days. The more he ran, the more power he gained, and the steady rise of his speed was palpable. So if he was honest, Kiyose's warning didn't really click. But he obediently answered, "Got it."

"Prince is the opposite. You're not running enough," Kiyose said. In his training log, Prince had written "treadmill" at least every other day, instead of his evening jog. "Your honesty is a virtue . . . but doesn't this basically mean you skipped jogging and read manga instead?"

On some evenings, Prince would barricade himself in his room with his piles of manga and refuse to open the door even when Kiyose invited him to a jog.

"Yeah, but I swear, I really am reading on the treadmill," Prince said, desperate to justify himself. "Besides, I feel like my legs are starting to tone up a little lately."

"Let me see." Kiyose bent down to inspect his calves.

"Haiji," Yuki chimed in, "you better do something about that habit of yours. You can't just go around touching people's legs without warning."

"Hmm." Kiyose straightened up. "It's true, I can see you're improving a bit during the morning jogs and the main practice. But it's not good to jog on a treadmill with a book. It'll ruin your form, and you won't get a feel for running on the road. From now on, you should join us for the evening jogs, too."

Pressed down by the quiet intensity of Kiyose's persuasion, which left no room for arguments, Prince could only promise to participate in the future. Kakeru was relieved. He wanted Prince to run outside as much as possible. There was enough weight on the floor of his room just from the manga collection, but now he'd brought in a treadmill to boot. Whenever he jogged in his room, the ceiling over Kakeru's room creaked threateningly.

"Unlike the honest prince, there's a king who has submitted records full of falsehoods and window dressing," Kiyose announced.

Everyone laughed and looked at King. "Crap," King muttered, sheepishly prodding the ground with the tip of his shoe. "But listen, I couldn't run at all, and my time wasn't going up. Thought I might get in trouble, so I tweaked the numbers to make it look better."

"It's only been two weeks since we started practice. You won't see progress that quick," Kiyose assured him gently. "For quizzes, you have to build up your knowledge bit by bit and sharpen your technique to press the buzzer fast enough, right? It's the same with running. Cheap tricks won't cut it. What matters is daily practice to level up your endurance and technique. And the courage to look at your own abilities right in the face. That's what saves you in the real race. I know you're following the training plan properly, so it's okay to write the numbers as they are."

"I will next time." King nodded.

"As for the rest of you, there's nothing I have to say in particular. Ah, except Nico-senpai."

"Yeah?" Nico was fixing his shoelaces, but he paused and looked up.

"You haven't been eating very much."

"'Course I have."

"It's not good to lie. Who do you think does the cooking here?" It was Kiyose, of course. No one could hide anything from him; the ruler of Aotake prepared not only the training schedule but also meals for all the residents.

"Well, I'm big-boned, y'know?" Nico mumbled an excuse, scratching his face. "I gotta lose some weight."

"No need," Haiji declared firmly. "You're getting a good workout at practice, so you'll get fit even if you keep eating as you've always done. Going on an extreme diet increases the risk of injury. It's better to eat balanced meals."

"All right. But if I can't get in shape just from the training, I'm gonna limit what I eat."

"According to my calculation, you should definitely be light enough by the summer, but if that doesn't look feasible, let's think about it," Kiyose conceded. "Whatever you do, please don't do anything reckless."

Shindo, who was listening to their exchange, looked puzzled. "Is it an advantage to be lighter? Doesn't thinner mean less strength?"

"Of course, impossible diets are out of the question," Yuki answered, ever the theoretician. "You get anemic, and that puts more burden on your heart, so it's too dangerous. But as a rule, it helps to shed some excess weight. When you burn extra fat, it heightens your cardiorespiratory function. Take race cars—you want to make the engine more powerful and the body as light as possible. Same thing."

"That makes sense," Shindo said.

"Yuki's right," Kiyose confirmed, looking around at the group. "It's just like a race car going on repeated test runs, so that the team can fine-tune the body's balance and the engine's performance. We build up our bodies by running every day. If you chase after rapid progress, it can backfire more than you think. Keep that in mind."

He went on to explain a range of methods for the group to prevent injury and maintain their physical condition: "If your muscles give off even a little heat after training, cool it down with ice at once. Never forget to do stretches and massages. Take supplements for nutrients that tend to be deficient, like iron." When he'd gone over everything, he said, "That's all for today. Let's head home."

On their way back to Chikusei-so, Kakeru ended up running next to Nico. On top of his weight concern, Nico was trying to quit smoking. He seemed heavy with pent-up stress; Kakeru wished he could bring up something lighthearted to chat about. He cast about in his head for a topic, but nothing came to him.

"What do you think we're having for dinner, Kakeru?" In the end, it was Nico who spoke up first.

Kakeru was disappointed. *Running really is the only thing I'm good at*, he thought. "It's probably curry. Haiji asked me to get a pack of curry roux from the shopping arcade before practice."

Something flickered at the back of his mind. *The shopping arcade.* He remembered Musa's suggestion that he come to watch their evening jog. It could be a nice distraction for Nico. "Would you like to run with me tonight, Nico-senpai?"

"Is that a pickup line? What's gotten into you?" Nico teased.

Yuki, who was running a few steps ahead, looked back at them. "Where're you gonna take us, honey bunny?" he joked, deadpan.

"The shopping arcade," Kakeru said. The three of them usually jogged by themselves, so they decided to go together to check out what "interesting" thing was happening with the group joggers.

Dinner, as expected, was curry. Kiyose never cut corners in anything, and cooking was no exception. Before the practice, he had simmered the chopped onions until they were soft and syrupy, and he made his own blend of curry sauce by mixing together a few different kinds of roux that Kakeru had bought.

Nobody noticed the depth of the flavor, however. Everyone was too ecstatic over how the curry was packed with pork belly strips. No one paused to appreciate the colorful aesthetic of the salad before gobbling it up.

"Why do I even bother?" Kiyose grumbled as he piled the empty plates in the kitchen sink, indignation and grief mingling on his face.

"I'll have a tiny bit more," said Nico, reaching for the rice cooker. He'd decided to eat his fill now. "Doesn't matter what you feed these guys. Just give 'em meat. Lots of meat."

There was no space in the kitchen for everyone to sit together. Anyone who came late and didn't fit at the main table pulled out a small low table and sat in the hallway right outside the kitchen.

Kakeru was still eating when Shindo and Musa came down. The main table was already full. The twins were almost starting on their dessert, but they didn't show any signs of moving aside. They were squabbling over what to pour over the strawberries: condensed milk or milk and sugar.

Kakeru simply couldn't ignore the pecking order, so he picked up his bowl, spoon clamped in mouth, and moved to make space for the upperclassmen.

Shindo stopped him hastily. "It's all right, Kakeru."

"There's no hierarchy at Aotake," Musa added. "That's why it's so comfortable here. Don't you think?"

"Yes." Kakeru sat down and went back to eating. For someone who'd lived in a track and field dorm for all three years of senior high school, it was unthinkable that senior students would sit in the hallway while their juniors ate at the table.

In Kakeru's experience, younger students were expected to take care of small chores for the older students, like washing their shoes and doing their laundry. And the seniors always bathed first, of course. Kakeru had gone along with the protocol. If dealing with these trivial duties meant he could focus on his training in peace, he didn't particularly mind.

When he became one of the upperclassmen himself, he didn't want the younger students to wash his shoes. For a runner, those shoes were invaluable and indispensable. He couldn't understand how his seniors had found it so easy to entrust their shoes to other people.

Teammates in the same year as Kakeru talked about him behind his back. They complained that he was "a poser" who was "messing up the order." Kakeru paid no attention to them. No one could come close to his speed. He was content just to be a senior, free to run without any constraints. *Let them talk*, he thought.

His teammates saw him as aloof and kept their distance from him. In other words, he was somewhat isolated.

But at Chikusei-so, he could breathe easy. Nobody cared who was born in what year. They were free to say whatever they wanted to each other. Just now, too, Nico had settled the twins' quarrel with a bold move—throwing in equal amounts of condensed milk along with milk and sugar.

"How could you, Nico-senpai?! I wanted to have it with milk and sugar!"

"Well, it's in there."

"I *definitely* wanted condensed milk."

"Like I said, it's in there."

Leaving them to their pointless quarrel, Kakeru got up to help Kiyose with the dishes. "What time do you usually run through the shopping arcade, Haiji?"

"Eightish. How come?"

"Oh, nothing."

Musa winked at Kakeru as he came to put his plate in the sink.

Kakeru, Nico, and Yuki went to the playground park near the entrance to the shopping street. It was boring to jog in circles around the little park, avoiding the sandbox, the slide, and the swings, but that was the only way they could keep an eye on the street.

When they'd done about thirty laps under the dim streetlights and were just starting to feel dizzy, Kiyose appeared, the Chikusei-so joggers trailing behind him. They turned the corner and went down the wide shopping arcade that led to the train station. The group was stretched out in a long line, some lagging behind others, but Prince was just about keeping up.

"They're here," Kakeru remarked.

"Let's stalk them," Yuki said.

The trio left the park and entered the shopping arcade. The narrow street was packed with small shops on both sides, run by locals: a bakery with the shutters down after a busy day, a fishmonger who was attracting passersby with lively calls to sell off the stock before closing time, a corner bar starting to fill up with people as the night began.

The streetlights, shaped like quaint bonbori lamps, threw a warm orange glow on the scene. The place was bustling with people walking home from the train station and shoppers out for special offers just before closing hours.

"Prince is way too slow," Yuki grumbled. "It's hard *not* to overtake him."

The three of them slipped past Prince, going behind a crowd of people so as not to be seen. They managed to sneak by King without blowing their cover, too.

"Look, it's Haiji." Yuki jerked his chin to point ahead. Kiyose was running toward them. "Why's he coming back?"

"It's too soon for him to be here if he made a U-turn at the station," Kakeru said.

The trio hung their heads and tried to let him pass, but of course, Kiyose had to notice them. "What are you guys doing, sneaking around?" he said, pivoting to run alongside them.

"And what are *you* doing, Haiji?" asked Kakeru.

"I came to check on the guys at the back," Kiyose replied.

As always, he was a hawk-eyed supervisor. Kakeru got a little worried. *How much is he really running to keep an eye on everyone else? His leg doesn't seem like it's fully healed yet.*

While Kakeru was lost in thought, Kiyose and Yuki were carrying on their conversation.

"Kakeru said there's something interesting happening with the group joggers, so we came to check it out," Yuki said.

"Ah, you mean—that?" Kiyose pointed ahead. They could make out Shindo and Musa in between the passersby, running side by side.

"What the hell are they doing?" Nico cocked his head, puzzled.

Shindo and Musa, running down the middle of the street, wore white T-shirts with something written on the back in big black letters. Kakeru squinted at the letters, which read:

We're Running for Hakone Ekiden!!
Kansei University Track and Field Club
Seeking Supporters

"They've even done proper lettering . . ." Yuki observed.

"Shindo's handiwork," Kiyose explained, keeping his breathing steady. "I told them not to bother 'cause it's embarrassing, but they persuaded me. We need the funding. They said they have shirts ready for all ten of us."

I'd rather die, Kakeru thought. Though Shindo always seemed so calm and quiet, apparently detached from the hustle and bustle of the world, it turned out that he was quite suited to practical work. "Who knew Shindo would be so driven about collecting money?" Kakeru remarked.

"Running can reveal hidden sides," Kiyose laughed, then called to the pair running ahead of them. "Shindo, Musa. These three want to help with our PR."

The trio hastily shook their heads to show that was a lie.

Musa waved at Kakeru, who caught up with them. "You can have Shindo's special T-shirt, too, Kakeru. Also, look over there."

A bicycle was weaving through the people on the street. A girl about the same age as them, her hair pulled up in a ponytail, her eyes fixed on something straight ahead of her, was pedaling with all her might. Even from a distance, glimpses of her face in profile were enough to show that she was beautiful, with clear, balanced features.

"She's the daughter of the grocer, Yaokatsu," Kiyose said.

"How do you know her?" Kakeru, who'd been distracted by the girl, looked sideways at Kiyose.

"I've been buying groceries on this street for all the cooking I do at Aotake. You get to know people."

"So you've talked to her before?"

"Along the lines of 'This daikon has impressive leaves,' or 'Here's 200 yen in change,'" Kiyose replied, a smirk tugging at the corner of his mouth. "Are you interested in her?"

"Not particularly." Kakeru looked ahead again. The girl was still pedaling toward the train station.

"Thanks to this, we're kind of celebrities around here," said Shindo, stretching out his shirt to show them. "We run in a line every day on this route, so all the shopkeepers who recognize Haiji call out to us. They say, 'Aren't you the students who live in that run-down house? You've got yourselves an interesting project there.'"

"And our landlord's a regular at the Go parlor down the street," Kiyose added. "I hear he's been going around telling anyone who'll listen that the Aotake residents are taking on Hakone Ekiden."

Kiyose and the landlord seemed to have a strategy: to rope in the local townspeople so that the Aotake members would think twice before dropping out. Kakeru marveled at their prowess in securing their foothold. As the first person who agreed to join, Shindo was taking the initiative in the advertising efforts. A swift current was sweeping the carefree, happy-go-lucky residents of Aotake along, straight toward the Hakone Ekiden. *Are we really going to be all right?* Kakeru felt a little uneasy. But he was also glad and encouraged to hear that people outside Chikusei-so were showing interest in the group's Hakone challenge.

"These days, she always comes by when we jog," Musa said, gesturing at the Yaokatsu girl on the bike. "Guess who she's here for . . ."

Kakeru, Nico, and Yuki followed his gaze far up the street. The runners in front of the girl were—

"The twins?!" Kakeru exclaimed in surprise.

"And which one?!" Nico added.

Musa shrugged. "Who knows?"

"Does it matter which one? They look exactly the same," Yuki pointed out coolly.

Love's in the air. Kakeru could sense it, though Jota and Joji seemed to be completely oblivious as they ran side by side. He made a mental note to drop them a hint that they'd better not skip baths.

In any case, one thing was certain. The daily joggers of Chikusei-so were starting to become a familiar presence for the people of the shopping arcade.

IV

TRACK MEETS

Spring to early summer was track meet season. Almost every week, there were track meets for setting official records hosted by universities (kirokukai) and competitive races cosponsored by corporations (kyogikai).

With the short-term goal of the kirokukai meet just around the corner, everyone put their backs into practice more than ever. Now only Prince and King were jogging with Kiyose in the mornings and evenings. The rest of the group could wake up without Kiyose's pot-banging—at least for the most part—and were eager to follow through with their regimen each day.

Kiyose guided each of them in different styles according to their personalities, though always with a light touch. For Shindo, who took pleasure in making steady progress fulfilling his quota, Kiyose devised a more detailed plan. With Yuki, he engaged in lengthy discussions about training methods until Yuki's theorist instincts were satisfied. Because Jota was the type to thrive on praise, Kiyose often called out to him during practice, and with Joji, who kept going even if he was left alone, Kiyose avoided the subject of running altogether.

By and large, Kiyose was letting them run as they wished. He gave them a thorough explanation of the training plan and merely offered a bit of advice to those who needed it. This way, he kindled motivation in each of them. Kakeru felt as if he were witnessing a magic spell at work. Kiyose didn't use force or punishment, and he waited patiently, ever so tenaciously, until they got in the mood for running. Never in his life had Kakeru seen a coach use an approach like this.

If only Haiji had been my coach when I got into track, I might've been a much faster runner by now, Kakeru thought, as he watched the Chikusei-so members slowly but surely shorten their running times.

Yet, at the same time, Kiyose's attitude felt too soft for Kakeru. Kiyose was dealing with newbie runners, still practically amateurs. If he didn't push them harder, they wouldn't improve fast enough to be ready for the prelim. Kakeru was frustrated. *Is he really serious about Hakone? Why doesn't he show it?*

One night, they were all drinking together in the twins' room when Kiyose made an announcement. "Most of you can now run five kilometers in under seventeen minutes without fail."

No matter how spent they were from practice, they would gather as a group and clink glasses at least once every ten days. All of them liked to drink, so it was an easy way to blow off steam.

"But we're a team of beginners," Kiyose went on. "You might get nervous at your first race. I signed you up for a few track meets, so you can get some practice. No need to stress out over it—just try to finish the run within seventeen minutes, that's all."

Prince, who was sitting next to Kakeru with his nose in a manga, leaned over and whispered, "Why is Haiji so hung up on seventeen minutes?"

"You need an official record of running 5,000 meters in less than seventeen minutes to qualify for the Hakone Ekiden prelim," Kakeru murmured back. Prince was clueless about the rules, apparently. "You have to run in official races and track meets to get an authorized record."

"We've talked about this before. Have you forgotten already?" The rim of Yuki's glasses flashed. He shot Prince a look, as if to add, *You don't have any trouble remembering manga titles.* "It looks like Haiji's focusing on just getting into the prelim," Yuki went on.

"Yeah, looks like it." Kakeru nodded.

"Well, I won't argue that that's reasonable." Yuki took off his glasses listlessly and wiped the lenses with a pristine handkerchief. "But what about you, Kakeru? Aren't you going to run in the ICs?"

Kakeru was silent.

Prince asked, "What's that?" But Yuki walked off toward Nico, who sat in a corner twisting wire dolls. Prince still waited for an answer, open book in hand.

"It's short for *intercollegiate*. It's a track and field championship between universities," Kakeru explained. "There's the Kanto IC in May and the national one in July."

"Why don't we all run there?"

"Those are for top-tier student runners. You need an even better time than for the Hakone prelim to be eligible."

"Hunh." Prince turned back to the manga on his lap with a puzzled frown. "But that's no problem for you, is it, Kakeru?"

Of course it wasn't. But Kakeru just gave a half-hearted laugh and let Prince's comment slide.

Kiyose went around the room handing out a sheet of paper to everyone. It listed all the dates of various track meets organized by universities. Kakeru dropped the paper on the floor as if it were too heavy. Forget about intercollegiate championships—he didn't even want to show up at these normal track meets. They would be swarming with students from universities with powerful teams. If he went, he'd be bound to run into his former teammates from senior high. He wasn't ready for that yet.

Holding up the schedule, Kiyose explained, "First, there's the track meet organized by the Tokyo Taiiku University. Then at the beginning of May, Dochido University. Two weeks later, Kikui University. If those aren't enough, there's another Tokyo Taiiku meet at the end of June. There's no rush. Stay calm and break through the seventeen-minute wall."

"But the Dochido one's gonna eat into Golden Week. We're supposed to be on holiday!"

"And the last one's right in the middle of the rainy season. I don't wanna run in the rain."

Jota and Joji were quick to complain, but they didn't really mean it. Practice had built up their confidence. Their eyes blazed with determination: *We'll definitely break that record at the first race!*

"One thing to note—if you want to aim for the intercollegiate race, you'll have to go full throttle from the first one at Totai. That's the latest you can get a record to qualify for the ICs," Kiyose said. "It won't count toward the IC points, but as a track athlete, it's an important experience to participate in the ICs. What do you think, Kakeru?"

Kakeru sat in a daze. When Kiyose pressed, "Is anything wrong, Kakeru?" he snapped out of it and looked up from the handout. "No, it's nothing," he said.

"So, what's an 'IC point'?" Joji piped up, and Kakeru was released from Kiyose's searching gaze.

"I didn't tell you before, but . . ." Kiyose began, straightening up and raising his voice to make sure everyone could hear him. "The competition at the Hakone Ekiden prelim isn't just about the total time of all ten members of each team."

The others had been chatting among themselves, but now a hush fell over the room. Everyone turned to Kiyose with a puzzled, questioning look.

"There are ten slots for the teams that make it through the prelim to the main Hakone race," Kiyose continued. "But one of those teams is actually the 'select team.' It's a system that saves the athletes who ran really well at the prelim but belonged to teams that didn't make the cut. To put it bluntly, it's a scratch team."

"Which means, in reality, only nine teams can proceed to the Hakone Ekiden?" Shindo asked.

"Exactly. And as for the teams that place seventh or lower in the prelim, IC points will count toward their total time to decide their final ranking. It's super complicated, so I'll keep it simple: basically, the teams that achieved good results from the IC championships get IC points. The better their results were at the ICs, the more they get subtracted from their total time at the prelim. Some teams have managed to cut down their total time by more than five minutes thanks to their IC points."

"So does that mean that even if you rank high in the prelim race itself, you might end up getting pushed out of the main Hakone race if another team climbs up the ranks with the IC points?" Jota asked.

"Yeah. The Hakone Ekiden airs on TV over New Year's, so it's good press for universities. That's why they often try to round up the best athletes, and all they care about is getting them to Hakone efficiently. The IC points system is also meant to deter those kinds of universities from focusing only on Hakone. It's supposed to encourage them to regularly participate in track meets and cultivate athletes who can handle running on a track course—not just the Ekiden."

"Smells like greed," Nico said with a wry grin.

"I see money gets tangled up in everything," Shindo sighed, realizing just how important the group's promotional initiatives were.

A slightly dampened mood descended over the room. But King blurted out, "All right then. Haiji, Kakeru, you go run in the IC races and rack up those points."

"Not an option." Yuki dismissed him ruthlessly. "We're a tiny underdog team. They award IC points according to each team's ranking and how many people competed from that university. No matter how fast Haiji and Kakeru run at the ICs, it won't change a thing."

"That's troubling. We don't have any money, and we can't get points from the IC races. What's left for us to do?" Musa looked dejected.

"It's okay." Shindo pulled himself together to cheer Musa up. "All we have to do is rank in the first six places at the prelim. That way, we won't be affected by the IC points. We'll tackle the competition head-on with nothing but our total time, just as an underdog team should."

"Well said, Shindo." Kiyose nodded, looking pleased.

"I thought getting our time down was our big problem right now," Yuki pointed out in a low voice.

"Anyway, we better run at those track meets and shorten our time step by step," said Nico, warping more wires into figurines. "As for you two—Kakeru, Haiji, why not go run at the ICs and scare the shit outta them?"

"Yeah! Go grab those points," King said again.

"But, King, we just said they can't get points by themselves," Jota retorted.

"Goes in one ear and out the other," Joji grumbled.

Still, Kakeru didn't open his mouth. He didn't have the presence of mind to respond to King right now. As he stared at the name *Tokyo Taiiku University* on the sheet of paper, the thought struck him. *Didn't Sakaki go to Totai?* The image of his high school teammate's face flashed in Kakeru's head. Gloom fell over him as if he'd plunged straight into the rainy season.

If he entered the Tokyo Taiiku track meet, he'd certainly have to face Sakaki. *What would Sakaki do then? Now that he's at a university with a strong track team, would I still be able to beat him?*

Under the pretense of going to the toilet, Kakeru slipped out of the twins' room, went downstairs, and slid open the front door. The gravel in the yard shone under the light of the stars. It felt as if something was inviting him—toward the path of white light; to the depths of his own heart.

He almost broke out in a run, but he remembered he was wearing sandals and stopped. He heard Nira padding out from under the engawa of the main house.

Letting out a small breath, Kakeru started walking slowly toward the dog. Nira pressed his wet nose on Kakeru's toes. Kakeru crouched down and stroked the dog's warm coat.

Suddenly, Nira's tail went wild. Kakeru heard footsteps crunching on the gravel behind him. He knew who it was without turning around: Kiyose.

Kiyose squatted next to Kakeru and tickled Nira between his ears. Nira huffed through his nose in delight. Kakeru waited for a while. But Kiyose didn't say a word, so Kakeru made the first move.

"Do you really mean to enter me in the track meets and IC races?" Kakeru asked.

"Of course. We're headed for the Hakone Ekiden, after all."

"I bet it's gonna get ugly. People will come at us."

"How come?" Kiyose asked calmly, kneading the flabby bits around Nira's neck.

Kakeru looked at Kiyose. "You know, don't you, Haiji? You must've heard. What I was like back in high school."

"That you were a really fast runner?"

"That's the bright side. I'm talking about—"

"Kakeru." Kiyose cut him off. "Listen. It's not your past or your reputation that's going to do the running. It's *you* who's going to run. Don't get distracted. Don't look back. Be stronger."

Kiyose rose to his feet, straightening his knees with a little groan of pain. Kakeru and Nira looked up at him. The spring constellations glittered above him like a noble crown.

"Stronger . . . ?" Kakeru asked.

"I believe in you." Kiyose smiled, then strode back to Chikusei-so.

Kakeru mulled over Kiyose's words, stroking Nira's back. Plenty of people before had told Kakeru to run faster. But no one had ever told him to become stronger. What did it mean to be *stronger?*

Kakeru couldn't say. But Kiyose said he believed in him.

A tiny flame flickered up inside Kakeru, where he had been frozen over for a long time. The flame curbed the torrent of violence always seething inside him and kept at bay the voice that tried to lure him into a dark place. Kiyose's words were charged with a quiet power that seemed to blow away Kakeru's fears and anxieties.

"Right," he murmured, rising to his feet. He was never good at sweating the small stuff anyway. So he might as well just run. Even if he had to face someone unpleasant, even if they made him feel miserable, all he had to do was to shrug them off and keep running. Running was all he *could* do.

Kakeru bid Nira good night.

Kakeru wasn't so scared or reluctant to run at the track meets anymore. In fact, he was even starting to look forward to putting his running to the test.

As the day of the track meet at Tokyo Taiiku approached, Kakeru's excitement grew. It was his first real battle in a long time. He was confident that his practice up until now had been thorough and comprehensive. Even so, thoughts raced around his head every night before he fell asleep: *What if seeing an old teammate shakes me up so bad I can't concentrate on the race? What if my runner's instinct has gotten rusty, and I put on a spurt at the wrong time? My results turned heads in the high school track world, but can I really compete at the university level?*

When he closed his eyes, he was flooded with worries, and he flung aside his duvet to sit up. Desperately trying to resist the urge to dash out of the house to start jogging, he sat all alone in the midnight darkness, telling himself to calm down.

Don't think about anything. Just visualize the race. All you have to do is run. Feel the movement of every muscle in your body, and keep pushing forward.

As soon as he remembered the familiar rush of running in a race, the heat of that moment, his hesitation faded away, and he was as impatient to get out there as Nira was to go for a walk.

Alongside the training, Kakeru never skipped a lecture. It was Kiyose's theory that someone who couldn't earn their course credits had no chance at achieving good results in running. When it came to get-togethers or drinking parties, Kakeru kept turning them down because he had practice. The other Chikusei-so residents were pumped up for the track meets, too. They came straight home after classes and jumped right into their workouts.

Soon, word spread around, not only among the townspeople at the shopping arcade but also on campus, that a bunch of guys living in that ramshackle apartment were serious about running.

The day before the Tokyo Taiiku track meet, Kakeru asked a friend from his foreign language class to answer the roll call for him in a few different classes.

"Whatcha up to, Kurahara? Skipping tomorrow?"

"I'm going to a track meet."

"Oh yeah, aren't you running a marathon?"

"Uh, not exactly a marathon . . ." Kakeru almost explained that it was the Hakone Ekiden they were aiming for, and tomorrow he was going to run the 5,000-meter track race, but he thought better of it.

Once he came to Kansei, for the first time in his life Kakeru realized that for people who had nothing to do with track, there wasn't much difference between a marathon and an ekiden relay race. When they talked about track events, they even laughed in disbelief: "You really run *five kilometers*? Like, round and round the track?" It didn't make any sense to them. In their eyes, it was like a bizarre ritual of dubious origin.

The reality had come as a shock to Kakeru. *Track's a really important part of my life. But for most people, it's barely a blip on their radar.* At the same time, he also found it amusing. Runners like him were sweating every day, pushing themselves to the limits, in an endeavor that didn't mean much to most of the population.

So when his classmate asked him about the marathon, Kakeru just gave a noncommittal laugh and replied, "Yeah, well, it's kind of like a short version of a marathon. Can I count on you, then?"

"Sure thing. Good luck," his classmate said earnestly. Kakeru could tell that even though his friend didn't quite understand what it was about, he was cheering Kakeru on for real.

That night, Kakeru lay still in shallow sleep. It was the kind of sleep that was stretched taut, sharpened to a point. *This is good,* Kakeru thought, as he drifted in and out of consciousness. He felt every excess piece of him getting stripped away, transforming his body and soul overnight into a creature made for running.

He'd tricked himself into thinking he'd forgotten it. But he still had the fight inside him: the blazing fire before a race.

The Chikusei-so residents crammed into the white van to go to Tokyo Taiiku University.

"Got everything you need? Uniforms, shoes, change of clothes, wristwatches?"

"All good!" They hardly had any space to move inside the van, but they held up their bags to show Kiyose.

"By the way, who's driving?" Nico asked.

"Me." Kiyose got in the driver's seat and buckled up. Yuki sat next to him, spreading out a map to do a final check on the route.

"Um, what about the coach?" Kakeru asked. He'd never heard of a coach who didn't accompany their team to track meets, not to mention their regular practice.

"He went to the Go parlor," Kiyose said.

An uproar broke out.

"But he's the coach!"

"Isn't he supposed to *coach* us?"

"Can we even call him a coach?"

"I've been wondering—what's a 'Go parlor'?" Musa asked Shindo.

As Shindo started to explain, King said, "Who could've guessed our landlord had a hobby like that?"

"You didn't know? But you've been at Aotake for years," Joji said breezily.

"Never had much contact with him till we started running," Nico said. "He was just the old guy who lives next door, pretty much."

"He doesn't have to be here." Kiyose carefully put the van into drive and stepped on the gas. "It's not like the coach is the one who's running."

The van zoomed out of the yard, and Nira watched them go, wagging his tail.

As soon as they were off, Kakeru realized why the landlord had stayed away. Kiyose's driving was problematic, to say the least. The van kept straying too close to the other lane, and there was an awkward jolt at every red light.

"Is this your first time on the road since getting your license, Haiji?" Kakeru asked. His head slammed against the window when they turned a corner.

"Keep left! Keep left!" Jota cried out.

"Can you all be quiet?" Yuki snapped, his face white. Sitting in the passenger seat put his life most at risk.

Nico dropped a live grenade. "Don't they say men who're bad at driving aren't so great down there either?"

"Isn't that a myth?"

"I think they've got a point, though," Joji and Jota chimed in. They blurted out whatever came into their heads.

"Where's 'down there'?" Musa asked Shindo.

"Never mind, just shut up!" Yuki shouted.

Kiyose didn't even seem to hear the chatter behind him. He was gripping the steering wheel for dear life, his whole attention riveted on the road.

Kakeru noticed Prince was leaning on his shoulder. "Prince? Are you okay?"

"I'm sick—throwing up."

"Hold on a second!" The van plunged into chaos. Jota thrust out a plastic bag and held it in front of Prince's mouth as Joji frantically fanned Prince with his hands. So much for concentrating before the race. Kakeru sighed and rolled down the window for Prince.

At last, they made it to Totai in one piece. The university campus was on an expansive tract of land on the outskirts of Tokyo, equipped with a well-maintained sports field. The group looked around in awe— Totai wasn't a sports science college for nothing. They registered at the reception area and received their numbered race bibs.

Joji noticed something on his bib. "Hey, Kakeru. There's a thing on the back, like a chip or something. What's this?"

"That's how they get your time. It automatically records it when you pass over the finish line."

"Wow! I thought they'd use a stopwatch."

"I think it's mostly automatic in big track meets and competitions. There's a lot of people in the race, too."

When they passed through the gate and got up on the stands, the women's short-distance race was underway on the track in front of them, and the long jump was taking place inside the track. Totai's cheer squad was chanting from the bleachers.

"Hunh. I thought there'd be opening and closing ceremonies that we'd all have to attend," Yuki remarked. "Is everyone allowed to show up whenever?"

"Well, we're here for a race, not a field day," Kiyose laughed. "We're meant to arrive in time for the event we're competing in so that we're in tip-top shape for our race."

They set themselves up in one corner of the stands and changed into their uniforms with the bibs attached. The uniform for the Kansei University Track and Field Club was a black shirt and black shorts with a silver line going down the sides. The name of their college was blazoned across their chests in silver. It was the group's first time wearing the uniforms.

"Looks cool," Jota said, inspecting the design with pride.

"What if girls start fangirling over us? We better be ready," Joji said cheerily, immediately stripping down and pulling on his new shirt.

"I see lots of girls from other colleges cheering from the stands. Let's run like crazy, Joji!"

Kakeru thought of the Yaokatsu girl, but he decided not to tell the twins about her for the time being.

"Once you get changed, go warm up. The race starts at half past two. Make sure you're back here by two," Kiyose said.

The group dispersed and started jogging. Kakeru ran around the sports ground with Kiyose. The Totai campus seemed to have everything you'd need for playing sports. Even just in their immediate surroundings, Kakeru could see three buildings that looked like gymnasiums.

If I'd stayed on the track team in high school, I might've gotten a referral for one of these colleges, Kakeru thought. *But which path would have been better? I'll have to find the answer through running.*

"Bathroom break," Kiyose said, swerving into the men's room at the edge of the playing field. Athletes couldn't help getting nervous before a race, and they would dash to the toilet multiple times. Kakeru had also gone a few times since they arrived, so he kept right on jogging.

Kakeru thought about the twins. *It's their first race ever, but they were still bantering as usual. Wonder if the reality hasn't hit them yet. Maybe they don't know how nerve-racking a race can be.*

Someone called out, "Kurahara!" Kakeru turned around to see a first-year in the Totai uniform, sitting near the path on the lawn. He seemed to be in the middle of stretches. It was Kosuke Sakaki, who had been on the track team at Sendai Jōsei Senior High in the same year as Kakeru.

I knew it, Kakeru thought. He didn't want to see Sakaki. He made a wide U-turn and stopped in front of his old teammate.

"Didn't expect to see you here of all places." Sakaki got to his feet, eyeballing Kakeru. "I didn't even think you were still doing track."

"It's the only thing I'm good at," Kakeru replied.

A vein on Sakaki's temple throbbed. "You haven't changed at all, have you? After all the mess you put us through."

Sakaki was short, and Kakeru stared at the top of his head. Kakeru noticed two whorls in his hair, but he kept his mouth shut. Sakaki scoffed when he saw the name of the university on Kakeru's uniform.

"Does Kansei even have a track team?"

Obviously. We're here, aren't we? Blood rushed to Kakeru's head. He couldn't stand being taunted by a guy who was slower than him. "Yeah. *I'm* the track team," he declared boldly.

The moment Sakaki shrank slightly at the quiet force in Kakeru's voice, Kiyose came back from the toilet.

"Kakeru, what are you doing?" he asked. "Don't slack off on your warm-up."

"I'm sorry." Kakeru apologized right away, like a docile dog. Kiyose held him tight by the scruff of his neck and by his stomach, just as he did the other members of Chikusei-so.

As he slipped away, Sakaki whispered at Kakeru, "Have fun running those playground races with your weak-ass *fwends*. It suits you."

"Hey, hang on!" Kakeru moved to chase him, but Kiyose grabbed the hem of his uniform.

"You've got a shorter fuse than you look."

Kakeru smoothed his shirt. "I'm sorry."

"Listen, Kakeru." Kiyose grinned so widely that he looked almost menacing. "There's an old saying that goes, 'What goes around in Edo, comes around in Nagasaki; insulted on the playground, take revenge on the track.'"

"What does *that* mean?"

"It means you never, ever forget an insult, and you pay them back in the race."

Is he actually fuming right now? Kakeru shuddered. He tried to think that it was the thrill before battle that was making him tremble.

When they had finished their warm-up and returned to the stands, the team gathered around Kiyose. Casting his eyes over them, he barked, "All right, it's time. Run with everything you've got!"

"Yeah!" Everyone roared, unusually in unison.

"Let's show the college track world who we are. That *we* are the Kansei University track team!" Kiyose declared.

So he was listening to what I said after all. For the third time, Kakeru said to him, "I'm sorry."

"It's fine as long as you get it," said Kiyose. "Just remember you're not alone."

In more ways than one, the Kansei team made sure that everybody knew who they were by the end of the track meet.

Kakeru's time came close to his personal best record in high school,

14:09.95 for 5,000 meters. Needless to say, he was the fastest among the first-years in the race. Even compared with the older students, he managed to rank third in the entire group—an impressive feat.

A student from the administrative committee brought over a simple podium and placed it on the side of the track. When Kakeru went up and received a certificate bearing his time, he felt a rush of excitement. Ever since he left the track team in senior high, he had been running by himself. Now he felt he got a tangible answer that the time he'd spent alone wasn't for nothing, that he'd been doing the right thing.

"You're Kakeru Kurahara, right? You went to Sendai Jōsei Senior High."

Kakeru looked up. A runner from Rikudo University was staring at him from his place at the top of the podium. He had a perfectly smooth, shaved head—Kakeru wondered whether it was a Buddhist college thing—and a rough stubble darkening his hollow cheeks. These features, coupled with his body, which seemed whetted into a refined, lithe figure, gave him the impression of a Buddhist monk who had devoted himself to rigorous training for spiritual enlightenment.

"I'd heard rumors about a fast runner. So you're at Kansei now. Keep up the good work."

I don't need you to tell me that, Kakeru wanted to retort. But the guy was clearly an upperclassman, so Kakeru just nodded and said, "I will."

"Looks like Kiyose's recovering, too."

The Rikudo runner looked toward the stands, where Kiyose was watching Kakeru on the podium. The twins were next to Kiyose, trying to snap some pictures of Kakeru with their cell phones. *We probably look like blurry dots at this distance*, Kakeru thought.

"Do you know Haiji?" Kakeru asked.

"I know him well. And I know that his run today is nothing compared to what he can do when he's on the top of his game," the Rikudo runner answered. "Keep an eye out for him. You're all set on going to Hakone, aren't you?"

The man stepped down from the podium, straightened his back,

and walked away. A group of Rikudo students in purple uniforms were
waiting for him by the gate, and they greeted him in unison with a bow,
cheering, "Congratulations! You did it!"

"You'd think he'd just gotten out of prison or something," Kakeru
grumbled under his breath. "Whoever he is, he's got a big mouth."

Kiyose's time was 14:21.51. This was much faster than his run on
the first day of practice. But, like the Rikudo guy, Kakeru also sensed
that Kiyose's knee wasn't fully healed. He might be wearing himself
out. Even though he advised Kakeru not to run too much, when it came
to his own training, Kiyose seemed to push himself beyond his limits.

When Kakeru returned to the bleachers, the Chikusei-so members
showered him with praise. All of them had shown they had enough
backbone. Though this was only their first race, most of them already
achieved their goal of under seventeen minutes. Musa in particular put
up a strong fight and made it under fifteen minutes. The twins and Yuki
came in around fifteen minutes, thirty seconds, while Shindo and Nico
finished under sixteen minutes, thirty seconds.

This meant that eight members out of ten were eligible to enter the
Hakone Ekiden prelim.

King came very close, but he went just over seventeen minutes.
He wasn't one to respond well to pressure. Perhaps weighed down by
the result, he was a little quiet. But if all went well, he would surely
make it under seventeen minutes at the next track meet.

The problem was Prince. He got dangerously close to dropping out
of the race altogether. He was lagging behind so much that the referee
mistook his slowness as a sign of dehydration and nearly stopped him.

When the crowd and other athletes realized what was happening,
they were astonished. *He's not even sick? He's seriously running as hard
as he can?*

"Is he really a track athlete? Which team is he on?"

"Apparently he's with Kansei."

As the spectators talked among themselves, Prince plodded on.

When he finally crossed the finish line at twenty-two minutes, the last one by a wide margin, the crowd erupted in a big round of applause.

"All press is good press," Yuki said with a shrug. "We really made a splash."

Prince collapsed as soon as he crossed the line and was carried up to the stands by Shindo and Musa. Even now, after the award ceremony, he still lay limp on the bench.

When they were ready to go home, Kiyose patted Kakeru on the shoulder and said, "Nice job. I saw that first-year brat from Totai sneaking out of here. Serves him right."

Kakeru had been so absorbed in the run that he'd forgotten all about Sakaki. *Haiji's pretty grudgy*, he realized, a little taken aback.

"The Rikudo guy who came first started talking to me back there. He sounded like he knew you, Haiji."

"Yeah." Kiyose nodded. "He was my teammate in high school, Kazuma Fujioka. He's a fourth-year at Rikudo now, the team captain. Rikudo rules over Hakone Ekiden. He's been the leader behind their win at Hakone three years in a row. And they look like they're well prepared to extend that record with a fourth consecutive win."

"Didn't know he was such a big deal. Is he that famous?"

"You're probably the only one in the track world who doesn't know Fujioka," Kiyose laughed. "You always zero in so much on your own run, you don't pay attention to what's going on around you. That kind of self-discipline can be good thing, but remember, it's worth observing other runners who're doing good work, too."

Of course, Kakeru was watching the way Fujioka ran during the race. His sharp, streamlined form, admitting no excess. His astute mind, reading the turns of the race with precision. He had steadily accelerated over the last two laps of the race, shortening the distance between himself and the one runner ahead of him. The runner in the lead was a Black international student named Manas from the invincible Boso University, also known as "the Ekiden Empire." Fujioka overtook Manas right before the finish line to win first place. Fujioka's time was 13:51.67. His speed and stamina were astounding.

Much to his chagrin, Kakeru didn't have the strength needed to keep up with the battle between Fujioka and Manas near the end of the race. His ability and experience were nowhere near enough.

I still have a long way to go, Kakeru thought. *I have to run harder*. He wanted to get as lean as humanly possible, grow a supple yet powerful spring in his step, and run like the wind. He wanted to run so tirelessly that people would wonder whether the air around him was denser with oxygen.

The thrill he had felt on the podium vanished in an instant, replaced by a restless hunger.

He longed to run faster, much faster—to attain new heights that no one had ever experienced before.

On their drive back home, Prince finally regained enough strength to speak. "You know, athletes might look nice and honest, but they actually play dirty. They were elbowing me and pushing my back as soon as the race started."

"Good thing you had so much space on the track at the end," Nico teased.

"Sure, but still," Prince mumbled, pouting. "Can you believe what this guy from Totai said when he passed me? He said, 'Get out of the way, you slug.' Arrrgh, it's pissing me off! Sportsmanship is a myth."

It's true you were sluggish, so what do you expect? Kakeru wanted to snap back. He couldn't find anything funny in their usual playful banter. Now that he'd witnessed Fujioka's formidable power, he couldn't help but feel that his teammates were too laid-back.

At this rate, it seemed doubtful that all ten of them could pull off the 5,000-meter run in less than seventeen minutes. Should they really be cracking jokes when even their place in the prelim was in jeopardy?

That phrase Sakaki had hurled at him—"playground races"—spun round and round in his head.

A tiny team of ten people, and a bunch of amateurs at that, running the Hakone Ekiden? It was never going to happen. Why couldn't I keep my anger under control back in high school? I should've stayed out of trouble and gotten a referral for a college with a strong track team. Then I could've trained with runners at a higher level, with better facilities and everything.

Fear gripped Kakeru. He felt that he was getting left further and further behind by the world of speed while he was chasing after a pipe dream with the Chikusei-so residents.

Kakeru sat brooding in silence as the rest of the group chattered on, unwinding after their first track meet. He didn't even realize that Kiyose was observing him in the rearview mirror from the driver's seat.

Once he started slipping, Kakeru struggled to get upright again.

His impatience clouded his judgment. He couldn't take a step back to assess his own condition. No matter how hard he practiced, he still felt that it wasn't enough. He ran and ran and ran, but he couldn't feel himself getting any faster. He wasn't cutting down his running times as much as he wanted to. He made sure he got enough nutrients from supplements, and he was running more than ever. *So why aren't I getting results?* His efforts only inflamed his frustration. But still, he couldn't stop running. The thought of spiraling down even more kept him on the move, too scared to rest.

Kakeru ran until the sky turned completely black, long after the group practice—like a fish that would suffocate if it didn't keep swimming, or a bird of passage that would plummet into the sea if it didn't keep beating its wings.

Kakeru continued to run as if he were possessed. At first, the others had looked on in awe, but soon they began to sense something abnormal in Kakeru's brutal training. They started calling out to him to go home with them.

"Let's call it a day, Kakeru," Joji said anxiously. "We're having tonkatsu for dinner tonight. Haiji went back ahead, so he'll have freshly fried pork waiting for us. Let's go home while it's still sizzling."

Kakeru answered in monosyllables: "Just a bit more." He shot off across the field into the gathering gloom, his eyes glinting like a demon spirit's.

Kiyose didn't say anything in particular to him. Sometimes he warned Kakeru, "You're running too much. Be careful." But the rest of the time, he stood back and watched without interfering. That irked Kakeru, too. When Kiyose suggested that he cut down on running, Kakeru felt Kiyose wasn't being serious enough. And it only fanned Kakeru's discontent that Kiyose didn't teach him exactly what he was supposed to do instead of running in order to become faster.

Despite feverishly pushing himself beyond his limits, Kakeru's time wasn't improving. In fact, it was getting worse. At the Kanto Intercollegiate Championship, he could run only about as fast as Kiyose, who was still nursing his injury. It wasn't an especially bad record, but for an athlete competing in an IC race, Kakeru had to call it mediocre.

They were already in the rainy season.

One night, when Kakeru came back from jogging in the rain, Kiyose called to him from the kitchen. Kiyose was sitting at the table, devising the next training schedule. The others had retired to their rooms, and the house was quiet. Tousling his drenched hair with a towel, Kakeru sat down obediently across from Kiyose.

"Let's call off the National IC. Both you and me," said Kiyose.

Kakeru was caught off guard. "Why should we? I want to run," he protested fiercely.

"You know you're not in good shape. Maybe you're a bit anemic from the intense training. You shouldn't strain yourself too much."

"But I'm not recovering from an injury like you are, Haiji. As long as I keep running, I'll get my rhythm back soon enough."

"I'm not so sure." Kiyose tilted his head, still surveying the training log. "I think it's useless for you to keep running in your current condition. You're not seeing yourself clearly enough. All you think about is how you compare with others and things like that. When you're in that kind of headspace, competing in the IC will only backfire."

"This is going nowhere." Kakeru slammed his fist on the table. "You do realize there's someone on the team who hasn't passed the seventeen-minute wall. It's not even clear whether we can qualify for the prelim. And you're telling me not to run the IC race? Where else am I supposed to set new records, then? Are you going to make me waste the whole year keeping pace with you people?"

"Are you only running to set records?" Kiyose threw down the papers. A hint of frustration and anger flickered in his eyes as he looked straight at Kakeru. "If that's it, you're the same as those micromanaging coaches who push their athletes into running until their legs fall off. That's exactly the kind of thinking you hated and fought against!"

"That's not true!" Kakeru shouted. He didn't want to be put in the same box as his high school coach. But he couldn't exactly articulate how he was any different. Kakeru did regard his teammates—the members who weren't getting any faster—as a burden, and a part of him mocked them as pathetic losers.

Kakeru desperately searched for the right words to make Kiyose understand. "There's no way we can get faster if we're just running together like some cozy club. Running for a track team at university level and aiming for Hakone are a whole different story from running as a hobby. We're not here to play games. We're competing in a serious race!"

"Of course. No one at Aotake is playing games. I certainly don't see us working toward Hakone Ekiden as a hobby or just for the hell of it," Kiyose parried with his usual composure. "Kakeru, what's making you so restless?"

"I'm not—"

"What's going on?" Prince popped his head through the kitchen doorway. He looked from one to the other, sensing the tension between them. "Fighting?"

"It's nothing," said Kakeru, getting up from his seat.

"You're still up? Do you want a drink or something?" Kiyose asked with a smile.

"Yeah, I got a bit thirsty." Prince opened the fridge, though he was still peering anxiously at them.

As Kakeru was leaving the room, Kiyose called after him, "About the IC race—senior's orders. Is that clear?"

"Yes," Kakeru answered. He crossed the hallway to his room and slammed the door shut.

Even when he lay down on the futon, sleep was slow to come. Tonight, as on other nights, a faint smell of rain seeped in through the thin windowpane.

At their third track meet, King managed to get his time to under seventeen minutes. Prince was the only one who hadn't. Under pressure, he was putting all his effort into practice. But in Kakeru's eyes, even that was far too little.

Why's he up so late anyway? Kakeru glared at the ceiling. Prince should have been keeping to a regular routine more than anyone else, and it was on him to get up early tomorrow to run hard. *I bet he's been reading manga again.*

Prince and Kiyose were talking in the kitchen, but after a while, he heard them going back to their rooms. Prince's footsteps creaked overhead.

Since it was an old, cheap house, everyone could hear everyone else going about their daily lives. It sounded like Prince was rummaging around in his hoard of treasure for a particular volume. Kakeru heard an avalanche of books tumbling down on the floor. *Put away your manga and go to sleep already.* Kakeru jerked the thin blanket over himself, curled up in a ball, and willed Prince to go to bed.

Presently, a whirring sound resembling a rickety windmill began to thrum in the air. Prince was jogging on his treadmill again, manga in hand. The noise kept Kakeru awake. He tossed aside his blanket, grabbed a pen lying near the futon, and flung it at the ceiling.

Such a small sound was lost on Prince; he kept on running on the treadmill. It seemed like he would go on forever.

In his own way, Prince was working hard. Though he'd hated running and constantly complained in the beginning, now he willingly jogged by himself in the middle of the night, without anyone telling him to. All so that the Chikusei-so team could enter the prelim and the Hakone Ekiden.

But Kakeru just couldn't bring himself to acknowledge Prince's efforts. To Kakeru, hard work that didn't produce any results was worthless.

Kakeru couldn't figure out whether he wanted to rage, cry, or laugh. He tugged the blanket over himself again and squeezed his eyes shut. Even when he pressed his hands over his ears, the creaking whirr of the treadmill rained down on him relentlessly from the room above.

At the second Totai track meet at the end of June, Prince achieved the time of 16:58.14. He had finally cleared the 17-minute hurdle. Now, every member of the Chikusei-so team was qualified to compete in the Hakone Ekiden prelim.

After the race, they were on cloud nine. They whooped and gave each other high fives, then whirled around in a circle holding hands. They kept spinning like they were performing a ritual to summon a UFO until Prince sank to the ground, exhausted.

Kakeru stood to one side, gazing at his teammates from a little distance. Of course, he was happy and relieved to have a ticket to the prelim, but he thought it was too early to celebrate.

Runners from other universities whispered to one another as they eyed the Chikusei-so team going wild.

"So they made it into the prelim. Not bad."

"But just look at them, they're never gonna go further than that."

"At least they'll have a nice memory to look back on, huh?"

They were snickering. It was the kind of laughter that was loaded with different undertones. Kakeru could sense them.

Sakaki from Totai spotted Kakeru standing apart from the circle and approached him. "Hey, heard your lame little group's trying to get to Hakone. Try not to embarrass yourself at the prelim."

Kakeru glowered at him. He wanted to bite back, but no words came.

"Kakeru." Kiyose called him over, waving his hand. Kakeru left Sakaki and went closer to the group. "You've put up a good fight, guys," Kiyose commended them calmly. "We're one step closer to Hakone. From now on, we'll focus on stretching out our distances at practice. But tonight, let's celebrate. Gather in the twins' room after you finish your evening jogs."

"Yesss!" the twins cheered.

Kakeru hid his icy response underneath his smile. *Another drinking party? We have those all the time.*

In his head, Kakeru went through their best official records so far:

Kakeru	14:09.95
Haiji	14:20.24
Musa	14:49.46
Joji	15:03.08
Jota	15:04.58
Yuki	15:36.45
Shindo	15:39.23
Nico	15:59.49
King	16:03.83
Prince	16:58.14

Most of them still weren't fast enough to compete with frontline runners. They were far below the threshold they had to meet if they were to have any hope of progressing beyond the prelim. That was the reality.

Now that the road to the prelim was clear, Kakeru grew more agitated than ever. When he was drinking with the group in the twins' room that night, the sake tasted bland. He sat alone by the window, feeling out of tune with the others' excitement.

The group had nearly finished the feast Kiyose had whipped up when they started to praise Prince, one after another.

"I was worried till the end, but you pulled through, Prince," said King.

"Your last spurt today—that was something! You crossed the line right in time," Shindo remarked.

"Yes. Watching your brave deed made me a little teary, Prince," Musa joined in.

As a prize for his achievement, the twins presented Prince with a prerelease volume of a weekly manga magazine, which they had procured at the shopping arcade especially for the occasion. Prince forgot all about the sake and was already poring over the book. Nico and Yuki were laughing at Prince's reaction.

Kakeru couldn't stand it. "Is it really worth raving about?" he muttered irritably. Eyes flew to him in surprise. He couldn't back down now, so he went on. "Prince's time is nothing to be proud of."

Without looking up from the magazine, Prince nodded in agreement. "Well, yeah, can't argue with that."

"What do you mean, Kakeru?" Jota fumed.

Even Joji, who was always sunny, firmly disagreed with Kakeru. "Don't you see? Prince got *so* much faster in just three months. At this rate, by the time we get to the prelim, he's going to whiz through five kilometers in a flash!"

"That's unrealistic," Yuki jabbed.

Kakeru ignored them and turned to Prince. "Do you realize what kind of position we're in? This is no time to be reading manga."

"You're absolutely right," Prince replied, shrugging him off, but the twins leaped to their feet in outrage.

"Stop it, Kakeru! You've been acting weird lately. You're kind of scary."

"Yeah, don't take it out on Prince. If you've got something to say, say it to all of us!"

"Fine, I'll say it!" Kakeru thrust down his cup and stood up. "Keep running like sloths, and we'll never get to Hakone! Never! But look at you, throwing a drinking party like everything's all good. How can you be so laid-back? I don't get it!"

"Calm down, Kakeru. You've been drinking with us, too," Shindo said, clutching Kakeru's ankle. "You're drunk, aren't you? Just sit down for a minute."

As for the twins, Musa was holding his arms up around them, trying to soothe them. Kakeru and the twins, the three first-years, were ready to pounce on each other, almost tearing themselves out of the older students' clasp.

"Who do you think you are! Just because you can run a little faster than us!"

"You're the one who told me to say it!" Kakeru retorted.

"You've crossed the line! It's not like everyone can just get up and start running like you do!"

"Wait till you put in more practice before you start talking like that! But who knows? Maybe no amount of practice can save *you*!"

"Kakeru, that's going too far," Nico cut in, rising halfway to his feet.

"You jerk, you think you're all that?!" King was about to lunge at Kakeru, but he was a split second too late.

Kiyose, who had been sitting in silence, shot up and grabbed Kakeru by the collar, as agile and ferocious as a leopard. "You doofus!" The others had no time to react. "When are you going to wake up?! Why can't you recognize that every one of us—including Prince—is putting everything into this! Why are you downplaying their commitment? Because they're slower than you? Is speed the only thing that matters to you? Then there's no point in running. Just go on a bullet train! Take a flight! That's a lot faster!"

"Haiji . . ." Stunned by Kiyose's fury, the whole room froze.

"You should see it by now, Kakeru. It's meaningless to chase after speed and nothing else. Nothing comes of it. Look at what happened to me. Someday you'll hit your limit and—"

He broke off mid-sentence. His grip on Kakeru's shirt loosened, and he staggered back.

"Haiji!" Kakeru darted forward to hold him up. "What's wrong?!"

Kiyose turned pale, and his eyelids drooped.

"Hey, Haiji! Wake up!" Kakeru slapped his cheeks, but he showed no response. "What do we do? He's unconscious!"

"What?!"

Panic broke out. Yuki seized Kiyose's wrist and checked his pulse. "Twins, get the futon out! Someone call an ambulance—no, it'll be quicker to call a doctor. Tell the landlord and ask for a doctor right now!"

"Don't die, Haiji!" Jota and Joji sobbed as they pulled out the futon.

Shindo and Musa ran to the window and shouted at the main house, "Mr. Tazaki! We need help!"

Prince scrambled downstairs to get some water, and King just scurried to and fro like a headless chicken.

Kakeru and Nico set Kiyose down on the futon. Even when Yuki told him, "Don't worry so much, he'll be fine," Kakeru stayed put near Kiyose's head. He didn't budge until the neighborhood doctor arrived.

It was well past his consultation hours, but he was an elderly physician who knew the landlord well. He hurried over straightaway after Tazaki's call. The doctor plowed through the group gathered around Kiyose and began his examination. He checked Kiyose's condition by lifting his eyelids, pressing a stethoscope against his chest, feeling for any sign of fever, and so on. Finally, he looked around the group and uttered a single word.

"Fatigue." He added, "It seems he fainted from anemia, but now he's actually asleep."

"He's . . . sleeping?" Everyone peered at Kiyose.

He was indeed breathing regularly, his chest rising and falling peacefully. Though they were relieved that it wasn't anything serious, they felt somewhat ridiculous for all the commotion they caused.

"Extreme fatigue from lack of sleep, I'd say." The doctor rummaged in his bag and swiftly prepared a syringe. "A nutrient injection is in order. Let him rest here for tonight. If anything happens, you're welcome to call me again. Well, take care. Try to keep him from working too hard."

The group thanked the doctor, and Yuki and Shindo saw him off to the front door. Kiyose remained fast asleep even when the needle of the syringe pierced his skin. The twins tucked him in under a thin blanket.

"It's my fault. I made him worry about me . . ." Kakeru hung his head and watched over Kiyose's sleeping face. He felt ashamed, frustrated at himself for not picking up on the signs. Even Fujioka from Rikudo had discerned that Kiyose wasn't in good shape. Kakeru had been so absorbed in his own running that he couldn't even see what was happening to someone who lived under the same roof.

Prince, sitting across from Kakeru on the other side of the futon, shook his head feebly. "That's not true. It's my fault. Even after all this time, I can't run any faster."

Everyone had sat around the futon in mournful silence, like the forest animals that gathered around the recumbent body of Buddha after he died and passed into nirvana. When Yuki and Shindo returned to the room, they shrank back from the funereal mood for a moment, but they joined the circle.

"Come to think of it, we've been relying on Haiji for everything," Musa said.

"Yeah, you're right." King crossed his arms. "Haiji took care of everything—all the admin stuff like registering for track meets, not to mention cooking for us."

"The supervisor, coach, and manager all in one," Jota said.

"We did have a lot on our plate just to keep up with the practice, but even then, we've been putting too much burden on him," Shindo brooded, with a guilt-ridden look on his face.

"Let's all pitch in from now on," Joji piped up, trying to lighten the mood, "at least take turns with cooking."

They all agreed.

"Well then, time to make peace," Nico said, looking back and forth between Kakeru and Prince.

"Sure," Prince said. Kakeru nodded reluctantly, feeling awkward at how childish he'd been.

"And you too, twins. Will you let Kakeru off the hook?" Yuki prompted.

Jota and Joji glanced at Kakeru sheepishly. They answered in sync, "Of course."

"All right, then it's a deal," Nico said. "Don't let Haiji's last wishes go to waste. Let's band together and go to Hakone."

"Yeah!" Everyone shouted in unison and reached out over Kiyose's futon to grab each other's hands in a tight grip.

"I don't recall ever dying. Don't jinx me."

Kakeru looked down instantly. Kiyose's eyes were open.

"Sheesh, what's all this fuss about?" he grumbled, shoving aside the tangle of arms over him and trying to sit up.

"Please, you need to rest." Kakeru hastened to push him down. "You blacked out, Haiji. The doctor said you were anemic from fatigue."

"Right. Sorry for the trouble." Kiyose looked up at Kakeru, who was peering down at him. "But it looks like you've all made up. Good."

Kakeru sat up straight, his legs tucked under him in the formal seiza pose, and bowed. "I'm really sorry. I've been on edge. I was feeling cornered."

"It's the noise leaking out from Yuki's room, right? I get it," said Nico, giving him a sympathetic look.

"If we're talking about noise, what about the creaks from the ceiling?" Yuki snapped back, and Prince flinched guiltily.

"It's not that," Kakeru blurted out. "I've been like this since before I came to Aotake. All I ever did was run, and I couldn't see much else around me." Even now, he didn't really know what he should do. If not speed, what guiding principle should he run by? He was still looking for the answer.

"But," he went on, lifting his face, "from now on, I'll aim for the Hakone Ekiden for real."

"*Whaaat?!*" The whole room shook. "What do you mean, 'from now on'? You weren't even serious this whole time?" Joji barked, ready to bite.

"Well, I just thought I might as well play along. That was it," Kakeru confessed. "I figured you wouldn't last long anyway—thought you'd all get tired of it and quit. Sorry."

"I'm amazed you could put in so much work with that mindset," Shindo murmured in awe.

"Running is the only thing I'm good at," Kakeru said.

He meant to be serious, but Yuki shook his head in mild disbelief, and King was baffled. "You're a total weirdo," he remarked.

"You're really something, Kakeru. So out there that it's actually funny," Joji said, stifling his laugh. That made Kakeru a bit indignant— *Why would I be 'funny'?*—but even Kiyose was nodding in agreement, so he didn't object.

"I can't quit reading manga, but I'll work harder, too," Prince declared, looking up.

A slight resentment still lingered in the air, but for the very first time, the same resolve flared up equally across the whole group.

Kiyose, who was gazing at their exchange, called to Kakeru. Kakeru drew closer to his pillow, still sitting formally.

"Do you know the best compliment you can give a long-distance runner?" Kiyose asked.

" 'You're fast?' "

"No. It's 'strong,'" Kiyose said. "You can't pull through a long-distance race with speed alone. The weather, the course, the twists and turns of how the race unfolds, your own condition, your state of mind. You have to analyze all these different elements with composure. You have to persevere and keep moving forward even when a stretch of the race turns painful. What a distance runner must have is strength, in the true sense of the word. To be deemed strong is our honor, and that's what we strive for as we run every day."

Everyone was still, hanging on to every word.

"After watching you run these past three months, I'm even more convinced," Kiyose went on. "You have talent and aptitude, Kakeru. That's why I want you to believe in yourself more. You don't have to rush. It takes time to grow stronger. You could even say it's a journey that never ends. Just as there are people who go jogging or run marathons even when they're old, the long-distance race is something worth working on over a lifetime."

Kakeru's passion for running always unsteadied his heart with volatile swings, like the inchoate impulses that stir in the depths of the human heart and threaten to erupt. But Kiyose's words penetrated the dim, shadowy undulations in Kakeru as vividly as a flash of lightning, setting off a cascade of light that illuminated him from within.

"But an old runner can't break the world record." Though he didn't mean to, Kakeru found himself arguing back, partly to hide his embarrassment.

"That's a bold statement," Nico joked, and Kiyose smiled as if to say, *What am I going to do with you?*

"That's what I used to think—until I got injured," Kiyose answered calmly. "They might not be able to set new records, but it *is* possible for old runners to be stronger than you. And that's where distance running gets deep."

Kiyose's words were directed not only at Kakeru but at everyone present. All the talking seemed to have tired him, and he closed his eyes. Jota and Joji cried out, "Haiji, don't fall asleep in our room!" and tried to shake him awake.

"Be quiet. Team dismissed," Kiyose mumbled.

Everyone except the twins shuffled out of the room. Kakeru was the last to leave. Just as he was shutting the door, he glanced back and saw the twins cramming themselves onto another futon that they'd taken out of the closet.

What does it mean to be "a strong runner"? Kakeru could understand that the kind of strength Haiji was talking about wasn't simply about muscle power. But it also pointed to something more than just mental fortitude.

Out of nowhere, Kakeru remembered a snow-covered field he'd seen when he was little. He woke up early one morning and went to a field in the neighborhood to discover the familiar landscape completely transformed by the snow that had settled overnight. Kakeru ran across the fresh, untouched expanse of white. Letting his heart guide him, he ran to make pretty patterns on the snow. That was the first time in his life that he felt joy in running.

Maybe strength was something beautiful that stood poised in a subtle balance, like the patterns on the snow he'd drawn that day.

As the thought crossed his mind, Kakeru trod softly down the stairs.

The next morning, clear blue sky stretched out overhead for the first time in a while. When Kakeru came back from his early-morning jog, Kiyose was feeding Nira in the yard.

Kiyose noticed him and said, "Welcome home."

Kakeru replied, "I'm back."

The fresh, dazzling light of the morning sun marked the beginning of another ordinary day.

V

SUMMER CLOUDS

"How are we supposed to practice in this crazy heat?"

"But if we slack off, we'll be homeless . . ."

Kakeru was in the kitchen boiling some somen noodles for lunch when he overheard snatches of conversation from behind him. It was Jota and Joji, who were sprawled out in the hallway near the front door.

Ever since Kiyose fainted, the Chikusei-so residents had begun to pay extra attention to their physical health. Once a month, they all visited the same neighborhood physician who had examined Kiyose and got tested for anemia. Their kitchen was well stocked with a variety of supplements, and every night before bed, the whole house turned into a veritable massage fest.

Still, there was nothing they could do about the heat.

Now that they'd finished their final exams for the first semester and dived into summer break, the temperature exploded to the boiling point. Chikusei-so, of course, wasn't equipped with air-conditioning, so all the doors throughout the building were left wide-open, even the front door. The residents were crawling around the hallways in search of any spot where they might find even a moment's respite from the heat.

The steaming hot air rising from the big pot clung to the skin and turned into sweat. Kakeru quickly drained the noodles in a strainer and rinsed the batch under cold running water. He set down a bottle of mentsuyu soup base, a bottle of mineral water, and a bowl of ice cubes on the table.

"It's ready," he called out, wiping away sweat with the sleeve of his T-shirt.

The twins heaved themselves up. Jota took one look at the table and whined, "Now, that's just sad. Don't we have any garnish, at the very least? No scallions or ginger?"

"Haiji's picking some shiso leaves from the garden right now." Kakeru put the mountain of noodles in the middle of the table, then started banging on the bottom of the empty big pot with a ladle. Like frazzled, half-dead snakes, the other residents crept out from their respective corners of the house and assembled in the kitchen.

"Is Haiji climbing up a mountain to pick them or something?" Yuki grunted.

"Shindo is missing, too. I wonder what happened to him?" Musa said.

"Still can't believe how brutal the landlord was. He didn't have to get *that* angry," Joji said.

"You had it coming, though," King countered.

Somehow, they all managed to heave a deep sigh while slurping up their noodles.

After Kiyose passed out, the landlord had tried to enter Chikusei-so to check on him, but Shindo and Musa desperately kept him back from crossing the threshold.

The landlord grew suspicious. The next day, he sneaked into Chikusei-so while the residents were all away at the campus. And as soon as he stepped inside the front door, he discovered the gaping hole in the twins' floor right above his head.

For the landlord, the time-worn apartment building was as precious as his own child, and his grief at seeing the damage was profound. He summoned the residents and announced, "I need money for repairing Chikusei-so. I'm going to raise the rent to gather the funds."

"Nooo!"

"Don't 'nooo' me! How about, 'We'll dazzle everyone in the Hakone Ekiden and pull in a big sponsor who'll build us a new dorm!' Do any of you whiners have the guts to say *that*?"

"There's no way we'd find a sponsor that generous," Jota, the real culprit behind the hole in the floor, started to mutter, but one glare from the landlord shut him up.

"Clearly, you all have too much pep for your own good, so Hakone should be an easy win, eh? If you don't want the rent to go up, make sure you get into Hakone. No excuses."

With any more provocation, the elderly landlord might drop dead, so everyone obediently answered, "Yes, sir."

"I can't just move out now," Prince murmured at the kitchen table, thinking of his treasured collection. "We've got to keep the rent low. I do want to go practice more . . . but to be honest, isn't it suicidal to run in the summer? What do other track teams do?"

"Most of the time, they go somewhere cool for training camp. Like Hokkaido," Kakeru replied.

"Hokkaido!" Joji breathed dreamily. The mouth-watering images of crabs, sea urchin roe, and ramen waltzing through his mind were so obvious that everyone could almost see them reflected in his noodle soup. Kakeru cleared his throat; he decided it was best to pull Joji back into reality to keep the mental damage minimal.

"That's not an option for us. We don't have the money."

Crestfallen, Joji gulped down the rest of his somen along with the half-melted ice. Just then, Kiyose and Shindo rushed into the kitchen.

"Where've you been, Haiji? We're done eating already," Nico said.

"Let's get out of the Tokyo inferno. We're going to a training camp," Kiyose declared, thrusting a clump of shiso leaves on Nico.

"To Hokkaido?!" the twins leaped to their feet.

"No, Lake Shirakaba."

Though not as enticing as Hokkaido, Lake Shirakaba was also a famous summer retreat in the highlands of Tateshina.

"But where would we get the money?" Kakeru asked.

"Some people in the shopping arcade volunteered to help us," Kiyose explained. "The owner of Batting Cage Okai is letting us stay at their summer house by the lake. Yaokatsu and the others will cover our groceries during the camp. And we'll take the Aotake van there and back, so it's not going to cost that much."

"Don't worry about our finances," Shindo assured them. "I've been advertising our challenge to the folks at the shopping arcade and the university. I'm sure we'll keep getting more backers. Besides, Nico-senpai's wire dolls are selling even better than I expected."

"What?" Nico gaped. He'd been shredding the shiso and sprinkling it on the bowls that still had somen left in them, but now he paused in midair. "You've been selling them? Where? And who in their right mind would buy something like that?"

"I asked a general store to stock them, and they're turning out to be pretty popular with girls. Like creepy-cute talisman dolls." Shindo smiled. "Hope you'll keep them coming."

"Woohoo! Training camp! Training camp!" Jota and Joji jumped up and down, grasping each other's hands. Prince had already disappeared from the kitchen. Apparently, he'd gone back to his room to start picking out which manga volumes to take to the camp. Each in his own way, they all indulged in daydreams about an exciting summer trip.

A refreshing breeze rustling through the lakeside forest. A beautiful girl in a white summer dress sits across from me in a swan boat, while I bite into grilled corn on the cob. Even when autumn comes, our love will go on. We'll promise to meet again in Tokyo in a teary farewell in the silver birch grove . . .

Joji's fantasy shattered when they arrived at Lake Shirakaba. "Why does life have to be like this?" he sulked. The summer house where they would be staying hadn't been used for a long time, and it was in a state of disrepair.

They had traveled in the white van, with Kiyose behind the wheel. After arriving at the house, which was nestled in a pine forest by the lake, they spent the rest of the day cleaning up the rooms. Once they had wiped the floors, scrubbed the bath, and swept the soot from the fireplace, they seemed to have breathed a bit of new life into the log cabin.

At first glance, the cabin amid the clump of trees had looked more like a wild den built by a bear than a summer house. But their efforts had made it look passable as a human dwelling. Kakeru felt relieved as he piled some branches he'd foraged in the fireplace.

"Joji, your fantasies are too corny," Jota said, his face smeared with grime. "I knew there'd be a catch."

As far as they could see during the day, the Shirakaba Lake resort seemed to attract mostly families with kids and elderly couples. The flock of abandoned swan boats were swaying in the gentle ripples of the water, accompanied by the tunes drifting from the small amusement park nearby.

"It's nice that it's cool here, but it's actually chilly after sunset," Musa observed, pulling on a hoodie over his shirt.

When Kakeru lit the firewood, the group gathered around the fireplace of their own accord. It was pitch-black outside the windows, and only the rasping of the treetops could be heard.

After gazing at the fire for some time, Kiyose said, "I've already prepped dinner. All that's left is popping in the roux. Let's go for a run before that."

"Curry again?!"

"I don't wanna! I'm too tired from cleaning!"

"What if we get run over by a car in the dark!"

Of course, Kiyose would have none of their protests. He herded them to their shoes and out onto the dirt trail winding through the forest.

"We don't even know the paths that well yet." Nico scratched his head. "Which way's the lake?"

"If we walk downhill, we'll get there eventually." Yuki led the way, and the rest jogged behind him in single file.

Kiyose, bringing up the rear, gave them directions. "One lap around the lake is 3.8 kilometers. Do three laps at your own pace, then come back to the cabin for dinner."

"Got it." When they got to the paved road by the lake, they started jogging at their usual speeds. The souvenir shops and the little museums along the road were already closed for the day. All the buildings were unlit, except for a couple of large hotels. They couldn't see much of the scenery, so they felt their way along the unfamiliar route.

Kakeru ran next to Kiyose, tracing the gentle curve of the dark road. Their only point of reference was the water lapping the shore.

Kakeru had no qualms about running on an unfamiliar road in unfamiliar air. For him, getting a sense of distance was second nature. As long as he knew that one lap meant 3.8 kilometers, he could intuit roughly how far he had run, based on his own speed and how his body felt. The pleasant thrill of running on unknown terrain coursed through him.

"Where's our coach?" Kakeru asked Kiyose. "Is he at the Go parlor again?"

"Who knows? He'll probably join us sooner or later." Kiyose cocked his head a little. "I don't know why, but he doesn't want to get in the car when I'm driving."

When they had set off from Chikusei-so that morning, the landlord had seen them off from the yard. Though he'd looked on in satisfaction as the donated groceries were loaded onto the back of the van, he himself had refrained from climbing in.

"You've gotten so much better at driving, though," Kakeru said, but regretted it immediately, realizing it came off as a backhanded compliment.

Still, it was true that Kiyose's driving skills were improving at an incredibly rapid pace. On their first few drives after the Totai track meet, the group had felt as though they were strapped into a space shuttle that was doing aerobatics. Tensing up or nearly passing out was the norm, while feeling safe enough to sleep in the van was unthinkable. But some of the passengers had actually dozed off on the road to Lake Shirakaba.

"I'm a quick learner with anything," Kiyose said, unperturbed. "I'm a perfectionist, I can't help going all out on research and practice."

Kakeru remembered the myth that Nico had brought up on that first ride. *Uh, does that mean he's the same down there . . . ?* Kakeru had to wonder, but he didn't dare pose the question. He merely nodded and replied, "Sure. I can see that."

Kakeru and Kiyose passed the slower runners and were the first to return to the cabin. After three laps around the lake, they didn't mind the damp, chilly night air of the highlands anymore. They loosened up their muscles with a massage, then Kakeru ran a bath while Kiyose pressed a plastic bag full of ice against his right calf. This was to prevent inflammation of the strained muscle.

"How's the leg?" Kakeru asked.

"All good." Kiyose smiled. "Go ahead, you can wash first."

Kakeru had gotten out of the bath and swapped places with Kiyose to stir the curry pot when the others came back from their jog. They tore off their sweaty T-shirts and swarmed the bathroom.

Their fighting over the shower and off-pitch humming echoed all the way into the kitchen. Kiyose seemed to have been pushed out of the bathroom. He reappeared in the kitchen, hair still wet, and popped open the lid of the rice cooker.

Kakeru and Kiyose worked together to set the large table made of solid timber. A massive pile of curry and rice, a salad, milk mixed with protein powder, and peaches for dessert. Everything had been provided by the stores in the shopping arcade.

The others, refreshed by the bath, gathered around the table. Just as they picked up their spoons to start eating, Kiyose said, "Wait a second. Someone's missing."

They all looked at one another. Musa and Shindo weren't there.

"That's odd. Even Prince is back already."

"I don't think there was anyone behind or in front of me when I was doing my last lap," Prince said, puzzled.

"Don't tell me they got lost in the forest?" King stood up and peered out the dining room window.

"Did anyone see them on their way back here?" Kiyose asked.

No one had. Nico went upstairs. They heard him switching on the lights on the second floor so that Musa and Shindo would have something to guide them back to the cabin through the woods.

"Where could they be?"

"Maybe we should go look for them," the twins suggested anxiously.

"No, we can't have anyone else go missing. Let's wait for them a little longer." Even though he stopped the twins from going, Kiyose was so worried he couldn't sit still. He went to open the front door and stared out at the forest path sunk in darkness. He strained his ears for the rustle of footsteps, but nothing came. Though the curry was steadily cooling, dinner was the least of their concerns.

Kakeru stood still beside Kiyose on the threshold. Nico came back downstairs and gave Kiyose's shoulder a pat. "No worries—even if they have to sleep in the woods, it's not gonna kill them. It's only one night."

Just then, the back door banged open. They spun around to find Musa and Shindo striding in from the side of the kitchen behind the dining space. The back of the kitchen was a steep slope, and there wasn't even a trail there. No one had expected them to come in from that side.

Musa and Shindo shouted at once.

"Bad news!"

"They're here too! The guys from Totai!"

The group all pulled themselves together and sat around the table. Musa and Shindo told everyone what they'd seen over dinner. They had stumbled across Tokyo Taiiku's clubhouse farther up the mountain.

"It looked like a brand-new building," Shindo said. "We saw the lights and thought it was our place, so we walked up to it. Then we saw the Totai guys having dinner through the window."

"By the way, grilled meat was on their menu," Musa added. "They appeared to be having the highest-quality Wagyu beef."

King shoveled the ground pork curry into his mouth without a word.

"Why did you climb up the mountain in the first place?" Kiyose asked.

"It wasn't on purpose."

"We just got lost in the dark," the pair said simply.

"Shindo, I thought you were used to mountains?"

"I am . . . but I also have a horrible sense of direction."

"Me too. It was so bad that back home, my parents made me promise never to go to the savanna, even when friends invited me," Musa said.

As Kiyose rubbed his temples in consternation, Kakeru whispered to him, "What are you going to do? Weren't you planning to give Shindo the mountain-climb leg at Hakone?"

"Yeah," Kiyose groaned. "We might just witness the first live broadcast of a stray runner in the history of Hakone Ekiden."

"They do have those escort vehicles to guide the runners, so I doubt that," Yuki sneered, "but in the worst-case scenario, we'd have to count on Shindo's animal sense of smell. Sniff out a beast trail through the woods of Mount Hakone and make a beeline for Lake Ashi."

"Oh, is that actually a thing?" Joji asked eagerly when he caught on to the conversation.

"Of course not. You're disqualified if you veer off the route," Kiyose chided.

"It used to happen back in the day," King jumped in to flaunt his knowledge of trivia. As a quiz maniac, he'd done some research on the Hakone Ekiden. "Back when they only had, like, four schools participating in the race, in the Taisho era. The story goes, every team put in the most effort on figuring out the best shortcut on the mountain. Even the Hakone Ekiden started out as your simple, no-frills race—there was no radio broadcast or anything like that."

"Isn't that cheating?" Prince asked as he peeled a peach.

Nico chuckled as he helped himself to more rice. "Exactly the sorta thing college students would think up."

Kakeru imagined those students in the 1920s running on wild animal trails, competing fiercely with their rivals but also devising tricks to give themselves a little boost. Silly, playful students, not so different from today.

"Let's say we look for a shortcut once we break through the prelim—" Yuki started.

"Like we said, that would be cheating."

"Anyway, our problem is Totai. What are we going to do about those guys?"

"We'll definitely run into them on the road around the lake tomorrow," Shindo murmured. Kakeru was silent, but his fighting spirit flared up inside him. He was determined to show the Totai team who was the better runner, even if they were only jogging.

"Don't get in a fight," Kiyose warned. "There's only one lake here. We should give way to each other and run in peace."

The Chikusei-so team slept crowded together on the second floor, wrapped up in blankets. They woke with the birdsong. After stretching, they went out for their prebreakfast jog in the clean, fresh air. No sooner had they reached the lakeside road than they bumped into the Totai athletes.

Dressed in matching tracksuits, the Tokyo Taiiku track team had just finished their morning meeting in the empty parking lot of a souvenir shop before it opened for the day. About fifty people were getting ready for their jog; they lined up in neat ranks according to the level of their abilities.

Their head coach, as well as several people who looked like assistant coaches, got into a few different cars that were apparently going to cruise alongside each group of runners. The first rank of runners, consisting of upperclassmen, began to jog. There was a clear order to everything they did.

Joji didn't try to hide his admiration. "That's impressive," he said.

As for the Kansei track team, their long-distance runners consisted of just the ten residents of Chikusei-so. They had never held a formal meeting before practice, and their coach was as absent as ever. Plus, their outfits were a motley collection; the twins were sporting brightly colored souvenir T-shirts from Hawaii.

Sakaki, the first-year at Totai, seemed to have noticed them. He whispered something in a teammate's ear. It quickly caused a stir among the rest of the group, and many of them, especially the first-years, kept glancing back at the Chikusei-so team as they jogged in front of them.

"I don't know, this is making me self-conscious," Musa mumbled. King, who was easily unnerved, looked like he wanted to turn around and head back to the cabin.

"Let's go." Nothing could daunt Kakeru. *When it comes to running, I'll never fall behind anyone. No one in the world can make me back down.*

"Where do you get that energy this early in the morning?" the others grumbled. But they started jogging, too, as though dragged forward by Kakeru. Kiyose called out to them, "Leave Kakeru alone. Keep to your own pace."

Kakeru let out a small laugh. Sure enough, going against his own instructions, Kiyose swiftly caught up with Kakeru. Sakaki was jogging ahead, beckoning to them behind his back.

"Don't take the bait," Kiyose said.

"I can easily overtake him."

"Stick to your own rhythm. We'll go easy. Hold a pace of five kilometers in twenty minutes this morning."

Kakeru looked at Kiyose. Kiyose wore a serene expression on his face, looking straight ahead as he ran. He seemed to be concentrating on listening to the voice of his own body. For Kiyose, once he was in the zone, the pack of Totai students and the cars that occasionally passed by ceased to exist. He was completely absorbed in the motions of his own body as it made its way through the narrow space between the pine forest and the lake.

"Got it," Kakeru replied. He pushed Sakaki out of his head. Five kilometers in twenty minutes. He focused all his senses on how his muscles, heart, and lungs worked when he ran at that speed. It was a comfortable pace. It was slow enough that he could feel the blood circulating throughout his body and brain.

Birds sang in clear, liquid trills to the rapidly rising sun. The breeze that blew from high above the mountains made small ripples across the surface of the lake.

I wonder what strength really is. Kakeru found himself going back to the question. *Take Haiji's calmness, for example. He's running in his own world, unwavering, in perfect self-command. I can run faster than him, but I'm not sure if I'm stronger. I'm too hot-headed, and too obsessed with winning.*

Kakeru wanted to find out—to know what he was missing, to know what made someone strong. It was the first time he'd ever wanted something like that. Until now, he had always run as if something were chasing him, driven forward by the compulsion of his own body.

There was nothing uniform about the Chikusei-so team. But Kiyose led them with a strong yet flexible command, without binding them up or forcing anything on them. Kakeru turned to look behind him. The group was running along the lakeside road. Their abilities still varied greatly, but they were all jogging with a solid form and intense concentration. Though they had endlessly moaned over their practice back in the spring, after three months of hard work, they now resembled a proper track team.

Kakeru turned to face forward and looked down a little. He stretched out his senses to feel the movements of his body, from his toes striking the ground to the arc drawn by his fingertips as his arms sliced the air.

If I keep following Haiji, I'm sure I'll see something new—something I've been looking for all this time, that shines bright in the dark.

Led by Sasaki, the Totai first-years began to play tricks on the Kansei team to interfere with their practice. They spread out in a horizontal line across the road to block the way. Then they clustered around Kakeru to put pressure on him. Whenever the coaches or the upperclassmen weren't looking, they found different ways to taunt him.

Kakeru didn't particularly mind. He'd grown used to such harassment during club activities and races in high school. If they surrounded him, all he had to do was speed up and shake them off. If they blocked the way, he merely had to pass them by sidestepping into the opposite lane.

But most of the Chikusei-so team were not much more than beginners. They didn't know the wily tactics involved in running a race. They were thoroughly intimidated by the first-years' underhanded maneuvers and were thrown off their stride.

At first, Kiyose had simply looked on, but he finally ran out of patience. "They're acting immature," he muttered when they finished their evening jog. He decided to take a stand.

The group of first-years, about twenty in total, were loitering in the parking lot of the souvenir shop. Kiyose boldly marched up to them. Kakeru and the others quickly followed suit. They had Kiyose's back.

The clear, melancholy tones of the higurashi cicada echoed in the twilight air.

"So we just gotta knock out two guys per person—that'll do it," Nico calculated, cracking his knuckles, and Musa flexed his ankles as they approached. The Totai students stopped talking and turned around. The teams faced off in the middle of the parking lot.

"We want you to stop interfering with our practice," Kiyose said quietly, breaking the silence.

Sakaki stepped up from the group. "And we don't want to hear any false accusations. Do you even have any proof that we got in your way?"

"We do," Yuki said, taking his cell phone out of his pocket and thrusting it in front of the Totai group. The screen showed an unmistakable photo of Kakeru looking cramped as he ran behind a row of Totai students who were taking up the entire sidewalk. "I was snapping some photos to study his form later, and I just happened to catch something interesting."

"I know how you feel, but leave your phone at home next time," Kiyose warned Yuki. "If you have anything extra in your pocket, that's going to skew your form."

Is that *the problem here?* Kakeru wanted to say. Yuki's overzealous research method made him cringe, but the sneak shot didn't seem to disturb Kiyose, who clearly had only running on his mind. *Scary.* Sakaki looked flummoxed and awkward, in equal parts.

Kiyose turned back to the Totai group. "That's all I have to say. I'd prefer not to have to show this blurry picture to your coach and captain. I hope you'll understand."

"Of course, crystal clear," Sakaki scoffed. "We at Tokyo Taiiku are working hard toward Hakone, and we take our practice seriously. We have no time to deal with amateurs who're just running for the hell of it."

"We think alike," Kiyose replied. Kakeru saw a blood vessel on Kiyose's temple throb. "It really is a nuisance when some people stoop to infantile tricks to meddle with serious practice."

Kiyose and Sakaki stood face-to-face, glaring furiously at each other. Kakeru whispered, "Haiji," and gently put a hand on his arm to calm him down.

"We obviously have a different idea of what 'serious' means," Sakaki taunted. "Why don't we settle it with a race? Ten of you and ten of us first-years run around the lake and see who gets the better time overall."

Kakeru boiled with rage at Sakaki's provocation. "Bring it on!" he roared. He knew Sakaki was working hard, but he couldn't just let him mock the Chikusei-so team like that. Seeing Sakaki's repulsive attitude was like seeing himself the way he was acting several weeks ago—and he couldn't stand it. This time, it was Kiyose who grabbed Kakeru's arm to hold him back. But Kakeru shook him off and kept going.

"You've got a problem with *me*, right?! Then why don't the two of us duke it out? Don't rope them in just 'cause you can't beat me!"

"As always, you're so full of yourself, Kurahara," Sakaki shot back without flinching. They were rearing to pounce on each other, so their teammates stepped in on both sides. Nico grasped Kakeru's arms from behind in a full nelson. Kakeru glowered at Sakaki, breathing heavily. Sakaki's teammates grabbed Sakaki's arms, but he was still kicking the air, trying to get at Kakeru.

"Is now really the time for fights?" Kiyose said quietly, addressing both boys. "Focus on training."

Sakaki extracted himself from his teammates' hold and straightened out his tracksuit. He looked at Kakeru, Kiyose, and the other Chikusei-so members in turn.

"Having fun?" Sakaki asked in a low voice. "You finally met some *friends* to run with. Is that fun for you, Kurahara?"

"That's enough," Kiyose interrupted, turning his back to Sakaki. "Let's go back."

Kiyose urged him, but Kakeru didn't move. *Friend?* Sakaki had no right to use a word like that. It enraged Kakeru and made his stomach churn. A sharp pang shot deep inside his skull. He tore himself away from Nico's hold and stood motionless, his glare fixed on Sakaki.

"Are you satisfied now?" Sakaki went on. "Running playground races with your nice friends who fuss over you?"

"It's not like that!" *It was* you *and the rest of them that always made a fuss over my speed.* Underneath the surface, though, the team back then had been consumed by a raging whirlpool of jealousy and rivalry. *I despised that track team in high school. You'd all pretend to be friends, but you'd stab each other in the back the first chance you got. I hated you guys so much it made me want to puke.*

Kakeru wanted to let loose the scream inside his head, but he was too infuriated to put his feelings into words. And in the back of his mind, a small part of him admitted he deserved whatever Sakaki had to say about him.

Sakaki can't forgive what I've done. Just live with it. Kakeru willed himself to swallow his rage, clenching his fists. *It was my fault he couldn't run in the last big race in high school, so it's no wonder he's mad at me. Just pretend it's Nira barking. Let him bark.*

"So *now* you can run along with your buddies, huh? Why couldn't you do the same that time? Why'd you make all our hard work come to nothing? All you had to do was hold back just a little bit."

Argh, I can't. Nira's cute, but Sakaki sure as hell isn't! Sakaki's reproaches quickly made Kakeru scrap any leniency.

"I can't hold back! That's just the way I am!" Kakeru sounded so vehement that even a lion might have turned tail and run from him.

He was the one who wanted to interrogate Sakaki: *Why did you just stay quiet and put up with that suffocating club?* Words came brimming up in his chest, but it always took time for Kakeru to voice them out loud. All too soon, his counterattack was trampled down by Sakaki, who charged at him with the force of a stampeding elephant.

"Don't flatter yourself, Kurahara!" Sakaki growled in a low tone. "Knowing you, you probably expected the best colleges to single you out. I bet you thought they'd invite you over, even if you couldn't run in the race, didn't you? Well, too bad. In the end, you're just an egocentric, selfish piece of—"

"I thought I said that's enough." Kiyose's glacial voice made them stop dead in what was starting to resemble a battle between fierce beasts of the savanna. Kakeru collected himself and stole a glance at Kiyose, who was standing right behind him. Kiyose's face was as blank as a sheet of ice. Behind him, the twins were flapping their arms, trying to signal to him to back down because Kiyose was about to explode.

When he saw that Kakeru's fire had been extinguished, Kiyose turned his chilling look to Sakaki. "I understand there are things you want to say. But Kakeru is a member of Kansei's track team now. I'd appreciate it if you'd refrain from lashing out at him. I won't let you hurt or disturb him."

Kiyose urged Kakeru to go home again, pulling on his shirtsleeve and pushing him toward the forest path. Kakeru started walking away with him.

"What did Kakeru do to Sakaki anyway?" King whispered.

"Dunno. But it kinda looks like everyone's got a thing for him," Jota murmured back. They gave free rein to their imagination. Kiyose told them to hurry up, so the rest of the Chikusei-so members turned to leave the parking lot.

"Be careful. He might betray you at the last second, too," Sakaki snarled at their backs.

Kiyose threw him a smirk. "At the prelim, we'll show you just how serious we are as a team of 'friends.' Oh, but maybe you'll be too busy scurrying around doing errands to watch the race. Well, best of luck on getting picked as a regular."

"Who's the immature one now?"

"He's got a twisted personality, that Haiji." Nico and Yuki muttered with a shiver. In the Kansei team, they never had to worry about internal struggles over getting promoted to being a regular member; there was no such thing.

"I suppose there are benefits to being a small underdog team," Musa said, pitying the sour-faced Totai first-years.

Kakeru stole a sideways glance at Kiyose. The vein on his temple wasn't bulging anymore, but he still looked grim, apparently lost in thought. *I've stirred up trouble again.* Kakeru tried his best to gulp down the heavy sigh that threatened to escape him.

"I'm sorry, Haiji."

"No need for you to apologize."

Maybe he's still angry. Kakeru faltered, and settled on a different phrase. "Thank you, Haiji."

"You're welcome."

That seemed to soften the curve of Kiyose's cheek. For the first time, Kakeru realized that it was better to thank someone in a situation like this. *He stood up for me, after all.* The thought washed away his rage and frustration. Feeling lighter, he broke out in a run.

"Draw a bath for us," Kiyose called after him. Kakeru raised a hand in response.

The wind of the highlands, carrying the night chill, whipped past Kakeru, but the warmth never left his body.

At dinner, Kiyose announced a change in their training routine. He had come to the decision that it was unwise to let the Totai group irritate them any further. He proposed different times for their morning and evening jogs, and they were also to avoid the road around the lake as much as possible for their main practice.

No one opposed these changes. Totai's provocation had made them even more fired up than before. If they could dive into training without interference, they didn't care where they had to go.

"But seriously . . . this is killing me," Prince wheezed. The Chikusei-so team was running up a wild, pathless slope. It was a route that Shindo had discovered.

"This feels more like crawling than running," Prince went on. "Tree roots sticking out everywhere, too. What if we sprain our ankles?"

"Anyone who twists their ankles on this kind of easy terrain just doesn't have good reflexes, and their ankles are too stiff. They're not cut out for running," Kiyose said matter-of-factly and gave Prince a push from behind. "Come on, we're almost there. Put your back into it and speed up a little."

Kakeru and Shindo were already so far ahead that Prince couldn't see them anymore. Even though the hill was so steep that it would have been challenging just to walk up it, Kakeru and Shindo had swiftly scaled the slope with a powerful spring in their legs, as well as stamina and agility.

"Don't lump me together with some ninjas," Prince grumbled, wiping his sweat.

Running up an incline every day would put too much burden on their knees, so Kiyose had devised a regimen that combined running up the mountain and running on a wide, flat course for optimum effect. With the latter, the focus was on running longer distances.

There was a hiking trail at a high altitude about two peaks away from Lake Shirakaba. It was a path near the summit where hikers could walk while enjoying the view. Though fairly even, it was un-paved and covered only with wood chips, which meant less strain on the knees.

Kiyose called it "highland training." He came up with the idea to do cross-country running there. On the days when they weren't running up the side of a mountain, they all piled into the van and drove to the hiking trail. The trail was slightly more than three kilometers per lap, so they did six laps to make twenty kilometers in total.

When they were running, just a small increase in altitude was enough to make them feel uncomfortably aware of oxygen thinning out. At first, King detested the highland training, dubbing it a "tour through hell." Prince would be in such a state by the end of the twenty-kilometer run that an elderly couple on a hike could overtake him. But their bodies gradually adapted to the terrain, and it was evident that they were steadily gaining strength.

Thanks to the regular routine and meals, Nico had succeeded in getting more fit. Since he'd managed to shave off the extra fat, his body was lighter, and his time improved.

Yuki, who liked to delve into theory, bombarded Kiyose with questions about the training. Once he was satisfied, he threw himself into practice without a single complaint. His success with the bar exam was proof enough that he had an aptitude for steady, repetitive work.

With their sunny temperament, the twins didn't see hardship as hardship. Shindo could bask in the thrill of running in the mountains, where he felt completely at home. Even Kakeru was impressed by the power in his legs and the tenacity that propelled him up the steep gradient.

In contrast, running up a hill wasn't Musa's forte. But as soon as he switched to the flat trail, his supple muscles revealed their full potential. With long strides, he kicked the ground as if he weighed nothing.

Even Prince, whose running capacity had been the biggest concern for the team, was improving his distances little by little. Now he could run up to ten kilometers without whining at all. It was remarkable progress. Kiyose's insight and forethought played a part in this. He had confiscated the manga that Prince had brought with him and made it a rule that he would be allowed to read them only on the nights when he had completed the full training.

Prince always said he'd suffocate without manga. He worked himself to the ground just to have those moments of happiness at night. His brave efforts could have moved anyone to tears.

Of course, Kakeru and Kiyose were making steady progress, shaping their bodies into vessels for running.

Because Kakeru was running more than the rest of the team, he often struggled to fall asleep due to chronic sore muscles. But when he thought of the pain and throbbing heat as a sign that new tissues were forming within his muscles, he was ready to endure anything. He even felt something that verged on pleasure. Each morning, when he set off running again, his progress was tangible. He could clearly feel himself leaping into the world of speed, deeper and higher than the day before.

The Chikusei-so members were now running longer distances than ever, with more perseverance. They were riding a good wave. As the fruits of their labor became palpable, this recognition fueled their motivation even more. While conquering new distances and times that used to be unbearably painful to run, they gradually discovered the thrill of moving their bodies. They became more and more engrossed in running.

As for the jogs they went on before dawn and after sunset to avoid clashing with the Totai crowd, everyone could handle the load with ease. The jogs were at a lower altitude than the hiking trail and set at a more moderate pace and distance than their main practice, so this routine was turning out to be a casual breather.

One evening, about halfway through the summer camp, a thunderstorm struck in the middle of their jog. Come wind or rain, long-distance races continued. Kakeru thought it would be good practice, so he ignored the bad weather and kept running around the lake. The lower temperature and higher humidity suited running; they made it easier to breathe.

But the thunder and rain grew increasingly violent. A flash of lightning cleaved the night sky near the horizon. Huge drops of rain pelted him relentlessly, and his skin began to hurt. He couldn't hear anything except the rain pouring down like a waterfall. The water splashing against the pavement shrouded the road in a white mist. Weather was fickle in the mountains, but Kakeru had never seen such a torrential downpour.

Within a matter of seconds, Kakeru looked like he'd gone swimming with clothes on. It was difficult to see ahead in the dark. Finally, Kiyose gave up on the jog and instructed everyone behind him to return to the cabin.

"Don't catch a cold. Head straight for the bath when you get back."

Kakeru stood near Kiyose and made sure the others were turning around to the forest path. He could barely make out their shapes through the veil of cascading water.

When he counted up to six, he realized something was wrong. The last one to pass him just now was Prince, who should have been at the rear end of the group. Two were missing. There was no sign of Jota and Joji.

"Haiji, the twins are missing!" Kakeru yelled.

"Where are they?" Kiyose had to shout over the roar of the rain.

"Maybe they're waiting out the rain somewhere. I'll go look for them! Go ahead without us, we'll catch up."

Kakeru retraced the road in search of the twins. When he ran, the raindrops struck his face even harder, and he felt like he was drowning.

He ran on for a while without seeing any sign of the twins. *Did I miss them in the rain?* As he came to a halt, there was a burst of light overhead, and a deep rumble erupted almost at the same time, making him flinch. He noticed a faint orange light out of the corner of his eye. It came from a public restroom in a parking lot on the shore of the lake.

Maybe they took cover there. Kakeru left the road and entered the concrete structure with a triangular roof.

The bathroom appeared to be empty. With the lights on, and the sound of rain slightly muffled, the narrow space felt inorganic and unreal, like a nuclear bomb shelter. Kakeru wiped his face with his hands and called out to the closed cubicles just in case.

"Jota, Joji, are you there?"

"Yup, in here," the twins answered in chorus from two adjacent cubicles. Kakeru was relieved. Turns out they hadn't been struck by lightning, and their charred remains weren't lying on the side of the road.

"What happened to you guys?" he asked. For a while, the sound of flushing continued, until the twins opened their doors and stepped out at the same time.

"Looks like our bellies got upset," Jota said.

"Started hurting like crazy all of a sudden. I dunno what we would've done if this bathroom wasn't here. Right, bro?"

"Totally. Pouring from the sky, pouring from our bowels." They both looked pale as they rubbed their stomachs.

"Too much milk," Kakeru concluded. Ever since they'd arrived at Shirakaba Lake, the twins had been guzzling down at least two liters of milk per day. The fact that the milk was a free gift from the shopping arcade had made them greedy.

Drenched from the rain, all three of them were starting to get cold. They had to get moving soon.

"Jogging is canceled. Think you can make it back to the cabin?"

"Uh, I'm not so sure about that," Joji whimpered.

"I'll squeeze my butt tight and get by somehow," Jota said with grim resolve.

They left the restroom and started jogging in the rain. They'd gone about five hundred meters when Jota stopped short. "I'm screwed."

Joji looked pasty, too. "Hey, Kakeru. Do you think we'd better go back to the restroom? Or press on to the cabin?"

"Huh?" Kakeru looked back at them, at a loss. The poor twins were hunched over stiff like a pair of shrimp. "Oh well, not much choice. Just do it behind one of those bushes."

"No way!"

"What would we wipe with?!"

"Don't worry, no one's around. Just use some leaves or something. You'll live."

"You wouldn't be so blasé if you were the one—"

"I'll get you for this."

Despite their grumbling, Jota and Joji were clearly in a critical situation. They clambered through the thicket up a gentle slope on the side of the road. They took similar measures twice more on their way back, and by the time they finally reached the forest trail leading to the cabin, the twins had let themselves go completely.

"I might as well streak now."

"Me too. If we have to stop and get it out so often, we should just go pantsless."

"Don't even try," Kakeru laughed.

As they cracked each other up with silly jokes, they ran toward the light of the cabin. The slight awkwardness that had lodged in them ever since their fight in the twins' room was washed clean by the heavy rain. They were all exhausted—the twins from diarrhea, Kakeru from worry—and it made them hyper in a weird way.

"We're back!" The moment they burst into the cabin, the twins flung off their shirts and shorts to make a run for the bath. Kakeru pulled off his drenched shirt, too.

A high-pitched scream pierced the air. Startled, the naked twins and Kakeru, who was just about to pull down his pants, stopped in their tracks.

In the dining room stood the landlord and a slender girl with long black hair—the girl from Yaokatsu.

"What do you think you're doing!" Kiyose hurtled out of the kitchen and steered the twins to the bathroom. The rest of the team, sitting around the TV, were cracking up. The Yaokatsu girl was covering her face with her hands, but Kakeru didn't miss it: her gleaming eyes were definitely peeking between her fingers.

"I'm Hanako Katsuta," she introduced herself later.

The twins, now out of the bath and properly dressed, grinned from ear to ear, echoing her name. "Hana, huh . . ."

What's so nice about "Hana"? Kakeru wondered. Hana *sounded like a flower, but turn it around and you get the kanji for* nappa, *so she's basically a leafy veggie.* But there was no denying it—Hanako was beautiful. Her clear doe eyes kept darting to the twins, and she blushed every time she looked at them.

Hanako was also a first-year in the Faculty of Letters at Kansei. "You guys were kind of the talk of the school even before summer, you know," she told them.

The dining table was overflowing with numerous dishes made by Kiyose and Hanako. Feeling refreshed after his bath, Kakeru sat down with an "itadakimasu" and reached for the stewed and simmered vegetables with chopsticks. The vegetables were chopped unevenly, and the flavoring was rather strong. Hanako was probably not so used to cooking. But of course, no one complained. After all, she had come all this way with the landlord in Yaokatsu's mini pickup truck, which was loaded to the brim with food from the shopping arcade.

"We brought you some meat, too. We can have yakiniku tomorrow," she announced.

"Is it beef? Are we having grilled beef?" The twins were quick to react.

"Yeah." She nodded, her cheeks flushing again.

"Whoop!"

"Finally! We're getting beef, too!"

Between their ravenous appetites and their sense of rivalry with Totai, Jota and Joji were pumped. Kakeru didn't get it. The twins had been so eager to get a girlfriend, but somehow they didn't notice an opportunity when it hit them right in the face. Seated next to Kakeru, Kiyose was making his disapproval known.

"What were you thinking, Coach? You seriously brought a girl to stay with ten rowdy young men?"

"You mean *eleven*," the crafty landlord replied, adding himself to the count.

"If you ask me, I'd say it's more like the twins who have to watch out," Yuki observed. The twins, having forgotten all about their stomachaches, were gamboling around the room, expressing their delight at the prospect of yakiniku. Hanako was all smiles as she watched them. But Kakeru felt gloomy for some reason. *What's wrong with me?* He wondered.

Nira lay on the mat by the back door, thumping his tail. He had come along, too, riding in the back of the truck, and he seemed happy to see the Chikusei-so residents again after so long.

The next day was perfectly sunny. Kakeru took a long, deep breath. The sweet scent of grass mingled with the clear, crisp air. White clouds dropped their shadows on the green face of the mountains, drifting toward the east.

The landlord and Hanako followed them to the hiking trail in Yaokatsu's minitruck. The whole team got more motivated than ever after learning that Hanako would be staying with them for a while.

At night, the men were packed like sardines on the second floor of the cabin. There was even less room for them now because they'd hung a sheet across a string on one side to make a private space for Hanako. Even in the cool night of the highlands, it was hard to fall asleep when they were all crammed together.

But every single one of them welcomed her wholeheartedly. Though they'd known her for only a short time, they could already tell just how much she was genuinely rooting for them, and she'd brought the support of the entire shopping arcade community with her.

"It's a miracle, isn't it? She's pretty inside and out," Shindo murmured.

"Yes, Hanako is very pretty," Musa agreed.

"But what I don't get is why she has a favorable impression of Jota and Joji." Shindo tilted his head, puzzled.

Musa also tilted his head. "Flavorful?"

"Uh-uh. Not flavorful, favorable." Shindo picked up a twig and scratched the word on the ground.

Nico, doing his prepractice stretches, commented, "You know, she might just have bad taste."

Kakeru smiled wryly. Even as they spoke, the twins were telling Hanako about their high-altitude runs, and she was listening intently, with *crush* written all over her face.

"So? Which one of the twins does she like?" Yuki asked Kakeru, gazing at the scene.

"I don't know."

"Ask her."

"Why me?"

"You're in the same year."

What kind of a reason is that? But Kakeru couldn't say no to a senior. He merely gave a noncommittal nod and walked off toward Kiyose to check on the details for the day's practice.

Kiyose was filling in the landlord about the training schedule. "We'll be doing eight laps around the course today—about twenty-five kilometers in total. Kakeru and I will do the first lap in twelve minutes, then keep increasing our pace, aiming for a ten-minute lap at the end. I'll give everyone specific instructions on their pace according to their levels. Even Prince, who's the slowest, will be starting the run at sixteen minutes for the first lap. How does that sound?"

"Fine, fine, I'm giving you free rein, Haiji. Do as you like." The landlord's attention had wandered somewhere else entirely. He was too busy gazing at Hanako in the distance.

"Is he really supposed to be our coach?" Kakeru whispered to Kiyose.

"Yeah, well, never mind," Kiyose laughed. "That's just the way he is. We can count on him when push comes to shove."

"Really?"

After a pause, Kiyose said, "Probably." Then he took off his tracksuit jacket. "Let's get started."

As the sun rose higher in the sky, its rays burned more fiercely. The wind was refreshing, but it was scorching near the peak, where there was hardly any shade. Hanako stood by midway through the course, handing out her homemade lemon water blended with protein powder.

Without stopping, Kakeru grabbed a bottle and took a gulp through the straw. He almost gagged on the grainy, sour liquid. *Sure, lemon and protein are good for the body, but who'd even think of mixing them together?* The powder separated from the liquid, and it felt like the granules might stick to the wall of his stomach.

"Isn't this insanely disgusting?" he murmured.

"Agreed." Kiyose's face also looked like he'd just seen the corpse of a cat run over by a car. "But you'd better drink up. Otherwise, we might get dehydrated in this heat."

They tossed their empty bottles on the side of the trail. They would retrieve them later for reuse. The pair were coming up to the members who were one lap behind them. Everyone was sagging. Kiyose called out to them as he passed by. "Your pace is dropping. But don't check your watches too much. Try to get the feel of it with your own body as much as possible."

"Keep your orders short and sweet, okay? It's too hot for this!"

Amid the shower of boos from the others, Kakeru and Kiyose maintained their set pace and completed twenty-five kilometers exactly as planned.

Even they were exhausted, breathing hard. They did an easy jog to cool down, then loosened their muscles with stretches. They pulled off their shirts, which were drenched in sweat, and wiped themselves with the towels they'd brought in their backpacks.

Once they changed into fresh shirts, they sat down in the shade of a tree. The others, who were still doing their laps, ran past them, one after another, panting hard.

"If it gets to be too much, don't push yourself!" Kiyose shouted. "Though no one's going to listen, are they?"

Not one of them stopped running. They were all intent on crushing their training goal. They were nothing like their former selves back in early spring.

Hanako walked over to them and sat down next to Kakeru. Kakeru worried that he smelled sweaty and scooted over a little to Kiyose's side. A small chuckle escaped Kiyose.

"How many kilometers do you guys run in a day?" Hanako asked.

"Depends on our condition and quota, but I guess . . . around forty."

"What?!" she exclaimed.

Kakeru jumped in surprise. Kiyose stifled another chuckle.

"What is it?" Kakeru glared at Kiyose.

"Oh, don't mind me." Kiyose, still smirking, feigned indifference and looked up at the sky.

"That's impressive," Hanako murmured in awe, then let out a small sigh. "I never knew you had to practice *that* much. I thought people who're good at endurance runs can just go and run marathons like it's no big deal."

"It's ekiden, not a marathon," Kakeru corrected her.

"Oh right, ekiden."

"Yeah." His face felt kind of hot. He could feel Kiyose shaking a little on his right, but he couldn't see his face. *Shit, he's definitely laughing at me*, Kakeru thought.

The twins ran past them.

"One more lap," Kiyose called out.

Hanako followed the twins with her eyes. Kakeru remembered that Yuki had given him a mission.

"Umm . . . you like the twins, right?"

"Gosh, how'd you know?!"

It's hard not to notice, Kakeru retorted in his head. He sensed that the same thought crossed Kiyose's mind at the same time.

"So, um, which one do you like?"

"What do you mean, which?"

"Well, you know—Jota or Joji, which one?"

"Both of them, duh!" Hanako blushed and slapped Kakeru's shoulder in embarrassment. His first thought was that she was kind of offbeat, and then his brain registered what she had just said.

"Huh?" Kakeru's voice flipped. "What do you mean, *both*? How is that okay?"

"Why not? They look the same. Totally my type."

"You've got to be kidding!" Anger welled up in him, and he sprang up. "They're not some onions going for 150 yen a pair! How can you like both at once—just 'cause you're into their looks? That's a bit heartless, isn't it?"

"Not a bad metaphor by your standards," Kiyose said to himself.

Hanako looked up at Kakeru with round, quizzical eyes. "How come?"

"Well, first off, the twins are two different people. Shouldn't you look more at, you know, their personalities and stuff?"

"Are personalities that important?"

"Obviously!"

"I'm not so sure. As far as I'm concerned, once I fall for someone, I don't really care about their personality." Hanako smiled happily. "I've gotten to know them a little better since last night. They don't have any weird quirks that creep me out, and their faces, pure perfection. Isn't that enough? I couldn't pick either one of them even if you told me to."

Kakeru felt drained and slumped back down against the tree. Kiyose was hiccupping now—possibly from suppressing his laughter too much.

"Hanako has a point," Kiyose said in between hiccups. "Sometimes, you can't help falling for someone no matter how mean they are or how much they make you suffer."

"Exactly." Hanako nodded eagerly, pleased to have someone on her side. "That's just love, right?"

The Chikusei-so members had finished their twenty-five kilometers and were coming back. "I'll go get the landlord. He said he'd take Nira on a walk and went off to the other side of the trail," Hanako said, leaving the shade.

Kakeru and Kiyose were silent for a while, watching the grass waving in the wind.

"Have you ever experienced something like that?" Kakeru asked.

Kiyose's hiccups had finally stopped. "You haven't?" He turned the question around, a hint of a laugh in his voice.

After a few beats, Kakeru said, "No, I haven't."

"Are you sure? What about running? No matter how painful it is or how much it makes you suffer, you keep at it. Isn't that the same kind of feeling as what she was talking about?"

Kiyose rose and walked out into the sun to the others, who were sprawled out on the ground.

"Come on, get up," he said, dragging them to their feet. "Don't skip the cooldown."

If Haiji is right, Kakeru thought, *if my feelings for running are like being in love—love is such a futile thing.*

Once you're spellbound, there's no escape. You're drawn to the object of your love whether you like it or not, and it makes no difference whether there's any hope of a reward. Without any idea of where you're headed, you're pulled in—like stars getting swallowed up by the deep, dark night.

Kakeru could never let go of running. No matter how painful it was, no matter how much he suffered, and even if there was nothing left to gain.

He stepped out of the shade to hand out more bottles of protein lemon water. The rays of the sun hit him straight on the head. Cicadas broke into a seething hiss all at once. The clouds were long gone, blown away by the wind.

The sky's so blue, he said to himself.

It was the height of summer.

VI

THE SOUL SCREAMS

Kakeru placed a cracked rice bowl on the edge of the hallway. Drops of water tapped the back of his hand. He shifted the bowl ever so slightly until it was just right, then stood up to survey the second-floor hallway.

There were donburi bowls and kettles and whatnot here and there down the entire hallway; the scene looked like some kind of voodoo setup. It was Kakeru's turn to go around Chikusei-so at regular intervals with a big bucket to collect the rainwater accumulating in these vessels.

The long rain of autumn, which was falling softly outside, produced a cacophony inside Chikusei-so. Kakeru sighed as he emptied the bucket in the garden. *The things you have to do when you're poor.*

"Can't we do something about all this noise?!" Nico groaned, scratching his head in frustration. "I can hear it dripping all night from my room. *Plip plop plip plop, plippity pop.* It's endless. I'm sick of it."

"Us second-floorers have gotten used to it," said Jota.

"Maybe you have a dull sensibility when it comes to sounds, Nico-senpai," Yuki scoffed, wiping his glasses. "There's some poetry in the sound of raindrops. Sometimes they tap out a fresh rhythm, and it makes me pause to listen."

It's not really the sound of raindrops, just leaks in the roof, Kakeru thought. But of course he kept his thoughts to himself.

"Well, the prelim is fast approaching now," Kiyose began, ignoring their complaints about the deteriorating building.

Everyone was gathered in a circle in the twins' room under Kiyose's orders. They had finished their practice for the day and had launched a drinking party. Their thoughts were still on the leak, but they turned to look at Kiyose anyway.

"Your hard work at the training camp has paid off. Every one of you is definitely growing stronger. Kakeru?"

"Ready." Kakeru had a sheet of paper with their records from practice, and he went down the list out loud. "Here's our personal best times for running 10,000 meters so far."

Haiji	29:14.00
Musa	29:35.00
Jota	29:55.26
Joji	29:55.28
Yuki	30:26.63
Shindo	30:27.64
Nico	30:48.37
King	31:11.02
Prince	35:38.42
Kakeru	28:58.59

Kiyose, who had been listening to the recitation with his eyes closed, gave a nod when Kakeru was finished. "Admirable progress, everyone. It makes me proud, seeing how far you've come as runners."

"Thanks to the summer camp, now I know what it's like to go to hell," said Jota.

"I'd be shocked if we couldn't run a bit better after *that* much practice," Joji added.

"We have a little less than one month till the prelim," Kiyose announced, looking around at each of them. "I believe most of you can improve your ten-kilometer time even more before then. Plus, you seem to have gotten used to running twenty kilometers as well—though, there is one exception . . ."

Prince shrank. He always started to flag when he passed the fifteen-kilometer mark; after that, his pace got steadily worse. But Kiyose didn't criticize him.

"All in all, we're in good shape. You've been building up stamina, strong and steady. Keep going at this rate, and we'll put up a proper fight at the prelim. Just make sure to watch out for any signs of injury. Let's all keep up the good work."

"Yeah!" Everyone cheered. "Not too hard, though," Joji added under his breath, and clinked his cup with Kakeru's.

Shindo took a slug of his local sake. "By the way, we got a request for an interview," he said.

The twins lit up. "No way! That's awesome!" "Who is it? Another newspaper?" they shouted over each other.

Back at Lake Shirakaba, the Chikusei-so team had been interviewed by a journalist for the newspaper *Yomiuri Shimbun*.

At first, a writer for a track and field magazine came to observe Tokyo Taiiku's training camp. Totai had narrowly missed out on the seed rights at the previous Hakone Ekiden, so the team had to climb up from the prelim this time. But because it was a solid team of competent athletes, it was virtually a given that Totai would pass through the prelim to Hakone. So the magazine was interviewing the group ahead of time.

The Chikusei-so members were coming out of the convenience store by the lake when they saw the Totai athletes getting interviewed. The students were lined up in the parking lot, and the journalist was taking a group picture. After the photo shoot, the journalist held up a recorder to the captain as he made some comments.

Though the middle-aged journalist was doing the work of both photographer and interviewer, and the captain was in a plain tracksuit, King was still riveted. "They look like celebrities," he murmured, rooted to the spot. Kakeru stopped alongside him and stared absentmindedly at the scene.

Eventually, the Totai team dispersed. The writer thanked the captain and started walking toward the corner of the parking lot where the Chikusei-so members were standing with plastic bags in their hands. "Oh," he said, noticing the group. "You must be distance runners, too."

"Can you tell?" Jota replied, looking tickled.

"I can see from your build. But you're not at Totai, are you?" He cast a puzzled look at their disparate T-shirts.

"We're the Kansei University track team," King answered, slightly nervous.

"And we'll be running the Hakone Ekiden, too." With his big smile and a childlike boldness, Joji said this like it was a done deal.

Kakeru was hiding behind Nico. He thought the journalist would laugh at Joji's remark. A team from a college that's never even made it to the prelims? Were they in their right minds? But he didn't laugh.

"Hunh." With a serious expression, the man looked at each of them. "Now, that's exciting. Who's the captain? Is this the whole team here?"

Though they'd never really declared anyone captain, everyone naturally looked at Kiyose. Somewhat reluctantly, he spoke up. "I'm the captain, Haiji Kiyose. This is all of us."

"Haiji Kiyose . . ." The journalist racked his brain. "If you're who I think you are, I heard you suffered an injury. So you're still doing track? And you back there, aren't you Kurahara, who used to be at Sendai Jōsei?"

Without answering, Kakeru shrank back farther behind Nico.

"And who are you?" Joji asked.

The man said, "Sorry," and handed Kiyose his business card. It read: *Track World Monthly Magazine*, Editor, Shingo Sanuki.

"Can I talk to you guys for a few minutes? Are you trying to compete in the Hakone Ekiden with just ten members?"

Sanuki fired off several questions. He turned out to be quite a skillful listener, letting out an interested "hmm" when he heard the name of their coach. When they told him that their rent would go up if they didn't shine at Hakone, he laughed, "That sure is life or death."

The next morning before dawn, Sanuki appeared on the lakeside road to watch the Chikusei-so team's jogging routine. When they were all done with their laps, he approached them.

"You really make an intriguing team. Most of you are practically amateurs, but I can tell you have a whole lot of potential for growth."

Unsure whether he was praising or insulting them, everyone stood without saying a word. But Sanuki nodded to himself with obvious enthusiasm.

"It's teams like yours that add more spice to the Hakone race. I'm afraid we only have space for an article on Totai this time, but there's a journalist I know at a newspaper. I'll tell him about you."

"A newspaper!" King gulped.

I don't like where this is heading, Kakeru thought.

Sanuki was true to his word, and he didn't waste any time. Around the end of their training camp, a journalist from *Yomiuri Shimbun* came to Lake Shirakaba to call at their cabin. As one of the sponsors of the Hakone Ekiden, the newspaper often published feature articles related to the event.

"I heard about you from Mr. Sanuki at the *Monthly*. My curiosity was piqued, so I decided to make use of my holiday to pay you a visit."

The reporter introduced himself as Masaki Nunoda. He had a mild demeanor and seemed to be about the same age as Sanuki.

"'*Monthly*'?" Prince mumbled. "That's what they call *Track World Monthly Magazine*? Who's gonna know what it's about? Besides, it clashes with *Monthly Shonen Magazine*." The Chikusei-so members assumed he was going on about manga again and ignored him. Kakeru slipped into the kitchen, away from the dining room.

"It's not feasible to write about you on the Sports pages, since you haven't exactly passed the prelim yet. But I think our readers would be drawn to a story about a small track team working toward Hakone Ekiden. Unfortunately, it'll only be in the local edition in Tokyo, but I'd be delighted if you would agree to an interview."

Finding it difficult to refuse Nunoda's earnest proposal, Kiyose gave in. Nunoda quickly called in a reporter from the local edition and a photographer. They asked about things like the team's day-to-day life and their determination to compete at Hakone. Mainly the twins and King gave the answers. The photographer took some pictures of their practice by the lake and a group shot in front of the cabin.

The article was published, accompanied by a large photo, on the very same day that they returned to Chikusei-so after their long training camp. Shindo and Musa were thrilled, going out to buy lots of copies. The team cut out the article and hung it up in the Chikusei-so kitchen. They handed out copies to the shopping arcade denizens, too. They even pinned a clipping to the noticeboard on campus without bothering to get permission. Of course, Shindo and Musa made sure to send a clipping to their families back home, enclosed with a letter.

The response was enthusiastic. The impromptu group of supporters from the shopping arcade became even more excited about the team's endeavor, and the university began to take notice. Most of the Chikusei-so residents received calls from their families.

"Both Mr. Sanuki and Mr. Nunoda are definitely going to cover us more closely from the prelim," Shindo said, pouring more sake into his cup. "But this time, we got a request from somewhere else. A TV station."

"TV!" King exclaimed.

"Someone from Nippon TV got in touch with me. They broadcast the Hakone Ekiden. Apparently, they cover the prelim as well. They told me they're going to follow several teams competing at the prelim with a camera—the teams that are especially noteworthy."

"Whoa . . . and they chose *us* as one of them?" King was already trembling.

"What a joyful occasion." Musa looked visibly moved.

"I haven't given them an official answer yet," Shindo said. "I mean, it'll defeat the purpose if we get too distracted by the TV camera. We need to focus on the race. I wanted to ask you guys what you thought first."

"I vote *yesss!* Let's go on TV!" Jota's hand shot up.

"Why in the world would we turn it down?" Joji followed up.

As for King, he already had beads of nervous sweat on his face as he checked his own appearance. "I was thinking I should go get a haircut soon."

"I'd also like to appear on TV." Musa smiled. "If I record it on a videotape and send it to my family, I'm sure they will all be excited."

"I think it'll be good for us, too," Shindo said. "It would make our parents happy. But more than that, it's great publicity. I bet we'll reach a lot more people this way."

"That's true." Kiyose crossed his arms. "What about the rest of you? What do you think?" He looked at the other members, who still hadn't expressed their preferences.

"If you guys wanna do it, I'm easy either way." With the composure of a real grown-up, Nico remained grounded at the mention of TV.

Prince gave a throwaway answer. "I don't mind either. I don't care about TV anyway." He was interested only in manga.

"Seriously?" King yelped. "We might even meet one of those announcer girls! You know how hot they are!"

"I don't really know any," Prince replied, looking bored.

Jota and Joji jumped into the discussion. "Wait, aren't they too famous to come to a prelim?"

"You never know. Who's the sportscaster girl at Nippon TV?"

Kiyose stayed out of the announcer talk and turned to Kakeru and Yuki, who still hadn't broken their silence. "The answer's already clear by majority vote, but let's hear your opinion."

"But it's settled, isn't it?" Kakeru sighed. "There's no point in me saying I don't want to."

"Aw, why not, Kakeru?" Joji asked. "If we go on TV, our parents are gonna be stoked, and we'll get the girls' attention—what's there to complain about?"

"That's just how *you* picture it," Kakeru mumbled, a half-hearted argument.

"Not everyone cares about making their parents happy, you know," Yuki muttered. His voice didn't have its usual sarcastic sting.

Everyone went quiet for a moment. The group sensed something bitter in Yuki's words. Realizing that their eyes were on him, Yuki quickly returned to his usual self.

"Can't imagine anyone who's as greedy as you guys when it's about stealing the show. Well, there's no use arguing now. I won't say no if that's what you all want."

When Hanako heard the news that a TV camera would follow the Chikusei-so team at the prelim, she cried out, "Oh no! We have to redo the banner!"

"What banner?" Kakeru asked. Kakeru and Kiyose were in the Chikusei-so kitchen, unpacking the box of unsold vegetables that Hanako had brought over.

"Everyone from our street is so excited to go cheer for you guys. My dad and the plasterer painted a banner for the prelim. But you know how the kanji for *Kan* in *Kansei* is pretty dense? The plasterer was like, 'What do we do, Katsu? The letter's gonna look like a blob on the banner.' And my dad went, 'That's where puns come in.'"

In the end, they punned on the proverb "Taiki-bansei"—"Great talents are slow to ripen"—and wrote, "Taiki Kansei! Let's go KANSEI U!" The huge sign in bright red paint boasted that "great talents are ready to serve."

"That's a bit . . ." Kakeru had no comment.

"I know, it's gonna look pretty dorky," Hanako sighed.

Kiyose was laughing silently again as he peeled some satoimo taro.

"But anyway, that's great news," Hanako continued. "It means you're getting recognition for all your hard work. It's a big deal."

While they would attract more attention, that attention was bound to bring them more trouble as well. Without answering, Kakeru flattened the empty cardboard box.

Then the twins came in, and the kitchen sprang to life.

"Oh, didn't know you were here, Hana."

"Did you hear about the TV thing?"

"I heard. We'll all be there to cheer you on, and I'll tape the show, too." Hanako sat down at the table and started happily chatting away with the twins.

"Aren't you going to do something?" Kiyose whispered to Kakeru, slicing the tofu balanced on his palm.

Kakeru was mixing miso paste into the pot. Bewildered, he asked back, "What do you mean?"

"Oh, nothing," Kiyose said. "Hanako, why don't you stay for dinner?"

The other residents piled into the kitchen and sat around the table with Hanako. Those who didn't fit brought out the low table and sat on the floor. The menu was stewed satoimo and cold pork shabu-shabu.

"It's almost that time of year when you start craving sukiyaki instead of cold shabu," Jota said.

"With beef!" Joji chirped. Both boys heaped up the boiled pork in their bowls with wolfish appetites. The vegetables from Hanako added a splash of color to the meal, including the grated daikon—one white, one vermilion with ground chili mixed in.

"Oh, I almost forgot." Hanako put down her chopsticks and rummaged in her bag under the table. "It's not just veggies I brought today." She presented a big stack of photo albums. The twins took them and flipped open the paper covers.

"Pics from the summer camp!"

"And there's one for each of us!"

Each album had a name written on the cover. Kakeru also stopped eating and peered at the album bearing his name in Hanako's handwriting. There were group shots as well as highlights featuring each of them, all neatly arranged in chronological order.

"I was making copies and thinking about the layout, so it took a while to get them all ready," she said apologetically. The effort she'd put into making them was obvious. Everyone was moved and eager to thank her.

For a while, they were engrossed in the albums, swapping them around to see the others. The photos brought back vivid memories of the summer.

"Now that I look back on it, we did have a lot of fun."

"Ooh! You even got a shot of the Totai coach!"

"That's a sneak shot," laughed Hanako. The photo depicted a man with slicked-back hair, his feet planted wide apart on the ground, holding a bamboo shinai sword.

"That dude was super scary."

"He was a real tough drill sergeant. A fiend! But in a different kind of way from Haiji."

On the last day of camp, the Totai team had showed up at the hiking course. Things hadn't turned ugly: the Chikusei-so team was in the middle of a cooldown, having already wrapped up a cross-country run, and the Totai students had other things to worry about. The upperclassmen never paid attention to the Kansei team anyway, and the first-years were focusing on practice like small dogs cowering in fear. Their hellish coach was keeping a close watch on them, a fierce glint in his eyes.

"It was like a military drill," Musa remembered.

"And remember those maxims the guy was screaming? What were they again?"

"He was saying stuff like, 'Count yourselves lucky for running in this heat!' and 'Running is a battle for survival!'"

They all burst out laughing.

"Imagine having a coach like *that*. I would've quit a long time ago." Prince frowned.

"Are all track teams like that at other universities?" Musa asked.

"The coach at my junior high was," Nico said. "You gotta watch out for the ones with hair slicked back."

"Based on what stats?" Yuki commented frostily.

"I think most university teams emphasize their athletes' independence and voluntary practice," Kiyose explained, looking up from his album. "But schools like Totai do exist."

"That's what I don't like about sports clubs." Prince shook his head. "They're shackled in hierarchies—everyone has to obey the coach, no questions asked. Like slaves."

"Some people think they have to keep the students on a tight leash, or there'd be no order, and they'd slack off," Shindo said. "Same with high school—the strong teams always had a tough discipline."

"It's a tricky question, isn't it?" King said, snatching the last slice of pork. "If they're not strict, they can't win the game. But if it's no fun, people wouldn't wanna play sports. What do you do then?"

"That's ridiculous," Kakeru spat out in a low tone. "The kind of people who need strict rules or fun to run should just quit running."

"There you go again with the hyperbole," Joji chided.

"What do you think, Haiji?" Jota asked.

"If I thought being strict was better, I'd be tightening up your leashes, right?" Kiyose replied. Hanako, who had been listening to the exchange in silence, let out a small laugh.

"Found an embarrassing photo of Haiji," Yuki announced, holding up the last page of his album. It was from their last night at the camp, when they all went to the lake with some fireworks.

Kiyose was crouching down to light the senko sparkler when Nira panicked at the noise and scrambled right onto Kiyose's face. Kiyose toppled over on his back from the impact and tried to peel the dog off to no avail. The whole sequence was captured in great detail in three photos.

Kiyose blushed. "Why are those in Yuki's album?"

"I put it in everyone's 'cause it was funny," Hanako said nonchalantly. The twins both held up the page to show Kiyose and beamed.

"Starting tomorrow, we start training military-style," Kiyose said.

When it was time for Hanako to go back to Yaokatsu, everyone saw her off at the front door.

"It's getting late, someone should accompany you home," Musa suggested. Shindo nodded and looked at the twins. The twins didn't notice and were just nodding along in agreement. Someone had to give them a push. "Twins, go on," said Nico.

Jota and Joji looked a little surprised.

"Sure, we can go."

"Okay, let's go, Hana."

They set off with Hanako walking in the middle.

"Hopeless."

"How can they be so clueless?" The others grumbled to one another as they headed to their rooms. Kakeru was the last one to turn back from the door.

Kiyose glanced back at him. "Aren't you going to do something?"

"Again, what are you talking about?"

"Oh, nothing." Kiyose almost laughed, but it faded from his face. "Do you think I'm too soft, Kakeru?"

Kakeru didn't understand what Kiyose meant by the question. Kakeru paused as he was taking off his shoes and looked up at Kiyose. His face was obscured in shadow, the light of the hallway behind him.

"You see it, don't you? We're actually on the borderline—there's no guarantee we'll be able to get through the prelim. Should I have pushed them to run more? Even if that meant binding them to strict rules—?"

"I know you don't believe in any of that." Kakeru cut him off. He stepped on the ledge to the hallway, leaned against the wall, and looked at Kiyose's profile right in front of him. "You don't like playing drill sergeant, and you think no amount of force can make people run. Am I wrong, Haiji?"

"No, you're right." Kiyose looked down for a moment, then up at Kakeru, and smiled. "Sorry, I got a bit unsure of myself there."

"There's still time. I'm sure everyone will get even faster by the time we run at the prelim. We'll make it through."

As he tried to lift Kiyose's spirits, Kakeru wondered what had made him worry. *It's not like him.* Kiyose was always striding forward toward his goal, full of conviction, aloof from the rest of the world. It was the first time he had betrayed any hint of doubt. Kakeru guessed that the conversation over dinner had brought the question to Kiyose's mind but couldn't see what would be weighing on him when they had already come so far.

"I—" Kakeru felt that he hadn't said enough and desperately searched for the words to express what was inside him. *I—what?* He got stuck after the first syllable. He wasn't used to putting things into words. Kiyose looked at him while he tried to gather his thoughts into something coherent. There was a distant look in Kiyose's eyes, as if he was seeing his past self through Kakeru.

"I'm sick of being tied up," Kakeru tried again. "I couldn't breathe, it was killing me. I just want to run. That's all."

Not for any purpose. Just to run free, by his own will. Only to follow the voice that called to him from the depths of his body and soul, urging him to run.

"Sakaki looked like he's content with the strict discipline at Totai, but I'm not like him. If you'd acted like that drill sergeant, Haiji, I wouldn't be here right now. I would've left Aotake on the first day of practice."

Kiyose's eyes snapped back into focus on Kakeru. He lightly put a hand on Kakeru's shoulder and slipped past him. "'Night, Kakeru."

In the split second before Kiyose closed the door behind him, Kakeru could see that his back showed no trace of weakness or uncertainty anymore, just as always.

"Good night," Kakeru murmured and returned to his own room.

In preparation for the prelim, it was imperative for the Chikusei-so team members to let their bodies rest by degrees to fully recover from the strains of the summer. They still followed a solid training regimen through the autumn days, but unlike their summer camp routine, they didn't spend all their time running. Still, even Kakeru was beginning to feel a dip in his physical and mental strength. The fatigue set in with the pressure of the looming race. They had worked so hard—but what if things went wrong on race day, and it all amounted to nothing?

Unlike the previous track meets, the prelim was a one-shot bet. No do-overs. They wouldn't get another chance to try again if they didn't achieve the results they needed. This knowledge made Kakeru tense. It weighed down on his mind and body.

The training routine became denser. It was a matter of course for them to run twenty kilometers of cross-country, and on the track, they started practicing buildups—which meant when they ran seven kilometers in total, they would run the first kilometer at a pace faster than three minutes, ten seconds, then steadily increase their speed until they reached a pace of two minutes, fifty seconds for the end.

Because they had to accelerate more and more over a long distance, it was an extremely demanding run. The breathlessness that came in the middle of an endurance run as well as the wild pulse after a full-speed sprint assailed them all at once. It felt like having to play water polo while drowning. Prince threw up multiple times from the exertion.

Kiyose warned him every time to hold it back as much as possible. "You'll get in the habit of vomiting. Keep it in and keep running."

"I would if I could." Prince ducked his head down in the weeds growing by the track.

The twins went over to soothe him but ended up retching alongside him. "I feel like I'm choking on vomit," croaked Jota.

It was a disaster.

Yet, as they repeated the routine with reasonable breaks in between, they gradually adapted. Soon they could keep up with both the twenty-kilometer cross-country and the buildup training. They also went to the Showa Kinen Park in Tachikawa, the venue of the prelim, to do a trial run on the actual course.

One day, only two weeks before the prelim, Kiyose assembled everyone after a cross-country run. A chilly wind blew across the darkening field. The blades of grass had lost their vigor, leaving no vestige of summer. With no one to pick them, the fruits on the persimmon tree swayed in the breeze, the same color as the sunset.

"It's all about focus from here on out," Kiyose said. "Sharpen your focus and control yourself. On race day, you should be in peak condition."

"Easier said than done," Nico sighed. These days, he was struggling to curb his appetite; his nerves made him want to eat more than usual.

"I feel like my poor little heart is gonna hit its peak already." King had been suffering from constant spasms in his stomach, even during practice. "Hope I last till the race."

"You have nothing to fear," Kiyose assured them in a calm, gentle voice. "You've all done more than enough practice. All that's left for you to do is to use the pressure of the race as a whetstone to hone yourself. Picture yourself as a gleaming sword cutting through the race. Refine your blade to a thin, keen edge."

"That's a poetic way to put it," Yuki said.

"But effective," Prince said. "If you sharpen it too much before the prelim, you'll snap in half, but if it's still dull and unpolished on the day of the race, it won't get you anywhere. That's what you mean, isn't it?"

"Exactly." Kiyose nodded. "And how to find the right balance is one thing you can't pick up just by blindly throwing yourself into practice. It's a battle against your inner self. I want each of you to listen closely to your own body and mind, and sharpen yourself carefully."

That's it, Kakeru thought. *Maybe this is a part of the strength you need in distance running.*

In a long-distance race, you didn't need an explosive burst of muscle power; nor was the race about performing some special technique with intense concentration. Running a long-distance race merely involved putting one foot in front of the other and steadily making your way forward. All you had to do was to keep moving your legs forward for a certain distance—a simple act that most people have experienced at some point in their lives. As for the stamina needed for perseverance, that had already been acquired through daily practice.

But Kakeru had seen so many athletes around him who slipped out of shape either right before or during a race. They would start off at a steady clip, but out of nowhere, something would knock them off their stride. Or they might be in perfect physical condition but suddenly start losing their speed at practice three days before a race. He'd also seen people who caught a cold at the last minute, despite being extremely careful, and were crossed off the list of runners on the day of the race.

Those athletes had done everything there was to prepare at practice. All they had to do was show up and run. Yet they still sabotaged themselves, and Kakeru had never been able to figure out why. He himself had come down with diarrhea just before the last big interschool championship he participated in in senior high. It wasn't like he'd caught a chill or eaten anything spoiled; it was just that, for some inexplicable reason, his stomach suddenly got upset. Everything turned out fine—he still managed to run—but he could never shake off that question: *Why now?*

Now he could understand why. Most of those trip-ups, known as fine-tuning failures, boiled down to pressure. Regardless of how much you'd practiced, there was always that anxiety that rose abruptly to the surface and made you ask, *Have I done enough?* And as soon as you managed to convince yourself that you *had*, another fear consumed you: *But what if I mess up?* The more you whet the body and mind, the more fragile they become. You become more vulnerable to catching a cold or upsetting your stomach—just as a high-precision machine breaks down easily from some specks of dust.

To conquer your own doubts and fears; to hone yourself into a blade so keen and smooth that you can withstand any amount of dust—that must be one element of what Kiyose meant by *strength*.

Though Kakeru understood this in theory, putting it into practice was another matter. The more serious he became about running, the more he was challenged by the prerace nerves. It was a rather lonely process, coming face-to-face with his own mind and body—a constant solitary battle between compromise and excess.

In the end, Kakeru stopped brooding over it. The more he mulled over things, the more fear was generated inside him. He couldn't help imagining the worst-case scenarios.

People got scared of ghosts because they thought about them, imagining what they might be like. Kakeru disliked things that were nebulous. He didn't want to worry about what evaded him, those things that might just exist if you think they do. He wanted black-and-white answers. Something was either there or it wasn't—just as putting one foot in front of the other would always make you move forward.

Kakeru emptied his head and ran. He simply sank his teeth into practice, going through the motions of running over and over again, the movements that had already become a part of his muscle memory. He didn't know any other way to overcome the pressure.

The other Chikusei-so members didn't have as much experience as Kakeru, so they didn't have a proven method for relieving their nerves. Some of them, like Kakeru, trained even harder. Some burned incense while they slept. One reread every volume of passionate sports manga that he owned. Each in his own way, everyone was doing his best to make final preparations for the prelim.

Two days before the race, Kakeru could sense his level of concentration rising steadily.

The team's practice was lighter than usual that day, so that they wouldn't get too tired before the big day. Of course, they still went on their usual individual jogs in the morning and evening, but there was no group practice scheduled for the two days before the race. They had done everything that was to be done. All that remained was to loosen up their bodies while keeping an eye on their own conditions, firing up their drive and concentration ever higher.

At Joji's suggestion—"There's only one thing left to get us all ready"— the Chikusei-so team decided to drink together in the twins' room two days before the prelim. For them, it was the quickest way to ease their tension and strengthen their bond as a team.

Since the landlord was the coach, at least officially, they invited him, too. The old man had handed Kiyose some money for repairing the hole in the floor, but Kiyose had passed it to Shindo to add to the funds for the team. What with the costs for transport and accommodation, they needed all the money they could get.

They timed the landlord's arrival carefully. Just as he passed over the threshold of the building, Jota sailed past him with his nose in a magazine, open at the pinup spread. The landlord, distracted by the photo of a woman in a bikini, slipped off his shoes without glancing up at the ceiling and followed right behind Jota up the stairs. Their plan was a success. Kakeru and Joji, who had been keeping watch, gave each other a small high five.

They had appointed Prince to sit on the hole. Even if he wanted to go to the toilet or an earthquake struck, Kiyose and Shindo had strictly forbidden him to move from the spot as long as the landlord was present in the room. Prince was now obediently hiding the hole while reading manga.

Drinks were flowing. When they were all feeling mellow, Kiyose called out, "Now then, Coach, how about a word?"

The landlord, who'd been hugging a large two-liter bottle, staggered to his feet. Perhaps they were finally going to see the landlord act like a proper coach. Kakeru waited expectantly.

"So, the preliminary race is just around the corner, at long last . . . I'll tell you the secret to winning the race," he declared solemnly in a hoarse voice. "Put one foot in front of the other!"

Silence descended on the room. The landlord must have sensed the crashing wave of dismay and disappointment that washed over the group. He hastened to add, "Do that, and you'll get to the finish line eventually. That's all there is to it!"

"That's it?!" King flung down his cup.

"Is he out of his mind?" Yuki muttered.

"Can't we invite a more decent coach?" Nico grumbled.

Murmurs of discontent spread through the group. Kakeru tried to steer the talk away from the landlord. "Haiji, you were so sure from the beginning that with this team, we'd make it to Hakone. I used to think it was pretty much impossible . . . but what made you so convinced in the first place?"

"Hmm?" Kiyose looked up from his cup and smiled. "Because everyone can hold their drink."

"Huh?" The complaints about the landlord ceased in an instant, and everyone stared at Kiyose.

"A lot of distance runners can handle buckets of alcohol. I guess the metabolism in their liver works well. It's the same for you guys: you don't drink like fish—more like whale sharks. I'd been watching the way you drink for a long time, and that's how I knew you could do it."

"There's plenty of people out there who can drink a lot!" Shindo looked up at the ceiling as if to say, *I can't believe this*.

"*That* was your rationale for bringing us together?!" Yuki's voice cracked in anger. Kakeru groaned. He'd hoped Kiyose would restore everyone's morale, but it was backfiring.

"Did we really come this far just because you saw how much we could drink?" The shock nearly made Prince rise to his feet, but he quickly settled back down when Shindo warned him with a look. "That's like building a skyscraper on mud purely out of willpower."

"Of course that's not the only thing," Kiyose said, slurring his words. "I just discovered the gleam of your hidden talent."

"You're drunk, Haiji," sighed Kakeru.

"Ugh. Isn't there anything to give us a lift?" King slumped back on the tatami.

"Speaking of which, what's happening with Hanako?" Musa asked.

"Hana?"

"We get along well. Did anything happen?" the twins answered innocently.

The others whispered to each other, "These two still don't get it!"

"What about you guys, huh? Don't you have any girlfriends?" Nico, who'd been nibbling on a strip of dried squid for a while, asked in passing. "If you do, you better invite them to come root for you the day after tomorrow."

It was rare for anyone to mention a subject like that at Chikusei-so. They lived in such close quarters that they were careful to stay out of each other's private lives. That was part of it. But it was also because if someone did get a new girlfriend, he didn't have to spell it out—everyone else would find out about her sooner or later.

For the past six months, they'd all been so busy with practice that they had no clue about each other's personal affairs. Of course, even before that, no one brought back a girlfriend to his room because everything they said and did would be audible to everyone else.

The twins sang out, "We're still looking!"

Then how could you miss the candidate right in front of you? Kakeru wanted to retort.

King clammed up and hunched his shoulders.

"And what about you, since you wanted to know?" Yuki asked Nico.

"I don't have any energy left for stuff like that right now." Nico scratched his stubbled chin.

"Me neither." Shindo looked down. "I'm too busy running around negotiating with the supporters and the university. She might get tired of waiting soon."

"You have a girlfriend?" Kakeru was surprised. He couldn't really put the two together in his head: the steadfast and decidedly unflashy Shindo and the flowery flamboyance of romance.

"Shindo has been seeing someone ever since he started at the university," Musa explained. "I haven't had any luck, though. It's not easy to find someone who's willing to come back with me to my home country."

Not that you have to take it that far from the start, Kakeru thought.

"What about you, Kakeru?" Musa asked.

Kakeru shook his head. "Girls aren't interested in me."

"You look like you'd be popular, though," Musa observed.

"Um, what about you, Prince?" Kakeru hastily passed on the question to put someone else on the spot. But Prince was still absorbed in his manga.

"I'm only interested in 2D girls." Prince, born with the features of a pop idol, was basically sitting on a gold mine. He glanced at Kiyose. "Though I've heard some rumors about Haiji going around in our faculty once in a while. He may not look like it, but he's actually pretty—ow!"

Prince yelped and held his tongue. Kiyose had flicked a peanut at him, hitting him right in the middle of his brows. No one dared to probe into the details. A thin smile played on Kiyose's face. "And you, Yuki?" he asked.

"Me—the guy with a bright future, a nice personality, and fairly good looks? Of course I have a girlfriend," Yuki answered casually. King shrank even more.

"Why don't you ask me?" the landlord piped up, filling his rice bowl with shochu. Just then, a ringtone went off. It was Yuki's cell phone. "'Scuse me," he said, leaving the room.

"Hey hey, is that his girl again?" Nico said. Kakeru had also noticed that Yuki was getting many calls lately.

"But then, don't you think he seems somewhat down these days?" Musa tilted his head, looking concerned.

Meanwhile, King had apparently decided to drown his woes in drink. "We're out of ice," he said, shaking an empty donburi.

Kakeru was sitting closest to the door, so he stood up. "I'll go get some."

When he went downstairs, he saw the front door was wide-open. Yuki was outside, talking on the phone. Kakeru could hear faint snatches of his voice. He seemed to be having an argument. Kakeru wondered what it could be about, but he treaded softly into the kitchen so as not to disturb him.

Kakeru emptied the ice cubes into the bowl and refilled the tray with water. Judging from how fast everyone was drinking, they might run out of ice again before long. He turned the temperature dial of the freezer to high and left the kitchen with the bowl.

The front door was still open. But he didn't hear Yuki's voice anymore. Kakeru hesitated for a moment, then slipped on a pair of sandals and popped his head out the door.

Yuki was squatting at the side of the entrance, gazing up at the night sky.

"I got ice," Kakeru called to him gently. "Let's drink some more."

"Sure," Yuki replied, but he didn't budge. He still stared vacantly, gripping his phone.

"Was it bad news?" Kakeru crossed the threshold and crouched down beside Yuki, wrapping the bowl in his arms.

"No," Yuki said. "My parents saw that article in the paper. They keep badgering me to come home once in a while."

"Where's your hometown?"

"Tokyo."

In that case, it should have been a quick trip to go see them, and there was surely no need for him to live in a rickety dorm like Chikusei-so. Kakeru remembered how Yuki had said he didn't even go back home for New Year's. He guessed there were some personal reasons behind this.

The air vibrated with the incessant chirping of insects hidden in the grass of the garden.

"Why aren't you so big on the TV interview?" Yuki asked.

"Hmm . . ." Kakeru had to think for a moment. "I have a lot of enemies. My parents and my teammates from high school—they probably don't even want to see my face. I'd rather not do anything to attract attention if I can help it."

"Sounds like you've gone through a lot. I thought you were just a track maniac." Yuki was scathing, but he didn't ask any more questions.

"That's the problem. I've been such a track maniac that now I have to sneak around dodging interviews," Kakeru laughed.

They heard a commotion break out in the twins' room. People were shouting and scrambling around. Kakeru and Yuki looked up and rose to their feet. "Wonder what's going on?"

The second-floor window opened, and they heard Kiyose call out, "Yuki! Are you there?!"

"I'm here. What happened?"

"Call the ambulance!" Kiyose saw Kakeru and Yuki standing below and waved his arms to hurry them. "The landlord coughed up blood!"

Kiyose flung on a zip-up hoodie and accompanied the landlord to the hospital.

Everyone was accustomed to the "early to bed, early to rise" routine now, so they struggled to stay awake. But they all waited up for Kiyose, worried about the landlord's condition.

When Kiyose finally returned to Chikusei-so sometime after midnight, he was surrounded by everyone just outside the front door. His face oozed fatigue as he gravely shared the news with the group.

"He has a stomach ulcer. Hospitalized for a week. They told me it was caused by stress from excessive tension."

"Stress?!" Joji's voice flipped. "Stress over what?"

"Our laid-back coach who doesn't look bothered about anything is *stressed?*" Jota cocked his head, too. *Got to be from too much drinking,* Kakeru thought.

"I have serious questions about the cause, too . . . But I suppose the landlord has been concerned about us, in his own way." Kiyose rubbed his temples. "Anyhow, that's the way it is. So, the day after tomorrow—actually, it's already tomorrow—we'll head to the prelim without our coach."

"Well, we don't really mind."

"Won't make much difference either way," the twins said, and Kakeru nodded.

"Didn't you say we could count on him when push comes to shove?" Kakeru whispered to Kiyose.

"I said, 'Probably.'" Kiyose shrugged off his hoodie wearily, as if to say, *Oh well, what can I say?*

VII

THE PRELIM

"It's a nice day." Kakeru did a full stretch and took a deep breath in the crisp autumn air.

The weather forecast he'd heard on the radio as he left Chikusei-so predicted it would be 55°F, with humidity at 83 percent. There was barely any wind. At this time of year, in the middle of October, there were often days like this with comfortable conditions for running. *The ideal day for a battle*, Kakeru thought.

Joji stood beside Kakeru, gazing at a family walking by with a picnic blanket. Because it was a Saturday, the park was already filling up with people who had come to watch the prelim, coupling it with a walk or a pleasant day out.

"They look so cheerful. And here I am, my bladder out of order," Joji said.

"Are you okay?"

"Nothing's coming out." Joji must have gone to the toilet at least ten times since he woke up. It was probably useless to tell him not to be nervous. The drums of the cheer squad for each university were booming across the Showa Kinen Park in Tachikawa. Whether the team liked it or not, it was impossible to ignore the fact that the preliminary race was about to begin.

By that afternoon, they would know whether they would compete in the Hakone Ekiden. Kakeru couldn't find the words to soothe Joji's high-strung nerves, so he only said, "Same here."

Jota was lying on his back on the lawn a little way off, his eyes closed. He seemed to be awake; his hands on his stomach twitched from time to time. The Chikusei-so team had woken up when it was still dark outside and rode on the train for about an hour to reach this park. But Kakeru felt wide-awake. His mind was sharp and clear.

"I'm going to do one more jog. What about you, Joji?" Kakeru asked.

"I'll go to the bathroom," Joji replied. Kakeru parted with Joji and left the lawn to jog through the extensive park grounds.

Athletes from other colleges were warming up, too, intent on getting the feel of the land. Every time he spotted the blue tracksuit of a Totai student, Kakeru felt an unpleasant jolt in his pulse. He didn't want to see Sakaki. If Sakaki provoked him again before the race, Kakeru was sure things would escalate into more than just a squabble.

Waves of people pressed toward the starting point of the race. Everyone was getting ready to cheer for their favorite team or athlete. Sparks flew between the cheer squads as they vied for the best positions to rally for their teams. Clad in black high-collar school uniforms, they brandished big flags and fanfare instruments.

By now, Kakeru had sufficiently warmed up. He felt he had to keep moving, but it wouldn't help to tire himself out before the race. He forced himself to stop jogging and returned to the lawn near the starting line.

The Kansei team's corner of the lawn was easy to find, marked as it was with the infamous banner hoisted above it, the handiwork of the Yaokatsu owner and the plasterer. The townspeople from the shopping arcade were sitting on a blue tarp, waiting for the shot of the starting pistol. The Chikusei-so residents had also assembled there, having finished their prerace preparations. Spaced out at reasonable distances, the bases of other universities dotted the lawn, each with a raised flag in school colors, flashing the name of the university in bold white letters.

"Our banner's pretty cool, huh?" King said to Kakeru as soon as he spotted him. Kakeru thought, *Is it?* But when he noticed that King's fingers were trembling, he decided just to say, "Yes," and nod in agreement.

"In fact, if you trace the history of our college back to its roots, Kansei University got its name from the founders' respect for the spirit of Matsudaira Sadanobu, who brought about the Kansei Reforms . . ."

Endless trivia streamed out of King's mouth like a broken tour guide recording. He was clearly jittery. Kakeru sat down, nodding along and chiming in at the appropriate places without really listening. Hanako had turned the square of tarp into a comfy space with blankets and bottles of water.

"I'm sure you know the drill because we did a test run here, but I'll go over our strategy for today," Kiyose said. Shindo and Musa were admiring the camera crew's equipment but quickly drew closer to Kiyose. Kakeru drew a simplified map of the course on a whiteboard.

"What's that, a maze?" Prince said, squinting at the drawing.

"The course is simple," Kakeru said, partly in objection to Prince. He pointed at the board and launched into his explanation. "First, we start from the base of the Self-Defense Force right next to the park. We'll do two laps around the runway and taxiway. Then we'll enter normal roads and go along the street toward the train station, under the elevated railroad of the monorail, then back to the park. After one lap inside the park, we finish next to the open field."

"We couldn't do a test run inside the base, but just think of the runway and taxiway as a humongous track," Kiyose advised. "Two laps make five kilometers. Since it's the first time we'll run there, and there's nothing around it that we can use as a benchmark, you might struggle to get a sense of the distance. We'll see how the race develops, but one thing to watch out for is getting dragged forward too much by other runners who start off fast. Make sure you think about your own pacing. When you pass under the monorail, that's about ten kilometers. The halfway point is at 11.2 kilometers, and when you're just inside the park, you'll hit fifteen kilometers. There'll be a water station, but if you miss it by any chance, don't worry about it too much. From that point on, it's all down to how much energy you have left. There's a lot of small ups and downs inside the park. Put on a spurt and dash to the finish line as fast as possible. Every second counts."

"I have a question." Musa raised his hand. "What kind of time do we need to get in order to pass the prelim? It would be helpful to have a rough idea."

Kiyose was reluctant. "I'd rather not say—I don't want you to feel too pressured . . ."

"These guys could do with a bit of pressure. If you just let them do whatever they want, they'll be running like sloths in slow motion," Yuki said. "It varies by year depending on the weather and how the particular race unfolds. But in general, if our total time is around ten hours and twelve minutes, we're safe."

"What?!" the twins shrieked. "Hang on, doesn't that mean each of us has to run twenty kilometers in just over an hour?" Jota said.

"That's running one kilometer in a little more than three minutes!" Joji cried out.

"And remember, we don't have any points from the intercollegiate championships," Nico added. "If our total time ranks lower than seventh place, IC points will come into play, so there'll be a higher likelihood that rankings will flip. We'll want to wedge ourselves into sixth place or higher, where the ranks are settled purely by the total time from this race."

The group was shaken, but Kiyose was quick to reassure them.

"Don't worry. Kakeru and I will cut down on our total time as much as possible. There's a lot of people in this race, so you should stick together as a group from the beginning and hold a steady pace. As we do the lap around the runway, those who are weaker will surely fall behind. No matter if they're too fast or too slow, make sure you don't let other people affect your pace."

"Got it," Joji replied, like a good boy.

"One more thing," Kiyose said. "I'll give you a sign if the group in the lead is going too fast, but otherwise, you better try to sink your teeth into the people in front of you and keep up. If you let go, chances are low that we'll make it past the prelim. All ten of us must run the whole race with everything we've got. That's our only hope."

Most of them hardened their resolve at his words, but King and Prince already looked intimidated. "Do you think we can do it?" they whispered to each other. "Sounds like hell . . ."

"Mind if I ask a question, too?" The Yaokatsu owner raised his hand. Hanako murmured, "*Dad*," and tried to shush him, but he plowed on. "Those fellas from other schools look like they've got more people wearing uniforms than you bunch. What's up with that?"

"Yeah, I was wondering the same thing, Katsu," the plasterer joined in, looking around at the crowd. "By my count, both Totai and Saikyo's got twelve guys in uniform. But we only got ten."

"I was hoping no one would notice." Kiyose smiled wryly. "Each team is allowed to enter a maximum of fourteen runners in this race. Then on the day, they take into account the members' condition and such, and narrow it down to twelve."

Yuki pushed up his glasses and elaborated on the system. "And out of those twelve participants, the race times of the top ten get counted into the team's total. In other words, they have two extra spots for insurance."

Since the Kansei team had only ten members, they would be disqualified from the race and lose their ticket to Hakone if even one of them failed to reach the finish line. Prince clutched his stomach, his face becoming ashen as the weight of responsibility hit home once again. Kakeru, in contrast, felt his eagerness for battle rise to a climax; he could barely restrain himself from breaking into a run.

"Let's all do our best," Joji said brightly, having given up on his bladder. "To avenge the spirit of our landlord!"

"He's not dead," Kakeru murmured.

Soon it was time for them to convene at the starting line.

"Let's get going," Kiyose said.

"Aren't we gonna get in a huddle and yell or something?" King asked restlessly.

"Do you want to?"

"Well, uh . . ." King hedged. He was too conscious of the TV camera following their every move, and he seemed to feel the need to do something dramatic.

Kiyose got his drift. *"Mount Hakone is the most savage in the world!"* he shouted. "Right, let's go."

He strode off, as calm as ever. The others followed suit, some of them stunned by Kiyose's outburst, others stifling a laugh.

The people of the shopping arcade saw them off.

"Go get 'em!" they cheered. "Show 'em what you got!"

"We'll be waiting at the finish line!" Hanako called out. The team waved in response just to her. Once the race began, the spectators were to cross the wide park toward the goal. Hanako and the others were planning to move their gear over and secure the team's space on the field.

"What was that about? Grinning like goofballs when it's a girl cheering for 'em," the Yaokatsu dad and the plasterer sulked.

All the cheer squads were thundering over each other now. A helicopter hovered overhead. TV cameras were stationed at various points throughout the course. Bikes with cameras were ready to film the athletes as they ran. The escort car, equipped with a loudspeaker and a TV camera, was on standby at the front. The crowd was buzzing with anticipation as they waited for the runners to pass by.

The Chikusei-so members couldn't help but cower a little at their first exposure to such a festive and feverish race.

"Never would've thought even the Hakone prelim would be so popular," Shindo remarked, deeply impressed.

"You know what shocked me?" Joji said. "I went to the bathroom with Prince earlier, and I saw people lining up in front of the cubicles for the first time in my life. In the men's room! All the guys running today, popping in and out one after another."

"I had the wrong idea about people who play sports." Prince was still rubbing his stomach. "I used to just assume they had muscles for brains, but they actually seem to have delicate sensibilities."

Jota had a spring in his step now, as if he hadn't been lying on the lawn like a corpse earlier that morning. He seemed to have overcome his nerves by concentrating hard on the race itself.

"So, it's time to take our first step toward victory at Hakone," he said.

Victory? Kakeru cast a sideways glance at Kiyose. Even if they succeeded in passing the prelim, it would be impossible to win first place at Hakone with this team. Kiyose noticed Kakeru's look and smiled a little. His eyes told Kakeru not to say anything that would sap the team's morale now.

The starting point was packed with participants. The front rows consisted of universities that had lost out on seed rights by a narrow margin at the previous Hakone Ekiden. Kakeru could make out the blue Totai uniforms through the mass of people. The Kansei team was starting from the rear end of the crowd.

Surveying all the teams from the back, Kakeru noticed that the runners' physiques varied greatly. The athletes in the front rows, from universities that regularly competed at Hakone, had sinewy bodies from which all unnecessary flesh had been stripped away. Some athletes from other universities toward the back of the crowd were visibly heavier in build, or the shape of their leg muscles suggested that they might not have done enough training yet.

The biggest difference of all was in the expressions on their faces. The athletes from the so-called weak universities seemed as though they were getting stage fright. They already looked unconfident even before the race began. *It's brutal*, Kakeru thought. Although distance running was one sport in which there was a higher chance of success from sheer effort, the harsh reality was that one's inborn physical potential and talent did play a part. On top of that, athletes' access to an environment where they could focus on their training and thrive as runners—with high-quality equipment and facilities as well as instructors—also depended on external factors, such as how well funded their university was.

Still, the athletes gathered there all possessed the same firm resolve: they were determined to compete at Hakone. No matter their position or background, they all had to stand behind the same starting line in this world of running. Each one of them would be forging the future with his own body, right then and there, whether it spelled success or failure.

That was why the sport was so thrilling, but also painful—and more than anything else, liberating.

Kakeru looked around at the Chikusei-so members in their black-and-silver uniforms. They had no excess flesh. Light, supple muscles stretched thin over their bodies. They stood their ground, even in comparison to the members of the teams that were Hakone regulars. Each of them possessed the body of an organism whose sole purpose was to run. They didn't look apprehensive anymore. Their eyes were gleaming with curiosity and drive.

We're ready, Kakeru thought.

There was nothing more to think about. When the race began, he would run. That was all. Kakeru looked straight ahead and waited for the gunshot.

At 8:30 a.m., the race began.

At once, 415 athletes from thirty-six universities started running. The battle for the Hakone Ekiden had commenced.

Out of all the contestants, only nine universities could proceed to Hakone. Kakeru kicked the ground in powerful strides. *We'll get there, no matter what.*

The race took off at a swift pace.

Kakeru and Kiyose were in the first group of runners leading the race, a cluster of about twenty to thirty people. Kakeru was itching to put on a spurt. Kiyose, running next to him, warned him to stay calm, and Kakeru managed to hold himself back.

Two Black international students from Saikyo University were at the top. They quickly left the first group behind and were already turning the first corner of the runway. The third runner, who bravely chased after them, was Kimani, a Black international student from Kofu Gakuin University, another regular at Hakone. Kimani was Kofu Gakuin's ace athlete. He had run the renowned second leg of Hakone three years in a row. As he watched Kimani speed far ahead of him, Kakeru could sense the pride and determination of an ace runner in his final year at university.

As if the top three runners were pulling them along by an invisible thread, the first group sprinted through the first kilometer in two minutes, forty-nine seconds. Considering that the whole race was twenty kilometers long, this was an extremely fast pace. The runway was so expansive that it was difficult to judge the distance. One after another, those who couldn't keep up fell behind, and by the time they were rounding the second corner, all the runners were already stretched out in a long vertical line.

Kiyose checked his watch and glanced behind him. The other members of the Chikusei-so team were running in the third cluster, along with about seventy to eighty people.

Kiyose shifted right up to the outer edge of the course to make himself more visible to the members running behind him. He held up his right hand, palm facing down, signaling at them to "hold back." Following the code they had agreed on beforehand, he flashed several numbers in succession with his fingers: *Keep your pace under three minutes, ten seconds per kilometer for the first five kilometers. The rest is up to you.* For the last part, he brought his hand close to his temple and made rock-and-paper shapes back and forth. Kiyose noted that Yuki and Shindo gave a nod and spread the word to the others around them.

"Are we going to ease the pace as well?" Kakeru asked.

"Will you?" Kiyose asked back.

"No." Kakeru didn't have the slightest intention of doing so.

Kiyose gave a light pat on Kakeru's back. "There'll be a change once we get on the normal road. When that happens, don't mind me and make your move."

Hanako had gathered up their belongings and was now cheering on the Chikusei-so team as they did two laps around the runway. So vast was the course that when the runners were on the farthest end of it, they looked no bigger than tiny peas. But when they approached, a rumble shook the ground. As they whizzed past, she could feel their breathing and the heat steaming from their perspiring bodies.

Hanako was stunned, stopwatch in hand.

They sure are fast! They were even faster than when she pedaled as hard as she could on her bike. They shot past her so quickly that she could barely bring their faces into focus. And they were about to run twenty kilometers at that very speed.

The three Black athletes passed by, and about forty meters after them, the first knot of runners came. She spotted Kakeru and Kiyose. Both carried their bodies with lightness and economy, and they looked calm, like they were only getting started. The crowd around her called out, "Let's go!" Hanako opened her mouth to shout, too, but nothing came out. A lump was stuck in her throat.

She saw the twins in the third group. The eight members of Chikusei-so were sticking together, clinging on so as not to lag behind, striving to get even a narrow lead over the others.

"The leaders are going at two minutes, forty-nine seconds! Hold your own pace!" she shouted to them. She realized she was almost in tears.

Until now, she had never imagined that the sight of someone running could be so beautiful. What a primal and solitary sport this was. No one could support a runner. It didn't matter how many people were watching or whether their teammates were running right next to them. In that moment, each runner was utterly alone, a single entity engaging the full mechanism of their body to keep going.

By the time they had completed two laps, five kilometers into the race, the distance between the top three runners and the first group had increased to more than one hundred meters. A middle-aged man standing near Hanako clicked his tongue and grumbled, "Shoddy Japanese runners."

That's not true, Hanako wanted to say. *Can't you see? There's no difference between the runners in the lead and everyone following them. Can't you see how earnest they look, how determined they are to test their limits? Not a single one of those runners is "shoddy."*

She clenched her fists tight and chased the Kansei uniforms with her eyes. *Don't let them win. Please don't let them win, guys.*

She didn't really know who it was that she wanted them to win against. Was it a battle against their rivals and other universities, or against the peanut gallery on the side of the road, or against their own selves? Whatever it was, she wished fervently for their victory. She didn't want them to lose against anyone or anything.

"Come on, Hana," her father urged her. "They're all doing well, see? Let's go wait for them at the goal."

The plasterer sniffled and gave a nod. It was the first time they had seen track athletes running up close. Blown away by their speed, they couldn't help being moved by the sight of the Chikusei-so team holding their own in the battle.

Those fellas might look like they're always fooling around, but they're dead serious. They've really been putting their all into running. Seeing them run brought this home to the shopping arcade townsfolk.

They made their way across the park, bringing their blankets and water bottles with them. They had to secure a good spot on the field and get ready to welcome the runners when they finished the race.

Hanako blinked back tears. It was no time for crying. The race had only just begun. She had to believe in the team and do her part.

Clutching the tarp, Hanako strode briskly, making her way through the tall grass wet from the morning dew.

The race entered a new phase after the five-kilometer point, when the runners reached the normal road. The first group began to spread out. They had been maintaining their high speed, neither getting closer to the three leaders nor falling farther behind, but some of them couldn't sustain the pace.

The first group was whittled down to about ten people, and both

Kakeru and Kiyose were securely among them. They were surrounded by star athletes from Totai, Kikui, Kofu Gakuin, and other universities. Kakeru noted that Sakaki wasn't one of them. He was unmoved. He didn't feel a sense of superiority over Sakaki, let alone sympathy. He merely observed that Sakaki couldn't keep up. *But I'm going to push harder. I'm going to leave this group behind.*

Around that time, the staff in the escort vehicle were marveling at them. "Look there! A couple of Kansei runners are in the first group. They're putting up a good fight." But of course, Kakeru and Kiyose had no way of knowing they were attracting such attention. They were absorbed in the silent push-and-pull tactics between the other runners, always alert for the next move in the race.

Big track teams had enough members who weren't running to place them at strategic locations along the course; these athletes could convey information about their teammates' respective positions in the race and pass them instructions on pacing from the coach. But Kansei had limited resources. Kiyose had to pay attention not only to his own running but also to the others at the same time. Occasionally, he looked back to check on them. The second and third groups had also dispersed now. Those who had dropped out of the first group joined those who hung on in the later groups.

Judging from their expressions, Kiyose could tell that the twins, Musa, and Yuki still had more energy to spare. Shindo and Nico looked self-possessed, intent on maintaining their own pace. King was struggling but still keeping up. Prince, however, seemed close to the breaking point. The Chikusei-so members were starting to spread out in a vertical line like the rest of the runners.

If the team tried to stick together any longer, there would be a risk that the slowest members would drag everyone back.

The first group passed the seven-kilometer mark. Their pace for the past kilometer was three minutes, five seconds, slightly more reserved than their speed at the beginning of the race. It was likely due to the pack mentality; the runners were wary of getting spent by the time they reached the latter half of the race. What's more, Kimani, the third leader, who was running a short distance ahead of them, had slowed down.

Kiyose estimated that some runners from the first group would put on a spurt just past ten kilometers. It was a given that Kakeru and Kiyose would rise to the challenge, but he also had to consider the impact that would have on their teammates behind them. There were bound to be runners in the first group who would run out of stamina and fall behind. Kiyose had to make sure that the Chikusei-so members wouldn't be thrown when that happened.

Kiyose edged toward the center line of the road and signaled to the group behind him, swinging his right arm in a big, circular motion. *We'll make a move soon.* He brought his hand close to his temple and fluttered his fingers. *You can spread out, too.* Then he made a fist and gave a thumbs-up. *Best of luck.*

Everyone raised their hands a little to signal that they understood— except Prince, who was too overwhelmed to respond.

"Kakeru," Kiyose whispered. "At ten kilometers, it's going to be the first critical point of the race. Don't fall behind."

Kakeru nodded. He could sense it coming from the change in the breathing of the other runners around them. The battle to secure the most strategic position to bolt ahead of the group was becoming fiercer. They were hyperalert to each other's movements, restraining each other, waiting for the opportune moment.

The sidewalks were lined with spectators, even when the runners got far from the station and approached the raised path of the monorail. But the crowd's cheers sounded distant. The noise caressed Kakeru's ears like the murmurs of the sea and quickly slipped away behind him. He was focused on the race. Once again, he became keenly aware that his body was moving especially well today.

Sometimes, even when his body felt light, the result of the race didn't reflect his feeling. On the contrary, there were times when he felt out of shape, but his pace turned out to be quite fast. No matter how much practice he put in, it was not uncommon that, during a real race, his body and brain wouldn't align properly, giving him these false impressions.

For the first time since the race began, Kakeru glanced down at his watch, just to be sure. He had been holding a pace of two minutes, fifty-seven seconds so far. It wasn't a trick of his senses. *I really am in great shape today. Even when the pace of the race goes up, I can push harder. I'll go faster.*

Kiyose seemed to detect Kakeru's confidence instantly. "Whoa, whoa," he said, as if he were calming a horse. "Wait for it, Kakeru. Once we're past ten kilometers, you can do whatever you like."

If they put on a spurt too early, it would be self-destructive. "Got it," Kakeru answered, and he made himself hold back without dropping the pace.

Just as Kiyose had predicted, there was a movement in the first group as soon as they passed under the monorail and the ten-kilometer sign came into view.

Kikui's third-year and Totai's captain sped up. Everyone except Kakeru and Kiyose was flung off.

Kakeru clung to the two runners competing with each other, using them as a windshield. After about five hundred meters of running that way, he murmured, "I'm going." Kiyose nodded without a word.

Kakeru rounded them on their right and shot past them. He kept running to his own rhythm. He didn't have the time or the inclination to look behind him. It was enough to hear their receding footsteps to know that he was leaving them behind, becoming the sole runner in fourth place.

It felt good. Ripping through the wind, pounding on the road. This moment was his and his alone. *It's a world only I can experience, as long as I keep running.*

His heart was burning up. He could feel it pumping blood to the very tips of his fingers. *Still heavy. You can do better than that.* He willed his body to transform even more. Like a fleet-footed beast that hurtles across a grassy plain, ever tireless. Like a silver light that illuminates the darkness.

Kakeru cornered the turning point at 11.2 kilometers with perfect efficiency, like a cutting-edge, streamlined machine. Losing any speed would have been a sin—his whole being was made for running.

Kakeru already held Kimani within firing range.

Meanwhile, Kiyose watched enraptured as Kakeru gained momentum right in front of his eyes. *Just look at that run. The beauty of a being who was born to run.*

The sight of him easily transcended any resentment or envy. Kakeru was like another species—a far cry from Kiyose himself, who was bound by gravity and desperate for air.

Kiyose wanted to scream, but he swallowed it back. *You are the only one. The only one who can embody what it means to run, as you're doing now. The only one who can spur me on and show me a new world. It's just you, Kakeru.*

Though he wanted to catch up to Kakeru, it was impossible for Kiyose, whose damaged leg was a ticking time bomb. He matched his pace with the two runners from Kikui and Totai. The pair were doing their best to recover from the shock of being overtaken by Kakeru just after their spurt. It remained to be seen how this turn of events would affect them when they came to the undulating course in the park. The only way forward for Kiyose was to preserve his energy and bet on the final stretch of the race. He had to give his full attention to his own run now—no more checking on the others.

But Kiyose could sense what they were feeling. The other eight members had definitely seen Kakeru flying out of the group. He knew they were electrified by Kakeru's run, a streak of dazzling light.

After Kakeru turned around at the halfway point, Joji looked at him straight in the face. His breathing was steady, and his face looked calm, as if he were only jogging. But Joji noticed his eyes were different. Kakeru's black eyes were gleaming, exalted with the joy of being in the midst of a run.

He probably doesn't realize how he looks when he's running. Joji felt both envy and affection at the same time. *And what about me? Is my run as pure as Kakeru's?* So simple, so absolute as to be almost merciless. *I want to run like that,* Joji thought. *I want to run like Kakeru.*

Nico was bowled over by Kakeru as he whizzed right past him. He'd known Kakeru was good, but this was something else. *When he really gets down to business, his speed is out of this world.* He was breathing, irrefutable proof that there were chosen ones in the world.

But I'll fight to the end, too. Nico pumped more oxygen into his lungs, which were starting to scream in pain. At least in his will to run he could keep abreast of Kakeru.

The runners in the Kansei uniform were bound by fervor and strength. With Kakeru leading them toward the goal, they pressed on in formation like a glimmering constellation in the night sky.

After securing their space on the open field, Hanako hurried to the course inside the park. The cheer squads were jostling each other near the finish line. Spectators had also swarmed around the area in droves, awaiting the athletes' arrival. Birds flew away from the woods in the park, startled by the sudden hubbub.

Hanako finally spied a gap in the wall of people about fifty meters before the finish line. She squeezed through, saying "excuse me" as she went, and made it to the front row. Since she was wearing a Kansei tracksuit, the crowd assumed she was a staff member and happily made space for her.

Hanako checked her stopwatch: fifty-seven minutes, thirty-five seconds since the start of the race. *It must be early still,* she thought. *They're running twenty kilometers, after all—surely they'd take longer.*

But moments later, the roar of the crowd swelled like a wave. The cheer squads pounced on the opportunity, swinging their flags and singing their school anthems at full blast.

The top runner emerged from the green shadows. It was the Black student from Saikyo University. He was followed by another Black athlete.

"Amazing . . ." Hanako breathed. The two runners completed the twenty-kilometer race at fifty-eight minutes, twelve seconds and fifty-eight minutes, twenty-eight seconds, causing a stir among the crowd. Their physical prowess deserved to be called invincible.

She wondered how the Chikusei-so members were faring. As she clapped for the runners who had finished, she stretched out her neck to peer at the course.

A figure appeared, turning a curve. Hanako let out a scream. She was speechless.

It was Kakeru.

The third runner to enter the final stretch was none other than Kakeru Kurahara.

Some spectators had been whispering, "Wouldn't be surprised if the Black runners snatch the top places." Now the crowd went wild, far more than they had for the first two. They erupted in thunderous cheers. Swept away with the rest, Hanako called out, "Kakeru! Kakeru!"

Kakeru didn't seem to hear anything.

The sound of his panting whipped past her in an instant. Kakeru was looking straight ahead, his eyes fixed on the goal. He sprinted the last fifty meters as if it were a short-distance race. The crowd was overwhelmed by his run, which radiated his persistence and determination.

For a moment, a hush fell over the crowd as if a saint had passed by.

Hanako checked her stopwatch. Kakeru had completed the race in fifty-nine minutes, fifteen seconds. Kimani came in five seconds later. Kakeru had triumphed over the Kofu Gakuin ace.

The crowd was buzzing with excitement.

"That was a Kansei guy. I've never even seen a team from there at Hakone."

"They've got one hell of a runner."

He's Kakeru. Kakeru Kurahara, and he's only a first-year, Hanako felt like boasting to anyone who would listen. But there was no time for that—the next athletes were already emerging at the straight line of the final stretch.

When he passed the fifteen-kilometer point and entered the park, Kiyose revved up his speed just as he had planned. The runners from Kikui and Totai sped up almost simultaneously, but he had no intention of yielding to them.

He felt a slight discomfort in his right shin when he increased his speed uphill. *Shit*. But he kept his breathing steady and his face smooth. If the other two sensed even a hint of his weakness, it would be over. Every second was precious. It was no time to be concerned about an old wound.

Kiyose didn't hold back. He kept accelerating. The blaring tunes of the cheer squads were crashing into one chaotic cacophony. He was vaguely aware of a few familiar faces from the shopping arcade shouting from the side of the course, though he couldn't catch any words. Kikui's runner took the lead by the span of a step. Every time the soles of Kiyose's feet struck the ground, he felt a dull pain in his shin. Even so, he held on.

"Haiji!"

He was certain he heard Kakeru call to him. He poured the last of his strength into his leg muscles and tumbled across the finish line. With great effort, he moved aside not to get in the way of the other runners and felt his shin with his palm. It was burning. He came in sixth place, tied with the Kikui runner. The time was exactly sixty minutes.

When Kakeru crossed the finish line, a staff member handed him a water bottle and rushed him to the side of the course. If he lingered near the line, he would get in the way of the oncoming athletes.

How's everyone else doing? He hovered indecisively under the trees at the side of the finish line. There was another wave of cheers, and Kakeru caught a glimpse of the Kansei uniform beyond the crowd. It was Kiyose.

"Haiji!" Kakeru shouted and leaped out on the narrow path to the field where runners were directed after they finished. Kiyose was crouched on the ground. Kakeru dashed over in surprise. "Are you okay?"

Kiyose wasn't too out of breath. Those who finished near the top were seasoned athletes with skill and endurance, which meant they could complete a race at their own pace without getting completely drained. It was virtually unthinkable for someone of that level to be gasping for breath and unable to move after a race. Judging from Kiyose's even breathing, Kakeru said, "It's your leg."

In an attempt to relieve even a fraction of the strain on his muscles, Kakeru poured the water from his bottle onto Kiyose's shin. He lent Kiyose a hand. Kiyose stood up and began to walk with a slight limp.

"Well done, Kakeru."

The first thing that came out of Kiyose's mouth was praise. Kakeru nearly cried, given there were more pressing things to talk about.

"Thank you," he mumbled, looking down. Kiyose laughed and ruffled Kakeru's hair.

"Let's go cheer for the guys."

"But shouldn't you cool your leg—?"

"No need. Come on."

Kiyose slipped through the gaps in the crowd. Kakeru followed suit, apologizing as he went.

A fierce, neck and neck battle was underway among the runners around eightieth place. The fate of their team hinged on the total time of ten members—everyone was desperate.

"The twins! They're here!" Kakeru saw their Kansei uniforms among the knot of runners. Hanako was on the other side of the course, jumping up and down.

Jota and Joji were both gritting their teeth as they crossed the finish line.

Next came Yuki, Musa, Nico, and Shindo, placing between 80th and 100th. King pulled through and came in at 123rd.

"So far so good," Kiyose murmured. Prince, however, was nowhere to be seen. More and more teams among the Hakone regulars had at least ten members who were finished.

"We'll be in trouble if he doesn't show up soon." Kakeru jogged in place restlessly. He wanted to run again—if only they could swap places. When was Prince coming? How much longer? He was hoping against hope, his eyes boring into the shadow of the trees, when finally, Prince appeared.

"He's shaky . . ." Kiyose frowned. Prince had long gone over his limit, and his eyes were bleary.

"Run, Prince! You're almost there!" Kakeru shouted, hoping his voice at least could guide him to the goal.

"I know, duh." Prince was fighting back vomit as he advanced, flailing his limbs as if he were drowning. His fingers felt strangely cold. *Where has my blood gone?* he wondered in a daze. *I probably look like a corpse right now.*

He was clearly anemic. But he clung on, refusing to break down. It was twenty meters to the finish line. If Prince stopped running, the Kansei team would be disqualified. They had no backup member. If they couldn't go to Hakone because of him, his manga collection would likely meet the dreadful fate of a bonfire. He had to avoid such an outcome at any cost.

Prince screwed up every shred of his willpower. The effort screwed up his stomach, too, and he was assaulted by unbearable nausea.

He couldn't be bothered about a few hundred people watching him anymore. He let himself go and vomited. He heard some of the women in the crowd screech.

"Don't throw up! *RUN!*" Kiyose's angry bellow rang through the air.

You're a monster. This is why I hate sports clubs, Prince cursed in his head, wiping the corner of his mouth with his hand. Of course, he wasn't about to stop moving his legs. *Why do you think I've followed along with everyone, even though I hate sports? Why do you think I've spent all this time on running practice like an idiot?*

To compete in the Hakone Ekiden, that's why.

Because I thought, for at least once in my life, I wouldn't mind sharing a dream with you people who have muscles for brains . . . !

Prince crossed the line at 176th. He crumpled to the ground and blacked out.

The Chikusei-so members were sprawled out on their tarp in the field. Less than half of them had checked their own finish times on their wristwatch. The rest had been too overwhelmed. Yuki gave up trying to pin down their total time.

"It could go either way." Kiyose calculated in his head while icing his shin. "If we average our rankings, we'd land somewhere around eighty-fifth or so. It's on the borderline."

"And if other borderline schools have enough IC points . . ." Nico scowled at the sky.

"It's not impossible that we drop out," Yuki said.

"We *caaan't!*" the twins wailed. Shindo and Musa were sitting quietly, apparently praying to their respective ancestors and guardian deities. King tugged at the grass. Prince was lying face down and didn't even twitch. Hanako and the townspeople sat around them, but they didn't have the heart to offer empty words of encouragement. All they could do was wait for the results.

Kakeru looked at the plastic bag Kiyose was pressing on his leg. The ice that they'd brought in a cooler had almost completely melted.

"I'll go get more ice. Maybe the stand over there would give us some."

He got up, eager to escape from the heavy atmosphere. Musa seemed to feel the same way. "I'll come with you," he said, tagging along.

They crossed the lawn toward the red-roofed stand. One glance at the other athletes' faces was enough to see how confident they were about passing the prelim. The teams who looked rigid were those on the borderline like Kansei. As for the teams whose total time was clearly far below the threshold, they were calmly waiting for the results announcement. Some of them were even cheerfully pecking away at the multitiered lunch boxes prepared by the manager girls.

There's all kinds of teams here, Kakeru thought. For some, running at the prelim was a goal in itself. They knew what the results would be even before they ran the race, so once it was over, they turned it into an event not much different from a picnic and just enjoyed themselves. *It's not like that's a bad thing—but we're different.* Kakeru was sure of that.

I definitely don't want to stop at the prelim. I want to go higher. I want our team to become even faster, stronger, and rise to the challenge at the Hakone Ekiden. That's what I've been practicing for, and I'm prepared to train even harder to make that happen.

"Do you think we'll make it, Kakeru?" Musa asked anxiously.

"We will. We'll go to Hakone," Kakeru assured him. Red-hot magma boiled in the pit of his stomach. Look how the team ran today, every single one of them giving it their all. *There's no way we can lose.*

Musa widened his eyes at Kakeru. "You seem to have grown stronger somehow."

"No, I don't think so," Kakeru said, shaking his head. "It's just—we ran pretty hard out there. So I think we'll be all right, that's all."

Musa nodded. "You're right. We *are* going to Hakone. All of us, together."

When Musa said it, it sounded like a happy fairy-tale ending or a prophecy they could believe in.

At the stand, Kakeru asked for some ice cubes, and the clerk gladly consented, scooping the ice into a paper cup because they'd forgotten to bring a container. "That was silly of us," Musa said to Kakeru. Just then, a group of spectators passed by behind them.

"Hey look, there's another Black runner. It's not fair, pulling in foreign students like that."

"Yeah, Japanese runners haven't got a chance when there's a bunch of *them* around."

They were whispering loud enough for Musa to hear. Musa's face stiffened, and Kakeru turned to argue.

"Let them be, Kakeru." Musa held him back. "I've heard similar opinions so many times, even just today."

"I can't let them talk trash like that!" Kakeru still wanted to chase after the men, but Musa gripped his arm.

"We shouldn't fight. The kind of runners they have in mind are the students who are invited based on their athletic talent. I'm embarrassed. I feel embarrassed for myself. They don't seem to notice the difference, but I'm not a fast runner. I don't have such a gift that anyone would envy. I'm just an average international student."

"That doesn't matter!" Kakeru fumed. "You, me, those runners who got first and second today—we all ran the same exact course. They can't just . . ."

Kakeru was frustrated but didn't know how to put it into words. He felt that those spectators had insulted all of them: Musa, who lived under the same roof as him; Kakeru himself; and those other international students with whom he'd never exchanged a word. Somehow, those people had insulted all runners who devoted themselves to the sport. Kakeru squared his shoulders in rage.

"Kurahara's right." A voice came from behind. Kakeru turned to find a spindly man with a smooth-shaven head standing there. "But don't pay them any mind. They're amateurs who don't understand what running is."

As Kakeru and Musa watched, the man bought a bottle of oolong tea from the stand. Kakeru had the feeling they'd met before. Without letting his guard down, Kakeru tried to place him. *I know I've seen this shiny head somewhere.*

"Fujioka from Rikudo . . . !" The name came back to Kakeru. Kazuma Fujioka, captain of the Rikudo University team, the invincible team that

won the Hakone Ekiden multiple years in a row. Kakeru hadn't seen
him since they'd met at the Totai track meet in the spring. *What's he
doing here?*

Fujioka, apparently reading the question in Kakeru's eyes, said,
"Observing the enemy. The Kansei team has grown much stronger now.
It looks like you might even make it to Hakone." Fujioka showed the
dignity and composure of a true champion.

"It looks like it," Kakeru answered confidently, his competitive side
rearing its head.

Fujioka locked eyes with Kakeru, who stood his ground. Then Fujioka
turned to Musa. "Don't mind the lot of them. What they say is foolish."

As Fujioka walked away, drinking his tea, Kakeru called out, "Foolish how?" What the men had said about Musa got on his nerves, but
he couldn't grasp exactly why it made him so angry. Fujioka seemed
to understand where Kakeru's unease came from. "Please, I want to
know," Kakeru said.

Fujioka paused and stared at Kakeru, amused. "Fine," he agreed,
turning around to face them again. "There are at least two reasons why
it's ridiculous. First, their assumption that it's unfair to bring international students into the team because the Japanese athletes can't compete against them. What about the Olympics, then? What we're doing
here is a serious athletic competition, not some field day at kindergarten
where kids hold hands and step over the finish line all together. It's only
natural that individuals have different physical abilities. Yet sports are
still a realm of equality and fairness. Those people don't have an inkling
of what it means to compete in the same sport, in the same ring."

Musa was silent, listening closely to Fujioka's every word. Kakeru
was blown away by Fujioka's calm, articulate analysis.

"And the second thing they are misguided about is this: they think
it's all about winning," Fujioka continued. "So as long as a Japanese athlete wins first place and gets a gold medal, everything's fine? Certainly
not the case. The true essence of the sport lies somewhere else entirely.

Suppose I got first place in a race—but if *I* felt that I lost to myself, then that wouldn't be a victory. People's times and rankings change from one day to the next, with every race, just like that. Who's to say who is number one in the world? Isn't it because we hold firm to an ideal or goal within ourselves that we keep on running?"

That was it. Fujioka's words dispelled the fog inside Kakeru. That was what had snagged in his mind and infuriated him. Fujioka was impressive. He had effortlessly untangled and expressed in words everything Kakeru had felt and wanted to say.

"You haven't changed at all, Fujioka," a voice called from behind. Kiyose had approached Kakeru and Musa without them noticing.

"It wasn't my place to speak, as an outsider." Fujioka bowed to Kiyose in a stoic manner and turned once again to leave.

"I appreciate it," said Kiyose.

Fujioka glanced back over his shoulder, and a smile flickered at the corner of his mouth. "I see you've assembled quite the team."

"Uh-huh."

"I'll be waiting at Hakone."

Fujioka disappeared into the trees. Throughout their conversation, he exuded an aura befitting a champion, resolute and imperturbable. Stray thoughts flitted across Kakeru's mind—*He might as well say "I'll be waiting at nirvana," the way he goes on,* and *He came all this way, but he's not staying for the results?*—but he hurriedly bowed to Fujioka's retreating figure. Musa thanked him and also gave a deep bow. Fujioka's words had invigorated them, like a powerful gust of wind blowing away a thundercloud.

"You didn't even take a bag," Kiyose said, holding up a plastic bag. Kakeru apologized and poured the ice cubes from the cup into the bag. Kiyose wasn't limping anymore.

"So he's called Mr. Fujioka. He's an admirable person," Musa said, deeply moved.

"As you can see, to keep winning at Hakone, you need mental strength and intelligence in the truest sense of the word," Kiyose said, then chuckled a little. "Though he was always oddly zen. Imagine a high schooler nicknamed 'Training Monk.' It's a bit grim, right?"

Kakeru and Musa exchanged looks and nodded.

The spectators and athletes were starting to gather around the large display board near the finish line.

"It's almost time for the announcement," Kiyose said.

"Let's go." Musa trotted toward the Kansei base. Kakeru matched Kiyose's pace, treading carefully across the lawn. Though he wanted to know how they had done, the results were out of their hands now, and nothing could change that. What dominated his mind instead was Fujioka's presence.

Fujioka's power to put emotions into words. His level-headed insight that enabled him to carefully analyze the doubt, anger, or fear inside himself.

Fujioka was strong. The speed of his run was exceptional, but more than that, the strength of his spirit from which his run derived was formidable. *While I'd been throwing myself blindly at running, Fujioka had probably been pursuing the sport at a much deeper level, constantly scrutinizing himself.*

Kakeru felt a peculiar sensation rush over him. He felt utterly defeated and inspired in equal measure.

What I've been missing is words. All I've ever done was let whatever was bothering me hang around like gray fog. From now on, that has to change. I'll become as fast as—no, faster than Fujioka. And for that, I need to know myself, who I am as a runner.

That must be what Kiyose means by "strength."

"I think I'm starting to get it," Kakeru said.

"All right." Kiyose looked satisfied.

A student in a high-collar school uniform clasping a megaphone climbed up onto the podium. He reverently opened the sheet of paper containing

the results of the race. He was a student on the administrative committee of the Inter-University Athletic Union of Kanto. The assistant, a
female student, stood at the ready on one side of the display board. The
whole assembly awaited the announcement, brimming with hope and
anxiety.

"We will now announce the universities who have passed the Preliminary Race of the Tokyo-Hakone Round-Trip College Ekiden Race.
First place—Tokyo Taiiku University."

The Totai crowd let out boisterous cheers. An older student slapped
Sakaki with glee. Their team had stuck together throughout the race,
and every member had finished in a good position. It was a win that
displayed the high caliber of their members: their strength as a cohe-
sive group.

The assistant slid out the large white panel from the first place slot on
the display board. The row showed the university's name and the total
time of ten of their members: ten hours, nine minutes, twelve seconds.
Their ranking, averaged across the ten members, was forty-ninth.

"Just as I expected—it was a really fast-paced race," Kiyose groaned.
Kakeru saw from his expression that it was looking doubtful for their
team. He clenched his fists.

"Second place." The presenter read on dispassionately. "Kofu Gakuin
University."

From a different part of the crowd came another outburst of cheers.

"That kid," King humphed, "he likes to put in a dramatic pause
between the rank and the college name."

"I wish they'd stop putting on a show and just get on with it." Prince
was quick to complain now that he had finally revived.

"Argh, I'm gonna explode!" The twins and Hanako were huddled
together, trembling like fledglings that had fallen out of a nest.

They had announced the colleges up to fifth place, but Kansei's
name still hadn't been called. All the universities that had been named
so far were Hakone regulars. If Kansei didn't make it into sixth place,
IC points would come into play in deciding the seventh to ninth places,

so there was a real possibility that the rankings wouldn't reflect the pure total time of today's race.

"Sixth place . . ."

"Come on, come on, come on!"

"Say Kansei! Say Kansei!"

Their urgent prayers went unanswered. The presenter intoned, "Saikyo University."

"Nooo!"

"Is it over? Are we done?" Nico and Yuki looked up at the sky. Kiyose was staring at the display board without a word. He stared so hard that his piercing eyes might have seen through the white panels that covered the seventh to ninth universities.

"In accordance with the regulations, the seventh place and below were determined by subtracting the IC points of each university from their total time. Seventh place—Jonan Bunka University."

Kakeru almost went weak in the knees, but he somehow managed to stay upright. *It's not over yet. Still two more places left.* He felt pain in his right shoulder. He turned to find Shindo digging his fingers into it. Musa was half burrowing his head against Shindo's arm, muttering something in his mother tongue.

It's all right. We have to make it. Kakeru reached over and patted their backs.

"Eighth place—Kansei University."

Kakeru thought he'd heard wrong. King pounced on him. Kiyose thrust his fists high and grinned from ear to ear, his usual calm mask slipping. Musa and Shindo fell helplessly to the ground. Nico and Yuki high-fived each other, while the twins and Hanako slapped Kakeru all over, screaming at the top of their lungs.

As he was jostled by the others, Kakeru saw it, clear and unmistakable. Their name, "Kansei University," glowed brilliantly on the board. He glimpsed a single tear roll down Prince's cheek as he stood outside the circle.

We did it. The fact finally reached his brain. *We can run at the*

Hakone Ekiden. Before he knew it, Kakeru was roaring from the pit of his stomach.

Kansei's total time was ten hours, sixteen minutes, forty-three seconds. The team's average ranking was eighty-sixth.

The actual time of Jonan Bunka in seventh place was ten hours, seventeen minutes, three seconds, but the team had ranked above Kansei because of IC points. The last team to make it past the prelim, in ninth place, was Shinsei University with ten hours, seventeen minutes, eighteen seconds.

Kakeru gazed up at their time on the board and heaved a big sigh of relief and joy. Kansei University had accomplished the feat of seizing a ticket to Hakone on the very first try. And what's more, the team had done it with a total time that was worthy of seventh place.

Everywhere in the crowd, people were exclaiming in surprise.

"Kansei's actually done it."

"Did you hear they only have ten people on the whole team?"

"That's the one with the guys who came in third and sixth, right? I know their uniform already."

"Me too. The black one with silver lines. They're kinda cool."

Kakeru felt lightheaded, as if he were deprived of oxygen. The sensation continued even as they were clearing up their space on the lawn, and even as they were being asked to give comments in front of the TV camera one by one. He felt more breathless than during the race. He could barely walk straight.

They had only passed the prelim. The real race still lay ahead, about seventy-five days away, at the very beginning of the new year. He kept reminding himself of that, but he still couldn't stop the exhilaration overflowing inside him.

Kiyose had once said, "Mount Hakone isn't just some mirage." It really was true. The Chikusei-so residents had come so close now that, at last, they could see the real mountain right in front of them.

Still on cloud nine, Kakeru swiftly folded up their tarp. Jota and Joji were sitting on the lawn. With a cryptic frown on their faces, they were scrutinizing the results that they'd jotted down from the board.

"What's up?" Kakeru asked.

The twins looked up at him. "Haiji said we'll 'conquer the summit,' didn't he?"

"Huh? Did he?" Kakeru replied airily. But Jota wasn't satisfied.

"He did. But our time . . ."

"What about it?" Kakeru squatted next to them and put aside the tarp. "Let's wrap things up and go home. I bet we're having a party tonight."

"Kakeru, doesn't 'summit' mean winning first place?" Joji said with a despairing look. "Our time was ten hours, sixteen minutes, forty-three seconds. Totai's, in first place, was ten hours, nine minutes, twelve seconds. They were faster than us by seven minutes, thirty seconds—that's a big difference. And we're only at the prelim. What about the kind of teams that would come out on top at Hakone? How fast do they actually run twenty kilometers?"

"Would we get to that level before New Year's if we keep practicing?" Jota asked gravely. "Well? Tell us the truth, Kakeru."

No answer came to Kakeru.

VIII

WINTER COMES AGAIN

A team of only ten members made it through the preliminary race and earned their place in the Hakone Ekiden.

The news of the Chikusei-so residents' incredible feat spread like wildfire, not only throughout the world of university track but also among the general public.

Since 1987, when the Hakone Ekiden first began to be televised, this competition among the student runners in the Kanto region had become known to virtually everyone living in Japan. With its arduous course and the glamour of the nationwide live coverage during the New Year's holiday, the Hakone Ekiden inevitably captivated the whole population.

And now, a small team of ten was about to compete in this prominent race. How did they dream up such a reckless endeavor? What would they do if someone got injured or ill on the day of the race? What kind of training regimen did they follow, and what were they like in their daily lives?

A constant stream of curious people in the neighborhood and students who wanted to join the team came to visit Chikusei-so. Most of these students didn't have any experience in track and field. Many of them were driven by a temporary rush of inspiration after hearing about the team's achievement at the prelim.

Kiyose wrote a polite note declining any visits and put it up on the front door of Chikusei-so. He appreciated the students' interest in joining, but he knew it was just a passing craze. New members weren't eligible for the race if they didn't hold an official record, anyway. And all the rooms in Chikusei-so were already occupied. After careful consideration, Kiyose decided it was best not to bring in any new members so that the ten of them could focus on training and strengthen their bond as they worked toward Hakone.

As for the locals, the owners of the shopping arcade appealed to their neighbors to let the team practice in peace. Most people stopped knocking on their door, content just to peek in at Chikusei-so from the other side of the hedges. A few elderly neighbors left them some harvest from their vegetable patches, though they were more of an exception.

One morning, Kakeru stepped out of the house to go on his morning jog and found an offering of hakusai cabbages and nashi pears outside their front door. *Are we in some kind of folktale?* Kakeru thought, remembering stories about a grateful animal leaving offerings at someone's door overnight in return for a good deed. Nira, who'd watched the elderly neighbors come and go without a single bark, merely wagged his tail at Kakeru. The Chikusei-so residents never figured out who it was that left them these occasional gifts, but they gladly partook of them.

Of course, they were also inundated by media requests. It wasn't just the track and field magazines that got in touch with them—they were also approached by all kinds of media outlets, including general weekly magazines, newspapers, and TV stations. Kiyose and Shindo sifted through these requests diligently. They politely declined most offers, citing as the reason that they wanted to concentrate on their practice.

They did accept the interview requests from Sanuki at *Track World Monthly Magazine* and Nunoda from *Yomiuri Shimbun*, who had been supportive since the summer camp days. These two were well acquainted with runners' psychology, so they observed the team's practice unobtrusively and fired away pertinent questions. Positive articles about the Chikusei-so team appeared in their respective publications.

The twins and King were exuberant, clamoring for more interviews.

"Now that we're running Hakone, we better make a splash," said Jota.

"More important, you should get down to serious practice," Kiyose said sternly. "Otherwise, your run might be so pathetic at Hakone that when we're on national TV, you'll attract everyone's attention whether you like it or not."

Despite Kiyose's flat refusal, the twins didn't back down. "Boooo. We wanna go on TV. TV! TV!" they yelled. Kakeru, watching their battle unfolding over dinner, was impressed. His own mind was restless from the tension and thrill he felt just at the prospect of competing in the Hakone Ekiden. But the twins wanted to taste even more of the extraordinary, like getting interviewed on TV. Were they naive, greedy, or just fearless?

Before last spring, long-distance running hadn't been part of their lives, so perhaps the twins didn't realize how much weight the Hakone Ekiden carried.

The Hakone Ekiden had been held every year ever since its inception in 1920, except during wartime. Even in the postwar period, when food was scarce, athletes still passed on the relay sash—the tasuki— from one to another and ran to the top of Mount Hakone. That was how important the race was for a runner, its history spanning more than eighty races.

For student runners, the Hakone Ekiden was a source of inspiration, a dream. It was possible the twins didn't fully appreciate what it meant to participate in such an event. Despite not grasping its enormity, the twins had put in the work to seize the opportunity. They were certainly forces to be reckoned with. Kakeru admired them for that and found it funny, too.

Sandwiched between the twins, Kiyose was intent on eating his dinner while the brothers kept up their appeals.

"Come on, we've *got* to go on TV at least once!"

"Can't we even have a bit of a bonus? I mean, you did say . . ."

"What did I say?" Kiyose's chopsticks came to a halt. Joji suddenly went quiet. He squirmed a little, clearly itching to say something, but eventually, he shook his head.

"Nothing."

In the end, it was Kiyose who gave in, and the team agreed to the TV interview. Life at Chikusei-so was to be introduced in a five-minute segment on the early evening news.

The camera crew paid them a visit and took some footage of the apartment building, including the overflowing stacks of manga in Prince's room and the army of no-smoking wire figurines scattered around the perpetually unmade futon in Nico's room. They also filmed the team's practice in the field and asked them questions.

The twins and King did most of the talking.

"How do I put it . . . We were basically just going with the flow, though Haiji kind of blackmailed us into it, but anyway, before we even knew it, we were all running for Hakone."

"I eat honey lemon slices every day not to catch a cold."

"There's nothing special about our practice. I think our training plan is pretty similar to what track teams do at other universities."

As always, Kakeru stood inconspicuously to the side, just outside the camera's frame.

"Why're you hiding, Kakeru?" Yuki asked.

"Oh, no reason," Kakeru laughed, hedging the question. Nico, who had been watching over the interview, turned around to face Kakeru.

"Don't tell me you're some wanted criminal on the run."

"What? Of course not."

"All righty then." Nico eyed him dubiously.

"Putting that aside—don't you think the vibes have been off lately?" Yuki said.

Nico nodded. "Kind of, yeah," he murmured. Kakeru had noticed it, too. There was something awkward about the Chikusei-so team now.

The first-floor residents were the same as ever. And most of the second-floor residents applied themselves to training with the same attitude as before. But the twins were obviously feeling gloomy and frustrated about something—or rather about Kiyose.

It wasn't as though the twins were picking fights with Kiyose or giving him attitude, but they tried to keep a subtle distance from him. Kiyose talked to them as usual, but they didn't quite open up to him in the same way. Somehow, their trust in Kiyose seemed to have diminished.

This uneasiness between them spread through the entire house. Ever since the team had come back from the prelim, things had been strained.

"Wonder what's up with the twins," Nico said. "Kakeru, you're in the same year. Try asking them, make it look casual."

"Ask them what?"

"You know, what's on their mind and all that."

"Oh . . . right."

Kakeru assented, but if he was being honest, he felt the burden was too much for him.

Practice was becoming increasingly intense. For instance, they would run twelve kilometers, going relatively slow for the first five kilometers in seventeen minutes, then building up the pace until they reached a pace of three minutes, five seconds for the last kilometers. After that, they would do five sets of one kilometer in two minutes, fifty-five seconds, with two hundred–meter intervals in between.

Kakeru's plate was full just from thinking about his own run. The way he swung his arms, the angle at which he struck the ground, how loose or taut his muscles were—he always asked himself whether everything was in good order. When he ran, he was conscious of every cell in his body, alert to every step he took.

Of course, between practices, he also had to attend lectures on campus. It was hard to find the time or energy to think about how other people were doing.

One day, Kakeru ran into the twins at Tsuru no Yu. Kakeru and Kiyose were sitting in the large bath, the mural of Mount Fuji behind them, and chatting with the plasterer, who had happened to come in at the same time. The twins stepped in and went to the side with the showers to wash up first.

"So, Haiji, how're things going with the fellas at Chikusei-so?" the plasterer asked. He was soaking in the bath with his back to the showers, so he hadn't noticed the twins come in. Normally, the twins would have said something in greeting, but when they saw Kiyose sitting near the tap of the bath, they only gave him a silent nod.

"They're doing well," Kiyose answered.

"The first-years are putting on a good fight, eh?" The plasterer lifted his hands from the water and rubbed his face. "Kakeru's impressive, but you know, those look-alike twins. They've got some real speed, too, that's for sure."

Kakeru fretted over what Kiyose would say. Behind the plasterer, Jota and Joji had pricked up their ears. Distracted by the talk, Joji's hand slipped, squeezing out an enormous drop of shampoo onto his head.

"They really do," Kiyose laughed. "It's a bit odd to say this right in front of them, but yes, they do run well."

"Really?" Jota leaped up from his stool, and the plasterer turned around in surprise.

"Why would I lie?" Kiyose rose from the bath. Turning to the plasterer, he said, "We have promising athletes on our team, so I do hope the people of the shopping arcade will keep supporting us. I'll be heading out now. Excuse me."

Kiyose passed behind the twins, slid open the door, and disappeared into the changing room.

"He only praised us 'cause we're right here," Joji mumbled to no one in particular. But he couldn't hide his delight. He scrubbed vigorously, and his head was soon covered in a fluffy cloud of soap bubbles.

"What's going on, you two? You didn't even say hello when you came in." The plasterer contemplated Kiyose and the twins' demeanor, then turned back to Kakeru, who was still in the bath. "They're not fighting or something, are they?" he asked Kakeru in a low tone.

"Who knows?" Kakeru murmured, sinking down up to his shoulders. "I don't think that's what it is, but I'm not really sure . . ."

Maybe the twins had an issue with Kiyose, but they wouldn't be able to hold it in forever. They were the straightforward type; their childlike honesty made them open books. They were bound to explode, sooner rather than later, and spill everything to Kiyose. It wouldn't be too late to try to patch things up after that.

Kakeru decided to let the twins be. No need to poke at a dormant volcano. When it erupted, the team would see where the mouth of the volcano was. Then, they could make a clear judgment about how everything stood and in which direction the wind blew, and decide whether to evacuate or wait for the flood of lava to cool down. That was Kakeru's take.

In addition to their usual practice, the team also began trial runs on the actual course of the Hakone Ekiden. Since much of the route included roads with heavy traffic, test runs were prohibited, at least according to the official rules. Nevertheless, it would have been unwise to dive into the race without doing at least one trial run.

In the early mornings, when the roads were relatively empty, the Chikusei-so members piled into the van and drove to different parts of the race. They covered the area around Otemachi on some days, and the Shonan coastline on other days. Little by little, they ran fragments of the course to experience the roads with their own two feet. They etched on their bodies and minds the characteristics of the course, such as how it undulated and which landmarks marked what distance.

Kiyose seemed to have constructed a rough order in his mind as to who would run which segment of the race. When they were doing a trial run near Yokohama Station, Kiyose asked, "Kakeru, do you want to run the second leg?"

The part of the race between Tsurumi and Totsuka, passing through

Yokohama, was called the Star-Studded Second. It was usually run by the ace of the team. If a runner performed well at the Hakone Ekiden, whether he ran the second leg might even affect how much he stands out to scouts of corporate track teams looking for promising new talent.

"No," Kakeru replied.

He wasn't attached to the Star-Studded Second. Whatever segment he had to run, it was all the same to him. As long as there was a road in front of him, he would run with everything he had.

"All right," Kiyose said, and went back to checking the course silently for the rest of the run.

In late October, they went to Hakone for a trial run. A narrow road snaked up Mount Hakone. Though it was a little too early for the fall foliage season, there were massive traffic jams on the weekends.

Kiyose parked the van in front of Hakone-Yumoto Station and announced, "Right, everyone. Let's try running up to Lake Ashi."

"No wayyy!" the twins wailed, without missing a beat. "It's a tough climb even when you walk it! You're telling us to *run* there for twenty kilometers?"

"How about whoever's taking this leg of the race just do the run?"

The fifth segment stretched from the Odawara relay station to Lake Ashi, the culmination of the first day of the race. Most of it involved running uphill on Mount Hakone. In contrast, the sixth leg, which began the team's return journey on the second day of the race, was all downhill. The runners for these segments had to run over an elevation difference of more than half a mile.

Each university entered an athlete who specialized in climbing or descending mountains for the fifth and sixth legs. The route required not only speed but also the mental fortitude and physical abilities suitable for this particular environment. It was completely different from running on flat land. For the fifth leg, the runner had to have the tenacity to face the endless uphill climb without quailing. And for the sixth leg, the runner needed the guts to ride on the speed of the steep downhill without holding back. Naturally, both routes were especially hard on the legs, so it was ideal to pick someone who wasn't prone to injuries.

"The fifth leg has Shindo's name all over it," Prince remarked. "He's so good at uphills."

"Are you saying I should run by myself?" Even Shindo's face clouded over at the thought of the long climb.

"We're running up together," Kiyose declared. "Don't you all want to see what lies ahead, where the tasuki goes? This is Lake Ashi we're talking about. It's the most celebrated viewpoint around Tokyo, you know."

"I'll pass for now—I'll see it on race day," King said.

"Most of us won't see it on race day, though," Kakeru pointed out. "We don't have enough people, so besides our own runs, we'll probably divide the work between us. We'll have to accompany each other before the start of each leg."

"Then maybe I'll see it on TV the year after," Joji said, making a last-ditch effort, but Kiyose wasn't listening anymore.

"Come on, hurry up and get started."

Climbing Mount Hakone was more challenging than any of them had imagined. The uphill path twisted and turned, stretching on for what seemed like eternity.

Along with Kiyose and Shindo, Kakeru doggedly ran up the mountain. Kiyose was giving detailed instructions to Shindo about certain points of the course that would help him judge the distance, and what to watch out for. But the rest of the group took every opportunity to try to hop on the Hakone Tozan Railway. Eventually, they slowed down so much that they might as well have been walking.

"Keep up the pace," Kiyose told Shindo, then looked behind him. "What's going on? You're too slow." Kakeru stopped, too, and waited for everyone to catch up. From their cars, the people waiting in the traffic jam peered curiously at the group in tracksuits.

Goaded on by Kiyose, they somehow made it to the sign for the summit.

The highest point of National Route 1 on Mount Hakone was at an altitude of 0.54 miles above sea level. The road widened around the peak, and the view opened up. The wind—much more bracing than in Tokyo—blew over the field of silver grass, making the white-tufted blades sway like waves of the ocean. Kakeru zipped his top up to his neck.

Shindo was waiting for them a few steps from the peak.

"Oh, that looks like . . ." Musa grimaced. It wasn't just Shindo standing there. Several students in Totai tracksuits were loitering around the summit. They must have come for a trial run, too. Kakeru spotted Sakaki among the group, and his stomach turned.

Sakaki patiently waited until all the Chikusei-so members had assembled, then made his way toward the group. While Kiyose took no notice of him, Kakeru braced himself. The others glowered at Sakaki threateningly—not just the twins, but even Nico and Yuki, who usually maintained their cool composure.

Sakaki didn't seem to mind that he was hardly welcome. He stopped in front of Kakeru and addressed him cordially. "Hey, Kurahara. You were pretty impressive at the prelim."

Kakeru was taken aback. It had been a long time since Sakaki had talked to him without lashing out. Kakeru didn't know how to react—"Yeah," he mumbled, barely opening his mouth.

"Doing a trial run today? The Kansei team's that dedicated, huh. Let's both do our best on race day."

Sakaki was smiling up at him. *What's gotten into him?* Kakeru was perplexed. *All he used to do whenever we ran into each other was bug me. This is creepy.* But now that they were advancing to the real race, Sakaki might have changed his mind about the Kansei team and was ready to accept them. His grudge from high school might have melted away when he saw that Kakeru was still putting his 100 percent into running. *I'd be glad if that's how he feels.*

"Yeah." Kakeru nodded. After all, Sakaki was a teammate he had once run alongside. It hurt to be treated with such a prickly attitude for so long.

Sakaki cast a loaded look over the Chikusei-so members standing behind Kakeru. "You sure are dedicated, practicing so hard. We were just talking about you, actually. About what we'd do if *we* were on the Kansei team."

"What do you mean?"

Kakeru didn't see what he was getting at. What difference did teams make? Wouldn't they just practice and keep running wherever they were?

"I mean, no matter how much you practice, Kansei only has ten members," Sakaki went on, a smile still plastered on his face. "If even one of you gets sick and can't run on the day, it's game over. And on the off chance that you do come within tenth place in the race and get seed rights, the fourth-years will graduate, right? What would you do about next year?"

Kakeru was caught off guard. He had been completely focused on running the Hakone Ekiden with everyone at Chikusei-so and delving into his own run that he hadn't even thought about what came next.

He knew that there had been students who wanted to join their team after the prelim and that Kiyose had turned them away. But there was no telling how serious they were. There was no guarantee that they would return next spring and ask to join again. However hard they ran at Hakone, depending on the outcome of the race, come next year the team might not have any new members. In that scenario, the Kansei team would come to an end after only one year.

This reality that Sakaki pointed out sent a quiet shock through the Chikusei-so members. The twins' faces visibly stiffened. Shindo, Musa, and King exchanged worried glances. Nico and Yuki tried to shut Sakaki up by scowling at him, their eyes warning: *Keep out of it*. Only Prince remained unmoved. Squatting on the side of the road out of exhaustion, he yawned as though it had nothing to do with him.

As Kakeru had suspected, Sakaki hadn't forgiven him at all. He had approached the team with a smile only to shake them up.

This realization hit Kakeru with a sharp pang, but he couldn't just stand there looking dejected. He had to act. If there was any uncertainty in their minds, there was no way their team could perform at their best at the Hakone Ekiden. Kakeru glanced at Kiyose. Like a cool iron mask, Kiyose's face betrayed no emotion. He gave Kakeru a look that said, *You handle it yourself.*

It's all because of me that Sakaki makes these jabs at the Kansei team. Kakeru frantically cast about in his head for the right words to hurl back at Sakaki.

But before Kakeru could put his thoughts together, Sakaki said, "See ya," and returned to his teammates.

"He's certainly diligent, in a way." Yuki watched him go, mildly impressed.

"Just the fact that Kakeru didn't try to pounce on him is progress," Kiyose said, still in his iron mask.

True, Kakeru thought. *Not so long ago, I wouldn't have let him get away with sticking his nose in our business.* Kakeru had been so intent on looking for the words to argue back at him that he'd forgotten about the option of throwing a punch. *It would've been so easy if I'd just hit him.* He felt even more frustrated, but at the same time, he was bewildered by the change in himself.

Instead of violence, I'm trying to choose another way.

Kakeru felt unsettled, as if his fangs had been pulled out, but he was also a bit glad that he might be getting closer to resembling Fujioka from Rikudo.

"Don't worry about what he said," Kiyose told everyone. "We're almost at the lake. Let's go."

Mount Fuji, visible straight ahead, had bright white snow capping its peak. The group ran all the way down the slope leading to Lake Ashi.

As they ran, Kakeru heard Jota grumble, "It's hard *not* to worry about it, though," and Joji nodded.

Sakaki's words seemed to bring the rift within the Chikusei-so team into even sharper relief.

After a short break at the lake, it was time to attempt the downhill run back where they had come from. Even Kakeru was surprised. "We're not staying overnight?"

"How do we have that kind of money?" Kiyose replied. Prince edged back toward the bus stop. Kiyose laughed and said, "It's okay, Prince, you don't have to run. Running downhill is a common cause for injuries. Only those of us who might take the sixth leg will run down. The rest can take the bus back to Hakone-Yumoto and wait for us there."

Kiyose named the twins and Yuki.

"Are you saying you don't mind my legs getting hurt?" Yuki said, dissatisfied.

"You and the twins took the Hakone Tozan train from Ohiradai to Kowakidani, didn't you? Did you think I'd let you get away with that?" Kiyose said. "You must have some energy left for running down. And Yuki, your balance seems to suit downhills, too. Your center of gravity is low and steady, maybe because you used to do kendo."

Yuki held his tongue, but the twins were still whispering to each other.

"I'm exhausted. And we *still* have to run back?"

"What's the point of practicing this much?"

"If there's something you want to say, I'll hear you out," Kiyose said to the twins.

The twins shook their heads.

Kiyose was to accompany the twins and Yuki on their run. Kakeru grew worried about his injured leg.

"How about I go instead, Haiji? You shouldn't push yourself too much."

"I'll be all right, I'm going to take it slow. Go on, there's the bus." Kiyose herded the rest of the group onto the return bus.

The bus got stuck in traffic midway down the mountain, and the runners caught up with them. They were flying down the slope. Despite what he had said, Kiyose was closely shadowing the other three, giving them instructions and pointing out things to watch out for.

Sitting in the bus, Kakeru and the rest of the team gazed at the runners. The bus sometimes overtook them, sometimes lagged behind.

"Might've been faster if we'd all run down," Nico muttered, fed up with the bus crawling along.

"I refuse to get off," Prince proclaimed, guarding his seat. Musa and Shindo observed Yuki dashing down the steep gradient in long strides.

"I see, your hip joints have to be flexible for running downhill," Musa said.

"You need springy leg muscles, too," Shindo said, "and a sturdy back and knees to soften the impact of your feet hitting the ground."

King was unusually silent, staring at the twins running down with a serious expression.

Kakeru thought, *I get it now.*

What was the point of running at the Hakone Ekiden, Sakaki had said, when there was no team to pass it on to next year? But he had gotten it all wrong. Running was meant to be something purer than that: an act done for one's own sake.

In the context of an ekiden race, where one runner passed on the tasuki to the next, the purpose of running could expand from "for the self" to "for the team." But that was as far as it got.

In the end, one ran only for oneself. And whether their team would survive in the future would be irrelevant while they ran the Hakone Ekiden.

The very first people to come up with the idea of an ekiden race between Tokyo and Hakone, and put it into action, must have done so because they liked to run. There was no guarantee of what would happen to their team in the future or even whether the same race would be hosted the next year. And yet, because running inspired them, they were driven to start the Hakone Ekiden. They must have had faith that others who shared the same dream would follow after them.

That was why the doors of the Hakone Ekiden were always open to all universities in the Kanto region. This was a crucial difference from the Tokyo Big6 Baseball League, another intercollegiate championship with a long tradition. Because Hakone wasn't limited to certain universities, all runners who harbored the ambition to compete in it—even students from the newest colleges—had a fair chance.

What Sakaki probably wanted to say was "Devoting yourself to track with competent teammates at a powerful university is what serious athletes should do, and that's the whole point of running."

Sakaki's never outright wrong, but he's not like me. What I seek, what I want to discover through running, is something different. And that's all right, Kakeru thought. *It's not a bad thing to be different.* But he felt his chest tighten a little. Even though he and Sakaki had once run together as teammates, and they were both facing the same direction—at least in their commitment to running—there was something between them that was irreconcilable. It pained Kakeru to have to confront their discrepancy: their incompatibility, which had grown over the years, was now finally in plain view.

Kakeru and the others waited for the downhill runners at the Hakone-Yumoto parking lot. By the time everyone had gotten on the van to depart for Chikusei-so, it was already sunset.

Kakeru spoke up during the drive home. "When I was a kid, I used to watch the Hakone Ekiden over New Year's."

"Yeah, me too," Shindo replied, slightly puzzled by Kakeru's sudden inclination to talk.

"Ever since then, I always dreamed of running like that someday. I always wanted to compete in the Hakone Ekiden. I'm glad that my dream came true." Kakeru racked his brain to find the right words to reach his teammates. "That's why I don't think it matters what happens to the Kansei team next year. Even if we don't have enough people after the fourth-years graduate, that doesn't mean it's the end. Some kid might see us on TV somewhere and think, running is cool—the same way I did when I was a kid. Maybe that's good enough."

"Hang on," Prince said, "is this actually your answer to what that guy from Totai said back there?"

"Yes."

"You've gotta say this to his face," said Nico, scratching his stubble.

"Kakeru, you're slow at everything except running. You should practice using your brain a bit more," Yuki joked, stifling a laugh.

"Sorry."

"But you've come a long way—now you can actually say what you think," said Shindo, trying to back him up.

"Yes, well done," Musa joined in.

"They make you sound like a kindergartner," Jota teased, and Kakeru's face burned. Whenever he came up with what he had to say, it was always too late. He felt ashamed and annoyed at himself.

"But Kakeru," King said, poking his head out from the back seat. "Aren't you being a little idealistic?"

"Yeah," Joji chimed in, crossing his arms next to Kakeru. "Let's say some tiny tots get inspired and start running. What does that have to do with us? It's useless, right?"

Kakeru was almost swayed into nodding, but some part of him was screaming, *That's not true.* He hastily shook his head. "I think that's why the race is still going. Because it shows us an ideal," he said. "There's something captivating about seeing someone run. That's why Hakone Ekiden pulls people in. It makes them want to root for runners or start running themselves."

That was all that mattered: To run for the team, for the children watching on TV, and most of all, for oneself. To run in an ideal form with grace and strength.

"You really are like a rock, Kakeru." Joji let out a sigh that was part disbelief and part surrender.

Kiyose remained silent as he turned the steering wheel, and the van pulled into the Odawara-Atsugi Road in the falling night.

After their interview aired on TV, people started recognizing the Chikusei-so team more often, both on campus and in the neighborhood. Some people extended casual words of encouragement: "I saw you on TV!" or "Good luck." Others offered to help out if the team was short on staff.

New applicants seeking to join the team, however, had dwindled. The rumor that Kiyose was turning everyone away had probably spread among the students. Kakeru could only hope they didn't give up and would come back to Chikusei-so next spring.

The administrative preparations for race day were also well under-way. Kiyose and Shindo took the lead and planned out their course of action.

At the Hakone Ekiden, each university stationed its members along the course. At the fifteen-kilometer point of each segment, there was a member in charge of handing a water bottle to the runner. There were also assistants waiting on the side of the road; they relayed intel that could give contestants an advantage in the race. It was useful to have these messengers at strategic points on the route, passing on details such as the time differences between their runners and those around them in the race, or whether their runners should adjust their pace.

The water supplier was required to sprint alongside the athlete to hand them the bottle midrun. Since a complete amateur wouldn't be able to keep up with the pace, the team needed someone who could run to some extent. For this role, the short-distance runners in Kansei's track and field club were happy to help.

Kiyose and Shindo also considered which students to place along-side the course. Among the students who had volunteered to help, they picked out those who lived close to the route. The volunteers would be giving up part of their New Year's holiday to assist the team, so Kiyose didn't want to put too much burden on them.

Since the people of the shopping arcade were bound to come root for the team even if they were told not to, Kiyose felt encouraged to enlist their help for the messenger staff as well.

As the day drew nearer, Kiyose tackled the bits and pieces of non-running work that still needed to be done. Shindo assisted him in negoti-ations with the university, communication with the host of the race, the

Inter-University Athletic Union of Kanto, and the like. Hanako was quick and efficient in managing the volunteers who would be assisting the team on race day, instructing them on their roles and their individual schedules.

Kakeru was impressed by Hanako's aptitude for dealing with these organizational tasks. She had to communicate with so many people to monitor who was available and when, and to make fine adjustments so that everything would run smoothly on the day. He couldn't possibly have handled it himself. Apparently, she even cut back on her sleep to make sure the Chikusei-so team could run the race without any issues.

Although Hanako might have gotten involved only because she had a crush on the twins, now she seemed to be enthralled by the sport itself. She became an indispensable part of the crew, frequently visiting Chikusei-so for various meetings.

One time, when Hanako wasn't around, King blurted out, "She's always hanging out with us—doesn't she have any girlfriends?"

"She does," Kakeru answered. His voice came out gruffer than he'd intended.

Just the day before, he'd caught sight of Hanako at the cafeteria on campus. She was having lunch with some girls, happily chatting away and laughing a lot.

Can't you see how much she's doing to support us? She's prioritizing us over her friends. Kakeru knew King hadn't meant to be rude, but the thoughtless remark got on his nerves. Then he noticed something. *Why am I so angry?* He thought about it for a few moments and concluded he was tired from practice.

That night, in early November, Hanako was once again having dinner at Chikusei-so. Over dinner, she reported to them about how many volunteers were now on board and how they were to be positioned along the course. Kiyose and Shindo commented on her updates, and Hanako jotted down their responses in her small notebook.

Has she told the twins how she feels already? Kakeru wondered. While Hanako was engrossed in the prerace preps, the twins were focused on shoveling down food.

When their discussion with Hanako was finished, Kiyose made an announcement: "We'll participate in the Ageo City Half-Marathon the Sunday after next."

"Where is Ageo?" Musa asked.

"In Saitama Prefecture. It's a relatively large-scale race that many citizen runners compete in, too. They're inviting all the university teams entering the Hakone Ekiden. We get to participate for free, so it's a good deal. Plus, it'll be useful practice running on the road, and you'll get a feel for things like how to grab a good spot at the start of the race and how to run through cheering crowds."

Besides Kakeru and Kiyose, no one had ever run in a race where the course consisted entirely of ordinary roads. And in terms of the time of year, the Ageo City Half-Marathon was the perfect rehearsal for the Hakone Ekiden. Most teams set to compete at Hakone participated in Ageo as well.

It would be the first time that any of them ran more than twenty kilometers on the road for a race. Kakeru's competitive spirit soared at the chance to put the results of his training to the test. He was content to practice on his own, putting in the work day by day, but he still liked running races where he could compete with other athletes.

But the twins had a different idea.

"The Sunday after next? We have plans."

"We're putting together a casual soccer team with the guys from our foreign language class. We finally found a team to play against, so we're gonna have a game on the riverbank field by Tamagawa."

"Can you cancel it?" Kiyose asked.

"They wouldn't have enough people if we dropped out."

"There's still time, two subs shouldn't be hard to find. Besides, playing soccer when we should be focusing on practice? What if you get injured? You've been slacking lately."

Kiyose scolded the twins in a harsher tone than usual, frustrated by the awkward tension that had built up between them over the past few weeks. *What now?* Kakeru panicked. He aimlessly moved his chopsticks up and down in midair.

"Practice this, practice that. What's the point of practicing so much?" Joji slammed down his miso soup on the table. "It's just like that Sakaki guy said. Doesn't matter how hard we run at Hakone. Next spring, we won't have enough members anyway."

"Exactly," Jota followed. "You tricked us, Haiji. Working ourselves to the ground, day in and day out. It's stupid!"

"Tricked?" Kiyose clacked his chopsticks shut. "When did I trick you?"

"When this all started you said, 'We'll band together and conquer the summit.' You said, 'Let's aim for the top.' Remember?" Jota raised his voice. "But that's just not happening. I looked into it. Whatever we do, at our level there's no way in hell we're winning against Rikudo. We can't win first at Hakone!"

"What he said," King joined in, jumping on the bandwagon.

Kiyose seemed to be tracing back in his memory. After a brief pause, he nodded. "That's true. I did say that."

"See? You lied!" Joji said. There was a stir around the table.

Musa asked Kakeru under his breath, "Is it true? Do we have no chance at placing first?"

"Well . . ." Kakeru was reluctant to give him a definite answer, but Yuki, ever the logical one, was ruthless.

"Frankly, I'd say it's impossible. Our time is proof of that."

Nico had a big stretch in his seat. "If we look at each runner's personal best record," he said wearily, "it's easy to predict how the race will go and which team will win. These numbers won't be overturned unless a miracle or something drastic happens. You could say that's the boring part of long-distance races."

"Hmm," Prince hummed, reaching for the salad. "But in most team sports, whether it's baseball, or soccer, or basketball, you can't tell who's going to win except when there's a huge difference between the teams. Is the gap between us and Rikudo *that* big?"

"It is," Yuki replied. He had already analyzed the teams' data. "The regular members on the Rikudo team would be considered aces if they were to transfer to any other university. On top of that, they have a big pool of quality athletes. Even their reserve members—the backups who won't be entered into the Hakone race—are so good that if they were to run Hakone, there's a high chance they'd rank better than we would."

"So you're saying Rikudo is a group of elite runners, and we'll be up against the cream of the crop," Shindo said despondently.

"Depending on how you look at it, though, aren't we the lucky ones?" Prince remarked, munching on some lettuce. "The backups at Rikudo are fast, but they can't run in Hakone. We're a bunch of wimps, but we managed to pass the prelim, so we get to run Hakone. Even if we can't come out on top, I feel like it's more rewarding to actually participate in the race."

"It's a waste of time if we can't win," Joji retorted.

"What's the use in doing a sport where you know the outcome even before you start?" Jota rolled his eyes.

Kakeru frowned and finally entered the fray. "If you want to win so much, there's no time for playing soccer. You should put in more practice and run at Ageo, too."

"Here we go again with your idealism, Kakeru." The twins turned on him at once. "We're saying we just don't feel like practicing when it's pointless anyway."

"You can't make yourselves run if there's no chance of winning? What, are you guys gonna quit living just because you'll die eventually?"

"That's got nothing to do with it."

"It's the same thing. Same logic."

"It's com-*pletely* different. And don't even talk about logic. You don't know what logic is."

"I do!"

"No you don't, you *animal*! You only know how to run!"

"Step outside."

"Bring it on."

Kiyose tried to subdue them, but they didn't listen. The three of them kicked over their chairs as they got up, locking eyes across the table. Musa tugged at Kakeru's sleeve, but Kakeru flung him off. By now they'd forgotten the root of their squabble, and it was turning into a schoolyard fight over muddled arguments. Yuki and Nico watched the course of events with a smirk. Prince seemed impressed by Kakeru's outburst. "His one line about life and death was actually clever, color me surprised," he murmured. King sympathized with the twins, but he feigned ignorance. He wasn't about to get pulled into a brawl.

"Wait, wait a second!" Hanako frantically barred Kakeru and the twins, who looked more than ready to storm out of the house. All eyes turned to Hanako.

"Let's all calm down. I mean, it's not impossible that the whole Rikudo team will get food poisoning on race day. Right?"

"I'm . . . not so sure if that would ever happen . . ." Musa said tentatively.

"And the fact still stands. When it comes to competence, we can't win against Rikudo," Shindo sighed. While her words had done nothing to raise their morale, she had successfully deflated the volatile tension between Kakeru and the twins.

"Thanks for dinner." The twins put away their used plates in the sink and made for their room.

"You're right," Kiyose called to their backs, "I did say let's conquer the summit. But I didn't mean we'll win first place. You might think it's a bad excuse, but—"

"Never mind," Joji said, and the twins disappeared upstairs. His tone suggested that the twins were still uninterested in hearing anything else Kiyose had to say, but also that they were ready to put their issues aside and return to practice as usual. Kakeru slumped back down with a sullen face, not knowing what to do with the anger that had lost its outlet.

"Umm, I guess I'll head home, too." Hanako hastily rose from her chair, anxious to escape the uneasy silence. "Thanks for dinner."

She tried to put away her dishes, but Kiyose stopped her. "Kakeru," he said, "you should see her home." Normally, it was the twins who accompanied her back to Yaokatsu, but it seemed that they would be locking themselves in for the rest of the night. "The night breeze should cool you off."

Though Hanako assured them that she could go home by herself, Kakeru went to the entrance hall to put on his sneakers before she could stop him.

At the table, Yuki and Nico started gossiping.

"Walking alone with Hanako at night?"

"Hopefully he won't have blood rushing to his *other* head . . ."

"That's what I'm afraid of," Musa added, with a reproachful look at Kiyose. "What if he gets in a fight with the twins again over Hanako?"

"He won't," Kiyose replied nonchalantly. "Kakeru's a more loyal friend than he might look."

Kakeru, of course, was completely oblivious to their conversation about him as he traced the road to the shopping arcade, matching Hanako's pace.

Kakeru rarely walked anywhere. If he was going somewhere at a walkable distance, he would rather run. Whether he was heading to the campus or doing groceries at the shopping arcade, it was all part of his jogging. Since he usually dashed through the streets, he hardly ever slowed down enough to take a good look at his surroundings.

But walking with Hanako, he felt so slow that he didn't know what to do with all the time. He let his eyes wander around him, reading a doorplate lit up by a streetlight, observing the branch heavy with satsumas reaching out over the street. Hanako wore a light coat with a lavender scarf wrapped around her neck. *It's the color of akebi fruits*, Kakeru thought. He used to eat them often when he was a kid, running around hills and fields. They tasted like thinned-out sugar water—he could taste it on his tongue now.

"I'm a little surprised," said Hanako. A puff of white breath escaped her lips. Kakeru averted his eyes.

"About what?"

"I didn't think you guys ever fought."

"'Course we do. We're crammed in that tiny apartment, we run together every day. We're bickering pretty much all the time. Don't leave water in the little bucket in the bath, don't sniff other people's socks left lying around after practice, blah blah blah."

"Sniff people's socks?" Hanako chuckled. "Who *does* that?"

Joji. But Kakeru felt bad for throwing cold water on her crush, so he answered, "That's a secret." He worried that she might think it was him, but he couldn't help it.

"I don't know why, but I kinda had this idea that a lot of people who do long-distance are reserved and patient."

"I wouldn't say so. I'm hot-tempered, and the twins and King are chatterboxes."

"But you're pretty mature, Kakeru. Everyone at Chikusei-so is so gentle." Hanako kicked a pebble on the white line of the road. "So I was like, 'Oh, they have fights, too.' I was surprised but also relieved. I mean, you guys can run so fast even when it's like twenty kilometers, and now you'll be going to Hakone. I was feeling like you're getting further and further away from me."

Ah, Kakeru thought, *she really does like the twins.*

He furtively pressed a hand to his chest. *What is this?* He felt a sharp, hissing pain in his heart, like an ice-cold drink stinging his teeth—as though the flesh around his heart were burning from inside, raw and swollen.

They turned the corner of the park and entered the shopping arcade. Streetlamps lined the street on both sides. Artificial momiji maple leaves hung from them, their bright reds and yellows swaying in the breeze. Most of the shops already had their shutters down, closed for the day. Kakeru and Hanako walked down the deserted street in silence.

Three young men who looked like high schoolers darted out of a small, half-shuttered bookshop. Each of them had a big duffel bag slung over his shoulder. They sprinted off toward Soshigaya-Okura Station.

An elderly woman who had been sitting at the counter rushed out to the street after them.

"Stop! Shoplifters!" She tried to chase them, but she was no match for the young men, especially in her slip-on sandals. She noticed Kakeru and Hanako, rooted to the spot in surprise, and looked at them with hopeful eyes.

Hanako came to her senses. "Kakeru, catch them!"

"Uh, me?"

"Go, hurry!"

The high schoolers were running about fifty yards ahead now, but since the street was straight, Kakeru kept them in his sights. He broke into a run. The students seemed to have their guard down, assuming that the old woman wouldn't be able to chase after them. They were slowing down when they heard Kakeru's footsteps drawing closer. "Crap!" They started up again, fleeing as fast as they could.

But they were only amateurs, weighed down with heavy bags to boot. Kakeru had them within range in no time. He observed their run from behind. *I can catch them anytime I want.*

It was three against one, though. If he just sprang on them by himself, one or two might get away. And if they all ganged up on him, it would be unwise to get into a fistfight when the big race was coming up soon.

The best option was to make them give up on their getaway, Kakeru decided, and ran right up to the trio.

"Hey there," he called to them, still running. They spun around in shock and hastily sped up. For Kakeru, though, they were like tortoises trying to quickly shuffle forward. "At this rate, I could keep chasing you guys for another eighteen miles at least."

The high schoolers were creeped out by this stranger who was casually talking to them without so much as panting. "What the hell?" one of them sputtered.

Ignoring his question, Kakeru went on trying to persuade them. "You might as well give up. Just apologize to the bookshop lady and ask her to forgive you."

The train station was coming into view. Kakeru saw two police officers in uniform running toward them from the koban box in front of the station.

"Stop right there!" the officers shouted, arms wide-open. They seized two of the high schoolers, and Kakeru reluctantly grabbed the other one. "Open your bags."

The students gave up their struggle and obeyed the officers' order. Their bags were packed with manga. They had likely stolen the books just to sell them off, with no intention of reading them. *If Prince was here, he'd be furious*, Kakeru thought.

"You there—well done. Can you come with us to the koban? It's just around the corner," a young officer said to Kakeru with a smile.

At first, Kakeru murmured, "No, I'll just . . ." but there were only two officers against three shoplifters. He had no choice but to follow them, keeping a tight grip on the high schooler's arm.

"Kakeru!"

Kakeru turned around. Hanako was speeding toward them on her bicycle. The old woman from the bookshop was riding on the carrier behind her. It turned out that Hanako had called the police from her cell, and the koban officers had received the alert. *Won't she get in trouble for riding double?* Kakeru wondered, but the officers turned a blind eye.

Climbing down from the rack, the old woman thanked Kakeru. "I hear you're an athlete running in the Hakone Ekiden. You saved the day, dear."

The high schoolers were to be taken to the local police station. The officers had to draw up a report, so the old woman accompanied them.

"Would you mind coming along to the station? You might get a certificate of appreciation."

Kakeru shuddered at the prospect and frantically refused the invitation. The officers looked disappointed, but Kakeru left the scene without even mentioning his name. Hanako followed him, pushing along her bicycle.

"You were amazing, Kakeru. The bookshop lady said there's been so many shoplifters lately, she didn't know what to do. She was really grateful you went after them."

Kakeru looked down a little as he walked. It wasn't like he'd meant to do anything good. He was just good at running, that was all. He only chased them because Hanako asked him to—no different from a dog running after a Frisbee out of reflex.

Hanako was so happy about Kakeru's feat that he felt his throat constrict.

"I don't really get it," he said in a low voice when it became unbearable. "I've shoplifted before, too. I don't think it's necessarily a good or bad thing. I don't really know."

Kakeru was still looking down, but he sensed Hanako look up at him, wide-eyed.

"All I care about is running. Everything else fades away pretty quickly. I'd shoplift if I got hungry, and I'd punch people if they got on my nerves. You said everyone at Chikusei-so is gentle. But that's not me. Just like the twins said, I only know how to run. I'm an—"

"If you were an animal, you wouldn't be worrying over how you don't know the difference between good and bad," Hanako said quietly. "You're too harsh on yourself, Kakeru. The bookshop lady was so thankful you jumped in. Everyone at Chikusei-so is inspired by your run, and they trust you. Don't you think you can put more faith in that?"

When they reached Yaokatsu, she said, "Thanks for seeing me home. See you later," and waved to him with a smile. Kakeru watched her disappear into Yaokatsu's side door. He realized he'd had his hand in the air, mirroring hers, and his ears grew hot.

He ruminated over what Hanako had told him: to believe in the people around him. Come to think of it, Kiyose had once told him to believe in himself more. He had a feeling that they both came down to the same thing.

Another fight with the twins, Kakeru thought. In high school, he'd clashed with Sakaki and the track coach because they couldn't understand each other. Kakeru was quick to lose his temper. For him, running was a vital part of his life. He spent almost all his waking hours on running. So whenever he found himself at odds with people over things related to running, he overreacted. Their disagreement made him feel as if they had invalidated his entire existence.

But I can't keep going like this. They were two sides of the same coin: his anger, on one side, and, on the other, his fear and lack of confidence. When Kiyose and Hanako told him to believe, they must have meant he shouldn't be afraid to accept himself and others.

I can't grow stronger just by running. I have to take control of myself— like Haiji and Hanako, who use words to try to tell me how they really feel. Kakeru renewed his determination to change.

He ran the rest of the way back to Chikusei-so.

The next afternoon, a journalist for the *Yomiuri Shimbun* community pages came to visit. The bookshop lady had been so touched by what Kakeru had done that she called the newspaper's office. The newspaper decided it would also be good press for the Hakone Ekiden, so they set aside some space on their pages to report the incident as a little heartwarming story.

The twins forgot all about their fight and congratulated him: "That's awesome, Kakeru!" Prince also gave him his props, commenting that "shoplifting at a bookstore is a crime that must be eradicated."

Yuki, on the other hand, teased Kakeru. "For once, you had Hanako all to yourself—wasn't there something else you should've done before catching shoplifters?"

Kakeru couldn't exactly turn away the journalist, so he accepted the interview. The article was published under the headline "Kansei Athlete for Hakone Ekiden Catches Shoplifters," along with Kakeru's headshot.

In mid-November, when people were beginning to put on thick winter coats, the Ageo City Half-Marathon was held.

Packs of athletes from invited universities arrived at the Ageo Sports

Park Athletics Stadium in microbuses. The Chikusei-so team made their way to the venue in their usual white van. This time, they were accompanied by the landlord, who had been convalescing from his stomach ulcer at home. Hanako brought out the Yaokatsu minitruck especially for him; he still refused to get in any vehicle when Kiyose was behind the wheel.

The exterior of the Athletics Stadium looked like the Colosseum. Each university team had laid out a tarp in its passageways to secure space for changing into uniforms and resting.

There were food stalls around the park, and a festive mood filled the air. The whole area in and around the park was bustling with spectators and contestants.

The landlord bought a pack of takoyaki as soon as they arrived. He addressed the team between mouthfuls of the steaming hot treat. "Today's goal is to familiarize yourselves with how things go in a road race, so no need to focus on speed. Feel free to run at a comfortable pace, everyone."

The landlord glanced at Kiyose, who nodded. Kakeru guessed what was going on. The landlord had merely relayed Kiyose's instructions. Since there was friction between the team members, Kiyose had chosen to take a step back.

In spite of their issues with Kiyose, the twins did join the team for the Ageo race. They seemed to have found replacements for the soccer game. True to their cheerful and loyal nature, they didn't ditch the team or break their promise, even while rebelling against Kiyose.

The half-marathon began at 9 a.m. on the stadium track. The invited athletes alone numbered roughly 350 people, and on top of that, there were the amateur citizen runners. When the shot was fired, it took some time even to cross the starting line.

A massive crowd was swarming around the starting point, lined up in the order of their bib numbers. Even in their tank tops and shorts, no one felt the cold. Kakeru saw the Totai group ahead. He stared at the back of Sakaki's head for a while. He was too far away for Kakeru to make out the two swirls in his hair.

Kiyose was teaching Prince about potential pitfalls and how to secure a good position at the beginning of a race. "Careful not to trip over if someone pushes you from behind. There's no need to get ahead of people in a rush. Instead, shadow some runners who match your pace and use them as a windshield. In your case, you don't have to think about putting on a spurt. The most important thing is sticking to a pack and trying not to fall behind as much as you can."

Prince nodded dutifully. *Haiji might be thinking of putting Prince in the first leg*, Kakeru thought. In the first leg of Hakone, the first runners of all twenty teams would set off together from Otemachi. Since they would start out in a pack, the segment was suited for a runner who wouldn't shy away from competing against others while keeping a close eye on everyone's pace.

Compared to the kind of athletes running at Hakone, Prince's time was definitely not on the fast side. How effective would it be to put him in the first leg?

While Kakeru was mulling this over, the pack finally began to move forward. By the time they did a half lap around the track and entered the road, the participants had spread out, and it became easier to run.

They passed through a quiet shopping arcade along the old Nakasendo route. Kakeru felt the flow of the river nearby and the greenery of the golf course. Under the cloudless blue sky, the wintry wind felt refreshing against his body as it heated up.

It felt good to run on roads with regulated traffic. Kakeru soon got into rhythm, hitting wide-open strides. People came out of the houses along the course to cheer for them. Children who had been playing in a small park sprinted after them, trying to catch up.

There were three water stations. Rows of paper cups were ready on the long tables, and the volunteer staff were reaching out to hand them to the runners. The runners were going faster than a bicycle. Since Kakeru wasn't used to this, it was tricky to grab the cup. He edged toward the sidewalk as much as possible, but most of the water spilled out from the impact when he took it.

Still, what little water was left felt cool and sweet.

Just before the halfway point, he passed Sakaki. Sakaki threw him a look, but Kakeru pretended not to notice. It was the coach's view—in other words, Kiyose's—that they shouldn't strain themselves in this race. *Besides, it looks like I'll never get along with Sakaki. I better just let him be*, Kakeru decided.

Kakeru was carefully observing the Rikudo athletes. As expected, they had good form, but they all seemed to be backup members. Kakeru turned to one of them, presumably a first-year, who had turned the halfway point at around the same time as him. "Where's Fujioka?" he asked.

The first-year was taken aback at his sudden question, but he seemed to recognize Kakeru. "The regulars are gone for altitude training in Kunming," he explained.

"Kunming?"

"In China."

"Whoa." Kakeru was stunned. *Rikudo really is on a whole different level*. He wondered whether they wouldn't get diarrhea there. Though he couldn't imagine Fujioka, with his inhuman discipline and training, making such a blunder.

The first-year sped away. Kakeru felt like humming along as he kept to his pace of three minutes, three seconds per kilometer. Fujioka was bound to return from China even stronger than before. Kakeru was impatient to confront him at Hakone. *I'll prove which of us is faster at the big race.*

The runners returned to the stadium to cross the finish line. Since the Kansei team had held back their speed, their rankings weren't great. But they got the hang of racing on the road. Even Prince, the slowest of the group, looked satisfied after completing the race. He had managed to run about the same distance as one segment at Hakone without breaking down. This fact seemed to have instilled confidence in him. Kiyose's strategy of entering the team's inexperienced members in a half-marathon paid off.

The event's host offered all the invited teams bento boxes and bananas for lunch. Shindo and Musa went to pick them up from the administrative committee's tent and came back with a cardboard box full of bananas.

"That's a lot of bananas," Jota and Joji said, peering into the box.

Hanako saw the stickers on the bananas and remarked, "These are quality," appraising them like the grocer's daughter she was.

As a quick way of refueling calories, bananas made the perfect post-workout snack. As they were wolfing down one banana after another, someone approached them. It was a man in his thirties, dressed casually like the other onlookers.

"You're the Kansei track team, aren't you?"

Joji stuffed his third banana into his mouth. "Yef, we are." He munched, looking up at the stranger. "Can we helf?"

"Is Kakeru Kurahara here?" the man said, his eyes fixed on Kakeru. He seemed to know Kakeru's face already. "I'd like to have a little chat."

Kakeru stood up and took his business card. It read: *Truth Monthly*, Shuji Mochizuki.

Most of the group assumed that the journalist wanted to ask Kakeru about the incident with the shoplifters, but Kakeru knew better. This journalist had come because he'd sniffed out Kakeru's past.

"You're from Sendai Jōsei Senior High, aren't you?" Mochizuki began. From the corner of his eye, Kakeru saw that Kiyose changed color and rose to his feet.

"Yes," Kakeru answered.

"So, you caught some shoplifters the other day. I saw it in the papers." Mochizuki arched his eyebrows in an exaggerated show of admiration. "They're saying you're a sportsman through and through, with a strong sense of justice. Folks in your hometown, too—especially the people around your old track team."

Kiyose stepped up next to Kakeru and confronted Mochizuki. "I don't remember giving you permission to interview our teammate."

"Don't worry, I won't take long," Mochizuki chuckled. But there was a caustic glint in his eyes. "Mr. Kurahara. You ran in the interschool championship when you were in your second year of senior high and achieved glowing results. But you quit the track and field club in the very beginning of your third year. Why was that?"

"Leave him alone!" Kiyose bristled, but Kakeru stopped him.

"It's fine, Haiji." Kakeru couldn't run or hide from the past. As long as he stayed in the track world, that incident would keep following him around. He'd already steeled himself for this when he decided to aim for Hakone with the residents of Chikusei-so.

"You've done all the research, haven't you?" Kakeru said to the journalist. "It was because I punched the coach."

"From what I heard, you broke the coach's nose. And what's more, you turned down recruitment offers from several universities and quit the team. Even though the coach tried to deal with the issue privately because he was afraid it would turn into a scandal." Mochizuki scrutinized Kakeru's face. "Tell me, what were you so dissatisfied with? What beef did you have with the coach?"

Kakeru was silent. His coach back then was well known for his harsh, spartan method of training and his micromanagement of his athletes. Of course, no one could deny he was a capable coach when his team produced results that justified the measures.

Kakeru, however, didn't get along with him from the start; he was irked by the coach's obsession with records. And so, when he walked into the locker room and stumbled on the coach berating a first-year student whose injury had made it difficult for him to return as an athlete, Kakeru couldn't stop the blood from rushing to his head. That first-year student was on a sports scholarship. If he was forced to quit the team, he might not have been able to stay at the school. To Kakeru, it seemed that the coach was just being a bully and taking advantage of the student's weakness.

But in retrospect, Kakeru realized that incident might have only been a trigger—merely a convenient igniter to set off an explosion of all the pent-up anger inside him. For in the instant Kakeru punched the coach, the only thought he had in his head was *I can finally end it.*

He didn't hit the coach for the first-year student. There wasn't a grain of heroism in Kakeru. He didn't even stop to think about how awkward the first-year might feel if an older student hit the coach because of him or how the other members of the team would blame him. Kakeru wasn't driven by a sense of justice or by sympathy. He merely used violence for his own gratification. Just to let out all the frustration and rage that had built up inside him. The moment the cartilage in the coach's nose cracked against his fist, Kakeru felt liberated.

"An act of violence in a high school track team," the journalist pressed, "and a well-reputed team in the track world, at that. Word got out, and since you didn't deny the charge, the track team had to refrain from club activities for a while. I wouldn't be surprised if the people involved back then still bear some ill will toward you. Obviously the coach, whose nose *and* record suffered, would be one of them—and your teammates who had to withdraw from races."

"What do you want to ask Kurahara exactly?" Kiyose cut in. "Even if what you say is true, shouldn't you be questioning the attitude of the school that tried to sweep it under the rug? Or how about the larger context—that some high school track teams put results above everything else? The excessive restraints and coercion they use to control the student athletes, which risks crushing young talent?"

"Are you the captain of the Kansei team?" Mochizuki looked at Kiyose, sizing him up. "Did you know about Mr. Kurahara's history of violence? What do you think of him?"

"He's a gifted athlete. More than that, he's a true friend we can trust."

A true friend. Something inside Kakeru quivered at the phrase, as if somebody had shaken him awake in the middle of a pleasant sleep. Floating in the lingering folds of his dreams, he felt a pang of regret at being jolted back into reality but also relieved to find the face of a good friend looking back at him when he opened his eyes. A tangle of emotions welled up inside him, and he faltered, uncertain how to take everything in.

But Kiyose was too focused on Mochizuki to notice. He stood his ground against the journalist, unyielding. "Please leave. If you want an interview, you can go through our PR managers."

PR managers? A murmur ran through the Chikusei-so members, who had been watching the scene unfold. Shindo and Hanako raised their hands as if to say, *Yes, that's us.*

"We'll have to decline your interview request," Shindo said. King added, "You betcha," with a nod. The landlord stayed out of it; he was busy eating his bento lunch, aloof and carefree. It was impossible to say whether he was troubled or amused by the situation.

"Ugh, you ruined the bananas," Nico grumbled, throwing a scornful look at Mochizuki.

The journalist smiled wryly and said, "Fine, just one last thing. You'll be running at Hakone soon, Mr. Kurahara. Anything you want to say to your coach from Sendai? Like, 'in your face!' or whatever."

"I have nothing to say." Kakeru shook his head quietly. He had no intention of apologizing, nor did he have any desire to triumph over the coach. He wasn't about to start boasting that his own abilities were enough to survive in the world of track; he didn't have to obey an instructor like him. "I regret what I did. That I couldn't think of any other way to deal with the problem than knocking him down. That's all."

A week later, *Truth Monthly* published a two-page spread with the headline "What's Happening to High School Sports?!" followed by a provocative subheading: "Stories Behind the Spate of Scandals." The articles touched on various incidents among prominent schools in the Koshien baseball tournament and soccer championships, including the past troubles of the track team at Sendai Jōsei:

"The student runner K—who recently had a taste of the limelight when he caught some shoplifters—is an athlete with a promising future, set to participate in the upcoming Hakone Ekiden. But rumor has it that he, too, sparked off a violent incident in the past. The coach of the track team at Sendai J Senior High School refused to disclose any details, only suggesting 'It's all in the past now,' but . . ."

The article prattled on in this vein. Even a reader who didn't have anything to do with the track world would easily guess who the writer was talking about.

"I bet the coach leaked it," Joji said in disgust, hurling the magazine. Musa tried to console Kakeru. "It's not worth our attention."

Kiyose and Shindo were busy dealing with inquiries from the university and the supporters' group. The landlord, too, was going around everywhere and apologizing for the commotion. When Kakeru found out and apologized to him, he said proudly, "Not to worry, it's part of my job as the coach." He let Kakeru go without so much as a warning.

Since Kiyose took a firm stance to protect Kakeru no matter what, Chikusei-so remained peaceful. Kakeru knew that the sensation stirred up by the article would die down in time, but that didn't change the fact that he'd brought trouble on the team.

Still, everyone at Chikusei-so treated him as they always had. This only strengthened his resolve to do his best run at Hakone, and he carried on with his training.

One night, the Chikusei-so team assembled in the twins' room after practice for a drinking party. Kiyose was supposed to make an announcement about their official entry in the Hakone Ekiden.

Kiyose himself had gone off somewhere after practice, so Nico and Jota were left in charge of the cooking. Guessing they must be cooking up a storm of pub grub to go with the alcohol, Kakeru left the twins' room and was about to go help in the kitchen when his phone rang. His home number in Sendai flashed on the screen.

Since Kakeru had come to Tokyo, his parents had never once called him. He'd sent them a quick postcard to let them know his new address, but that was it. They still paid his tuition and put the bare minimum to get by in his bank account, so he had to be content with that. His parents had pinned their hopes on him. They'd expected their son to be a track athlete of impeccable conduct and to go to college on a sports scholarship.

When he pressed the call button, he heard his mother's familiar voice. "Kakeru?"

"Yeah?"

"You were in the tabloids, weren't you? How many times do I have to tell you not to do anything that brings the wrong kind of attention? Your father's angry, too, you know. Are you listening?"

"Yeah. Sorry."

"Just try to imagine how we feel living over here—what would our neighbors think? Put yourself in our shoes."

"I will."

"What are you going to do for New Year's? Are you coming back?"

"No, I'll be running in Hakone. I don't think I'll have time for that."

"Oh, I see." His mother was clearly relieved. "Fine. Take care."

For a while, Kakeru stood motionless in the middle of the staircase, clutching his silent phone. Spaced out, he didn't even notice Yuki standing by the front door.

"Uh, sorry," Yuki said. "I didn't mean to eavesdrop." He was holding a bag from a record store in Shimokitazawa. Yuki made time for music no matter how busy he was.

Kakeru replied, "It's all good," and climbed down the rest of the stairs to join Yuki in the hallway.

"Was that your folks?"

"Yes. They're mad at me for making the tabloids."

"Well, you're the man of the hour," Yuki laughed.

Maybe I can tell Yuki. Yuki was the only one who hadn't been happy about their interviews. He might lend an ear to Kakeru's oppressive thoughts. "Things aren't going well with my parents," he said off-handedly.

Yuki was quiet for a moment. "I see. Same here," he said. "In my case, I guess you could say they're overprotective. My mom remarried. He's not a bad guy, and it's not like I don't care about my little sister . . . But it's a bit late to have a new family thrust on me. When they fret over me, I don't know what to do. To be honest, I kind of want to stay out of their way."

"How old is your sister?"

"Five."

"She's that much younger?"

"Yeah. Don't know how my mom still had the energy." Yuki pushed up his glasses with a weary air. "Generally speaking, family tends to mean trouble. It's best not to expect too much of them and keep a reasonable distance."

Yuki headed to his own room. Realizing that Yuki was giving him advice, Kakeru replied, "Yes."

Just as he turned to peek into the kitchen—which had been raucous with the sounds of streaming water and clanging saucepans during their whole conversation—Yuki came back. "By the way, Kakeru," he murmured, gesturing at Kakeru to come over to the edge of the hallway. "On my way back, I saw Haiji at the train station in Seijo."

Did he have something particular to buy? Seijo had a station where express trains stopped, but the Chikusei-so members didn't go there often. They tended to prefer the neighborhood around Soshigaya-Okura Station, which had a relatively homely air with a jumble of buildings.

"He went to see an orthopedic doctor by the station," Yuki said.

Kakeru felt an unpleasant jolt. He pictured Kiyose's old scar that ran down his right shin. Kiyose did look like he was in pain after the prelim. The tabloid incident and all that practice had pushed this worry out of Kakeru's head.

"I don't know much about track athletes' injuries," Yuki said with a frown, "but maybe he's not fully recovered?"

In any sport, first-rate athletes would likely experience some kind of injury. Track wasn't an exception. The intense training always went hand in hand with risk. The harder runners practiced, the sharper and more brittle their bodies became.

"If he's seeing a doctor, they should stop him from doing anything reckless, so it might actually be safer that way . . ." Kakeru murmured.

"Do you think Haiji would listen to a doctor? Especially now."

He's got a point, Kakeru thought. Kiyose must have felt a certain level of discomfort or even palpable pain to choose to go to a doctor. He might ask the doctor to prescribe something to keep the pain at bay, but Kakeru had the feeling Kiyose would ignore any warnings the doctor might give him.

"You're right. I'll try asking him later," Kakeru assured Yuki.

By the time they were all gathered in the twins' room, Kiyose had slipped back into Chikusei-so without their noticing. Kakeru carefully sniffed the air around Kiyose to check for that pungent, minty smell of pain-relief patches, but he couldn't detect anything. All he got was a comment from Kiyose: "You're a weirdo."

"We're getting a lot of background noise these days," Kiyose began, looking over the assembled members sitting in a circle. "Well, just ignore them. All we have to do is prove ourselves with our run."

"Whoop whoop, Haiji!" the twins hooted, already a little tipsy. "'Leave our Kurahara alone.'" They were mimicking Kiyose's response to the *Truth Monthly* journalist. Ever since that incident, they'd started to regain their trust in Kiyose.

"It's almost the end of November. We don't have much time till Hakone," Kiyose went on. "From now on, staying in good shape will be more important than ever. Make sure you don't get any last-minute injuries."

At the word *injuries*, Kakeru couldn't help but exchange glances with Yuki.

"Kakeru, can you explain how the official entry works at Hakone?" Kiyose asked.

Kakeru shook off his worries for the moment as everyone turned to look at him. "First, we submit our entry list to the organizer by December tenth, naming up to sixteen people per team. At this stage, we don't reveal who's going to run which section of the race," Kakeru explained. "Then we submit the section entries by December twenty-ninth. Each team narrows down their runners to fourteen members, and we register ten of them in their respective segments. The remaining four are treated as backups. On the day of the race, we'll be allowed to change who runs which leg. The final lineup will be announced one hour before the start—that's for both the first day going up to Mount Hakone and the second day going down. The only exception is that once a runner is taken out of a section, they can't be reregistered for another one."

"I don't get it. What does that mean?" Joji asked.

Kakeru thought about it a little and tried to reframe the rule in simpler terms. "Let's say Fujioka on the Rikudo team was registered for the second leg as of December twenty-ninth. If they want to make some last-minute changes on race day, they won't be allowed to put him in any other leg. If Fujioka gets sick on the day, he can only swap with one of the four backups. Even if he's all better the next day, he won't be allowed to run any part of the race."

"That makes sense." Musa nodded. "On the flip side, if Mr. Fujioka is among the four reserve runners as of the twenty-ninth, we can be certain that the Rikudo team will change their lineup on the day of the race."

"Exactly," Kiyose said. "If a strong runner is in the reserve list, he's either in poor shape or the team's going to pull a hidden ball trick by swapping a runner at a crucial part of the race. When the first lineup goes public on the twenty-ninth, all the teams will analyze it and re-evaluate their strategy. They'll try to read between the lines, get at their opponents' true intentions, and switch tactics if needed."

"Can't let our guard down right up to the race, huh." King sounded intimidated. "Does that have anything to do with us, though? We've only got ten members. What tactics could we use?"

"True. In our case, we'll have to show our cards early on, with the entry on the twenty-ninth." Kakeru looked at Kiyose anxiously. The Kansei team had no backups, which meant that once they registered for their respective segments, there was no chance of switching places. He wanted to know what Kiyose thought about their position.

"We're not the only one with a small team," Kiyose said with perfect composure. "There are pros and cons to changing the lineup on race day. It doesn't always go down well when you're suddenly told to run. As a matter of fact, many teams follow a principle of not making any changes to the section entries unless there's an emergency. As long as you're aware of the fact that these tactics can come into play with the lineup, it's better to be certain about which leg you're running at an early stage. That way, you can get in the right headspace."

"I guess you've already decided which leg each of us will run?" Yuki asked.

"Yeah," Kiyose replied, then straightened up. "We can talk if you have any objections, of course. But for now, I believe this is the best combination."

Kiyose pulled out a note from his pants pocket and spread it out in the middle of their circle. Everyone leaned forward eagerly to peer at the list, letting out murmurs of surprise.

To Hakone (day 1)

Leg 1	Otemachi—Tsurumi	Prince
Leg 2	Tsurumi—Totsuka	Musa
Leg 3	Totsuka—Hiratsuka	Jota
Leg 4	Hiratsuka—Odawara	Joji
Leg 5	Odawara—Hakone	Shindo

From Hakone (day 2)

Leg 6	Hakone—Odawara	Yuki
Leg 7	Odawara—Hiratsuka	Nico
Leg 8	Hiratsuka—Totsuka	King
Leg 9	Totsuka—Tsurumi	Kakeru
Leg 10	Tsurumi—Otemachi	Kiyose

"Me, run the second leg? I can't do that." Musa shuddered. "The second leg is for the ace of the team, isn't it? Why not Kakeru?"

"Putting Prince first is a pretty bold move, too . . ." Joji tilted his head hesitantly.

Even Prince himself mumbled, "Why would you throw away the race from the very beginning?"

Kakeru took one look at the lineup and understood Kiyose's intent. *Haiji's betting on the latter half of the race. He really is going for the seed rights. And if the race goes as he expects, we might get more than that. With this lineup, we might even rise higher than tenth place . . . !*

Though they were an underdog team with no guarantee that they'd have enough members to continue next year—a random group of amateurs who'd just managed to crawl up to where they stood now—Kiyose's ambition knew no bounds. He was constantly aiming higher, confidently leading the residents of Chikusei-so toward a single dream and purpose. He was always striving to reach new heights in running, and his sights were set on the summit: on conquering the Hakone Ekiden, the ultimate cross between individual and team sports.

Kakeru could sense just how serious Kiyose was about this battle, and he clenched his fists as tight as he could. That was the only way he could stop himself from getting swept away by the rush of excitement.

"No one else can take the first leg, Prince," Kiyose said gently. "You remained undaunted at the track meets and the prelim—maybe because you have no interest in three-dimensional things. The first leg attracts a lot of attention, so you're a perfect fit. Plus, you managed to keep up with all the practice even though you were slow as molasses. If you have to compete neck and neck with our opponents, I'm sure you can hang in there."

There he goes again with the backhanded compliments, Kakeru thought. But Kiyose's expectations for Prince were meant in earnest. Prince seemed to sense that, too, and a light kindled in his eyes.

"But the first leg's usually been fast-paced in the past few years," Yuki interjected. "It could be the same this time, too. Won't the other teams prioritize speed when they choose their first runner?"

"We also can't rule out the possibility that they'll go in the opposite direction this year and try taking it slow. It's a gamble," Kiyose readily admitted. "But even if Prince lags behind, there'll be plenty of time for us to recover if it's just the first leg. That's why I put strong, reliable members from the second to fourth legs. As for the fifth leg, Shindo's an obvious choice, right? I'm confident that Musa and the twins will carry the race forward to that handoff with solid runs."

"But the second leg is for the best of the best. I'm not sure I can bear such a heavy responsibility." Musa didn't seem convinced.

"What do you think?" Kiyose threw the question to Kakeru instead. "It looks like Musa wants you to run the second leg."

"No. I think Musa is the right choice," Kakeru answered firmly. "He's had to deal with so much pressure, but he never let it get to him and has stuck to practice all this time. Even though he'd never done long-distance before, now he can run ten kilometers in just over twenty-nine minutes. Besides, he always knows what to say to keep me going." In terms of hard work and character, Musa would excel over any other athlete. No one deserved to be called the ace more than him.

"You're too kind, Kakeru," Musa said bashfully, but the vote was unanimous: he would run the second leg.

No one opposed the twins running the third and fourth legs, and the pair themselves were keen on the idea.

"The third leg—that's the one that goes by the coast, right? I'll get ocean views," said Jota.

"I wanna eat some kamaboko at Odawara!" Joji chimed in.

Everyone agreed the fifth leg was for Shindo, but the problem was the downhill climb of the sixth. "Why put me in the sixth leg?" Yuki demanded an explanation.

"When we did the trial run the other day, your posture was balanced and steady. Most people get a bit nervous when they sprint down a slope that steep. They tense up and lean back, but you didn't." Kiyose glanced at Yuki's legs, crossed on the floor. "And on top of that . . . you have thick legs."

"What?"

"Don't get me wrong, it's a compliment. Your lower body has to be strong enough to handle the sixth leg—otherwise, it's out of the question."

"You make it sound like sturdy legs are my only asset. What if I get hurt?"

"I don't see a problem with that. You've already passed the bar. You probably won't have time to run at serious track races after graduating."

"Come on, you can't be so cruel . . ." Nico cut in, but Yuki was surprisingly unfazed.

"Fair enough," Yuki said, concurring with Kiyose. So long as it made logical sense, Yuki would have accepted any reasoning, however heartless. It was a method of persuasion fine-tuned to Yuki's mindset. Kakeru was once again in awe of Kiyose's dexterity in manipulating people.

"As for Nico-senpai in the seventh leg and King in the eighth," Kiyose went on, "by the time we get to that stage of the way back, the runners will be spread out, and it's likely that you'll be running all by yourself in some parts of the course. You won't be able to see anyone else running around you. I trust Nico-senpai and King can keep running steadily at their own pace, without getting impatient or letting their guard down. And it's around then that competition for the seed rights will start getting more heated. These sections aren't flashy, but they're definitely important."

"Are you still aiming for the seed rights?" Joji asked timidly.

"Of course," Kiyose said. "Now, for the ninth leg, we'll have Kakeru. It's 'the other second leg' that's considered the ace's turn on the return route. As the one who roped you guys into this in the first place, I'll take the responsibility of running the tenth leg as the anchor."

Kiyose kept his words brief for Kakeru and himself, but Kakeru felt the full force of everything that Kiyose was pouring into the Hakone Ekiden—as well as what kind of run they would have to perform in the ninth and tenth legs.

Kakeru looked at Kiyose. Kiyose gave him a nod.

"That's all from me. Any questions or comments?" Kiyose said to the group.

No one raised a hand. Kiyose's conviction was infectious. As the Hakone Ekiden turned into a tangible reality, the fire inside them began to blaze.

"Good. Everything I've told you is top secret till the lineup announcement on the twenty-ninth. I want all of you to visualize your own run and thoroughly research your own section." Kiyose took his sake cup and invited everyone to drink up. "With this team, I know everything will go well. Jota, Joji."

The twins looked up in response.

"I promise I'll show you the summit. No—we'll all see it together. Look forward to it." Kiyose smiled like a fearless king.

Later, when the drinking party reached its climax, Kakeru sidled up to Kiyose. "Haiji, aren't you having trouble with your leg?" he murmured.

"Why do you ask?" Kiyose replied calmly, helping himself to more sake.

Kakeru didn't know what to say. Kiyose would never complain to him. But Kakeru still couldn't shake away the doubts swirling inside him.

Kiyose had told Yuki that he probably wouldn't have time to run at serious track races after graduating. Kakeru wanted to press Kiyose: *Weren't you actually talking about yourself back there? Aren't you planning to tackle this race ready to give up on running forever?*

He shuddered just to think about it. For Kakeru, losing his ability to run was the same as dying. He guessed the same went for Kiyose.

But Kiyose only smiled at him. "There's nothing for you to worry about. Come on, drink up." He poured more sake into Kakeru's cup.

Lost for words, Kakeru downed his anxiety with his drink. Kiyose was wearing his old dotera jacket, the one with the frayed sleeves. Soon, Kakeru would have spent all four seasons with the residents of Chikusei-so.

Kakeru recalled the night he met Kiyose for the first time—the beginning of everything.

Emotions he couldn't put a name to grew in his chest, as if he was nostalgic for the past and eager for the future all at once.

The Chikusei-so residents remained committed to their training in December, too. They quietly passed the end of the year, all together in their run-down house.

On New Year's Eve, they went to a local temple to strike the bell bidding goodbye to the old year, and on New Year's Day, they ate Kiyose's homemade ozoni soup.

With every passing hour, the air around them grew taut with tension, but even that felt invigorating. Because they weren't alone. At Chikusei-so, all the team members could feel the presence of the others with whom they had practiced and shared their lives all this time.

They were never alone. Until they started running.

But they had teammates who would always wait for them, however long it took—to watch over their run from start to finish and welcome them back when they returned.

That was the essence of the ekiden.

At last, on January 2, the Hakone Ekiden began.

It was the culmination of the battle that the team of ten had fought over the course of the year. At the same time, it was the beginning of their first and last battle: a fierce struggle that would live on as legend as long as the Hakone Ekiden existed.

IX

INTO THE DISTANCE

January 2, 7:45 a.m.

In just fifteen minutes, the Tokyo-Hakone Round-Trip College Ekiden Race would begin.

After the roll call twenty minutes before the start of the race, Prince made his way toward the underground passage for the subway. In the small hours of the morning, he could jog on the sidewalks aboveground to loosen up. But now it was impossible. Countless people were swarming around the *Yomiuri Shimbun* head office building in Otemachi to catch a glimpse of the opening of the Hakone Ekiden.

The throng of spectators—including the cheer squads of each university, the event staff, and ekiden enthusiasts who looked positively thrilled to see this time of year come round again—formed a continuous mass along the moat of the Imperial Palace, all the way from the *Yomiuri Shimbun* headquarters to the Wadakura Gate of the palace grounds. The deep beating of drums shook the air, accompanied by the school anthems of each university. Flags and banners flaunted their vivid colors in the cold wind whipping through the office buildings. The crowd's energy and anticipation were mounting.

"Where are you going?" Kiyose, who was accompanying Prince,

stopped him. ."You should be warmed up by now. Don't tire yourself out before the race even starts."

"Yeah, but I get too anxious if I'm not running." Prince stamped his feet in place. "I didn't think there'd be *this* many people."

Kiyose had never imagined there would come a day when Prince, of all people, would voluntarily keep running. He smiled at Prince to put him at ease. "You've practiced enough. You'll be fine. Did you go to the bathroom?"

"Multiple times." The side door to the *Yomiuri Shimbun* building was kept open for the athletes and staff to use. "Every time I go, it's jam-packed with people running the first leg."

"That just means you're not the only one who's nervous. You have nothing to worry about."

Kiyose led Prince to the back of the building so that he wouldn't catch a chill from the strong gusts of wind. There were fewer people at the back, and the two of them jogged lightly, side by side. Plastered on the wall was the final lineup of the race, announced at 7 a.m. that morning.

"Rikudo didn't put Fujioka in the second leg, huh?" Prince remarked, puzzled. Rikudo had entered Fujioka among the backups, though he was the captain and the strongest athlete on the team. No one had heard any rumors about him getting injured—could it be that he was ill? All the other teams had been keeping a close eye out for his name, but it was absent from the final lineup for the first day of the race.

"They're probably going to put him in the ninth or tenth leg," Kiyose said.

Rikudo's stance seemed to be to carefully assess the situation. If anyone could stop the team's successive victories at Hakone, it was Boso University. Boso's lineup made it clear that they were betting on the first day of the race, the journey to Mount Hakone, to go for the win.

With such a formidable list of athletes from Boso, even Rikudo would face a fierce battle on the way to Hakone. It was possible that Rikudo would let Boso come out on top for the first day and focus on seizing the second day as well as the overall victory, which would be determined by the total times over both days. No doubt Rikudo would decide where to enter Fujioka based on the team's ranking at the end of the first day, as well as the time difference between Rikudo and Boso.

"But for now, don't even think about Rikudo." Kiyose pressed a light hand on Prince's shoulder. "Come on, let's go back to the starting line. Remember what I told you?"

"Yeah." Prince nodded firmly, then took off the thick bench coat that hung below his knees. Upon seeing the black-and-silver Kansei uniform, the spectators moved aside.

The cold didn't touch him anymore. As the first runner, he had the tasuki strung over his left shoulder and across his body. It was a black sash with *Kansei University* embroidered on it in silver. The plasterer's wife had spent weeks working on it, ever since the Kansei runners had passed the prelim.

Prince touched the tasuki. Each of them would pass it on to the next, and all ten of them would do everything they could to make sure it returned to this very spot tomorrow without breaking the link.

Kiyose adjusted the length of the tasuki so it wouldn't get in the way when Prince ran. He tucked the extra part in the waistband of his shorts.

"Prince. I'm sorry I dragged you into this and made you come all this way," Kiyose said.

The cheer squads started blaring music even louder. The staff shouted out, "Runners, on your mark!"

"That's not what I wanna hear, Haiji." Prince grinned. "Wait for me at Tsurumi."

Prince handed his coat to Kiyose and went to stand at the starting line along with the other nineteen athletes running the first leg.

Otemachi, Tokyo, 8 a.m. Weather: clear sky. Temperature: 34.3°F. Humidity: 88 percent. Wind: 2.46 miles per hour from the northwest.

A momentary hush fell over the crowd. The starting shot was fired. Prince broke into a run. There was no need to look back. The only way to forge the path of their journey—the first Hakone Ekiden of Kansei University—was for him to press onward on this road.

As Kiyose had predicted, the race began at a slow pace. Prince could see Tokyo Station on his left as he passed the Wadakura Gate. The roar of the crowd crashed into him like a wave and broke away behind him, carried by the sharp winds that whistled through the skyscrapers. The group ran on the damp ground, still spread out in a horizontal line. Their pace was three minutes, seven seconds per kilometer. It was a speed that Prince could keep up with.

Perhaps because of the wide road, he felt like he wasn't moving forward no matter how much he ran. He could sense the nervous tension among the other runners around him, watchful for who would be the first to shoot ahead of the group, keeping each other in check. Prince willed them to stick to the slow pace.

The wind gusts through the office buildings made it feel colder than it really was. Remembering Kiyose's instructions, Prince shifted so that he was running right behind a slightly bulky runner from Teito University. Prince couldn't spend too much energy on securing an advantageous spot; it would just be another burden for him on top of his slow speed. He quickly found a position that afforded him some protection from the wind, then focused his attention on keeping up with the pack.

The pace remained steady even as they crossed the Intersection at Shiba Go-chome and entered Dai-Ichi Keihin. The group passed the five-kilometer point at fifteen minutes, thirty seconds.

The teams' coaches were bringing up the rear in their respective coach vehicles. At certain points of the race, the coaches were allowed to say a few words to the athletes through their cars' loudspeakers: once just after the first kilometer, then every five kilometers throughout each leg, and once more at the last kilometer. But none of the coaches gave any instructions until the runners had passed the five-kilometer point.

That was how taut the tension was among them. Even the coaches felt it would be reckless to speak too soon.

The runners from Rikudo and Boso were contending for the lead position, but every time they tried to dart ahead, they were soon swallowed back into the rest of the group. The first leg was 21.3 kilometers long, and of course, the Hakone Ekiden had only just begun. If their spurts backfired and they ran out of steam, it would put a strain on their teammates who were running the next segments. This reluctance to make a big move held back the whole pack.

Prince completely forgot about the escort car and the TV cameras. His entire being concentrated on moving forward, maintaining a veneer of composure as he clung desperately to the group.

Meanwhile, Kiyose had taken the JR train from Tokyo to Shinagawa and had just switched over to a Keihin express train. Carrying Prince's jacket in his arms, Kiyose jammed in his earbuds to catch the radio. He tuned in to the sound of the TV coverage and discovered that the group was still sticking together. "Yes!" he shouted in a small voice. The other passengers turned to stare at him, but he didn't care.

The broadcaster and the commentator sounded somewhat baffled as they discussed the slow pace of the first runners.

"Nothing's happened in the race so far, has it?"

"I think the stronger athletes can step up their game and start running like they're going for a new record."

"Keep your crappy advice to yourself," Kiyose lashed out. He couldn't help it. *Slow is good. No one make a move. Stay together as a group all the way to the finish.*

His cell phone rang. It was the landlord calling from the coach car. Kiyose picked up immediately, hoping Prince hadn't started falling behind.

"What should I do now, Haiji?" the landlord drawled in a leisurely tone.

"What happened?"

"We're almost at ten kilometers. What should I say to Prince?"

"Does he look like he's struggling?" Kiyose gripped the phone.

"Naw. We just passed Yatsuyama Bridge, but he's holding on tight. The pack's still going just the same, everyone running side by side."

"Then no need to say anything."

The Yatsuyama Bridge came just before the eight-kilometer point. The bridge was an overpass that formed a gentle slope across the railroad tracks. If the group was still together after that, it was highly likely that they would stay that way until they reached the most challenging part of the first leg: the Rokugo Bridge. *Hang in there, Prince,* Kiyose called to him in his head.

"But all I've done so far is sit here and say nothing. Not a peep. How's that for being the coach?" The landlord sounded bored. "At this rate, I might as well be getting a lift to Hakone."

"If you sit back and watch over us, that's more than enough. You can be our rock—stay calm and dignified. If Prince starts struggling, encourage him."

"How? Don't tell me I gotta sing the school song, I'm tone-deaf."

"No coach in this day and age would sing the school song to hype up a runner," Kiyose sighed. "Could you pass on a message to him from me? Tell Prince I have something to tell him, so he should come to Tsurumi even if he has to crawl his way to get there."

It was at the fifteen-kilometer point that Prince heard Kiyose's message, bellowed through the loudspeaker in the landlord's gravelly voice.

Something he wants to tell me? Let's hear it, then.

It was getting harder to breathe, but Prince flared up again. He managed to snatch the water bottle from Kansei's short-distance runner, who informed him, "Exactly three minutes for the past kilometer." The pace was rising. It was clear now. The crucial turn of the race would come at Rokugo Bridge, at 17.8 kilometers.

When they had just passed twelve kilometers, it seemed there might be a twist in the race. The runner from Eurasia University darted forward, and the group began to stretch out in a line. But without missing a beat, Rikudo and Boso followed close behind him, and the others were also pulled forward. In the end, everyone remained in the pack.

Everything hung on Rokugo Bridge. This unspoken understanding bound the whole group.

Rokugo was a large bridge, spanning 488.08 yards over Tama River. The road went uphill leading up to the bridge and turned downhill at its other end. By then, the runners would have already covered nearly twenty kilometers, making the elevation especially tough on their stamina.

When they finally began their climb at Rokugo, Prince's legs suddenly felt like lead. He was shocked by how hard it felt to move. He gasped for breath and swung his arms, trying anything to propel himself forward.

There was a shift in the rhythm of the group. The breathing of the stronger athletes fell quiet for an instant, and just as Prince sensed something was coming, the runner from Yokohama University put on a spurt. Boso and Rikudo followed suit.

The group spread out in no time, stretching in a straight line. *How do these people have that much energy left?* Stunned, Prince could only look on as the top runners sprinted farther and farther away. He wanted to chase after them, but it was impossible. The leaders reached the downhill part of the bridge and gathered even more speed.

Prince remembered Kiyose's prerace advice: "Stay calm. If you can hang on until Rokugo Bridge, the rest of the way won't make such a big difference in time. Just focus on finishing the run at your own pace."

That's right. I'm still just a beginner. It doesn't matter how much the others can speed up. All I can do—all I have to do—is keep running with every fiber of my being.

The top runner was already about 100 meters ahead of him. But Prince didn't give up. He held on to hope and ran with dogged persistence.

Did I just say "still just a beginner"? Does this mean I actually want to keep doing track? Even though I got roped into it and running hurts like hell?

Prince let out a small laugh as he gasped for air.

The soft, warm touch of sunrise fell on his face.

At the Tsurumi relay station, Kakeru and Musa huddled together, staring intently at the screen of the portable TV. The owner of the electronics store in the shopping arcade had lent it to them for free.

"Ah, they're leaving Prince behind," Musa said sadly. When Prince slipped out of frame, Musa leaned forward as if he wanted to follow Prince with his eyes for as long as possible.

"But there shouldn't be that much time difference between him and the top runners." Kakeru watched intently, burning Prince's brave run into his memory, then looked up at Musa. "You can close the distance in the second leg, Musa."

"Yes. I'll do my best."

The first runners would start arriving at the Tsurumi relay station soon. Musa pulled off his knit hat and scarf. It was 37.9°F. While there was hardly any wind, and it was sunny out, Musa felt bitterly cold. Following Kakeru's advice, he decided to run wearing arm warmers that covered his elbows down to his wrists. If he got too hot, he could take them off and go back to just his running uniform.

"Have you had enough water? Even if you're cold, you have to be careful not to get dehydrated during the race."

"If I drank any more, I'd have to pee and flee midway through," Musa laughed. It was the first time Kakeru heard him use slang that way.

Kakeru laughed with him. "That doesn't sound like you."

The broadcaster's and the commentator's voices came from the portable TV.

"As for the second leg, each team has entered its ace runner, or a runner of that caliber. A whopping eleven runners out of twenty hold records of ten thousand meters in under twenty-nine minutes. We'll also see four international students in this segment."

"Manas from Boso University, Kimani from Kofu Gakuin, Jomo from Saikyo, and last but not least, Musa from Kansei."

At the mention of his name, Musa and Kakeru looked at the TV and saw themselves on the screen. They spun around in surprise. The TV crew had crept up on them from behind. Musa smiled awkwardly at the camera.

"Kansei's Musa stands out from the others. An international student on a government scholarship, he studies in the Science and Engineering Department, and believe it or not, before last spring he had zero track experience. The Kansei team is taking on Hakone with just ten members, but most of them are newcomers to the sport."

"And they managed to come this far—it's incredible. What a team." The camera cut to the studio, where the commentator was nodding eagerly. "Training must've been insanely tough."

"There's a great deal of personality packed into the Kansei team. It's their first-ever Hakone—keep your eyes peeled for their performance."

A commercial break started, and the TV crew left. Being introduced on TV seemed to make Musa nervous again. *Not good. I have to find a way to distract him*, Kakeru thought.

Kakeru's cell phone went off. It was Shindo, calling from the Odawara relay station, where he was waiting for his turn to run the fifth leg. Kakeru pressed the button to answer and handed the phone to Musa.

"Hey, Musa, I saw you on TV," Shindo said. His voice sounded rather muffled.

"How's your cold?" Musa asked anxiously, and Kakeru brought his ear closer. Shindo had come down with a fever on New Year's Eve, and he still wasn't feeling well that morning.

"I'm fine. But what about you, Musa? Your nerves must be going haywire right about now."

"Yes, a little," Musa replied. Even miles apart, it was as if Shindo could sense how Musa was feeling. The strength of their bond amazed Kakeru.

"Listen, Musa. Think of something fun," Shindo said through his stuffy nose. "Once we're done with this, we'll finally get our New Year's holiday. I'm thinking of going back home during the winter break. Would you like to come with me?"

"Can I? Isn't it a time for being with family?"

"My parents are looking forward to meeting you. We do live in a village in the middle of nowhere, though. There won't be much to do—other than play in the snow. We can make yukidaruma."

"What's a yukidaruma?"

"Oh right, you've never made one before. Then that settles that—let's spend winter break at my place together."

"Yes." Musa nodded. "Thank you, Shindo." When Musa hung up, all traces of doubt and fear had disappeared from his eyes.

The crowds on either side of the course cheered even louder. The first runners were coming into view. Kakeru and Musa approached the road.

Kiyose came running from the direction of Keikyu Tsurumi-Ichiba Station. When he found Kakeru and Musa, he let out a big sigh of relief. "Looks like I made it." He looked at Musa. "How're you feeling?"

"Better than ever," Musa answered boldly.

"Good." Kiyose checked Musa's face and his shoelaces for any sign of disarray. "Prince will probably come in last. But don't let that get to you. Just run as you always do."

"That's good news for me. If I'm already last, it can't get any worse," Musa joked. "Besides, I'm better suited to chasing than being chased."

"That's the spirit," said Kakeru, taking Musa's bench coat.

The Rikudo runner was the first to arrive at Tsurumi. The relay station was located in front of a police koban box along the side of the Dai-Ichi Keihin road. It was a plain, tree-lined road, extending in a flat, straight line, so they had a clear view of the runners drawing closer.

A staff member who had just received the news of the runners' positions hastily called out the names of the universities. The first-leg runners would reach them in that order, so the second-leg runners took their places on the changeover line and waited for their teammates.

Rikudo's tasuki passed from the first runner to the second. It was one hour, four minutes, thirty-six seconds since the start from Otemachi. Next came Yokohama University, Boso, then Eurasia, almost at the same time. Since they had all been packed together for most of the route, it was an extremely close race.

Musa did some stretches. Kakeru leaned out into the road. One after another, the runners of the first leg passed on the tasuki, and the second-leg runners hurtled away. Prince was still nowhere to be seen. Thirty seconds had gone by since Rikudo's handoff.

"It's Prince!" Kakeru shouted. He could make him out in the shadow of the escort car. The staff member called out the remaining universities.

Musa said, "I'll go now," and stood at the changeover line. He held up his hand toward Prince.

Prince was pushing on, swinging his arms wildly for momentum. When he noticed Musa ahead of him, Prince took off the tasuki like he'd just remembered it was there. The rubber in his waistband snapped back against his side, giving him a light whip, as if it wanted to spur him on.

I'm almost there, Prince thought. *Just a little more.*

Musa and Kakeru were screaming his name. Kiyose stood still next to Kakeru, waiting for Prince to reach them.

Prince crossed the changeover line and pushed the tasuki he'd been gripping into Musa's outstretched hand. Musa was already running. The tasuki linked Prince and Musa for a split second, then slipped away through Prince's fingers.

Prince could hardly breathe. He couldn't even keep his eyes open. *Who's panting so much? Is that me?*

He came to a halt and almost toppled over headfirst, but someone caught him in an embrace just in time.

"I take back what I said at Otemachi," Prince heard Kiyose say right next to his ear. "What I really wanted to say was this. Thank you for coming with us all this way."

"That's better," Prince murmured.

Kakeru and Kiyose took the Keikyu express train to Yokohama, then the JR train to Odawara. Their team was understaffed, so they were circling ahead to Lake Ashi to be there for Shindo when he finished his part of the race.

They were reluctant to leave Prince, who was still wiped out, but he urged them to go. "Don't worry about me, just go on to Hakone. I've already finished my run. I'll head to the hotel by myself when I feel ready to walk."

Prince's job was to go to a hotel near Yokohama Station and keep an eye on the live coverage to follow how things stood in the race. Kiyose and Kakeru were to return to the same hotel that night to prepare for their runs the next day.

Once they made sure Prince was hydrated and recovered enough to sit up, Kakeru and Kiyose left Tsurumi.

The bench coat that Kiyose had carried over from Otemachi was back on Prince. Now Kakeru was carrying Musa's bench coat. It was meant to be for Shindo when he reached the finish line up on the mountain. The team was short not only on staff but on gear as well.

The Tokaido line was crowded with people: spectators chasing after the Hakone runners and families on their way to shrines for hatsumode, their first visit of the new year. Though the seats were mostly taken, Kakeru found an empty spot in a four-seater booth and made Kiyose sit down. Kiyose pulled out a notepad and pen from his bench coat pocket.

"Prince's time?"

"One hour, five minutes, thirty-seven seconds," Kakeru answered, checking his wristwatch. Kiyose jotted down the numbers.

"That's eleven seconds' difference from the Dochido University runner just ahead of him. And one minute, one second after Rikudo in the lead," Kiyose said. "There'll still be plenty of chances to make up for it. Prince put up a good fight."

When Prince handed the Kansei tasuki to Musa at Tsurumi, he was last out of twenty teams. The select team of the Inter-University Athletic Union of Kanto—composed of athletes who ran well in the prelim but whose teams hadn't made the cut—wasn't counted as part of the team rankings. For this team, only the times of the individual runners would remain as an official record. So, strictly speaking, the Kansei team had finished the first leg in nineteenth place, but in effect, the team was last in the race.

Still, just as Kiyose had said, the time difference wasn't significant, and there was still hope of turning things around. The slow pace of the first leg had been a blessing for Prince and the Kansei team. The race had only just begun.

Kakeru had the portable TV, but it didn't get good reception on the train. "Try this," said Kiyose, handing him a small radio. Kakeru was twisting around the knobs to try to pick up a station when Kiyose's phone rang. It was King, who was accompanying Jota at the Totsuka relay station.

"Haiji, it's getting crazy out there! Look at the TV!"

"We would if we could . . ." Kiyose muttered.

The Star-Studded Second was plunging into a dramatic turmoil.

Rikudo and Boso were running in the lead. But the runner from Manaka University, who'd taken the tasuki in ninth place at Tsurumi, was storming past the others and catching up to the top two. In contrast, the runner from Yokohama University, who had been in second place at Tsurumi, dropped back by a wide margin.

A fierce three-way battle was unfolding between the leaders, each as determined and undaunted as the other. Meanwhile, there was also some dynamic movement among the group who followed in their wake.

The runner from the Jonan Bunka team, who had started off from Tsurumi in eighteenth place, was sprinting at a pace that approached the all-time course record for the second leg. The other runners around him also kept up a fast pace, desperate not to be overtaken or left behind.

Musa, who'd started last, was almost catching up to the runners from Dochido and Jonan Bunka. A student staffer standing on the side of the road held up a placard that read "1 km." Musa checked his wristwatch. He'd run the first kilometer in two minutes, forty-eight seconds.

It would be impossible to run the whole twenty-three kilometers of the second leg at this pace. He knew full well that he'd struggle in the latter half of the course, but he wouldn't be able to bring up their ranking if he faltered this early in the race. The Dochido and Jonan Bunka runners passed Teito, and Musa soon followed suit. That meant he had already closed the seventy-meter gap between Teito and himself since he'd set off from Tsurumi.

The road was surrounded by huge masses of people. Musa thought, *Now I know what* kuroyama no hitodakari *looks like—"a crowd as big as a dark mountain."* Rows upon rows of people filled the sidewalks as far as he could see, waving the small paper flags that the newspaper company, a cosponsor of the event, had handed out. Everywhere he looked, he saw radiant faces, all of them cheering for the athletes who passed by in a flash. The excitement in the air far surpassed that surrounding the prelim and the Ageo City Half-Marathon.

So this is the Hakone Ekiden. And what it means to run the second leg, the ace race.

Musa was elated. He wasn't born in this country, and there were people who didn't welcome his presence. He knew that. *But what a place I'm in right now, in this moment, where everyone's free and equal. We're all sharing the same time and space—both the runners next to me and the runners in the lead, though they're so far ahead I can't even see them.*

After having endured such long and intense training, they had all transformed themselves into organisms whose sole purpose was to run. The same wind was whipping past all their bodies in that moment.

What Fujioka had said was right. If Musa had simply stuck to his studies in the Science and Engineering Department, he wouldn't have been able to experience such a thrill or this sense of unity—or this stir-ring inside him, like blood boiling in his veins, that rush known only to those who ran in earnest.

The crowd roared even louder, and Musa finally realized he'd passed by Yokohama Station. He was 8.3 kilometers in. *How did I run so far already?* The elevated highway that had been obscuring the sky swept past, drawing a large curve and receding to his right. Pale sunlight fell on him from the open sky. Musa kept running next to Jonan Bunka and Dochido, feet striking the road that was now turning dry.

Musa was on a roll, riding the rhythm. The fact that the landlord had instructed him to hold back his speed at the five-kilometer point—and that Gonta Hill, the most challenging part of the second leg, was waiting ahead of him—had slipped clean out of his mind.

"He's going too fast." Kiyose pulled out his earbuds and called the landlord.

"He-*llo* from the Coach Mobile."

"Did you tell Musa what I asked you to at five kilometers?"

"Take it down a notch, Haiji. I did tell him, in fact. But he just wouldn't listen. So what am I supposed to do?"

"Please tell him again to slow down at the ten-kilometer point." Kiyose hung up and leaned his head back on the hard seat of the train. With a sigh, he knitted his brows and squeezed his eyes shut. "He's too caught up in the moment."

Kakeru placed a hand on the back of the seat, crouched down a little, and checked the view streaming past them outside. "No sign of the sea yet. We're lucky there's no wind today."

Kiyose opened his eyes and stared up at Kakeru, as if to say, *Laid-back much?*

"I'm sure Musa will realize before it's too late. Let's believe in him," Kakeru said, still gazing out the window.

Kiyose pushed his earbuds back in and muttered, "Guess that's all we can do."

Of the ten segments that make up the Hakone Ekiden, the second one, starting from Tsurumi and finishing at Totsuka, is the longest, at twenty-three kilometers. It isn't just the length that makes it challenging. A hill called Gontazaka, which extends no less than one and a half kilometers in a constant climb, awaits the runners fourteen kilometers into the race. Gontazaka is followed by small ups and downs, and then in the last three kilometers of the course comes another hill.

As the longest course of the relay, and with the many undulations toward the end of it, the second leg is worthy of the title "Star-Studded Second," both for its difficulty and for its drama. Runners who take on the challenge must excel not only in their running capability but also in their indomitable spirit and perseverance. The course also requires a quick mind to grasp and respond to turns in the race, as well as the agility to adjust one's form in line with the ups and downs of the terrain.

Musa ran the relatively flat part of the course at a good, steady beat. After passing the Yokohama Station, he was still carried by the same momentum when he went straight into Gontazaka. Then four seconds into the climb, he realized, *Oh, it's Gontazaka.* It suddenly felt much harder to lift his legs, as if someone had attached heavy weights to them.

Though he'd been running abreast of Jonan Bunka and Dochido until that point, the gap between them grew wider and wider. Musa hastily tried to keep up with them, but he had a feeling it wasn't within his power.

What have I been doing? Musa finally became aware of the cold wind blowing against his face. The arm warmers clung to his skin, soaked with sweat. *It seems I got carried away.*

Like a breath of wind coming in through an open window, swaying the curtains and clearing the dusty air inside, Musa's surroundings swept into his senses. The small corner stores dotting the side of National Route 1 here and there. The deafening cheers of the spectators who formed a continuous wall along the course. A peaceful suburban scene during the New Year's holiday.

Musa reminded himself of what he had seen on TV with Kakeru back at the Tsurumi relay station. Eleven runners competing in the second leg could run ten kilometers in less than twenty-nine minutes. Jonan Bunka and Dochido were among them. If he tried to keep up with them head-on, he'd only end up destroying himself.

The twins had asked what fun there was in a sport with results that were predictable based on the athletes' credentials. *But this is different,* Musa thought. Even if plain numbers often made it clear who was the faster runner, this wasn't a track race. This was an ekiden. *I was given the tasuki, and now I'm running not to break the link.* An ekiden was a different story from a 10,000-meter track race, where every runner would start running at once, going round and round on the flat track. The course he was running now, the twenty-three kilometers full of ups and downs, was merely one-tenth of the journey from Tokyo to Hakone and back again.

His part of the race was nothing more than the first chapter of a story that was still being written. *I shouldn't get ahead of myself. I should just run in a way that's fit for a first chapter. In other words, stay calm and steady, and bring up our position as much as I possibly can. Though I can't compete against the fastest runners in terms of speed, I can still pay close attention to how the race is unfolding and stay alert for any opportunities.*

First, I should hydrate myself properly at the fifteen-kilometer point, Musa decided. He'd thought it was freezing, but after running at such a high speed, he was drenched. *And what next? . . . Oh yes.* Musa recalled the warning that Kiyose had given him:

"Be cautious when you go down Gontazaka. If you've been going steady until then, you should be able to climb up the hill with the same momentum. But don't let that trick you into pelting down the hill—that's a surefire way to tire yourself out. Instead, you should restrain your speed a little when you go downhill and save your strength for later. The *real* challenge of the second leg, the part that decides whether you win or lose, is the uphill over the last three kilometers. Be patient till you get there and keep chasing the other runners."

Understood, Haiji. Musa nodded to himself and concentrated on climbing Gontazaka. The highest point of the hill was nearly 183.7 feet above sea level. Yokohama Station was 8.2 feet above the sea, so that meant he was sprinting up an increase in elevation of more than 175 feet nonstop.

The fifteen-kilometer point of the course came just before the peak of the hill. A short-distance runner wearing the Kansei tracksuit and a water supplier's bib signaled to Musa, holding up the event's official water bottle.

In the brief moment when he ran alongside Musa to hand him the bottle, the water supplier shared some vital info. "You're eighteenth right now. Seven runners in a group up ahead. You can do it."

Musa nodded and slowly took a big gulp of water. He drank enough not to feel weight in his stomach, then tossed the bottle on the side of the road.

He was eighteenth now. That meant he had passed another runner after Teito while he was running on air. The cluster of seven runners ahead of him must include Jonan Bunka and Dochido. They'll likely keep pressing forward, far beyond the rest. Who were the other five runners?

Making use of Gontazaka's gradual downward slope, Musa strained his eyes ahead of him. Dochido had shot out of the pack, and the broadcasting car followed his trail as he began to leave the others behind. The teams' support vehicles were busy maneuvering their way to their respective athletes to give instructions for the fifteen-kilometer point. Musa couldn't make out the runners very well because of the cars blocking his view, but it did look like several people were running neck and neck.

Musa moved slightly closer to the center line of the road. From this angle, he could see one of the runners in the shadow of a car, wearing the vertical green-and-white-striped uniform of Eurasia University.

Eurasia? If I recall, they left Tsurumi in fourth place.

It was then that Musa realized that there had been a major upheaval in the team's positions.

If the Eurasia runner had dropped so far behind, he must be struggling badly. Perhaps he was sick or the pressure was crushing him—whatever the reason, he hadn't managed to find his rhythm.

The broadcast vehicle moved farther and farther ahead. Dochido and Jonan Bunka must have left the group behind. Musa judged it would be feasible for him to catch up to the remaining five. He could overtake them. *Don't rush it. Close the distance bit by bit.*

The landlord's raspy voice came from the coach car behind him. "*Musa!* Don't tell me you've got your balls scrunched up stiff like some pumped-up racehorse!"

The loudspeaker fell quiet for a few moments. The monitoring staff riding in the same car must have warned Tazaki about language. With a cough, the landlord resumed, "Do you remember what Haiji told you, Musa? If you do, do three somersaults right now."

How did we end up with this wacky guy as our coach? Musa laughed. The laugh made him relax, and he could feel his thoughts becoming unclouded.

Musa raised his hand lightly and gave a thumbs-up to the coach car.

At the Totsuka relay station, Jota and King sat together on a tarp, watching the broadcast on their portable TV.

"They don't show much of the lower-ranked teams, do they? Wonder how Musa's doing?" King said.

"Well, no wonder. There's just too much happening with the top runners." On the screen, the Manaka runner had just begun to leave Rikudo and Boso behind. "But I'm sure Musa will pull through."

Just then, the team rankings at fifteen kilometers flashed on the screen. Kansei was eighteenth. If they discounted the select team,

Kansei was now in seventeenth place. The camera switched to the battle among the lower-ranked teams. Musa was steadily gaining on the five runners ahead of him.

"Told you!"

"All right!" Jota and King gripped each other's hands in excitement. "C'mon, Jota, we gotta get moving. Musa might get here faster than we think."

"It's better for me to stay still before a race, I think." Jota had finished his warm-up jog long ago, so he stuck to doing stretches with his legs out in front of him. "By the way, how's your job hunt going?"

"Why bring that up now?"

"I'd get too nervous if I don't talk about something else."

"You're gonna make *me* break out in a cold sweat." King sulked, but for the present, it was his mission to protect the peace in Jota's mind before his turn in the race. Grudgingly, he answered, "It's not going. You think I've got time for that with all this running?"

"Seriously? What are you gonna do? Gap year and keep hunting?"

"I might have to do fourth year again." King hugged his knees and looked up with a sigh. A feathery cloud hung in the wintry blue sky. "Hope my folks let me." His sigh came out in a small, wispy cloud, momentarily floating in the air before melting away.

"Ooh, do-over." Jota drew up his knees like King and rocked back and forth. "If you're gonna stay, let's run at Hakone next year, too."

"You idiot, we haven't even finished this one and you're already on to next year? I'm not gonna. I'd never find a job." King shot down Jota's suggestion. Then, after a pause, he murmured, "You . . . think you can do it again next year?"

"I will." Jota rose to his feet. "Why wouldn't I?"

Jota's eyes blazed, more serious than ever before. *This guy, he's gonna do it,* King thought. The fervent fire in Jota, burning ever brighter as he waited for his turn, ignited King, too.

"All right." King got up and stretched his knees. "Let's do a light jog for the end, Jota."

The two of them started running to and fro, weaving through the crowd around the bustling relay station.

Musa was running up the hellish hill stretching over the last three kilometers of the course. The only thing that kept him going was his relentless determination.

He overtook the Eurasia runner just before the hill. Now he was surrounded by the runners from Tokyo Gakuin, Akebono, and Kita-Kanto Universities and the select team. He couldn't see who was running ahead of them. He had no idea whether the others were so far ahead that they were simply out of sight or whether they were obscured by the event vehicles and the shape of the terrain.

In any case, all he could do was keep an eye on the movements of the four runners around him. If any of them made a move, he'd respond without missing a beat. He could sense that his competitors had the same thing on their minds: they wanted to shoot out of the pack if they could, to pass on the tasuki to the next runner as fast as humanly possible. All four of them were waiting for the right moment to strike.

Musa had come so far. He didn't want to be the first to fall behind the group, especially now that he was so close to the finish.

He had already reached his physical and mental limits, but pure tenacity made him cling on at the same speed.

The Totsuka relay station was midway up the hill. Just five hundred meters left. The noise barrier obstructed his view to the left. But the growing number of spectators, almost overflowing from the sidewalks, told him that the relay station was drawing near. He noticed that the select team runner in front of him was sweating even more than he was. All the runners around him were breathing heavily—and so was he, of course.

This was his only chance. Musa swerved around the select team runner and emerged as the leader of the pack. He poured everything he had left into this burst of speed.

As long as he could cross the line and pass on the tasuki to Jota, it didn't matter whether Musa collapsed on the spot. *Though I'm nowhere near the course record, this is the best run I can muster now. It's time for me to show what I can do, to throw everything I've got at the final stretch.*

His chin pulled up and his form became ungainly, but it was no time to think about how he looked. He could see the changeover zone. He could see Jota slowly raise his hand. Musa leaned in, thrusting forward his upper body, and sprinted even harder. He didn't know when he'd pulled it off his shoulder, but Musa found himself gripping the tasuki in his outstretched fist.

"Ran like a true ace," Jota said, taking the tasuki and slapping Musa's arm. Musa heard Jota's light footsteps bounding away from the asphalt where he collapsed.

When he came to, he was lying on a tarp. He seemed to be in a parking lot of a ramen shop and a secondhand car dealer. Still foggy, he thought, *I didn't think the relay station would be in such a humdrum place.* The place was buzzing with the event staff, the runners who'd just arrived, and their teammates who were there to support them. It seemed Musa hadn't been out for too long.

"You awake?" Musa's field of vision was filled with King's face, who looked like he was about to cry. "You fought hard, Musa."

King filled him in on everything that had happened. Musa had come out on top in the group at the end of the course, reaching Totsuka in thirteenth place. He'd overtaken seven teams and had run the whole twenty-three kilometers in one hour, ten minutes, fourteen seconds. Out of the twenty athletes who ran the second leg, he got the twelfth best time.

The Kansei team was now in thirteenth place overall. They were twenty-seven seconds behind Shinsei University, in twelfth place, and only six seconds ahead of Tokyo Gakuin, in fourteenth. The team still couldn't let their guard down, but Musa's charge gave them hope.

"You should've seen Jota." King sniffed, rubbing his nose, which was red from being out in the cold for so long. "He got so pumped up watching you run."

I'm glad. So I managed to put in a good run after all.

Musa nodded without a word, a tremor in his lips. He thought that if he opened his mouth to speak, he wouldn't be able to stop the tears from pouring out.

Kakeru and Kiyose got off the train at JR Odawara Station and were walking through the station to switch to the Hakone Tozan Railway.

"Okay, got it. Thanks, get some rest." Kiyose finished the call with King and clapped his phone shut. "He says Musa is awake now. They're about to head to the hotel in Fujisawa."

"That's good," Kakeru said, relieved. He'd been worried sick since he'd seen Musa crumple to the ground at Totsuka on TV. King had been too much in a panic to answer any calls, but eventually, he rang to let them know that Musa was all right.

Kiyose and Kakeru bought the tickets and went through the gates. Kiyose checked the departure times on the electronic noticeboard. They had about ten minutes until the Odakyu line to Hakone-Yumoto arrived.

"Didn't you have to call Jota before he ran?" Kakeru asked.

"Well, the twins should be fine on their own. Knowing them, they'd call me if they were worried about anything."

Fair enough, Kakeru thought. On the platform, he saw some people dressed up in special kimonos for the New Year's holiday.

"Our biggest problem right now is Shindo's condition." Kiyose pulled out his cell again to make a call before the train arrived. "Yuki?" Kakeru asked, and Kiyose nodded. When the call went through, Kiyose said, "It's me."

Kakeru reached over and pressed a button on Kiyose's cell to put it on speakerphone. He figured no one would mind since there was enough bustle around them to drown out their voices. Kiyose cocked his head to one side, wondering what Kakeru had just done. Kakeru pulled Kiyose's hand so that he held the phone up in front of them.

"How's Shindo?" Kiyose asked.

"I don't know," Yuki answered. "I can't see his face, and he's refusing to let me check his temperature. Not well, that's for sure."

"What do you mean, you can't 'see' his face?" Kiyose said with a frown. "You better be keeping him company."

Yuki was supposed to be with Shindo at the Odawara relay station, waiting for Shindo's turn to run in the fifth leg. Kiyose sounded impatient. They were so close now, but they couldn't go see Shindo in person.

"He's right next to me," Yuki said. "But he's got half his face covered with a towel. Plus, he's wearing masks over the towel. One normal mask for colds *and* another one for hay fever—you know, those big ones that pop out like a tengu spirit. So I can't really see if he looks red or pale, let alone much of his face. Hey, can you breathe okay in there, Shindo?"

Apparently, Shindo was subjecting himself to full quarantine mode so that he wouldn't infect Yuki with anything. There was a shuffle on the other end as Yuki handed his cell to Shindo.

"Hello," said Shindo. His voice sounded low and muffled, like some kidnapper demanding a ransom.

"How high is your fever?" Kiyose asked, getting straight to the point.

But Shindo didn't budge. "I'm totally fine. I don't have a fever," he insisted. "Is Kakeru there?"

Kakeru stepped closer to the phone. "Yes?"

"If you're able to, could you get some masks on your way here? I'll leave the ones I have on now with Yuki."

"For someone who doesn't have a fever, you're acting rather cautious," Kiyose commented.

"How come Haiji can hear me?" Shindo sounded unsettled.

You're on speakerphone, Kakeru explained in his head. "Don't worry, I'll get some," he said out loud.

"Drink as much as you can, Shindo," Kiyose instructed. "Even if it means you wet your pants midrun, that's better than getting dehydrated."

"I'd rather not do either," Shindo laughed, then hung up.

Staring at his cell, Kiyose remarked, "Quite a useful feature."

"Didn't you know you could do that?" Kakeru said, switching off the speaker for him.

"I never even noticed."

What did he think that button was for? Kakeru wondered as he ran to the kiosk on the platform. By the time he had bought the masks and returned to Kiyose, the train to Hakone-Yumoto was just coming in.

Kiyose got on, looking a little downcast. "Wish I could tell him he can bow out if it's too much."

Stowing away the masks in his pocket, Kakeru followed Kiyose onto the train in silence.

For Jota, his twin little brother, Joji, had always been the other half of his soul.

Their parents never mistook one son for the other. When they were young, the brothers often played pranks on grown-ups, Jota pretending to be Joji and Joji, Jota. But their parents never failed to tell the boys apart.

Wonder how they did that, Jota thought. There were times back then when even Jota had looked at his own reflection in the mirror and gotten mixed up between Joji and himself.

Their parents never compared them, either. They treated the boys as two completely separate individuals; in the parents' eyes, it didn't make sense to compare their sons.

It was natural for their parents to think of their children that way, a given. But when he got older, Jota learned that there were some parents out there who couldn't adopt that stance. Some parents compared their children with each other and regarded them as possessions. Jota was glad their parents were never like that.

Having the same face didn't mean they shared the same soul.

It was thanks to the way their parents had treated them that Jota could accept that fact as though it was the most natural thing in the world. Jota loved his twin brother simply as another person, a separate individual who was also his closest companion.

Jota and Joji had always been together. They shared a bedroom, went to the same schools, played soccer side by side. They'd fought as many times as they'd made up, and they hung out with the same friends.

Jota knew mostly everything there was to know about Joji: his favorite foods, the little mole on his right ankle, when he had his first kiss and with whom. He also knew that Joji's personality was totally unlike his own.

Jota and Joji had many friends. People around them probably saw them as cheerful, fun-loving brothers. That was true, and Jota had no objections to being seen that way, but he felt those adjectives didn't quite fit his own personality.

Joji was more artless than Jota.

Joji could brighten up a room and make people relax just by being there. Whether he was angry or happy, he showed his emotions in an honest, straightforward way without any hidden motives.

Jota didn't wear his heart on his sleeve as much as Joji did. Sometimes he was calculating; he behaved in a certain way because he thought people would like him more. People like Joji—carefree, easygoing, living in the moment—were harder to come by. This was one thing that made Jota feel even more affectionate toward his brother.

Joji probably doesn't know it yet, Jota thought, *but it's about time we started going our separate ways. We've done everything together our whole lives. But we can't keep going like this forever.*

Jota crossed the Hamasuka intersection and continued southward, entering the Shonan coastal road. As soon as he turned onto it, he felt the wind blowing straight in his face.

In studies and in sports, Jota and Joji were practically at the same level. So naturally, they had gone to the same senior high and had both been regulars on the soccer team.

But running was different. Joji was more cut out to be a runner.

Right now, there wasn't such a big gap between their speeds. But because Jota knew Joji better than anyone, he could see it already: *This is probably as far as I can go, but Joji will get even faster. He can reach a world that I could never see. He has all the makings of a great runner, and besides, it looks like he just can't get enough of running.*

Loved by many, Joji had a big heart, spacious enough to feel the same affection for everyone. But when it came to running, Jota was surprised by how much passion and tenacity Joji had shown for it.

At first, Jota had assumed Joji would get bored of track soon enough, but Joji kept running, day in and day out. Though even Kiyose didn't seem to notice, Jota knew that sometimes, Joji sneaked out of the house late at night to practice by himself. He'd slip out of his futon, careful not to wake Jota, and jog for about an hour before coming back.

When the twins were alone in their room, Joji constantly brought up Kakeru. He'd rattle off comments like "Kakeru's run was really on fire today" and "Wonder how I could run like that." Eager to inch closer to Kakeru, he'd strike a pose on the tatami and ask Jota to check his form. Joji's eyes shone bright in moments like these.

Jota and Joji often got into it with Kakeru, partly because they were in the same year and didn't have to hold anything back. To Jota, Kakeru seemed naive and single-minded to a fault. Sometimes this irked Jota and made him lash out.

But Joji looked up to Kakeru. He locked horns with Kakeru only because he was too shy to admit how much he admired his teammate.

You're all grown up now, Joji. Jota felt both lonely and proud. His little brother's biggest rival had always been himself. Each of them had sought to surpass the other, and they'd stimulated each other that way for as long as Jota could remember. But now, Joji had finally discovered another rival, a model to aspire to, in Kakeru.

If they hadn't tried track, they'd never have known. They could've kept going together for much longer, with their sights set on the same things.

But this is where we part, Joji.

Jota had kept running this far, pulled along by Joji's zeal. With the Chikusei-so residents, the twins had succeeded in reaching Hakone. Joji, Jota was sure, would keep climbing up, striving to attain what lay beyond—reaching beyond the point that Jota would never be able to cross, for that realm in the far distance.

Oh well, I don't mind, Jota thought. *No matter what happens, Joji will always be my little brother. I've got to embrace it. Let him leave the nest, become independent. All I can do is to run the best I can right now—and give him a parting gift. He's about to embark on a long journey to seek new heights.*

Jota hoped that one day, Joji might win. Though it might take many years, Joji could become a runner as good as Kakeru, or even better, an invincible runner, faster and stronger than anyone else. Jota didn't know what he himself would be doing then. But he was sure about one thing, at least. He would be rooting for his little brother from the bottom of his heart, just as he was now.

He came to the part of the coastal route that was bordered by a long grove of black pines and broadleaf evergreens, which functioned as a barrier against sand blowing from the beach. The trees cut off the ocean from view. Now only the salty smell in the wind told him he was running near the sea.

They say this leg is boring, Jota thought, *but it's actually brutal.*

Most people saw the third leg between Totsuka and Hiratsuka as an in-between stage. The route turned south from National Route 1 at Higashi-Matano. After passing Fujisawa Station at the seven-kilometer point, the course continued through nondescript roads downtown. It turned right at the Hamasuka intersection, headed down National Route 134, commonly known as the Shonan coastal road, where the same monotonous scenery continued for some time. Since there weren't many houses along the road and it was far from any train stations, this was one section of the Hakone race where there were some large gaps in the line of spectators.

For Jota, it was tough to run when no one was watching. The more people looked to him in expectation, the more his motivation was boosted. Another aspect that made this course challenging was the contrast in terrain. The route leading up to the coastal road had small ups and downs, whereas it became almost completely flat and linear along the sea.

It was 42.3°F. He was still running against a headwind. Since it was a clear, bright day, Mount Fuji might have been visible in the distance, but he couldn't spare any energy to look for it.

Yup, Jota thought, *Hakone Ekiden is definitely better on TV. You should watch it when you're lazing around at home and pecking at some osechi or something. And around the third leg, you can take in the aerial shot from the helicopter—a panoramic view of the sea, the never-ending road, Mount Fuji. That's the way it should be.* It was a serene, magnificent scene, which stirred up that New Year's holiday spirit.

But now that he was running it himself, Jota couldn't believe how much of a grind it was.

After grabbing the tasuki from Musa at the Totsuka relay station, Jota's Hakone Ekiden started off with an uphill climb from the outset. The runner from Kita-Kanto University, who'd received the tasuki in seventeenth place at Totsuka, stormed past Jota. But he didn't mind. The Tokyo Gakuin runner, who'd started six seconds after Jota, also outstripped him, but he kept his cool. *Running on hills isn't for me*, he thought.

He knew that the Kita-Kanto athlete was a top-tier runner even among all the third-leg contestants. Jota had had a thorough look at the data on his fellow runners that Yuki had shared with him. It would have been a losing battle if he'd tried to keep up with that runner. Getting bullheaded would only land him in trouble. As for the Tokyo Gakuin runner, the guy was already panting when he went by. *I can catch up to him later and turn the tables*, Jota thought.

Jota could see far ahead of him on the coastal road. He already had a clear view of the four runners in front of him: Tokyo Gakuin, Shinsei, and two more who seemed to be falling behind in the ranks, Maebashi Institute of Technology and Jonan Bunka.

At the fifteen-kilometer water point, the Kansei student yelled, "You're gaining on them!"

All right, I can do it. Jota felt a fresh wave of energy flow down through his legs.

The landlord, who had been quiet until then, shouted from the coach vehicle, "Jota! Are you concentrating? Is your head wandering off somewhere?"

It has been—about Joji and stuff. How'd he know? Is my form off?

"Here's a message from Haiji. The last kilometer is where you've got to stand your ground and pull through. Don't let anything throw you off, whatever you see. Over and out!"

So Haiji was behind it. It made sense to Jota now. *No way the landlord would've noticed.* Kiyose must have been watching on the portable TV and decided to give Jota a little kick.

But what did he mean about throwing me off? What's waiting ahead?

Jota felt a thrill run through him. Kiyose knew him so well. He just couldn't resist going to check for himself whenever he heard there was something stimulating to be seen.

He could rebel against Kiyose all he wanted, but in the end, Kiyose had Jota dancing in the palm of his hand. It got on Jota's nerves a little, but it also made him laugh.

First, he passed Tokyo Gakuin and Shinsei.

At 18.1 kilometers came the Shonan Bridge over the Sagami River. The sand-barrier grove came to an end, and Jota could finally see the vast expanse of the sea out of the corner of his eye. Wild, white waves broke near the mouth of the river, where fresh water and seawater clashed and swirled into one.

Jota was almost catching up to Jonan Bunka and Maebashi. He decided to strike once he crossed the bridge, then he turned his attention even farther ahead.

And there he was: the runner from Tokyo Taiiku.

Jota could see his blue uniform lined with light blue—a uniform that had been too far ahead in the race to see until now.

Jota couldn't reach the runner yet. But he could get nearer. He could close the distance as much as possible, then pass it on to Joji. Jota thought of Sakaki, the Totai member who tortured Kakeru and went out of his way to provoke the Chikusei-so team. Sakaki had always infuriated Jota. Jota felt sorry for Kakeru, who clammed up in front of his old teammate, unable to think of a good comeback. *I may be the kind of guy who holds grudges and obsesses over stuff, but at least I'm not a sneaky asshole like Sakaki.*

I don't have anything against the rest of the Totai team, but as long as Sakaki's one of them, that makes them our rival, our enemy, who deserves to be clobbered to the ground. Of course, we're nothing like Sakaki. We'll take them head-on. Fight it out in the race.

Jota charged forward, mounting an aggressive attack. He came neck and neck with Jonan Bunka and Maebashi. They didn't let him pass so easily. But Jota didn't care about those two anymore. His attention was focused solely on the runners farther ahead, Kikui and Totai.

Jota saw the sign marking 20 kilometers. The 21.3-kilometer course of the third leg was coming to an end. Jota suddenly recalled Kiyose's words. *What's that thing he was talking about? The thing that might surprise me?* When he dove into the final kilometer, he realized what it was.

The last part of the course was a straight road, so the Hiratsuka relay station rose into view. When there was a target in sight, it made him feel as though he wasn't getting any closer, no matter how much he ran. *Keep calm. Hang on tight, pull away from the runners next to me, and pass on the tasuki to Joji as fast as I can. Make every second count.*

But something else happened that startled Jota even more. Around two hundred meters to the relay station, he noticed Hanako on a bicycle, speeding along on the sidewalk to keep up with him. She was pedaling with all her might behind the rows of spectators.

"Jota, you're almost there!" Her voice rang out over the commotion.

Hana never tells us to "keep going" or "give it all you got." Because she knows we're already working as hard as we can. Why does she root for us so hard?

Jota pictured her face smiling up at him, and he almost blurted out, "Oh!"

Like a divine revelation, the realization descended upon him.

Could it be that Hana likes me?

When he thought about things in that light, it made sense why Yuki and Nico smirked suspiciously whenever Hanako came to Chikusei-so and why Musa was so insistent that the twins see her home every single time.

But hang on. It was always me and Joji taking her home together. And Hana looked perfectly happy with that.

So then, which of us does she like?

Jota's head was spinning in excitement and confusion. He was still too wrapped up in his tangle of thoughts to notice when he left Jonan Bunka and Maebashi in the dust.

Not long before, Joji and Nico had been stunned as they stood at the Hiratsuka relay station, gaping at Hanako careening away on a bike.

"She's gone," Joji remarked.

"Yup, she's gone," Nico agreed.

Hanako had been waiting with them at Hiratsuka, but when she caught on to the fact that Jota was coming closer, she flew off. She practically commandeered a bicycle from one of the spectators, saying, "I'll give it back in a second!"

"She's a nice girl, huh?" Nico said.

Before she went, Hanako had been as thoughtful as ever, making sure Joji felt comfortable before his race. With Nico's assistance, she provided Joji with drinks and blankets, and when Joji was doing stretches, she chatted with him to take his mind off the race and ease his nerves.

Frank and good-natured, Hanako had already won Nico over. He felt like a father nodding approvingly at the girl who was to marry his son.

The question is, though, Nico wondered, scratching at his stubble, *which twin does she like?*

Since Hanako had chosen to keep Joji company at the relay station, Nico had surmised that she liked Joji, but then she went off to cheer for Jota, too. And she didn't just "go off"—she flew off like she couldn't keep still, even snatching a bike from a stranger.

So which one is it? Or could it be both?

Such thoughts were what had prompted Nico to comment, "She's a nice girl, huh?"

All smiles, Joji only said, "Yeah, she sure is."

Are you kidding me? He's still not getting it. Nico sighed and turned his attention back to the top runners who were arriving at Hiratsuka: Manaka, Rikudo, and Boso, in that order. Before the race began, everyone had expected the first day to be a bitter battle between Rikudo and Boso, but they were now getting ambushed by the Manaka team, which was putting up a surprisingly good fight. It made the crowd go wild.

The next runners were fast approaching behind them.

"Look! It's Jota, he's passing them!" Joji cried out.

"Let's see," Nico said, leaning out into the road. Jota, in his black-and-silver uniform, had just overtaken Jonan Bunka and Maebashi. He was sprinting so fast that Hanako was struggling to keep up on the bike. Meanwhile, the other runners were handing off their tasukis one after another.

"Oh yeah, he's running all right." Nico slapped Joji on his back. "You're up next. You ready?"

"Bring it on. Can't let Jota steal the whole show. I'm gonna *run*, baby!" Joji said brightly, loosening up his ankles. There was still a good deal of distance between Kansei and the two teams ahead of them, Kikui and Totai.

"Be careful not to push too hard just because Jota climbed up the ranks. It's not gonna be easy for someone with your ability and time to overtake them. Just count yourself lucky if you can narrow the gap."

"Gotcha." Joji nodded, then stepped out on the handoff line at the staff's announcement. Nico stood by, awaiting Jota's arrival and Joji's departure.

Totai came into Hiratsuka in ninth place, three hours, nineteen minutes, fifty-eight seconds after they'd set off from Otemachi. Ten seconds later, Kikui handed off the tasuki in tenth place. Then fifteen seconds after Kikui, Jota passed on the Kansei tasuki to Joji.

They were three hours, twenty minutes, twenty-three seconds into the race. The Kansei team had hauled themselves up to eleventh place. Jota left a remarkable record of running 21.3 kilometers in one hour, four minutes, thirty-two seconds—the tenth-best time in the third-leg group.

Nico, however, was in too much shock to celebrate Jota's feat. Jota, running toward them with a spine-chillingly fierce look, had exclaimed just as he was handing over the tasuki, "I think Hana likes us!"

"What?! No way!" Joji yelled as he sprinted away.

Nico felt pricked all over by the funny looks people were giving them. "Hey, are you guys taking this seriously?" he grumbled, wrapping his arm around Jota's shoulders. He dragged him off to hide in the back corner of the relay station, away from the stares.

"'Course we are," Jota retorted, gasping for breath, his hands on his knees. "How come you never told us?"

"That Hana's crushing on you guys?"

"Yeah. Or am I just imagining it?"

"Probably not. But man, why here, why now? Talk about bad timing. What if Joji gets distracted?"

"What might distract him? Did anything happen?" Nico and Jota turned around upon hearing the voice, clear as a bell. There Hanako was, having returned the bike to its owner. She wiped the sweat off her forehead and beamed at Jota. "You were amazing."

Jota, who was squatting on the ground, turned bright red down to

the nape of his neck. He got up awkwardly and mumbled, "Uh, thanks."
He couldn't even look her in the face.

Nico scratched his head, at a loss. *Seriously? If Jota's like this, chances are Joji's not much better . . .*

"Looks like it's time to call Haiji," he said.

Hanako gave Nico a quizzical look.

Kakeru and Kiyose were waiting in front of Hakone-Yumoto Station
for the bus to Lake Ashi. They had to go all the way up Mount Hakone
before the traffic was restricted for the race. There was a long line of
cars going up the road up the mountain; clearly, they weren't the only
ones who had thought ahead.

"We're eleventh, Haiji!" Kakeru turned up the volume on the portable TV, trying to stamp away the cold.

The broadcaster sounded animated, too. "Manaka University has
come out on top at the Hiratsuka relay station, passing on their tasuki
in first place. Rikudo University, with their sights set on seizing their
fourth consecutive victory at Hakone, came in second with a delay of
nineteen seconds. In third place is Boso University, with only fifty seconds separating them from the leading team. Wow, what a plot twist
in the third leg. Don't you think, Yanaka?"

Yanaka, the commentator, took over. "Oh yes. We expected this
year's race would be a one-on-one battle between Rikudo and Boso,
but now Manaka is entering the fight. I'm excited to see how things
are going to play out in the fourth leg, then the fifth up the mountain."

"The Hakone regulars are all lined up from the fourth to tenth
places: Dochido, Daiwa, Kofu Gakuin, Saikyo, Kita-Kanto, Tokyo
Taiiku, and Kikui. Any one of these teams could rise in the remaining
legs to Mount Hakone, and come out victorious for the return journey
tomorrow—even the overall race."

"And we can't take our eyes off Kansei University in eleventh place," Yanaka said, unable to hide his enthusiasm. "They were last in the first leg, but they've been steadily climbing up the ranks ever since. Even though they have only ten members on the team, every single one of them has nerves of steel. They did a great job of matching each runner to the course that suits his particular skill set. In fact, it's not out of the realm of possibility that they could secure seed rights for next year—or rise to even higher ranks."

"Not to belabor the point, but who would have thought this dark horse would put up such a strong fight? Yanaka, the Kansei University has three fourth-year students on their team. Even if they can win seed rights, what would happen to them next year? They wouldn't have enough members."

"That's a fair point," Yanaka chuckled. "It's extremely rare that a team with only ten members competes in the Hakone Ekiden. This is the only time it's happened since the race has been televised, at least. Who knows—if they get seed rights, they might have to ask the fourth-years to repeat their year."

"Well, desperate times," the broadcaster quipped.

"I'm just kidding. But I don't think it'll be a problem," Yanaka said, his tone growing a little more serious. "After their impressive performance in this race, I'm sure there'll be new students who want in. There are benefits to being part of a strong team at a prestigious institution, but it's also nice to have universities like this where young people who've never run before are given a chance. After all, the whole purpose behind the Hakone Ekiden is to foster runners who can hold their own on the international level and to expand the scope of the long-distance track world in Japan."

"This guy knows what he's talking about," Kiyose murmured at the TV.

"Who is he?" Kakeru asked.

"You really are clueless, aren't you? Yanaka was an ace runner at Daiwa University about thirty years ago. He ran in the Olympics, too, representing Japan in the marathon. Now he's an adviser for a corporate track team, I think."

"Hunh." *I guess when they've taken on the world, it shows in what they say*, Kakeru thought.

The camera switched to the fourth-leg runners, zooming in on Joji.

"Why's Joji grinning like that?" Kiyose said.

"He does look kind of goofy."

"Come to think of it, Jota's face was bright red at Hiratsuka. Maybe from the effort?"

"He's not the type to get nervous like that, either. Wonder what happened?"

Just then, Kiyose's phone rang. This time, Kiyose himself switched to speakerphone as soon as he picked up.

"Hey, Haiji. We've got a bit of a situation here." It was Nico.

"What's wrong?" Kakeru blurted out.

"Oh—Kakeru? Did I call your number by accident?"

"No, this is my phone." Kiyose didn't bother explaining the speaker mechanism. "Did something happen?"

"Hmm, so Kakeru can hear everything I say, huh. I don't know if I should say it then."

"Never mind him, out with it already," Kiyose demanded.

Picking up on the irritation in Kiyose's voice, Nico gave in. "It's the twins. They've figured out that Hana has feelings for them. So as you can imagine, Jota's in la-la land coming back from the race, and Joji's in la-la land going into it."

Kiyose glanced at Kakeru. *Why's he looking at me?* Kakeru wondered.

"*Now* they figured it out?" Kiyose sighed at the phone.

"Uh-huh, right on cue. So, what do we do?"

"I guess there's nothing we can do, now that they know. I'll keep an eye on Joji's run, and if push comes to shove, I'll think of a way to intervene."

"All right. I'm about to start heading to the inn in Odawara with Jota. Is it still okay for Hana to go to Yokohama?"

The plan was for Hanako to spend the night at the same hotel in Yokohama that Prince was staying at. Once Joji finished the fourth leg, he would also join them, as well as Kakeru and Kiyose later in the evening.

"Yes, we can stick to the plan," Kiyose said.

"Anything you want me to say to Jota?"

"Nothing. His run was perfect."

"I'll tell him that."

When he hung up, Kiyose said, "So, Kakeru," and cracked his neck. "You and Joji better play nice tonight at the hotel. Not sure if Prince and I would be enough to handle a brawl between you two."

"Uh, why would we fight?" Kakeru asked, genuinely puzzled.

Kiyose stared at him for a few moments. "So in the end, you're the last one to get it," he laughed. "Finally. The bus is here. Let's go."

"What are you talking about, Haiji? Hey, wait up!"

The two of them got on the bus, which would take the old road up to Lake Ashi. They sat side by side on the two-person seat. The bus took the roundabout route, winding along narrow roads, but it was probably a better way to go up since it wasn't as congested as National Route 1.

The reception for both the TV and the radio gradually deteriorated as they became hemmed in by the mountains.

Kiyose turned the radio antenna this way and that, as if he were trying to strike a vein of water, before eventually deciding it was a lost cause. "Looks like we can't get updates till we reach Lake Ashi." He pulled out his earbuds and leaned against the window. "Just hope Joji shakes off any impure thoughts and focuses on his run."

"Impure thoughts? That's a bit over the top," Kakeru said with a wry smile. So Hanako's feelings had finally reached the twins. *Surely that's got to be a good thing. Yeah, it is a good thing. Then why do I feel like there's this fog hanging over me? Feels like something's gripping my chest. It's like when I'm frustrated that I can't run as well as I want to. When my body can't burn off all the fuel I have, and useless heat gets trapped inside.*

Kakeru clammed up and endured Kiyose's gaze on the side of his face. Kakeru braced himself. He knew Kiyose was going to tease him again. Kakeru was itching to run. He wanted to be free from hazy feelings, those fuzzy things he couldn't put into words, and feel the wind on his body.

The bus was warm and stuffy with the heat on. Kakeru felt vaguely uncomfortable, the way he felt when he wanted to doze off but kept getting pulled back from the brink of sleep. He sank lower in his seat, wishing he could hide from Kiyose's eyes.

"We have to pull Joji's focus back to the race," said Kiyose. His tone was more serious than Kakeru had anticipated, so he looked up. Kiyose was gazing out the window, not at him. The cedar branches jutted out so close that they almost touched the pane. "What would *you* say to Joji, Kakeru?"

"Well . . ." Kakeru thought about it a little, then gave his answer.

What does that mean? Does Hana really like me?

Joji's head was full of Hanako.

Oh, but Jota said "us," didn't he? What did that even mean? Maybe he wanted to say "either one of us." Or did he mean, "Hana likes both of us as close friends"? If that's what he wanted to say, that's just silly. I knew that a long time ago. I like her as a friend, too. And I've been thinking it'd be nice to get closer to her.

Ahh, but then, what if she really like-likes me? Well, it could be Jota she likes, but what if she actually has a crush on me? What do I do? That would make me super happy. Should I just go for it and try asking her out?

The more Joji turned things over in his head, the wider his grin spread across his face.

Since Joji's thoughts were absorbed in a world of his own, his run was out of focus. He was totally unaware of where he was running. He didn't know he'd entered Oiso, got back onto National Route 1, and passed by the row of pine trees on Tokaido. The scenery streamed by without his seeing it, his body cruising on autopilot.

The fourth leg from Hiratsuka to Odawara was 20.9 kilometers long. It was one of the shorter segments of the Hakone Ekiden, but it was still crucial to stay alert in order to pass on the tasuki in a good position for the fifth leg uphill.

The course continued past Ninomiya and Kouzu on National Route 1, and the runners had to cross several small rivers that flowed into the Sagami Bay before they entered the castle city of Odawara. With every river, there was a small bridge, resulting in slight undulations in the road.

Joji was the type of runner who could get in a groove more easily with some ups and downs rather than a flat road. So even with his wandering thoughts, he somehow managed to hold a steady pace.

But now, he was missing the drive to chase after Kikui and Totai running ahead of him. The distance between him and the two runners had remained the same since they had left the Hiratsuka relay station. The only thing on Joji's mind was his wish to know how Hanako really felt about him.

One feature of the fourth leg was a dramatic contrast between the first and second halves of the course. The route along the coast leading up to the city streets of Odawara was relatively warm, congenial for running. But when the route left behind the city area and approached the foot of Mount Hakone, the temperature dropped sharply. The contestants had to run straight into the biting wind that swept down the mountain. The last three kilometers were a long, arduous climb. The last kilometer was especially steep, as though they were already on the mountain.

All the facts about the course—the topography he'd researched in advance, as well as his experience from the trial run—had fallen clean out of Joji's head. He had no space in his brain to think about the course right now, let alone devise tactics for the race.

Joji couldn't help it. His thoughts simply kept coming back to Hanako.

In general, Joji was on the popular side. He'd gone out with a few girls in the past. He'd liked all of them, of course, but somehow things sort of fell apart after a while, and the relationships faded away.

The cause lay in the fact that Joji had a brother who looked just like him.

For example, say his girlfriend came over. When Joji answered the door, the first thing she'd say was always "Umm, Joji?" The same thing happened when he was walking down the corridor at school with Jota, wearing the same uniform. Joji's girlfriend would never call him from behind. She'd circle around in front of them, look from one to the other, then talk to Joji.

It was true the brothers looked alike, so it wasn't the subtle pause that put off Joji. He just didn't like how his girlfriend had to try so hard to tell them apart.

He knew full well that his wish was self-indulgent, that he was being selfish and unreasonable. He didn't have any problems with having an older brother who looked like him. In fact, when he was little, he'd had fun pretending to be Jota to play tricks on their friends.

Even so, he tried his best to play up his "Joji-ness" in front of girls he liked. Every time a girlfriend took a moment to spot the difference between them, he felt a bit hurt. It made him want to ask her, *Do you think I'd try to trick you?*

None of the girls had meant any harm, and Joji knew he was overreacting. He'd never say any of this out loud.

He just didn't want to be compared with his precious brother. All he wanted was to be accepted for who he was: a guy who happened to have an older brother who looked just like him.

In that sense, Hanako was a little unusual.

She never mistook Jota for Joji or vice versa. Even when they were wearing the same tracksuits, even when they had their backs to her, she always called each twin by the right name, as naturally as breathing.

And she never pointed out the differences in their personalities either—just as someone wouldn't go out of their way to point out the distinction between Kiyose and Kakeru.

Once, Joji got curious and asked, "Hey Hana, how're you so good at telling us apart?"

"Tell you apart?" Hanako tilted her head, puzzled.

"You know, me and Jota. I guess we really look alike, even for twins. Our friends at school come up to me pretty often thinking I'm Jota."

"But the people at Chikusei-so never do that, do they?"

"Well, sure, 'cause we hang out all the time."

"Hmm." Hanako pondered over it. It was nighttime, and they were walking back to Yaokatsu from Chikusei-so. Jota, who was walking on her other side, seemed to be waiting for her answer with bated breath.

"I don't know. I've never thought about how to tell you apart or anything like that," she said eventually. "From the start, I always thought of you guys as brothers who were super close—and for me, it's totally normal to see you together. And, well, you're both . . . good-looking, too."

Ah! Joji almost yelled out midrun.

Yeah! She did say that. She called us "good-looking"! Maybe she really is crushing on us. Though I'm still not sure which one of us she likes.

Well, whichever it is, I'm happy either way, Joji thought. Nothing would change the fact that Hanako was a special person: someone who accepted him—all of him—just as he was, whether like or unlike his brother.

But then again . . . Joji sank again into his sea of thoughts. *I always thought she had a thing for Kakeru.*

That was why he'd been shy to make a move on Hanako despite all his affection for her.

Both at the summer camp and whenever she came over to Chikusei-so, Hanako often chatted with Kakeru. Joji knew how beautiful Kakeru's figure was when he ran. Joji felt a bit weird about describing it that way, but when he saw Kakeru run, he'd discovered for the first time in his life the strength and beauty of someone who dedicated himself to sport.

Kakeru might have been a track freak who probably couldn't help but march to the beat of his own drum, but there was something pure about him. *Kakeru can't make friends with people as easily as I can. But he always works hard to find the right words, and to get to know people and himself a little better. Kakeru lives the way he runs. Powerful, dead straight, inspiring hope in everyone who sees him.*

This was why Joji liked Kakeru, even though they got into fights. Joji always dreamed of the world he might be able to glimpse if only he could run like Kakeru. Hanako seemed captivated by running itself, so naturally Joji assumed she admired Kakeru, too.

Plus, Kakeru didn't seem all that indifferent to her either.

"Hey, Joji! Are you listening?! Oi!"

The landlord's furious bark snapped Joji to the present.

Huh? Where am I? He looked around. He could see the Totai and Kikui runners up ahead. He was just crossing a wide bridge over Sakawagawa, fifteen kilometers into the race. Soon, he'd enter the city streets of Odawara.

How did I get all the way here? The cheers of the crowd took him by surprise.

"Joji!" the landlord bellowed again. Joji waved a hand to signal he was listening.

Focus on the race. A Kansei student was handing him a water bottle; Joji grabbed it and splashed it over his head. He licked at the trickle of water as it traced the corner of his mouth.

"Don't ask me what it means, but here's a message from Kakeru," the landlord declared. "'If you're in love, run.' That's all."

You're one to talk. Joji stifled a laugh. *You don't even have a clue how you feel about her.*

But you're right, Kakeru. Now's the time to run—because I love it. I'll run for the sake of this whole crazy roller-coaster year, for all the people we've met along the way. I'll run so hard that I'll soak up all the heartfelt support and repel all the heartless insults we've gotten. I'll savor every moment of this run—the running we love so much.

Everything else will come later.

Joji sprinted through the quaint, tranquil streets of Odawara. The people of the neighborhood flocked to the course to root for them. *Must be an old tradition for these townies*, Joji thought. Though running might have played little part in their daily lives, they watched the athletes running through their neighborhood as intently as if they were participating in the race themselves.

I'm glad I got to run in the Hakone Ekiden. I'm glad that now I know what it's like to run with everything I've got.

When he turned right at the intersection in the Honcho district of

Odawara, he caught up to Kikui at last. The wind from the mountain chilled his damp hair, but even that felt refreshing. His next target was Totai.

Joji passed under the railroad bridge of the Hakone Tozan Railway and, with the Hayakawa River flowing on his left, he finally came to the steep gradient of the last kilometer. It was grueling. Since he'd been so distracted in the first part of the course, he struggled to find a good rhythm.

The Odakyu Romancecar rattled past him on his right, heading for Hakone-Yumoto.

Joji recalled what Kiyose had told Kakeru that summer: "Is speed the only thing that matters to you? Then there's no point in running. Just go on a bullet train! Take a flight! That's a lot faster!"

Back then, Joji didn't really get what Kiyose meant. But now he did. If he wanted to go to Hakone, he might as well sit on the Romancecar, munching on some frozen satsuma. It was less effort, and faster.

But that's not the point. Where I—we—want to go isn't Hakone. It's somewhere much further, deeper, and even more beautiful, somewhere only running will take us. Even if I'm not ready for it just yet, I hope I'll see that place someday. Until then, I'll keep on running. I'll run all the way through this painful last stretch and edge my way closer to that uncharted territory.

Joji didn't let the Kikui runner get away. He forgot everything else and threw himself into the run, catapulting up over the unrelenting hill.

A peculiar music began to drift down from the Kazamatsuri Station of the Hakone Tozan Railway, where the Odawara relay station awaited him.

"What's all that racket?" Kiyose asked.

Yuki clamped a hand over one ear and raised his voice at the phone. "We've got chikuwa and hanpen dancing around over here. Anyway, how's the weather looking on your end?"

People were swarming around Kazamatsuri Station to watch the tasuki handoff. The relay zone was set up in the parking lot of a shop selling products from a kamaboko company in Odawara. Human-sized surimi fish cakes—presumably they were company mascots—were bouncing to the music. With large-barreled drums booming out the battle beats, the carnivalesque atmosphere was almost at its peak.

The fourth-leg runners were beginning to arrive. Yuki was still accompanying Shindo, waiting for Joji, who would reach them soon.

The National Route 1 lay between the Hakone Tozan Railway tracks and the Hayakawa River, past Hakone-Yumoto and up toward the mountain.

"It's pretty cold here," Kiyose said on the other end. "It's just over thirty-nine degrees now, but clouds are coming out. Might drop a lot more."

That meant there was at least about three and a half degrees' difference in temperature between Kazamatsuri and Lake Ashi. Yuki decided that Shindo should wear a long-sleeve shirt.

"How's Shindo?" Kiyose asked.

"He's in the restroom. Oh wait, he's coming back. I'll swap." Yuki called out, "Shindo, it's Haiji," and waved his phone in the air. The spectators made way for Shindo as he returned from the shop's restroom—probably less because he was a Kansei member who was about to run in the race than because he stood out in his bizarre outfit. Shindo still had half of his face wrapped in a towel, with two layers of masks over it. Fever unsteadied his steps.

Just pop on a helmet, and he'd fit right into those Yasuda Auditorium student protest photos from the '60s, Yuki thought, holding out the phone to him.

Shindo took it. "Yes? I'm okay," he said in a hoarse, feverish voice that sounded far from okay. He exchanged a few sentences with Kiyose and hung up.

"What did Haiji say?" Yuki asked.

"He told me to make sure I grab water at the hydration points."

There was nothing else Kiyose could say. Yuki and Shindo both understood how Kiyose must be feeling. If Shindo dropped out of the race, the Kansei team's Hakone Ekiden would come to an end then and there. Shindo had no choice but to do everything in his power to reach Lake Ashi.

"Shindo! Yuki!"

A voice called to them over the bustle of the crowd. They turned to find the Yaokatsu owner walking toward them, with Nira on a leash. Since everyone at Chikusei-so would be gone for these two days, he was looking after the dog for them. Nira noticed Shindo and Yuki and wagged his tail with gusto.

"Joji's fighting for the tenth place with Kikui right about now," Yaokatsu said. He'd been waiting at the Odawara relay station with Nira since the morning. Shindo gave him a quiet nod, inwardly strengthening his resolve. It was obvious that Shindo was sick, so Yaokatsu didn't offer any empty words like "Are you feeling all right?" He looked on in silence as Shindo stroked Nira's head.

The beating of the drums grew even more frantic. The Boso runner was the first to pass on their tasuki. Next came Daiwa; the team was fifth at Hiratsuka, but they'd climbed up. The reigning champion of Hakone, Rikudo, was yet to be seen. The unexpected turn of events caused a stir in the crowd.

Twenty seconds after Daiwa, Manaka came in. Another seven seconds later, Rikudo arrived at last, having fallen to fourth place.

Shindo took off his bench coat and handed it to Yuki. He was wearing a silver-gray long-sleeve shirt under his running uniform. The farther he ascended Mount Hakone, the colder it would become. There were a few other runners in long sleeves, too.

"Time to go." Yuki accompanied Shindo toward the changeover line, holding the jacket in his arms. Kofu Gakuin, Dochido, then Kita-Kanto passed on their tasuki in succession. At that point, they were four minutes behind the lead, Boso. They still had a chance to overtake the top teams during the climb. It was a close race. Any team could come out victorious.

Shindo peeled off his masks and towel. "Please put these in a bag, seal it tight, and give it to Mr. Yaokatsu. It has germs on it, so don't hold on to it under any circumstances," he told Yuki.

Yuki thought this sounded a bit extreme, but Shindo looked completely serious. He was probably keyed up as his turn in the race drew closer. If he had anything to worry about, it would get in the way of his run. So Yuki simply said, "Will do."

Saikyo and Totai arrived. "Kikui and Kansei are up next," the staff announced.

Should I say it or not? Yuki vacillated, but as Shindo was about to take a step forward to the changeover line, Yuki stopped him, blurting out, "If it gets too hard, you can withdraw anytime."

Startled, Shindo turned to stare at Yuki's face. Yuki knew his words might make a fissure in Shindo, whose mind and body were already taut to the breaking point. But still, he had to say it.

Just for an instant, a clear light came into Shindo's feverish eyes. Yuki met his unwavering gaze. "No one's going to blame you for it," Yuki pressed. "If you think you can't make it, just drop out on the spot. Please."

"Okay." Shindo smiled, then went to stand at the handoff line.

Joji was sprinting with all his strength, neck and neck with Kikui. Neither yielded. They even stopped breathing for the last few steps and crossed the line at exactly the same moment.

"Shindo!" Joji shouted.

The silver letters of *Kansei* sewn onto the tasuki rippled in the wind. Shindo wordlessly gripped Joji's hand over the sash for a split second, then shot out of the relay station.

"His hand was burning," Joji murmured. Shindo's hand had held more heat than Joji's, even though he'd just run more than twenty kilometers. Joji watched him vanish into the woods, stupefied. *I'm an idiot. Why couldn't I stay more focused? I knew Shindo was sick. That he was waiting for me here, believing in me. I knew all that, so why couldn't I hand him the tasuki in a better position?*

The Kansei team reached the Odawara relay station four hours, twenty-four minutes, forty-seven seconds after they set off from Otemachi. They were now tied with Kikui in tenth place.

Joji had taken one hour, four minutes, twenty-four seconds to run 20.9 kilometers. Out of all the fourth-leg runners, his time ranked eleventh. Jota's time had ranked tenth, completing the 21.3-kilometer third leg in one hour, four minutes, thirty-two seconds. Considering the shorter distance, as well as the difference in their abilities, Joji should have been able to run at a much better pace.

Kansei had finally ascended to tenth place, but Joji felt only regret.

"Good work," Yuki told him. He could see Joji wasn't satisfied with his own run, but it wasn't the kind of situation in which a bystander could casually proffer words of consolation or encouragement. Seen from the side, Joji had completed his part of the race with flying colors: an achievement that kept Kansei's hope alive. Whatever self-reproach he felt, Joji had to find some way to come to terms with it himself.

"Yuki, I wish I could've done better," Joji said and bit his lip.

"Me too." Yuki took hold of Joji's drooping head and gave him a gentle shake. "I couldn't stop Shindo. I had to try, but in the end, he went anyway." Yuki led Joji to Yaokatsu and Nira, who waited for them away from the din of the crowd. "Chin up. No matter how hard you try, there'll be times when you fall short. But that's what makes things interesting, right?"

Kansei's Hakone Ekiden, Joji's regrets and delights. These would never end. There was no way they could end. As long as he felt he couldn't reach that elusive goal, there was an infinite number of nexts.

Joji wiped his eyes with his fist and straightened up. "You're right."

Now they would each make their way to their own destinations, to do what they had to do: Yuki to Lake Ashi, to prepare for his own run tomorrow; Joji to the hotel in Yokohama; Yaokatsu and Nira back to the shopping arcade in his mini pickup truck, to get ready for the wrap-up party tomorrow night.

The race would go on, and still more opportunities lay ahead. Joji waved at Yaokatsu and Nira, and started walking toward Kazamatsuri Station with Yuki.

Despite the deep chills Shindo felt all over, sweat kept streaming down his skin. His damp shirt felt cold in the wind, yet it didn't abate the flush of his body. Every time he took a step forward, the impact shot pain through his head, and he could barely breathe through his stuffy nose.

He was taking on Mount Hakone in delirium. Every sound and sensory stimulus felt distant, as if his head were swathed in some transparent, shock-absorbing cushioning.

Pain, torture, pain, torture. Those two words whirled around in his brain, trailed down his spine, suffused his entire body.

He ran the first kilometer in three minutes, thirty seconds. Even for an uphill course, it was a slow pace. The Kikui runner, who'd received the tasuki at the same time as Kansei, was long gone.

Once he passed through the onsen district of Hakone-Yumoto at 3.4 kilometers, his surroundings began to assume the aspect of a ravine.

At the Kanrei Domon Tunnel, the Yokohama runner passed Shindo. The tunnel stretched along a river, and its concrete wall on the right was shaped like arched pillars. Light streamed in through the gaps, forming a black-and-white world inside. Like a film with missing frames, the Yokohama runner passed him in angular movements. Shindo could only watch him go.

Once he reached the streets of the Tonosawa Onsen district, which still retained the air of a bygone era, there was an onset of curves, one after another. As the road twisted and turned, it also gained in elevation by degrees. Shindo strained his bleary eyes to try to determine the trajectory of his run. He had to trace the innermost part of each curve in order to minimize the distance.

His legs felt heavy and sore. His joints might be getting inflamed from the fever. But the real climb was yet to come. Shindo passed under the Deyama Iron Bridge of the Hakone Tozan Railway. Though his steps were shaky, he kept climbing up without a pause. His pace had dropped to three minutes, thirty-five seconds per kilometer.

He climbed the mountain along the Hayakawa River, and at the 7.1-kilometer point, he came to a hairpin turn at Ohiradai. A heavy groan escaped from the engine of the car trailing him. *Looks like I'm not the only one struggling*, Shindo thought dimly. *This climb is tough for cars, too.*

He entered the Miyanoshita Onsen district and passed the Fujiya Hotel. Both sides of the narrow road were packed with vacationers spending their New Year's holiday at the well-established hot springs hotel. Shindo was slipping down the ranks, and three teams had already outstripped him by this point. But the spectators cheered for him when he went by, yelling, "Go Kansei!" even though they were complete strangers. They had probably seen the team on TV and were rooting for the underdog.

Spurred on by the cheers, Shindo ran up to the intersection at Miyanoshita and turned left. What awaited him there was a slope so steep it almost sickened him to look up at it.

At ten kilometers came Kowakien, at an elevation of 1,968.5 feet. The elevation of the city of Odawara was 131.2 feet, so that meant he had just run up an altitude difference of more than 1,800 feet in one go.

This, however, was far from the end. The highest point of National Route 1 came after the 15-kilometer point, at an elevation of 2,867.45 feet. In other words, over the 20.7 kilometers of the fifth leg, the elevation increased by three times the height of the Tokyo Metropolitan Government Building.

The landlord had been quiet at the five-kilometer point, but now he broke his silence.

"Shindo, here's the thing about the game of Go."

What's he talking about? Is the fever getting to my ears, too? Shindo strained every nerve to listen to the old man's voice, which cracked a little in the loudspeaker.

"It's tricky to decide when to admit defeat. Suppose you realize that you're losing. The stronger a player you are, the more you put all your effort into devising the best way to accept defeat. You can try and venture a last-ditch maneuver to turn the tables, but if your opponent still parries your attack, that's when you surrender. Even if there are still empty spaces on the grid on the board, you end the game. But no one would criticize you if you did, or accuse you of giving up in the middle of the battle. Quite the contrary, in fact. If you surrender at the right time, you'll be praised along with the victor as a wise player who knows when to surrender. Because everyone will know you persevered until the very end, till it was time to let go."

Shindo realized what he meant.

"Are you suffering, Shindo? If you are, raise your hands. I'll get off this car right now and stop you from taking another step forward."

Shindo clenched his fists and shook his head. This was the ekiden. If all ten runners didn't finish their run, the battle would never be over. Surrender wasn't an option. However messy and undignified he might appear, and even if he missed the prudent moment to give in, he would still run. *I'll keep running as long as my legs still move. No, even if I were to collapse, I'd still crawl my way forward till I reach Lake Ashi.*

Sensing Shindo's determination, the landlord said no more and switched off his loudspeaker.

The curves in the road up to Kowakien had allowed Shindo to just hit his stride, as he could feel himself inching forward with each turn. But from here on out, there would be fewer curves and hardly any spectators. He would have to keep climbing on toward the highest point of National Route 1, a solitary runner on the desolate mountain, where snow still lingered on the side of the road.

He passed by the main gate of Keimei Gakuen. His breath came out in thicker, whiter clouds because of the high altitude. It was 37.4°F.

The wind blew at 6.7 miles per hour from the southeast. The sky was clear and bright.

Back home, his parents were probably following his run anxiously on TV. *It's all right, I'm going to go home once this is over. I'll come back with Musa to tell you all about how amazing a race the Hakone Ekiden is.*

At the fifteen-kilometer point, Shindo received a water bottle from the Kansei student and was informed that he was seventeenth, almost ten minutes behind the lead. He realized he'd been overtaken by two more teams at some point. His throat was swollen and constricted as he gulped down the water. He'd hoped he might feel a little better, but the water turned lukewarm long before it touched his stomach.

Teams that fell more than ten minutes behind the top team were required to begin at the same time on the second day of the race. He wanted to avoid that at all costs. The morale of his teammates who were running the return journey depended on it.

The road dipped, going downhill before rearing its head again toward the peak. Already almost spent, Shindo plowed on. He punched his cramping thighs as if to give himself a kick.

The shimmering surface of Lake Ashi was coming into view.

Shindo was on the last descent leading to the lake. He was no longer sure whether he was even moving forward. Footsteps pounded past. Another team had outstripped him.

Unable to shift gears from uphill to downhill, Shindo couldn't accelerate. Frustration ate at him. He didn't want to lose. No matter how humiliated he looked, no matter how many teams overtook him, he didn't want to lose to himself. Not here. That was the only thing that kept his legs in motion.

When he heard the crowds cheering at Motohakone and passed under the towering torii gate at 19.1 kilometers, he lost consciousness.

Nothing reached Shindo's senses—not the green of Onshi Park by the lake, nor the sight of Mount Fuji soaring beyond, nor the drums of the cheer squads beating along the final straight line of the course. Even pain was distant now.

Onward, onward, onward. This single word kept echoing in his foggy brain like an incantation.

It was just past noon when Kakeru and Kiyose arrived at Lake Ashi. The portable TV picked up a signal again just as the broadcast was showing Joji, running the latter half of the fourth leg.

Kiyose called the landlord in the coach car and Yuki at the Odawara relay station, passing along vital messages and instructions. Kakeru, in the meantime, was gazing at the lake a little way off.

With the view in front of him, Kakeru couldn't believe he'd been in a world of skyscrapers and asphalt only some hours ago. The lake gleamed silver as if coated by a thin sheet of ice, reflecting the sky and the gentle undulations of the surrounding mountains. A pleasure boat designed like a pirate ship drew a leisurely line across the lake, sending small ripples over the water. Mount Fuji, which rose over the scene, was capped in pure white snow and looked so vivid that it felt much closer than it really was.

It was a tranquil, beautiful sight—so much so that it felt unreal.

The parking lot of Lake Ashi, where the finish line of the first day of the race and the starting line of the second were located, set a stark contrast to the magnificent serenity of nature. The place was buzzing, packed with spectators and staff awaiting the fifth-leg runners. It was freezing out; the cold winds were blowing in over the lake, but the crowd was glued to the giant TV screen that had been set up especially for race day. Many of them were holding some refreshments—cans of beer sold at the sponsor company's stalls and bowls of steaming tonjiru prepared by the locals at what resembled a big soup kitchen.

The screen displayed the athletes running up the mountain road. Numerous broadcasting vehicles were working in tandem to capture all the runners, from the top to the very bottom, since the contestants had spread farther out once they reached the mountain.

The lead was the runner from Boso, who had been the first to leave the Odawara relay station. Rikudo followed next, regaining the team's rank over the course of the climb. Despite the unforeseen turn of events in the middle of the race, the results of the first day seemed to be aligning with prerace predictions that Boso would finish first, beating Rikudo by a close margin.

As for third place, the Daiwa runner, who had been the second to pass through Odawara, appeared to be a solid contender. Manaka, who was third at Odawara, had dropped far behind.

The runner attracting everyone's attention was Kikui. Though the team had tied for tenth with Kansei at Odawara, the runner had steadily gained in rank, and on the last downhill stretch to Lake Ashi, he finally moved up to fifth place. Even though he'd just finished running up a steep gradient, he showed no sign of slowing down. It was almost certain he would set a new course record. If he kept up his pace, he might even do the unprecedented and break through the wall of one hour, eleven minutes, thirty seconds.

Kakeru unconsciously clenched his fists. On the big screen, the camera zoomed in on Inagaki, the runner for Kikui University. He was only a second-year.

Kakeru was riveted. Inagaki ran with such a light spring in his step that he didn't seem to weigh anything, yet his run exuded power. He ran as if he were on flat land. His expression was undaunted, as though he could go even farther. He seemed to have enough strength in his reserve to run all the way up to Mount Fuji.

Fujioka at Rikudo wasn't the only one. The Hakone Ekiden was a race where runners like this emerged: athletes whom no one had heard of before but who burst onto the scene like comets hurtling across the sky, embodying for all to see what it meant to run.

Kakeru felt frustrated—but thrilled, too. *I want to run. Let me start running right now. Let me taste those new heights, those unknown reaches that not even Fujioka and Inagaki have seen.*

The view changed, and Shindo appeared on the screen. Shindo was also in the spotlight now, for completely different reasons. The Kansei team was now eighteenth, falling far behind. Shindo was on the verge of passing out because of his illness. Though staggering from side to side, he forged on desperately.

"Shindo . . ." Kakeru was at a loss for words when he saw his friend, blank-eyed, struggling to make out the route ahead of him. Shindo was in the middle of a battle, and no one could reach out and help him. Fighting for his own sake, and for the sake of the Chikusei-so members whom he'd been running alongside for the past year.

Kakeru had always thought that running was a solitary act. He still thought so now, and he was absolutely certain that it was true.

But it was also true that Shindo embodied what it meant to run on a level that had nothing to do with results or records.

Strength. The thought struck Kakeru. Maybe *this* was the strength that Kiyose was talking about. In essence, to run with strength was no different, whether in individual races or group ekiden.

The power to keep moving forward in the face of pain. The courage to keep fighting the battle within oneself. The tenacity to keep striving to overcome one's own limits rather than external records.

Kakeru had to admit it. Shindo *was* strong. If Kakeru had been running the fifth leg, Kansei would have been able to rise in the ranks. But that didn't necessarily mean Kakeru was superior to Shindo.

Shindo was strong. He was sacrificing his own body for his run, showing Kakeru the kind of run to aspire to.

Why do I run? Why do we run?

Kakeru never took his eyes off the screen.

Why can we never stop running even when it tortures us so much? Every particle of his body stirred restlessly, longing to feel even stronger gusts of wind blowing against him.

"Kakeru."

Kakeru turned to find Kiyose standing right behind him.

"Can you call the inn and ask them to lay out the futon before we arrive? And if they have a doctor they're familiar with on call, ask them to contact the doctor so that they're waiting for us when we get there."

"Got it."

Shindo was visibly dehydrated. It was a gamble whether he'd even make it to the finish line. Kakeru hastily pulled out his cell phone and dialed the lakeside inn. Kiyose went to the event staff to request a stretcher.

The cheers and the anthems surged.

It was five hours, thirty-one minutes, six seconds since the runners had set off from Otemachi. At last, the Boso runner broke the finish tape of the Tokyo-Hakone Round-Trip College Ekiden Race. One minute, thirty-nine seconds later, Rikudo finished second.

Kakeru stood by the finish line with Kiyose. They couldn't see the Kansei uniform yet.

"The landlord told me Shindo refused when he urged him to withdraw," Kiyose murmured. "I just want him to be okay. As long as he gets here safe, I couldn't care less about our time or ranking . . ."

One by one, the runners arrived at the goal. Their teammates welcomed them and guided them to the back of the parking lot, applauding their run.

Kikui finished fifth. Inagaki set a new course record of one hour, eleven minutes, twenty-nine seconds. Considering how even the Rikudo runner, who was second-fastest in this leg, came in at one hour, twelve minutes, and fifteen seconds, Inagaki's would be a difficult record for anyone to beat for years to come. It was a historic achievement.

The fear of being disqualified from the race hung over Kiyose and Kakeru. For them, the Kikui team's celebratory whoops for Inagaki's feat seemed to be coming from another world.

Totai came in seven minutes, forty-seven seconds behind the top team, placing eleventh at five hours, thirty-eight minutes, fifty-three seconds. The team stood well within the range to rise higher on the return journey tomorrow.

The broadcaster's voice could be heard from the large screen. "It's almost eight minutes now since Boso crossed the finish line. Once ten minutes pass, any team arriving after that will have to start at once at a designated time for tomorrow's journey back to Tokyo. How many teams will be hindered by the ten-minute wall this year? All eyes are on the finish line at Lake Ashi!"

As he spoke, Manaka, Teito, and Akebono arrived. Jonan Bunka came in not long after, placing fifteenth at five hours, forty minutes, fifty-six seconds.

"This is it." Kiyose's face stiffened as he stared at the big screen. "It's going to be ten minutes past."

The screen showed the runner from the select team; he was running for his life to make it across the line before the ten-minute cutoff. He dashed past the screaming swarm of people on the lakeside road and turned right at the traffic light onto the short straight path to the finish.

But time was merciless. At that very moment, ten minutes had passed since Boso made it across the line. Gasps of shock escaped the crowd. The runner knocked his head back for an instant but snapped forward again and sprinted past the tape at full speed. The time was five hours, forty-one minutes, thirty-three seconds. Because his team was late by a margin of twenty-seven seconds, they would have to start the race tomorrow with the other late teams at the appointed time.

"It's Shindo!" Kakeru pointed at the screen. Shindo was running with faltering steps behind the runner from Eurasia University. Kakeru and Kiyose sprang out of the crowd to the finish line.

Eurasia came in seventeenth at five hours, forty-two minutes, thirty-four seconds. Then, finally, Shindo turned the corner at the traffic light, his Kansei uniform becoming visible in the final stretch.

Shindo seemed to be following the noise of the crowd to stay on course, barely conscious of the way he was going. Every time he staggered, everyone watching held their breath.

Kakeru was dying to run up to him and hold him up. Shindo was less than forty meters away from the goal. Kakeru wanted to tell Shindo he had done enough and carry him to the doctor. But neither was allowed. The moment a teammate reached out and touched a runner, the team would be disqualified. The only thing he could do now was watch over Shindo and call his name.

"Shindo!" Kiyose yelled.

"Shindo, it's this way! You're almost there!" Kakeru shouted at the top of his voice to reach Shindo over the roar of the crowd. They watched as Shindo mustered every scrap of willpower he had left in him.

Shindo took the last five steps without wavering, planting every step firmly on the ground. As soon as he crossed the finish line, he started to crumple, but Kakeru and Kiyose were there to catch him. His body was burning like it was on fire.

"We need a stretcher, please!" Kiyose shouted. The staff, who had been watching, stunned, rushed over with a rolled-up cloth stretcher.

Kakeru splashed water from a bottle over Shindo's face, and lightly slapped his cheek. "Shindo, it's water! Can you drink? Drink something, please!"

Shindo's lips moved very slightly, so Kakeru pressed the open bottle to his mouth. But Shindo shook his head and refused. What he wanted wasn't water. He was struggling to tell them something, as if it was all that mattered.

As he was laying Shindo down on the stretcher, Kakeru realized that Shindo was trying to apologize.

"Why . . . ?" Kakeru cradled Shindo's head in his arms. He didn't want to hear that kind of thing from Shindo. "You finished your run, Shindo. Isn't that enough? For us—"

Running means everything.

The Kansei team's black-and-silver tasuki had journeyed 107.2 kilometers from Tokyo to Hakone and had now reached Lake Ashi. There was nothing more to desire.

Out of twenty teams, Kansei concluded the first day of the race in eighteenth place. It was five hours, forty-two minutes, fifty-nine seconds after the team had started from Otemachi. A difference of eleven minutes, fifty-three seconds separated them from the leading team.

"Can you please take him to the Ashihara Inn? He needs immediate medical attention," Kiyose told the staff, and they carefully lifted the stretcher.

A doctor who lived nearby was waiting to see them at the inn.

"It's a miracle he ran at all," he remarked, shaking his head in astonishment. "He's got a dreadful cold. And he took a double blow of fatigue and dehydration on top of that—no wonder he's knocked out. Well, he's young and strong, so I don't think we have to worry about it developing into pneumonia. Just make sure he gets plenty of rest tonight."

The doctor stayed until the IV drip was finished, then went home. Kakeru and Kiyose nursed Shindo. The landlord, who had arrived in the coach car, and Yuki, who'd finally made it to Lake Ashi once the traffic restrictions were removed, all gathered around his futon.

Shindo slept like a rock in their hotel room. When the clock struck three in the afternoon, he finally opened his eyes. The first word he uttered was "Mask."

Kakeru took out the masks he'd bought from his pocket. Shindo put one on and slowly sat up on his futon.

"I'm sorry," Shindo said. "I've been nothing but trouble—"

"No, it's me who should be apologizing." Kiyose cut him off firmly. "I didn't realize how much you had on your plate. I basically made you our spokesperson, even though I knew you were tired . . . I'm sorry I pushed you too hard."

If they were left to themselves, Kiyose and Shindo might have gone on apologizing to each other forever. Kakeru tried to think of something he could say to persuade them that it was nobody's fault.

"Now, now," the landlord said to the downcast pair. Kakeru hoped he might tap into the wisdom of his age and say something to resolve the situation. Instead, in a grave manner, he said, "In any case, tomorrow's going to be an uphill battle."

Rather than mollifying the two, his words rubbed salt into their wounds. "No, it won't," Kakeru snapped, throwing a threatening look at the old man.

"'Because *I'm* gonna run,' right?" the landlord teased him, then sat up straight. "Every race throws curveballs, it comes with the territory. What I'm talking about is support. Keeping your teammates company and making sure they're in good shape before their race is an important job. If Shindo's like this, who's going to look after Yuki before he runs the sixth leg? I'll have to go in the Coach Mobile, so I can't be there . . ."

"No need to worry." Yuki finally spoke up. "I like to think I don't need someone babysitting me to be able to run a race. My nerves aren't that fragile. Shindo can stay here and rest, no problem."

"No." Shindo shook his head. He wouldn't lie down again, so Kakeru draped Musa's bench coat, which he'd been carrying around all this time, on Shindo's shoulders. Shindo gripped the jacket over his chest. "I'll be fine in the morning," he said, determined. "I'll look after Yuki before his race. It's my responsibility."

The landlord studied Shindo's face for a few moments, then gave a nod. "All right. Then we'll let Shindo take care of Yuki as planned. Agreed, Haiji?"

Kiyose looked down. After a pause, he said, "Yes."

"Now that's settled, we should call the others," Kakeru said, trying to put on a cheerful voice. "I'm sure they're all worried about Shindo. They must be waiting for news."

Kakeru called Prince and Joji in Yokohama; Yuki called Musa and King in Fujisawa; Kiyose called Jota and Nico in Odawara. Huddled around in a circle, they brought their phones close together, so all ten of them could talk at once.

"Are you okay, Shindo?!" Musa cried out as soon as he picked up.

"We have *so* much time on our hands now. I've already finished reading all the manga I brought," Prince complained.

"Jota won't shut up about how hungry he is, it's driving me nuts," Nico grumbled. "Can we go out to get some kamaboko?"

"Hey, I want some, too! Can you get it for me, bro?" Joji chimed in.

"One at a time, guys," Kiyose barked at all the phones. "First, Musa. Shindo's doing just fine." Yuki handed his cell to Shindo. Shindo and Musa praised each other's perseverance. Kiyose turned to Kakeru's phone next and called out, "Prince. Has Hanako arrived at the hotel already?"

"She checked in a little while ago. She said she'll pop over to our room later."

"The twins know about Hanako now," Kiyose informed him.

"Hunh."

"Try not to leave Joji and her alone together till Kakeru and I get there."

"How come?" Prince was clearly getting a kick out of this.

"What if Joji gets carried away and asks her out or something? It might have repercussions for the race tomorrow." Kiyose glanced at Kakeru as he spoke.

Again, why look at me? Kakeru retorted in his head.

"Gotcha," Prince snickered.

"Right. Everyone, gather round your phones," Kiyose said. Kakeru put all three phones on speaker and lined them up on Shindo's futon. He could sense everyone leaning in on the other end.

"You all fought well today," Kiyose began. "Kansei made it to Hakone in eighteenth place. It's not a great position, but there's still hope to turn things around tomorrow."

"Yeahhh." A drawn-out cheer came from the other end. They sounded like they were trying to stifle their enthusiasm. Kakeru chuckled to himself. *We really are a stubborn bunch—or more like shy, I guess.*

"Those of you running tomorrow, be extra careful about keeping yourself warm tonight, and don't eat too much. That's it from me."

"It is?" King blurted out. "Don't you have something a bit more, y'know, *constructive* to tell us?"

"Nope." Kiyose smiled. "When you've come this far, all that matters now is sharpening your focus so you can give your best performance."

"So this is it, huh. It'll all be over tomorrow," Joji said, sounding a bit emotional.

"Stop it, Joji, you're gonna make us all sad," Jota sniffled.

Kakeru looked at the row of phones. "See you at Otemachi, every-one," he told them, letting those simple words carry everything he felt.

"See you there!"

What kind of expressions would he see on their faces when they saw each other again at Otemachi?

Kakeru couldn't wait to find out. It was the first time he'd ever felt this way. To be so excited to see someone. To be eager to run toward something, a place where someone was waiting for him, to get there as fast as possible.

I've never felt anything like this before. The delight of running. The sense of purpose that surpassed all pain, blazing in his core, unquenchable.

They would throw themselves into the race, all for the sake of reuniting at the destination, bound by the thrill of having run as one.

Tomorrow, we'll fight again with everything we've got.

The Tokyo-Hakone Round-Trip College Ekiden Race was only at its halfway point.

Kakeru and Kiyose left Lake Ashi. They had to trace their steps back to the hotel in Yokohama. Since the landlord had told them to preserve their energy, they took a taxi down the mountain to Odawara Station using some cash he had given them.

Kiyose was silent in the car. Kakeru guessed he was thinking about how the race would unfold tomorrow, so he stayed quiet, so as not to disturb him.

The undulating mountain road was already dipped in the color of night. Occasionally, the lights of the city flickered through the branches, spreading out over the world below.

"It sure is getting chilly. We might see some snow tomorrow," the driver murmured.

Even a slight snowfall meant the surface of the road would freeze over.

If it snowed enough to stick, the road down the mountain would transform into a winding ski slope. Would Yuki be safe on his sprint down?

Kakeru leaned close to the window, feeling the cool air of the evening through the glass. The dark sky was covered in thick white clouds.

From Odawara, they took the train on the Tokaido line. With no commuters on board, the train car rattled on quietly, illuminated by orange lights. Kiyose and Kakeru sat next to each other in a four-seat booth.

"We didn't get to jog much today," Kakeru said.

"Yeah. How about we jog around the hotel later?"

After the long day, punctuated by intense moments of tension and exaltation, their conversation became fitful. Kakeru began to feel drowsy. Swayed by the rhythm of the train, he found himself nodding off.

Just as he was about to be sucked into deep sleep, he heard Kiyose softly call his name.

"Yes?" When Kakeru turned to look at him, Kiyose had his eyes fixed on his hands, clasped together on his lap as if in prayer.

"Your name's perfect for you."

Kakeru was confused. His name, written with the kanji for *run*, could mean "to run fast"—but he couldn't figure out why Kiyose would bring that up now. "My pops used to do track, too—though I think he quit running once he graduated from high school and got a job."

"Was it your father who got you into running?"

"No, not really." It was only after Kakeru had joined the track team in junior high that he began to sense his father's expectations for him. He got into high school on a sports referral. When he quit the track team there, he and his father stopped speaking. Even when the Chikusei-so team won a place to compete in the Hakone Ekiden, his father hadn't given him a call.

"What's on your mind?" Kakeru asked. *What does he want to tell me?*

"It looks like it really was a gamble to tackle Hakone with just the ten of us," Kiyose said, subtly avoiding Kakeru's question. "They say strange beasts dwell in Mount Hakone, after all . . . But I ended up putting too much on Shindo—no, on all of you—just because I was stubborn."

Kiyose heaved a deep sigh, which shook Kakeru. He didn't really get where Kiyose was going with this, but he could tell Kiyose was feeling down.

What now? What do I do? Kakeru desperately racked his brain for something to say and blurted out, "It's too late for that." The moment he said it, he realized it didn't sound comforting at all, which made him panic even more. "Uh, what I mean is, we already knew from the beginning that we only had ten members . . ." Kakeru stammered, trying his best to string together the words. "We knew that, but we still came this far. Besides, we're not *just* ten. We have the people from the shopping arcade, our friends at Kansei—they're supporting us, rooting for us."

"You're right. I'd forgotten about that." Kiyose sighed again. This time, it was more like he was taking a deep breath to let fresh air fill his body.

"Kakeru—my father coaches track at a high school back in my hometown."

"Oh." Kakeru nodded along, though he was still perplexed. Kiyose was always so logical and rational, but tonight, he seemed to be flitting randomly from one subject to another.

"For me, running was always a part of my life. Something I'd always been meant to do ever since I was born," Kiyose continued.

His face, slightly downcast, looked somewhat pale, outlined by the dark window behind him. Kakeru focused all his attention on Kiyose to discern what he was trying to tell him.

"My parents had an arranged marriage," Kiyose said. "From what I've heard, my father mainly chose my mother because she seemed like she wouldn't get fat as she got older."

"Huh?"

The corner of Kiyose's mouth twisted up a little. "Genes for obesity are a runner's mortal enemy. That was his logic. Then he met my mother's parents and saw they were thin, too—that sealed it for him. All to create an ideal child for running. It's a bit out there, right?"

"Uh . . . it's pretty damn crazy." If he was honest, when Kakeru saw a woman on the street or an idol on TV, what drew his attention first and foremost was how fleshy she was. For a runner, it was a sin to get fat. Since he himself was constantly alert to the shape of his own body, he couldn't help immediately checking whether a girl had excess flab. It seemed to him that of all the people in the world, the ones most concerned about their weight were, in fact, long-distance runners, not women who made brief attempts at dieting.

But even Kakeru had never thought about the physique of his hypothetical future child. If he fell in love with a girl who happened to be chubby, he wouldn't forget about her just because of that. He found it hard to believe anyone would choose a wife based on whether she seemed unlikely to gain weight.

"Well, just like he wanted, I can eat all I want and never get fat." Kiyose rubbed his face with his hands. "My father's not a bad man, but he fixates on one thing and thinks it rules over everything else—that's the way he operates. A true track fanatic."

Kakeru didn't say anything. He knew he had no right to point a finger at anyone. Kiyose dropped his hands to his lap again and looked up at the empty luggage rack.

"I went to the high school where my father worked and ran on his team. He's the kind of coach that you don't like, Kakeru. A control freak with the students. He made me run all the time, day in, day out. But I couldn't say anything to him. Even when I started feeling some weird discomfort in my leg. Unlike you, I wasn't brave enough to stand up to him."

The train came to a halt at a small station. The doors opened and closed without anyone getting on or off, and the train started moving again.

"That fight I had with my old coach," Kakeru muttered, squeezing out his voice, "it didn't have anything to do with bravery. I just couldn't control my feelings, that's all."

"I wasn't totally serious about running." Kiyose looked back down. "I figured if I just did what the grown-ups told me and ran whatever distances that were required, I'd get faster. I wasn't putting my whole soul into running like you are. The only small act of rebellion I could do was to choose a university I liked that didn't have a strong track team."

Kiyose stroked his right knee with his palm, moving his hand slowly, as if all the pain of his past was buried there.

"When I couldn't run anymore, for the first time in my life I wanted to run from the bottom of my heart. This time, I wanted to think for myself instead of being ordered around. And I wanted to run toward a dream with other people—people who were also driven by a real desire to run."

"Haiji . . ."

"I couldn't have asked for better candidates than the people at Aotake. I wanted to prove it. That even if it's a tiny underdog team, a bunch of amateurs, they can run as long as they have the drive to. I wanted to prove that they don't have to be puppets to run on their own two feet—no matter where and no matter how far. And I've always dreamed of proving it at the Hakone Ekiden."

Kakeru closed his eyes. Kiyose must have had this ambition ever since he came to Kansei four years ago. His sheer determination broke against Kakeru like cold, wild waves.

"When you ran past me that night," Kiyose said quietly, "I thought I found the one. I wanted to shout out, *My dream is here, running right in front of my eyes!* As I chased you on the bike, I realized right away that you were Kakeru Kurahara from Sendai Jōsei. I decided to rope you in, knowing who you are and how you had nowhere else to go."

Why would you tell me this now? Kakeru thought Kiyose's scrupulousness was both comical and cruel.

He wouldn't have minded if Kiyose had kept the truth hidden and let him keep believing the lie. That Kiyose had called out to Kakeru because he seemed to be running free and enjoying it, that Kiyose hadn't even noticed who Kakeru was.

"Haiji." Kakeru opened his eyes and looked at Kiyose. "You taught me everything: where I belong, the path I should take. You taught me how to think for myself."

The train was slowing down. They were approaching Yokohama Station. Kakeru got to his feet, grabbed Kiyose's arm, and pulled him up. "Just know that I'm grateful to you for that."

They got off the train and walked through the crowded underground passage toward the east exit.

"Hey, Haiji," Kakeru said under his breath, as though he was telling Kiyose a special secret. "Let's run tomorrow. Like we've never run before."

No amount of lies or ulterior motives from the past could destroy the trust and passion that they'd built up together. No beast obstructing their way could make them falter or flee now.

Tomorrow was the day their dream would come true. All that remained was to run to their hearts' content.

"Yeah. Let's do it, Kakeru."

The two of them looked at each other and laughed. Then, side by side, they broke into a run and sprinted down the streets to the hotel.

X

METEOR

January 3, 5 a.m.

In a dimly lit room at the Ashihara Inn, Yuki changed into his Kansei uniform and tracksuit and picked up his bench coat.

He'd already been awake for two hours. Out of goodwill, the hotel had served him breakfast in the small hours of the night and kept the communal bath open for him. By the time the food felt comfortably digested, he returned to his room, which he shared with Shindo and the landlord.

He wasn't sure whether he slept at all. But his head was perfectly clear. Excitement and nerves formed a keen blade that whittled his body until it felt light.

I'm in a good headspace, Yuki thought. He'd had a similar sensation just before he passed the bar, too. When he was answering the essay questions during the exam, it was almost amusing how effortlessly his brain had absorbed the meaning of the questions and how the answers had practically written themselves. His hand glided over the paper almost automatically. Never in his life had he been able to output so smoothly the information he'd input into his head. It was an incredible feeling: a kind of heightened awareness, as if a kind of sixth sense had awakened in him.

Yuki could feel that he was on the verge of that same thrill and hyperfocus.

The return journey of the Hakone Ekiden would begin at 8 a.m. For the next three hours, Yuki was going to warm up gradually, so that he would be at peak excitement right in time for the beginning of the race. In the first two hours, he'd take things slow to ease his nerves, and in the last hour, he'd get into focus and rev up. That was his way of getting ready. It had been his method of choice for concentration since the days when he was studying for the bar exam.

The six-mat guest room was about a hundred square feet. It was crammed with futons for the three of them, laid put on the tatami. Shindo, still masked, slept soundly, his breath quiet and regular. When Yuki knelt down and gently touched his forehead, he was still a bit feverish. The landlord was sleeping like a log, though the sound of him grinding his teeth filled the room.

Careful not to wake them up, Yuki folded over his futon and put it away in a corner. He stood by the window and lifted aside the curtain just a little. There was a thin blanket of snow over the small, homely garden of the inn, and specks of snow were still falling from the dark sky like ash.

Yuki had never been skiing. He couldn't fathom why anyone would choose to travel somewhere cold in a cold season to stick some wooden boards on their feet. He thought it was a waste of time—he was better off studying at home—and more important, he and his mother didn't have the kind of money for going on vacations when they lived by themselves.

Do I have what it takes to sprint down a snow-covered slope? Too late to back out now. Maybe I should've given skiing a shot.

The windowpane clouded over at the touch of Yuki's sigh. The room was faintly warm from the heat the three of them gave off.

It's not just me, Yuki told himself. For the past several years, there hadn't been any snow on the Hakone roads at New Year's. Most runners—in fact, probably all the runners in today's race—wouldn't know what it was like to run down Mount Hakone in the snow. It would be a completely new experience for everyone. *I can do it. I can run.*

Repeating the words to himself like a mantra, Yuki picked up the Kansei tasuki from the tokonoma alcove. He thought it still felt a little damp from the sweat of the five runners who'd carried it up to Hakone.

Yuki folded the tasuki carefully and put it in the pocket of his tracksuit, then quietly left the room.

When he went down the corridor to the genkan foyer, he met the landlady of the inn holding a newspaper.

"Oh, already changed?" she said.

"Yes. I'll do my warm-ups now."

"Outside?" Her brows furrowed anxiously as she glanced out the window. It was still as dark as night. "But it's twenty-three degrees at the moment."

He immediately decided against going out. At that temperature, his muscles would stiffen from the cold.

"Would you mind if I use the space here?" he asked, gesturing at the empty lobby.

"Of course," she said gladly. "Would you like to read the paper? I asked them to deliver it especially early this morning."

Yuki began stretching on the floor of the lobby with the newspaper spread out in front of him. He let out a long breath as he slowly loosened his muscles and joints.

The Hakone Ekiden was featured prominently: how Boso University had emerged victorious by a narrow margin on the first day and how the return journey would prove to be a very tight race, given that Rikudo's claim to the throne was now in question and other teams were just as likely to triumph over the entire race.

A part of the feature also touched on Kansei under the headline "Team of Ten Takes on Hakone," accompanied by a photo of Shindo staggering up the mountain road. Yuki read the article while spreading out his legs and pushing down his torso.

"Consisting of only ten members, the Kansei University team hit an unexpected wall in the fifth leg. They fell far behind and concluded the first day in eighteenth place. However, with ace runners Kurahara in first year and Kiyose in fourth year still to come in the lineup, they have plenty of chances to make a comeback on the return journey. How will the brave battle of this small team end? It is sure to be a highlight of this year's race."

The writer's initials, *MN*, marked the end of the column. *Must be Mr. Nunoda*, Yuki thought. The journalist had been watching over their progress ever since he'd come to interview them at their summer camp.

Still plenty of chances. The Kansei team believed it themselves, but it was encouraging to hear someone else confirm it. Yuki placed the paper in the newspaper rack and concentrated on his stretches.

At 6 o'clock, Shindo appeared in the lobby. He was wearing Musa's bench coat and a mask. "Good morning," he said in a slightly raspy voice, then started pressing down on Yuki's back to help him stretch.

"You didn't have to get up so early," Yuki said.

"I thought you'd say that, so I asked Musa to give me a wake-up call." Shindo sat down next to Yuki. "It's snowing today."

"Yeah."

The two of them gazed at the gray specks fluttering down outside.

"How are you feeling?" Shindo asked.

"Good. You?"

"I'm feeling much better."

Yuki started doing sit-ups. Shindo held his feet in place.

"To tell you the truth," Yuki muttered, "my nerves are kind of killing me. I'd run away if I could."

"I felt the same," Shindo laughed under his masks. "How about listening to some music? Here, I grabbed your iPod from your stuff in the room."

Yuki took it and pushed his earbuds in. He tried listening to his favorites for a while, but even the world of music couldn't comfort him today.

"No good," he said, jerking out the earbuds. "I feel like some song

I hate might play on an endless loop in my head while I'm running. Probably some stupid downer like 'My Grandfather's Clock'!"

"You don't like that song?"

"It's way too slow and depressing. I don't like anything that doesn't go anywhere."

"I think it's a good song."

Yuki humphed and stood up to rotate his ankles.

Shindo looked up at him and suggested, "What if you remix any song that gets stuck in your head into something more upbeat?"

"You're really something, Shindo." Yuki was thoroughly impressed. "I can't get these worries out of my head. I keep thinking about all the worst-case scenarios, like what if I slip on the hill, or what if my shoelaces snap?"

"Knowing you, Yuki, I think you can even get the fastest time in your course."

"Why would you think that?"

"Because you've always accomplished everything you set out to do. Whether it's passing the bar exam or competing in the Hakone Ekiden, you said you'd do it and did just that." Shindo's eyes smiled. "So I'd like to hear you say it this time, too. Tell me you've got your eyes on the prize."

Moved by Shindo's quiet conviction, Yuki answered, "I've got my eyes on the prize."

"Okay, now you'll be fine. I'm sure you'll run at a great pace."

When he saw Shindo nod in satisfaction, Yuki couldn't help laughing. "Now I know how useless I was yesterday," he said. "You must've been feeling anxious before your race, too, but it's not like I was any help."

"At the end of the day, though, you're the only one who can put your anxieties to bed," Shindo replied, getting to his feet. "How about we go for a jog?"

They put on their shoes by the entrance and stepped outside. There was no hint of daybreak yet, but birds were singing in the forest. The dry, powdery snow brushed against their faces.

"Yesterday, you stayed with me until the moment I started running.

And I was all the better for it." Shindo pulled down his mask and breathed in the frosty air. "So today, I'll be sticking right by your side. All the way till you set off."

Yuki gazed at Shindo, at a loss for words. Yuki was simply happy.

"It gets chilly when we stay still. Let's start running," Shindo said, putting his mask back on.

"By the way, what's the landlord up to?" Yuki asked.

"He said he'd go take a morning bath."

"He's basically on a holiday."

"Wasn't he grinding his teeth so loud last night?"

Yuki and Shindo jogged together, chatting about this and that. In the flurry of snow, white clouds of breath hovered and drifted away along the dark lakeside path.

Kakeru felt restless.

Kiyose was acting odd. Kakeru had invited him to a jog after breakfast, but he'd declined, saying, "You go ahead. I have to make some calls."

Haiji, skip his morning jog? Something must be up. Seems he had trouble sleeping last night, too. It can't be his leg hurting again, can it?

With all these thoughts spinning in his head, Kakeru ran around Yokohama Station for about half an hour, then decided to turn back to the hotel. He would still have enough time to warm up even at the relay station. Normally, Kakeru would never cut his jog short even if he felt sick, but right now, he was too worried about Kiyose. Maybe Kiyose was about to do something reckless. Gripped by this premonition, Kakeru rushed back to the hotel.

In the lobby of the low-budget hotel, Joji was perusing the sports newspaper while watching the weather forecast on TV. He noticed Kakeru cross the lobby and press the elevator button. "That was quick," he said, coming closer. "It's not like you to keep your jog so short."

"Where's Haiji?"

"I think he's in his room. Prince and Hana are packing up together. I got kicked out. I have a feeling they're trying to keep me away from Hana," Joji said, pouting, but Kakeru wasn't listening anymore. He got on the elevator, and Joji tagged along, asking whether anything had happened.

The Kansei group had booked three guest rooms on the fifth floor: Kakeru and Kiyose took the room at the end of the hallway, Joji and Prince were in the room next door, and Hanako was closest to the elevator.

Kakeru stepped out on their floor, and in the hallway, he passed a man in his late thirties holding a black bag with a wide bottom. It hit Kakeru that the bag looked like a doctor's bag, and he glanced back at the man just as the elevator doors were closing on him.

That guy isn't staying at this hotel. He's a doctor, Kakeru knew instinctively. He must have come to look at Haiji's leg.

Kakeru hurtled down the hall and opened their door with the card key. "Haiji!"

Kiyose was sitting on the bed by the window. He looked up, startled by Kakeru's outburst.

Kakeru pounced on him. "Show me your leg! Right now!"

Kiyose was knocked over by the force of Kakeru's lunge, but Kakeru went right ahead and tried to roll up the leg of Kiyose's track pants.

"Wait, calm down, Kakeru! I can explain!"

Joji hovered at the threshold, gaping at the two of them wrestling with each other. Prince and Hanako heard the kerfuffle and popped their heads out of the room next door to peer into the hallway.

"What in the world?" Hanako asked.

Joji cocked his head, bewildered. "Don't ask me, I'm as lost as you are."

Kiyose finally managed to untangle himself from Kakeru's grip and gestured at the others in the doorway to come in. Everyone gathered around and sat down on the bed, in a chair, wherever they found space.

"Haiji. Wasn't there a doctor here just now?" Kakeru interrogated Kiyose from his seat on the bed.

"Yes, I'm not denying that," Kiyose sighed, as if to say, *I give in.* "He's a doctor I always go to. I'd asked him to come check up on me here. He gave me a painkiller shot."

"Your leg injury from before—it's still hurting?" Prince asked in surprise.

It was the first time Hanako had heard of Kiyose having any injury. She looked incredulous as she exchanged looks with Joji.

"What will you do?" Kakeru could barely keep his voice from trembling.

"I'll run, of course."

"Are you going to be okay being so reckless?"

"Now's the time to be reckless, don't you think?"

"But what if . . ." Kakeru faltered. He was scared that if he said it out loud, it might come true. "What if you can never run again?"

Joji caught his breath, and Prince looked down. Hanako remained perfectly still as she watched their exchange.

Kakeru fixed his gaze on Kiyose, waiting for his answer.

"It'd certainly be hard to cope with . . ." Kiyose's voice was quiet, and Kakeru could sense that he'd been contemplating the question for a long time already. "But I'll have no regrets."

I can't stop him, Kakeru thought. Even if Kakeru were to swap places with Kiyose, he would choose to run, too.

Kakeru steeled himself. *If this is the way it has to be, there's only one thing I can do. I'll make sure I'll put as little strain on Haiji as possible. In the ninth leg, I'll cut down on our time as much as I can.*

The rapt silence in the room was broken by Kiyose's ringtone. It was a short call. "That was Shindo on the phone. The final lineup was just announced at Lake Ashi. Rikudo entered Fujioka in the ninth leg, just as everyone expected."

Joji looked at Kakeru with a mix of anticipation and anxiety.

"Good," Kakeru said quietly. Blood rushed in his veins, coursing throughout his body, making his heart race with the thrill of competing against the Rikudo runner. Kakeru was finally going to confront Fujioka in the same arena. At the Totai track meet in the spring, he could only chase after Fujioka. But now, Kakeru would have the chance to put himself to the test, to show himself how much faster and stronger he'd become since then.

"Kakeru, don't let him beat you," Kiyose said.

Kakeru gave a firm nod.

It was just past seven now. They had to leave the hotel and go their separate ways: Kakeru and Joji to the Totsuka relay station, Kiyose and Prince to the Tsurumi relay station, and Hanako to the finish line at Otemachi.

"Are you okay with Joji going with you?" Prince asked Kakeru. "Do you want me to come instead?"

Of course, the point of his question flew right over Kakeru's head. "Why would I mind? Let's stick to the plan."

Though his offer for Kakeru's sake had been in vain, Prince didn't look put out. He only chuckled and shook his head: *As you wish.*

When they got to Yokohama Station, Kiyose turned to Kakeru. "About what I said back there," he began. "It's not as dire as you think, Kakeru. The painkiller is working, and it won't finish me off as a runner."

"Is that really true?"

"Have I ever lied to you?"

"Several times."

Kiyose frowned at the air for a little while, tracing back over his past deeds. "Don't worry, it'll be all right. This time it's the truth," he laughed. "I'm looking forward to seeing you run at Tsurumi."

Kakeru felt like telling Kiyose something. Gratitude, anxiety, resolve. But because words could not capture his feelings, Kakeru said simply, "I'll pass the tasuki to you as fast as I can."

With a quick wave at each other, the group parted for the time being. They ascended the steps to the platforms to make their way to their respective stations.

It was 8 a.m.

First, Boso started running at the gunshot. Then one minute, thirty-nine seconds later, Rikudo followed suit.

Each runner slung his team's tasuki over his shoulder again and set off in order, according to the time differences at the end of the race on the previous day. It was the beginning of their journey back to Otemachi, Tokyo.

Teams that fell behind Boso by more than ten minutes were forced to start running all at once on the second day—which meant that this year, the select team, Eurasia, Kansei, Tokyo Gakuin, and Shinsei had to depart ten minutes after Boso's start.

Kansei's total time was eleven minutes, fifty-three seconds behind Boso. Though they were to start ten minutes behind Boso with the other four teams, the remaining difference of one minute, fifty-three seconds would, of course, still be added to their overall time at the end of the race. Because of this system, it was possible that a team's actual ranking based on overall time might not match up to a runner's physical position during the race.

In effect, the return journey required the runners—especially those on the lower-ranked teams—to keep in mind not just the lay of the race that they could see with their own eyes but also the tricky mental arithmetic of their team's actual time. In order to raise their actual rank, they had to approach the race with a calm, analytical strategy.

Suits me, Yuki thought. Rather than competing face-to-face with others, Yuki preferred to devise a stratagem for how he could play to his strengths and achieve the intended goal, weighing various possibilities and coming up with tactics based on solid data. The sixth leg of the Hakone Ekiden, the mountain descent, was a good fit with Yuki's personality. Instead of getting distracted by the positions of the other runners that were visible to the eye, his task was to fight against time, an invisible opponent, and make full use of his technique to sprint down the winding slope.

Shindo kept his promise and stayed close to Yuki until the very end. Without being asked, he'd supported Yuki in all kinds of little ways—assisting him with stretches, massaging his calves so that they didn't stiffen in the cold, casually striking up conversation. Thanks to Shindo, Yuki was able to quiet his mind and focus his attention on the race.

The time for his departure was fast approaching. He took off his bench coat and handed it to Shindo. The temperature at Lake Ashi was 26.6°F. Powdery snow was still swirling down. The road was blanketed in snow, the ruts frozen over. Even with the long-sleeve shirt under his uniform, Yuki still felt the rush of cold press on him like a sudden change of air pressure. At least there was no wind.

Jonan Bunka was the last team allowed to start at their actual time gap from Boso. Then at the call of the staff, the remaining five teams hurried to the starting line to depart at the same time.

Yuki looked at the crowd on one side. Though almost swallowed up by the sea of people, Shindo was still watching him with a steady gaze.

"See you at Otemachi," Yuki said. Though the cheers of the crowd might have drowned out his voice, Shindo nodded back at him.

Ten seconds after Jonan Bunka, the five remaining teams started running at the signal. Yuki's glasses clouded over as his body heat flared, but the cold wind cleared it away in an instant.

A thin layer of snow covered the road. Anyone would have needed to be careful just walking on a flat surface, but running on it meant they had no time to check where their steps fell. Every time he took a step forward, Yuki felt the wet snow splash against his legs. Even wearing his lightweight shoes with cutting-edge features, he couldn't prevent his feet from slipping slightly when he kicked the ground.

The first part of the course was mostly uphill, going from the lake-side road to the highest point of National Route 1 in a little over four kilometers. Of the five teams that set out at once, Eurasia was the first to shoot out of the pack. Yuki followed without hesitation. When he checked his wristwatch, he was going at just under three minutes, twenty seconds per kilometer.

Considering the gradient and the poor condition of the road, he was a bit too fast. But if he didn't take the offensive here, the Kansei team would have no chance of rising in the ranks. *Besides*, Yuki thought, *the Rikudo guy must've been the only one in the sixth leg who can run ten kilometers in under twenty-nine minutes. That means speed isn't a major factor here.*

From the highest point onward, the sixth-leg course was almost all downhill until it reached the streets of Hakone-Yumoto. Even if you weren't that fast a runner on flat ground, sprinting downhill was a different story. Once you hit your stride, you'd gather speed whether you liked it or not. What mattered was the ability to keep your balance, the deftness to switch gears according to the angle of the terrain, and the unflinching fearlessness to gallop down the slope.

Going a bit faster on the first climb won't hurt. I can still save enough energy for later. Yuki assessed himself and kept pushing forward.

He left the lakeside and climbed up the road to the peak. Some smaller ups and downs came before he reached the highest point. Just as he passed the first mound, he checked his watch again. Kiyose had instructed him to run at a pace of three minutes, twenty seconds per kilometer when he was going uphill, but Yuki had been going at three minutes, fifteen seconds.

I can do it. Yuki was confident. His body felt light, and his legs adapted to the slight undulations like it was second nature.

The pack of lower-ranked teams now comprised six runners, having absorbed Jonan Bunka. Tokyo Gakuin and Shinsei were already falling behind.

All Yuki thought about was outstripping as many teams as he could. He no longer felt the cold. He shot straight up to the highest point.

On the other side of the hill, the downward path stretching over nearly fifteen kilometers awaited him, winding on and on through the whirling snow.

"Isn't he going too fast?"

At the Totsuka relay station, Kakeru was staring intently at the portable TV with Joji. On the screen, Yuki and the others were just passing the main entrance to the Flower Center at the five-kilometer point.

"But I heard it's pretty normal to run five kilometers in like thirteen to fourteen minutes in the sixth leg?" Joji said in his usual carefree way, but it didn't quell Kakeru's fears. That pace was when they really got going on the downhill run. When it was all downhill, it was hard for the runners to hold back their speed. If they managed to find a good rhythm, it was even possible to fly down a hundred meters in less than sixteen seconds. Though the length of the course measured 20.7 kilometers, the runners sometimes accelerated as though it were a short-distance race. That was the defining feature of the sixth leg.

But now, Yuki was already past the five-kilometer point in sixteen minutes, despite the uphill in the beginning and the hostile road conditions. Judging from Yuki's ability, this seemed alarmingly fast to Kakeru.

"I'll try calling Haiji," Kakeru said.

"You're such a worrywart, Kakeru," Joji said with a little shrug.

Kiyose's voice came through the phone immediately, the buzz of the crowd audible in the background. He seemed to have arrived at his relay station, too.

"Are you listening to the radio?" Kakeru asked.

"We figured out how to watch TV on Prince's cell. He never knew he could do that either. We're following the broadcast now—amazing what phones can do these days."

"Yes. Uh, that's not what I'm calling about . . ." Kakeru felt a bit dizzy hearing just how much Prince was in his own world and how technologically challenged Kiyose was. "Isn't Yuki speeding a bit too much?"

"Yeah. Wish I could call the landlord, but it's no use. The coach cars don't trail the runners down the mountain road."

"What are you going to do?"

"Nothing we can do. From here on out, he'll go downhill. He'd be an idiot to slow down at this point, so we just have to pray he won't slip and fall." Kiyose let out a lighthearted laugh. He'd apparently managed to drive away the murk of anxieties that had been plaguing him the day before. "More to the point, Kakeru, make sure you do your jog and warm-up routine properly. I need to call Nico-senpai and King now, so talk to you later."

The phone went silent, and Kakeru heaved a sigh.

"It'll be fine," Joji consoled him, taking his phone from Kakeru's hand. "You've got to put a bit more faith in us, Kakeru."

"Faith, huh." Kakeru flexed his ankles in circles, getting ready for a jog. "Now that you mention it, Hanako told me the same thing once."

"H-Hana?" Joji blushed right up to his ears. "Why bring her up?"

"Why? What do you mean?"

"Ugh, are you doing this on purpose, or are you really just clueless?" Joji lost his patience at Kakeru's left-field answer and turned to face him. "Listen, I like Hana."

"I know."

"You do?! How?!"

"Nico-senpai said so on the phone yesterday."

"Zero privacy even when we're not in Chikusei-so," Joji grumbled under his breath. Then he fired a question he'd been dying to ask. "And? What about you, Kakeru? Are you okay with me asking her out?"

Why does he have to check with me? It's like everyone's made up their minds that I have a crush on Hanako. Just as Kakeru's brain formulated this thought, it hit him. The shock sent him reeling, like that plummeting sensation on the brink of sleep.

I do like Hanako.

He'd been even slower on the uptake than the twins all this time.

But his feelings for her had always been such a quiet, natural presence in his heart that he hadn't even noticed it until now.

Kakeru had always held on to his memories of Hanako as if they were treasure pieces. The color of her scarf when they'd walked home together. Her profile as she gazed at the team's practice under the billowing clouds, which towered over the summer sky. Her slender back when he saw her for the first time, speeding down the shopping arcade on her bicycle.

Kakeru's gaze had been fixed on Hanako. And for all that time, Hanako's gaze had only followed the twins.

"So that's how it was." Kakeru was surprised by his own feelings, which he finally recognized, plain and simple.

"Uh . . . what are you talking about?" Joji asked hesitantly. Kakeru had suddenly gone blank and was now nodding to himself. It was a little weird.

"Nothing," Kakeru said, shaking his head. "Maybe you should try telling her."

He wasn't trying to be the bigger person. He just felt like clouds had lifted from the sky. Hanako would be happy to hear how Joji felt about her. And she might be just as happy to be approached by Jota, which might trigger a bit of a brotherly scuffle. But these things weren't any of Kakeru's business.

This wasn't a competition. Hanako's heart was just Hanako's. Joji's heart was just Joji's. Just as Kakeru's heart belonged only to himself. No one else could seize it or bend it against his will. The realm of the heart was free from judgment; there was no way of measuring what was felt inside of it.

Kakeru was glad to discover something inside himself, this gentle yet powerful emotion that had nothing to do with either speed or competition. This realization only made Hanako seem more dear to him. She was the one who'd taught him this unfamiliar feeling. If Hanako's love was requited, Kakeru would be happy, too.

Besides, I'm used to running long distances. Being patient is my thing. I can wait for my chance. Hanako might like the twins now, but that doesn't mean she will forever.

"You think so, too?" Joji replied. "Wahhh, what do I do? I'm getting nervous."

Kakeru really was patient when it came to what was most important. He relished what was, to his knowledge, his very first taste of love, as deliberately as a cow chewing the cud. Happily oblivious to what was going on in Kakeru's head, Joji strengthened his resolve to confess his feelings to Hanako.

Yuki was sailing down the mountain.

At first, he was wary of slipping on frozen snow and tried to run on the ruts, but that way he couldn't find the most efficient line through the curves of the road. If he was conscious of slipping, his body tensed up too much, putting extra strain on his muscles, and nothing good could come of it. In the end, he decided to stick to his usual methods of running and determining his trajectory through the course.

Who knew running downhill could be so much fun? Yuki thought. To feel this level of speed in your own living body. Even the specks of snow flying straight into his face felt like tiny pebbles pelting him—that was how fast he was moving. Using his entire body to keep his balance, he let the angles of the slope guide his steps. The rush he felt banished all thoughts of tripping from his head.

Kowakien marked the ten-kilometer point of the sixth leg. It also served as the broadcast point for TV. Though it was still early in the morning, and the weather was far from ideal, spectators had gathered around this area to cheer on the contestants. Yuki turned the curve after the Eurasia runner. He could hear the Shinsei runner sloshing right behind him.

Though Yuki, of course, had no way of knowing this, the broadcaster and the commentator Yanaka were scrutinizing the live footage and analyzing the run of each team.

"Now we're getting a view of the lower-ranked teams at the ten-kilometer point. What do you think, Yanaka?"

"Well, they're going at quite a fast pace. I thought the fastest of the course might be the runner from Manaka University, who's been rising steadily from twelfth place. But it's possible that the winner of the course prize might emerge from the lower ranks."

"According to our data, everyone except Tamura of Rikudo has an official record of running 10,000 meters in under thirty minutes."

"Time records on flat land don't get reflected as much on this downhill course. The runners have the strength to run ten kilometers in that amount of time, so all they need now is pluck. That's the deciding factor."

"Pluck, is it?"

"Yes. The speed and steepness that the runners feel are much more intense than what we can see through the screen. For them, it's like cycling down a sharp hill at full throttle with their hands in the air. What makes it even worse today is the slippery surface. They not only have to keep calm and maintain their balance but also have the guts not to kill their own momentum."

"Which of the lower-ranked runners do you think is close to getting the course prize?"

"It's a bit too early to say, but Iwakura from Kansei University is impressive. He has excellent balance from the waist down, and no excess sway in his upper body. Despite the tricky road, he's pushing head-on without pulling back. Definitely a model downhill run."

"I see. Let's see how much he can hold out when the road goes flat after Hakone-Yumoto. Now we'll turn to the leading teams."

As the altitude decreased, the snow began to turn into sleet. The road, too, was covered in muddy slush. Yuki noticed he'd just leaped over a pedestrian crossing in only two steps.

That crossing must've been at least four meters wide. I crossed it in two steps, which means I'm covering two meters in a single step. Yuki was blown away. *That's fast.* Since he was riding the momentum and literally flying down the hill, his strides were widening, too. He glanced at his watch. He'd been running at two minutes, forty seconds per kilometer for the past five kilometers.

One kilometer in two minutes, forty seconds. Yuki couldn't dream of running so fast on flat terrain. As far as he knew, Kakeru was the only one who could keep up a pace like that on flat land.

The cedar branches by the road were bending low, heavy with pillows of pure white snow. The tree trunks glistened black. The mountain had been transformed into a stunning monochrome world overnight. The scenery streamed past the corners of his eyes, a smooth, constant flow swifter than a film reel.

So this must be the kind of world Kakeru sees when he runs. Yuki felt his chest tighten.

Sure is lonely. The wind whistled past, almost drowning out every other sound, and the view slipped behind him in the blink of an eye. It felt so exhilarating that he wanted to keep running forever, yet it was a world he could experience only by himself alone.

For the first time, Yuki thought he understood why Kakeru became so engrossed in running, sometimes excessively. Imagine having the gift to run at such speed—you'd wallow in it like an addict. You'd never stop longing for a glimpse of an even faster, more beautiful world. That moment would probably feel like eternity. But it was too perilous. It was a harsh, dangerously beautiful world to seek in a mortal body.

With the help of Mount Hakone, I can see the gates to that world, Yuki thought. *But in the end, I don't think I'd ever want to get any closer than I am now.*

Swayed by Kiyose's enthusiasm, Yuki's past year had revolved around running. But all that would come to an end today. *I have my own way of living. Instead of striving to experience a fleeting, sublime moment of beauty, and honing my mind and body for that single purpose, I want to live among other people—even if the world around me isn't nearly as beautiful. That's why I took the bar exam to become a lawyer.*

Today's the last day. But I'm glad I got to experience this speed for the first and final time. A thin smile played on Yuki's lips as he sprinted down the mountain. *Kakeru, don't stray too far. The place you're running toward is beautiful, but it's lonely over there. Almost too much for a living soul.*

It'd be nice if there was something that could ground him, Yuki thought. Something to tie Kakeru down to the everyday lives of ordinary people, with their delight and pain. With his feet firmly planted on the ground, Kakeru would surely become even stronger, much stronger than he was now. Balance was everything—just as in running downhill.

When Yuki entered the Miyanoshita Onsen district and passed the Fujiya Hotel, he caught sight of something unexpected and let out a little yelp.

A big crowd of the hotel's guests were gathered outside, waving the little Hakone Ekiden flags. Some people were shouting themselves hoarse while shivering in the cold, wearing only the hotel's yukata and a light tanzen robe over it. Yuki spied familiar faces among the spectators: his mother, his little half sister, and his mother's second husband.

"Yukihiko!" his mother called out at the top of her voice.

"Go, big brother, go!" His sister was leaning forward in her father's arms, while her father eagerly nodded along.

This is so embarrassing . . .

Yuki passed the hotel in a matter of seconds, but he couldn't look up again for a while. *So they spent New Year's in style, huh?* He made a snide remark to himself to cover up his embarrassment. *I guess they didn't invite me 'cause they knew I couldn't come anyway, and they were planning a surprise. But man, that almost gave me a heart attack. Hope all these mics didn't catch their screaming. If Nico-senpai saw them on TV, I'd never hear the end of it. Well, I think he only has a radio, so I should be safe.*

Yuki suddenly felt amused. *Ma's face back there. She looked so intense, like she was running the race herself. It looked like she was about to burst into tears.*

Yuki had no recollection of his real father. His father had died in an accident shortly after Yuki was born, so his only memories of his father were the stories his mother told him and old photos. After his father's death, Yuki and his mother lived on their own. He really cared about his mother. When he was in high school, his girlfriend accused him of being "a total mama's boy," but Yuki thought, *Why wouldn't I be?* As far as he was concerned, any son who didn't cherish his mother couldn't be trusted.

Perhaps because he grew up watching his mother work late into the night, Yuki had one goal in mind from an early age: to get a steady job and let his mother live an easy life. Luckily, it was already evident as he continued in school that he had a decent brain. So he concluded that the quickest way to achieve his aim was to pass the bar exam and secure what was said to be the ultimate license for the ultimate career. He thought being a lawyer—working in the borderland between sentiment and logic—would suit him, and more than anything, the profession seemed lucrative. As soon as he entered senior high school, he devised his own program and began preparing for the exam. On top of his studies, he built up his stamina as well. Thinking it might be useful to gain some insight into the subtleties of relationships, he tried going out with girls, too.

Then one day, something happened to render all his efforts meaningless. His mother remarried. Her new husband was employed at a proper company with a proper salary, and his mother no longer had to work. She loved her new husband, and she looked perfectly happy. Yuki's stepfather had swept in and effortlessly accomplished everything Yuki had been hoping to do for his mother, and then some.

Inevitably, Yuki was devastated. Since he was the type who had to see something through to the end once his mind was set on it, his pride kept him from giving up on the bar exam. But he felt empty. The year after his mother remarried, his sister was born. Yuki, now in his late teens, felt squirmy and awkward at the same time. He left home when he started university, and he'd barely gone back since, not even for New Year's.

The sight of his family cheering for him made those trivial thorns that only he'd felt melt away. As if to reflect this change inside him, the sleet turned into rain.

Yuki's stepfather and sister always thought of him as part of the family. And the most important thing was that his mother was happy. *That's all that matters, isn't it? That's what I've wanted all along. So what if the way she found happiness wasn't the way I had in mind? It'd be childish of me to keep moping because of that.*

With no one to hear him, Yuki let out a laugh, mingled with white puffs of breath. He realized that he could now glimpse the back of the Teito runner ahead of him beyond the curve. No sign of anyone behind Yuki. He seemed to have left behind the knot of lower-rank teams.

Glancing at his watch, he confirmed that he was still going at the exact same pace. His heart and body felt light. *I can keep it up for the rest of the way down. The important part is whether I can hang on after Hakone-Yumoto for the flat three-kilometer stretch.*

Kiyose had advised him yesterday: "After the downhill, the flat road is going to feel like going uphill. That's where the real battle starts."

I think I'll be all right, Yuki answered in his head. *Today I feel invincible. There's nothing holding me back.*

The big drums were booming again at the Odawara relay station. Spectators were swarming the parking lot of the kamaboko company in front of Kazamatsuri Station, awaiting the arrival of the sixth-leg runners.

"Hey, did you catch that, Jota? The look on Yuki's face!"

Nico caught everything that happened in front of the Fujiya Hotel on TV, tuning in on Jota's cell phone. Haiji had called them earlier and alerted them to the fact that they could watch the broadcast on their phones, too. Even Nico, who was computer-savvy, only ever used his phone to make calls, and Jota used his only for calling and texting. Perhaps this was why they could all put up with life in a ramshackle dorm: they didn't have much interest in technological advances.

"Yuki's mom is a babe," said Jota, who was munching on a whole roll of datemaki fish cake. "If he keeps going like that, he might just get the top record in the course, right?"

"Yeah, though it doesn't look like he's aware of that. The Manaka guy's going just as fast as Yuki, so it's gonna be a close call."

"Ahh, I can't just sit around waiting! Wish I could let him know."

"How?"

"By telepathy or whatever." Jota put away his half-eaten datemaki in his duffel bag and peered at his phone with a serious expression. "It'll be your turn in less than twenty minutes, Nico-senpai."

The screen showed Boso in the lead, with Rikudo chasing him by a margin of about one minute, thirty seconds. Finally done with the descent, they were heading toward the Hakone-Yumoto Station. Manaka, who was going for the course prize, had risen to eighth place. He hadn't slowed down at all.

"How's Yuki doing?" Nico asked.

"He's not on the screen. Guess they won't show much of the low-rank teams till they make it to Hakone-Yumoto."

Nico told Jota to keep an eye on Manaka's time and started his final prep. He jogged casually around the parking lot, loosening up his body.

At 9 a.m., Boso was the first to reach the relay station. His time was sixty minutes, forty-six seconds. Next came Rikudo, then Daiwa. Nico hurried back to Jota, who was waiting near the changeover line.

"Yuki's on fire!" Jota was bursting with excitement. "He hasn't slowed down even on flat land. He's really crushing it!"

On the phone screen, Yuki was just swerving around the Teito runner at the fork from Hakone-Shindo. The Kansei team was now in fourteenth place, with Totai in full view straight ahead.

"All right, looking good!" Nico took off his tracksuit. The biggest question now was whether Yuki could snatch the course prize.

"What about Manaka?" he asked Jota.

"We'll see him soon." Jota looked up from the phone. "He's here!"

The red uniform of Manaka, who'd come running along the railroad tracks, was just about to veer away from the road into the relay station. Everyone knew he might land the course prize, so the cheers surged as he passed on the tasuki.

"Time?" Nico asked.

"Sixty minutes, twenty-four seconds." Jota read out the numbers on his screen. It was a good time considering all the snow on the ground. Even Rikudo's Tamura, who could run 10,000 meters in under twenty-nine minutes—the fastest record of the group—took sixty minutes, forty-eight seconds to complete the course.

One team after another entered the relay station. The live coverage showed Yuki fast approaching.

Almost there, Yuki. Nico stood on the handoff line, called up by the staff. It was a battle against time now. The Totai runner next to Nico took the tasuki and started running. He heard Jota call out Yuki's time, his eyes glued to his watch.

"Sixty minutes, seventeen seconds, eighteen, nineteen . . ."

Yuki emerged at the relay station. He was gritting his teeth, clasping the tasuki in his right hand. A spectator might have shouted Manaka's record to him. He was putting all his strength into the final stretch.

"*Yuki!*" Nico roared.

"Sixty minutes, twenty-four seconds!" Jota shrieked, causing a stir among the crowd. The tasuki hadn't reached Nico's hand yet. Yuki was one step short of the course prize.

But in that moment, Nico forgot about the time. Yuki's eyes were boring straight into his. Yuki wasn't thinking about the course prize at all. The only thing he cared about was passing on the tasuki as fast as he possibly could. Driven by that single purpose, he'd overcome the flat three kilometers. Nico understood. He could tell by the touch of Yuki's fingers on his, hot and damp despite the freezing wind.

"Well done," Nico murmured.

"I'm tired. You do the rest." Yuki slapped Nico's back and somehow found the strength to firmly plant his quivering feet on the ground to stop himself from collapsing.

"Yuki!" Jota grabbed a blanket from the staff and rushed forward to hold him up. "You were so close, but you killed it!"

Yuki gulped down some water and regained his voice. "Close? To what?"

"The course prize. Your time was sixty minutes, twenty-six seconds. If you were two seconds faster, you would've tied with Manaka."

"Right." *Two seconds*. Yuki laughed. A mere two seconds. A fragment of time that would slip away in a single breath. *So I missed out on getting first by a hair.*

"Never mind," Yuki said. "Those two seconds would've felt like a whole hour to me."

Jota almost cried when Yuki took off his shoes. Though the skin of their soles had grown so tough over the past year, Yuki had a blister at the base of his big toe that had burst, the skin peeling off and blood oozing out. It made Jota realize just how grueling it was to run down Mount Hakone.

"'Course, you've done more than enough," Jota said, choking up. "You were awesome, Yuki."

Yuki patted Jota's head and gazed out at the road leading to the city of Odawara. *I'm counting on you, Nico-senpai.*

Nico was replaying in his head the conversation with Kiyose he'd had over the phone before setting off from the Odawara relay station. Calm as ever, Kiyose had asked, "How're you feeling, Nico-senpai?"

"Pretty much the same as usual."

"That's good to hear. Then I hope you'll run the same as usual, too."

"Does that mean you're not expecting much from me?"

"Of course I am. It's just that Yuki is running much faster than expected, so don't let that affect you."

Nico humphed. He didn't think he was so hot-blooded as to lose sight of his own abilities, spurred on by Yuki's powerful run. "Well, I'll go at my own pace."

"Nico-senpai," Kiyose said, more solemnly this time. "If you could run just over three minutes per kilometer and hold the pace, that'd be ideal. I'm sorry I can't make things easier for you."

"You know, Haiji," Nico said, scratching his head, "if you're talking 'easy,' it would've been a lot easier if I never ran. I wouldn't have had to go on a diet, quit smoking, or any of that stuff. Whatever the pace, once you start running, 'easy' goes out the window. I'd say it's good enough progress that I got healthy. So whatever rank I end up in, I don't wanna hear any complaints."

"Got it." Kiyose seemed to laugh. "So, see you at Otemachi then."

Nico had told Kiyose the truth. It would've been easy if he'd never run. But Nico didn't regret getting back into track after being out of the game for so long. The pain of running mingled with the thrill of striving with the gang toward a single goal and turned into something sweet. For Nico, who had been leading an independent, self-sufficient life, earning money to pay for his own tuition, this was a long-forgotten flavor.

As he ran on, the wind from Mount Hakone blew against his back. The seventh leg, from the Odawara relay station to Hiratsuka, extended over 21.2 kilometers. The terrain was flat overall, so it was relatively easier to handle. Most of the route traced back the same roads as the fourth leg toward Tokyo, except for the bypass at Oiso Station, which made it slightly longer.

The first three kilometers to the city streets of Odawara were a downhill slope, albeit a gradual one. If Nico got carried away and sped up too much now, he'd suffer in the latter half. He tried hard to keep his excitement and nerves at bay, to hold a pace that matched his own strength.

That Haiji really does keep a close eye on people, Nico thought. Kiyose must have known that taking the tasuki from Yuki would get Nico fired up. And given Nico's stubborn pride, he'd hold himself back not to get too swept up in the moment early in the race. Nico's personality, the nuances of his relationship with Yuki—Kiyose must have taken those factors into account when he appointed Nico to the seventh leg. He must have also judged that on this course, which had fewer ups and downs, Nico would be able to do his best run with the least amount of strain on his legs.

It was still drizzling. Nico's hair was already drenched. It was easier to breathe on rainy days than on dry ones. It was lucky, too, that the wind had died down. He would've had more than just the run to worry about if bitter gusts had been blowing down from Mount Hakone to chill his rain-soaked body. The temperature seemed to be around 34°F. The seventh leg was known to deplete the runners' energy more quickly because of the swift transition from cold to warm. Thanks to the rain, that didn't seem to be much of a concern today, though Nico still had a long way to go along the coastline, and the temperature might rise a little by the time it was closer to noon.

The only problem is this wet uniform clinging to me. Nico frowned a little. It revealed the contours of his body so clearly that it made him self-conscious. He might as well have been streaking down the road. *Well, it's not like our uniforms cover much to start with.*

Nico cringed at track uniforms, those flimsy sleeveless shirts and shorts. Long-distance track athletes had slender physiques. Of course, their slim frames were packed with supple, powerful muscles, but just based on their superficial appearance, they were comparable to gazelles or serows. Runners like that looked sharp in these minimalistic uniforms. Unfortunately, Nico had a sturdy frame. His dieting had paid off, and he'd shaved off much of his flab, but he couldn't do anything about his broad shoulders, his prominent hip bone, or his hefty thigh bones.

And so, when Nico put on those thin scraps of fabric they called a uniform, he felt oddly exposed. And wet uniforms were the worst because they stuck to him like plastic wrap.

Give me a break. I'm not some thickset mermaid washed up on a rock. Nico wanted to dig a hole and hide. *Maybe I should've trimmed my leg*

*hair, at least. To think that the view of my bushy legs sticking out of these
tiny shorts is being aired on TV nationwide.*

He cast a sideways glance at the legs of the runner next to him. *This
dude's hair is under control. Does he have less body hair to begin with, or
did he do some grooming before the race?* The next moment, Nico was
struck by the fact that there was someone running *beside* him. Did
this person gain on him without his noticing, and was he about to get
outstripped? Nico whipped his head around to check who the runner
was, then faced forward again.

The runner beside him was from Totai. He must have taken the
tasuki at the Odawara relay station about ten seconds before Nico. *So
he's not gaining on me, I'm gaining on him.* Nico looked at his watch to
make sure he was holding his pace. *Good.* He nodded to himself. *Looks
like I can throw him off.*

But Nico couldn't see any other runners ahead of him. He had no
idea what position he was in, nor what Kansei's rank actually was if
he took into account the time difference from day one.

This battle feels even more slippery than my wet uniform, Nico
thought as he entered the city streets of Odawara. Swarms of spectators
buzzed on both sides of the road, waving the little flags. Nico spotted
someone—probably from the shopping arcade—holding up a Kansei
banner, shouting something, but the words were swallowed up by the
surrounding noise. He'd have to wait until the coach's advice at the
five-kilometer point to get any updates.

For now, Nico focused on keeping to his pace and leaving behind his
team's archrival, Totai. Had the landlord been the only one Nico could
count on for information, he would have been worried whether he'd get
anything accurate and useful, but Nico knew Kiyose, the unnamed coach
of the Kansei team, was standing watch behind the landlord. Kiyose must
be gathering the crucial data, advising the landlord on what to say to
alleviate Nico's pressure—even as his own turn in the race drew closer.

Nico had great confidence in Kiyose's competence as a coach. Kiyose
had the second-best time record after Kakeru on the Kansei team, but

where Kiyose excelled more than anything else was in observing and insightfully managing people. Without Kiyose, the Chikusei-so residents would never have thought of taking on Hakone, and they would certainly not have been able to come so far.

There had been many times when Kiyose invoked executive power over the Chikusei-so residents. But despite their lack of experience in track, he never criticized them unfairly, and he made sure to respect their feelings and pride. He had always accommodated their disparate personalities as he carefully showed them how to take the initiative in their own training.

It was because he himself had faced a setback in track before that Kiyose was able to guide their team of mostly novices. He guided them with kindness and strength, with conviction and passion for running. Nico had a full appreciation for Kiyose's leadership because Nico also ran track until the end of senior high.

When Nico entered university, he quit track once and for all. He couldn't see any hope for his future in running. Back in high school, he'd worked hard as a serious athlete. It was tough and tedious to run every single day, working toward certain milestones that he set for himself, but he liked how it felt to run.

His body, however, grew bigger, and his bones heavier. It didn't matter how much he liked to run. As long as the winners were determined by race times, there was always going to be the problem of how well his shape suited the sport. Of course, Nico could run faster than most men his age, but it was another matter to continue as a long-distance athlete and aim higher in competitions. By the time he was in the third and final year of senior high, the wall had become all too apparent. His body—with its robust frame and tendency to put on weight easily—wasn't made for long-distance running. No amount of hard work could have overcome that fact.

Promising runners joined their college track team, flourished in a corporate team after graduating, and went on to compete on the international stage. Just how many athletes could follow that kind of path?

The higher Nico aimed, the more he was dazzled by those natural-born runners. Because he had enough experience and training to be able to grasp the extent of his own abilities, he was forced to admit that he could never go beyond a certain level. He stood completely helpless before his own body, which continued to grow increasingly burly.

Nico's misfortune was that he didn't have anyone to tell him that he could keep running for himself, if not as a competitive athlete—that it was okay to enjoy running for its own sake. Nico was younger then. Because he had been single-mindedly committed to track, everything seemed meaningless if he couldn't achieve success as an athlete. And so, Nico had stepped away from running, disappointed in himself.

During his long life as an undergrad, he gained the necessary skills to survive on his own, as well as experiences outside of track. And what he learned was that it wasn't so bad for something to be meaningless. He had no interest in flaunting lofty ideals. Of course, as long as one chose to run, one had to win. But victory could come in many shapes and sizes. Getting the fastest time in a race wasn't the only form of winning—just as there wasn't a single set answer to what it meant to win in life.

It encouraged Nico to find that Kiyose held views similar to his own. Looking back at his high school days, when he was so bent on believing that there was only one path to victory, Nico thought his young self to be both cute and ludicrous. Distancing himself from track made him more mature. Then, inspired by his sympathy for and trust in Kiyose, he threw himself back into running once again.

Kiyose was a capable leader. He knew the pain of others as well as the ruthless nature of the competitive sports world. He was able to lead their motley crew, fully accepting the differences in what each of them valued, while also pulling them forward with fervor and fortitude.

Kakeru must be the one who keeps that flame burning in Haiji, Nico thought. Kiyose just couldn't leave Kakeru alone. And he was drawn to Kakeru's rare gift, which still shone even after it was wounded.

What amazed Nico was how well the pair got along. Nico wiped away the rain trickling down the line of his nose. Their rapport wasn't just about running. In various aspects of life, Kiyose and Kakeru seemed to inspire each other. That was how Nico saw them. Each was moved by the other's virtues and frustrated by the other's shortcomings. In other words, they had truly connected on a human level, as two individuals. Friendship, love—those pure and vital emotions—most definitely existed between Kiyose and Kakeru. They were bound to each other in running and in spirit. To Nico, it felt like a miracle that such a pair should meet.

Nico would never tire of watching Kiyose and Kakeru connect and clash, so noble in their steadfast pursuit of running.

That was why Nico had kept running with them over the past year. And why he was still running now, with all the strength he could muster. When they left the city streets of Odawara, Totai started slipping behind. Once they crossed Sakawagawa, the rest was a straight line along the coast. Would he be able to close the distance between himself and the next runner in front of him?

At the five-kilometer point, the landlord called out, "Nico, my man, you're the thirteenth runner in the course right now. Kofu Gakuin should be thirty seconds ahead of you."

If Nico remembered correctly, the seventh-leg runner for Kofu Gakuin had a record of 10,000 meters in just under twenty-nine minutes, twenty seconds. He was far above Nico's level. Trying to keep the gap from getting any wider was all Nico could do. He listened closely, breaking down the new information as it was fed to him.

"Now, Kansei's actual rank, if we add the time difference from yesterday," the landlord declared through the loudspeaker, "is sixteenth place, as of the end of the sixth leg!"

Still sixteenth, even with Yuki's run, the second-fastest in his course? The thought of the long road ahead of them staggered Nico. But they were still crawling up, albeit slowly. He couldn't give up now. He had to pass on the tasuki as fast as his legs could carry him.

"Here's a message from Haiji. 'There's still hope. Hold your pace.' Over and out!"

Nico raised his hand slightly to signal that he got it. *That's right.*

There's still hope. It was impossible for Kansei to win first place in this Hakone Ekiden. They'd sunk down to eighteenth on day one, and though they were already on the seventh leg, they hadn't been able to rise back up very far. Nevertheless, they could still aim to make it into the top ten and win the seed rights.

They weren't striving for the top ten just because they wanted a guaranteed place in next year's Hakone Ekiden. It was because they wanted some kind of clear resolution to their struggle, to see it through to the end. Never again would anyone claim that getting seed rights was pointless for a small team that might not have enough members come next year.

This had nothing to do with what was useful or useless, meaningful or meaningless. Right now, Nico was pouring everything he had into this run, all for the sake of defending his team's pride and leaving a mark of their endeavor over the past year.

Nico's arms, throbbing with heat, beat back the cold rain streaming down on him.

King, who was going to run the eighth leg, was at the Hiratsuka relay station with Musa. After finishing his warm-up routine, he jogged around the area, went to the bathroom, and generally refused to stay put. A big crowd was already gathering at the relay station and along the course. King was jittery.

Musa had decided it was best to let him be. No matter what Musa said, King kept trotting back and forth, like a hamster constantly spinning in its wheel.

Oh well, he'll tire himself out soon. It's not ideal to get exhausted before the race, but it seems I have no choice but to let him do as he pleases. King was more sensitive than he appeared. If Musa tried to make him sit down, King's nervous energy might get trapped inside him and explode.

Musa sat by himself on the tarp in a corner of the relay station, checking the developments in the race on their portable TV. He'd cheered when he saw Yuki's achievement, and now he was watching Nico's run, which the camera sometimes captured. Nico was currently running near Ninomiya, past the ten-kilometer point. Despite the many small ups and downs from crossing bridges over rivers, Nico was striding forward, his form steady and his eyes fixed straight ahead.

Finally, King seemed to regain a temporary peace of mind. He stopped jogging and came to sit next to Musa.

"How's it looking for Nico-senpai?" King asked, peering at the screen. Musa gave him a blanket.

"He hasn't dropped his pace. The gap between him and Kofu Gakuin is getting wider, though. The other runner is too fast."

Wrapping himself up in the blanket, King started stretching on the tarp. "And our rank?"

"It's still the same. He's running behind Kofu Gakuin, and in front of Totai, so he *looks* like he's in thirteenth place, but we're actually sixteenth in terms of our total time."

"Ah . . ." A murmur somewhere between an answer and a sigh escaped King. He pressed his forehead against his outstretched legs. When he stayed still too long, his body started trembling of its own accord from anxiety. "Yuki's run was really something, huh?" King said, forcing himself to sound cheerful to stop the trembling.

"It really was. Shindo must be happy, too." Musa smiled.

The two of them sat in silence for a little while, gazing at the scene around them. The place was like an ennichi festival, full of life, with the athletes, staff, and spectators milling about. Only the air around King and Musa was quiet, as if they were in a little pocket that existed outside of sound and time. They felt as if they were immersed in a glass aquarium, filled to the brim with nervous tension, cut off from the rest of the world.

A pair of legs in track pants appeared in their field of vision and came to a halt in front of them. When the two looked up, they found Sakaki from Totai sneering down at them.

"Well, well, well, from the looks of it, I expect this is going to be Kansei's first and final Hakone. You might even call yourself lucky that you don't have to worry about finding more members next year."

Sakaki's polite, calm veneer made it impossible to shrug off his venom. Seething, King almost jumped to his feet, but Musa grabbed his blanket to restrain him. Sakaki was also running in the eighth leg. Even though his turn in the race was drawing near, he took the trouble of coming over to talk to King. Musa sensed how high-strung Sakaki was under the pressure.

"It's too early to say," Musa responded mildly. "Totai's seed rights seem to be up in the air, too."

"Yeah, look at your team. You're trailing behind us," King added, his voice dripping in sarcasm.

"That's only what it looks like. Besides, come the eighth leg, you're toast," Sakaki said, full of conviction. "And not just you. I'll outrun anyone who gets in my way."

Oh yeah? Good luck with that, King retorted in his head. Out loud, he said, "Jeez, what are you getting so worked up for?"

Sakaki's brows jerked up like broken windshield wipers. "Of course I'm worked up. This is *the* Hakone Ekiden. I've been running all these years to compete in this race. Ever since I was thirteen! I know it's hard for people like you to understand—you're only here to play games."

"No one runs just to play games," Musa asserted and rose to his feet abruptly, startling King. Musa stood face-to-face with Sakaki. "And there can't possibly be a game so painful as this one. You must already know that, so why do you pick fights with us? King will be up soon. I would appreciate it if you didn't say anything to agitate him."

Damn, Musa, you tell 'im. Still wrapped in the blanket, King looked up at Musa's reassuring figure in admiration.

Some upperclassmen, reserve members of the Totai team, were hanging around behind Sakaki. When they were all at the summer camp, they hadn't spared so much as a glance at the Kansei team, but now it was different. "Hey, Sakaki, what are you doing?" they called out anxiously. But Sakaki showed no sign of turning around.

Suddenly, King felt sorry for Sakaki. For Sakaki, even his teammates must be rivals, just as much as Kakeru and the Kansei team. Sakaki dedicated everything in his life to running, fueled by his single-minded love for it, and thus he saw everyone around him as enemies. He couldn't open up or get close to anyone, always alert to everyone else's rankings and race times.

That was the only way Sakaki could engage in running, and King found it pitiful. He set aside the blanket and stood up.

"Hey, you having any fun?" he asked Sakaki. "Your lifelong dream is finally coming true—you're about to run in the Hakone Ekiden. But you don't look happy at all. Why's that?"

"Why would I be having *fun*?" Sakaki was unshaken. "This is a race."

"Yeah, but still . . ." King thought about how to get across to him. "Our captain, Kiyose, says this all the time: just being fast isn't enough. Long-distance runners have got to be strong. The way I see it, that means you better get a kick out of running."

"You're too soft." Sakaki raised his eyebrows again, as though he were scoffing at some toddlers playing in the mud. "Feel free to 'have fun' if you just want nice memories to wax nostalgic over one day. That's fitting for you people. But I'm not like you. I'll fight, and keep fighting, to win. That's what I run for. I refuse to degrade myself like Kurahara by stooping to the level of weaklings."

"Watch it, smart-ass!" King snapped, tossing his newfound pity out the window. But Sakaki only smirked and, having said his piece, promptly walked away. "He drives me up the wall," King said, gnashing his teeth.

"There's some reason to what he says, though." Musa tried to soothe him.

"Sure, you could say that, but he's freaking annoying. I'm gonna call Kakeru!" King pulled out his phone from his pants pocket.

Kakeru had just returned to the Totsuka relay station after a light jog. Since his muscles were loosening up, he was just thinking he'd be all set after some stretches and one more round of jogging when Joji, who was looking after their luggage, waved at him to come over.

"Kakeru, someone's calling you."

Kakeru took his phone from Joji and checked who was calling. He expected to see Kiyose's name, but it was King.

"Hello?" Before Kakeru could ask whether something had happened, King hollered from the other end.

"*Kakeru!* Make sure you finish first, all right?! Show that snot-nosed brat what's what and drown him in a sea of loser tears! Got it?!"

Once he'd spewed everything out, King hung up. He was so outraged that his voice leaked from the phone to people around Kakeru.

"What was that?" Joji asked.

"Beats me . . ." Kakeru exchanged looks with Joji.

"It's actually pretty rare for King to lose it like that, isn't it?"

"I think I've only seen him snap when he's watching those quiz shows on TV."

"Oh, I know." Joji pretended to press a buzzer. "You know Sakaki's running the eighth leg for Totai? I bet he mouthed off again at the relay station."

Kakeru thought Joji was right on the money. In a way, it was a good thing that King's fury pushed out his anxiety, but when Kakeru thought about how much Sakaki must despise him, he felt miserable.

Though Kakeru tried not to show his gloom on his face, Joji was quick to pick up on it. "Just let him say what he wants," he said, giving a light pat on Kakeru's back. "Though I do want you to win first, too."

"'Course, that's what I'm planning to do, but . . ." Kakeru sensed

Joji wasn't just cheering him on—he had something else on his mind. When Kakeru gave him a questioning look, Joji grinned sheepishly.

"I'm thinking of telling Hana when Haiji breaks the tape at Otemachi. Ahh, can't wait!"

I get it, Kakeru thought. *So that's why he wants the race to go on without a hitch.*

"But Joji, I'm not sure you can get to Otemachi from here in time, even if you really hurry."

"*Whaaat,* seriously?!"

"Probably. I watch it on TV every year, and a lot of the time, the eighth-leg runners don't make it to Otemachi from Totsuka before the end of the broadcast."

"Oh no! Uh, mind if I start heading to Otemachi now?" Joji blurted out, ready to abandon his supporting role for the sake of love.

"I don't mind, but I think if Haiji were to find out, there'd be a bloodbath."

"Yeah, you're right." Joji started squirming in distress. "I guess I'll be in big trouble if I don't stay with you till you get the tasuki. Do you think Hana would wait for me?"

Knowing Hanako, Kakeru was certain she'd gladly keep waiting for the twins to arrive for as long as it took, even after night fell, even if she got buried in a snowstorm. But he kept his thoughts to himself and only said, "I guess we'll see." He knew *he* was pretty clueless about things like this, but Joji's obliviousness was so frustrating, it was like watching an armadillo creep forward ever so slowly. Kakeru felt justified in teasing him a bit.

As Kakeru laughed inwardly at his own petty revenge, a voice came from behind. "The Kansei team always look like they're enjoying themselves."

Kakeru and Joji turned around to find Fujioka from Rikudo standing there. Apparently, he'd been listening in on them. He wore a wise smile, like the enlightened Buddha. His smooth-shaven head was gleaming as always, even under the cloudy sky.

"Hey, hang on, isn't this guy . . . ?" Joji tugged at Kakeru's sleeve.

"Happy New Year," Kakeru greeted him.

"And best wishes for the future, eh?" Fujioka replied in a slightly jokey way, but he soon turned serious. "The time has finally come, Kurahara. I'm going to break the course record for the ninth leg."

The declaration overwhelmed Kakeru for a moment. Fujioka wasn't simply announcing that he was going to win the course prize. He meant to reign over not only the contestants running the ninth leg today but also every athlete who had ever run the ninth leg in the history of the Hakone Ekiden.

Breaking the course record. That would mean leaving a new mark on the worthy series of records that generations of runners had built up over Hakone's long history. It meant becoming the one who rose above the rest; to change from the follower, who challenged those who came before, into the leader, respected and pursued by those who would come later. Such an achievement would be especially significant for the ninth leg, where the record had been static for the past five years or so. For an athlete running in Hakone, setting a new course record was to seize glory.

"Whatever record you set, I'll break it," Kakeru said boldly. "You'll probably only be the record holder for around ten minutes."

Even Joji trembled in shock and awe at Kakeru's audacious declaration of war. Rikudo's Fujioka would most likely take their tasuki and set off before Kakeru. But if Fujioka did achieve that new record, it would last only until Kakeru arrived at the Tsurumi relay station and crushed it.

Joji quietly observed the two runners, neither of whom showed any sign of yielding. Both Kakeru and Fujioka had the same spark in their eyes: a fierce determination to win and an eager anticipation to see how the other would run. It was a clash of pride in which no one could intervene.

Kazuma Fujioka of Rikudo, the defending champions of Hakone, and Kakeru Kurahara, the ace runner of Kansei, the motley crew. At the relay station, everyone in their vicinity was electrified by the furious fire of rivalry that blazed between them.

At long last, the moment had come. The fiery battle worthy of marking the finale of the Hakone Ekiden: a battle between two athletes who were born to run and lived to run.

Nico was running as fast as he could along the coast on National Route 1—a solitary runner, with no one in sight to chase after and no sound of footsteps on his heels to spur him on.

The sides of the road were packed with spectators. The landlord was right behind him in the coach car. At the fifteen-kilometer point, the Kansei student waiting for Nico with a water bottle told him the time gaps between the runners to the front and the rear of him. Still, Nico was alone. All he could do was keep running, buoyed by the crowd's cheers, which were torn by the gusts of wind from the sea. Echoing in his brain was Kiyose's instruction to hold a pace of just over three minutes per kilometer.

It's a solitary journey, running long-distance, Nico thought. The loneliness and freedom he felt was like voyaging under a starless night sky. No one else but Nico himself could feel his pulse racing to the very limit, his feverish skin drenched in sweat that never had a chance to cool, the rise and fall of his muscles in rhythm with the blood coursing through his veins. Until he ran all the way along the appointed path and arrived at the appointed place, he had to continue fighting a battle that no one else could comprehend, as a solitary figure that no one could touch.

I'd forgotten about it all this time—or I've been pretending I forgot—the heartbreak and the thrill of running like this. And it's the guys at Chikusei-so who revived it in me, who led me to a place where I can taste it again. Ever since the moment I quit track, I've been waiting. I was waiting for another chance, one more time. For someone to need me, to want my soul that loves

running, even while knowing my body isn't cut out for track. For a voice to
tell me that I'm allowed to run.

Nico knew that this would be his last run as an athlete. There was
no path for him as a professional runner. It would be difficult for Nico
to keep up with the intense training as well as to produce even better
results than he had already.

If a presence that could be called the god of track existed in this
world, Nico was neither chosen nor blessed. This painful fact was hard
to ignore when Kakeru was around. Nico wished from the bottom of his
heart that he could become a runner like Kakeru—the chosen one, the
celebrated—but that was an empty wish that would never come true.

Oh well, maybe that's all right, Nico thought. *Even if I'm not chosen,*
I can still love running. His irrepressible love for running glittered inside
him, as incandescent as the loneliness and the freedom inherent in the
act. *That's what I've won, and it'll stay with me for as long as I live. That's*
enough for now. I'll put everything I have into this last run, and today all
the thoughts about track that I've dwelled on for years will come to an end.

Nico veered north from National Route 1 in front of the Oiso Station and entered the bypass. When there was less than a kilometer
left to go, he got a clear view of a broadcast car ahead of him. In its
shadow, he caught glimpses of the runner from Maebashi, whose pace
was slipping. At the same time, Nico sensed a presence drawing closer
from behind. He didn't have to turn around to know who it was. Totai
was gaining on him.

Though he felt the urge to accelerate, Nico restrained himself. After
running twenty kilometers, much of his strength was depleted. *Stay*
calm. Just over three minutes per kilometer. Hold that pace for a little
longer. I'll make my move in the last three hundred meters.

Nico trusted his body's instincts. Like a migrant bird that can cross
the ocean even without any stars to guide it, he pressed onward toward
his destination, his strokes hitting a steady rhythm. The crowds grew
even thicker with the people who had spilled out of the relay station.

He could see that Maebashi had his chin pulled up. Nico knew by intuition. *This is it.*

Forcing his burning muscles to work harder, Nico put on a spurt and began his fierce pursuit. Totai followed suit, bolting forward as if pushed from behind. Nico could taste a hint of blood in his throat, but he endured his groaning bones and the pain racking his entire body. The crowd stirred, and Nico saw King jump out to the handover line. So did the next runners for Maebashi and Totai. The three stood in a row and called to their teammates hurtling toward them.

Nico took off the tasuki, now soaked in sweat. He gripped it tight like a lifeline. King was the only thing he could see. Nico ran straight toward the black-and-silver uniform.

The destination. I've finally come back to it.

"I'll get 'em, too, Nico-senpai," King murmured briefly as he took the tasuki and ran off without looking back. Nico nodded without a word and pushed King forward—on to Otemachi.

Collapsing into the bench coat that Musa held up for him, Nico stopped his wristwatch, which was still counting laps. He didn't need it anymore. He'd completed his journey across the world of competing in time.

The record of Nico's final battle was 21.2 kilometers in one hour, six minutes, twenty-one seconds. His time was twelfth in the course.

The Kansei team had passed on their tasuki in twelfth place at Hiratsuka. Maebashi came in four seconds later, tied with Totai.

Nico's dogged efforts raised Kansei's rank—both the visible rank and the actual one, including the time difference from day one—to fifteenth place. As for Totai, the team looked like they were lagging behind Kansei on the course, but their actual rank was still thirteenth. Rikudo and Boso were still fighting for the top, with Boso defending their leading position by more than a minute and a half. A gap of three minutes separated Daiwa, in third place, from Rikudo.

Would there be any upheavals among the leading teams? Which team would make it through the close race into the top ten and attain the coveted seed rights? With the time gaps between each team in a deadlock, the race seemed to be in the calm before the storm, the outcome of the battle still unknown.

Nico was lying on the edge of the relay station and gazing up at the eastern sky. Their hope was still alive. *King, Kakeru, Haiji: Run, run to the finish line at Otemachi. We're going to prove it. We're going to prove what made us run this far.*

Though he was utterly spent, Nico rose to witness the conclusion of the race. Musa, who had been sitting by his side in silence, held him gently by the shoulders and helped him up. The two of them packed up their things and left the relay station, which was still buzzing from the handoffs, and made their way to Otemachi.

Right before King set off, Kiyose called him and asked, "Are you nervous?"

"Wish you didn't ask that kinda thing. You've just reminded me I'm nervous."

"Sorry about that," Kiyose apologized. "But you're always on edge about something. The exam season's started, your essay deadlines are coming up, your part-time job interview's tomorrow, you might mess up the setting for taping that quiz show you're dying to see and miss it, the list goes on. I'm always impressed how you manage to find so many things to stress over."

"Are you trying to get a rise outta me?"

"Of course not. All I'm saying is, being nervous is your default state of mind, so no point in worrying about it now."

That's what I mean by riling me up. King opened his mouth to grouch, but a laugh came out instead. He didn't need to see Kiyose's face to know that he was smiling on the other end, too—he could tell just from the sound of his voice. "Hey, Haiji. Have you been job hunting?"

"Did it look like I was?"

"So whatcha gonna do? I guess a runner as good as you could get recruited for a corporate team? Or are you gonna do another year at college and run in Hakone again next year?" Even as he spoke, King thought, *Weird. Why am I so sure that the Kansei team is gonna compete again next year? Why am I dying to tell him, "I'm gonna stay for another year, so how 'bout you do the same? And let's run together one more time."*

"I haven't thought about what I'll do next, and I can't think ahead right now," Kiyose said quietly. "Running in the Hakone Ekiden—that's the only thing I've had on my mind for the last four years. Even now, I still feel like this is all a dream."

King was a tiny bit disappointed. Somewhere inside him, he was hoping Kiyose might say, "Of course I'll run again next year. You too, King." But he didn't want to give away how he really felt. Instead, he said, "With the hell we went through at practice? This better not be a dream."

"You've got a point," Kiyose chuckled. "King," he said, slipping back into his usual stolid tone, "the eighth leg is a tough course. Don't worry if others overtake you. The most pivotal part is the hill going up to Yugyo Temple just past the sixteen-kilometer point. Try to save your energy as much as possible up until then."

"Gotcha."

"Once Hakone is over, I'll help you with your job hunt."

"How?"

"I can press your suit flat under my futon overnight or iron your shirt, things like that."

"No thanks. See ya."

King handed the phone to Musa and took off his tracksuit. Kiyose hadn't said "Let's job hunt together," either. That felt vaguely ominous to King. It was as if Kiyose thought there would be no future after today.

Now just in his uniform, King shook his head a few times and looked up at the sky. It was covered in gray clouds that had advanced from the west, along with the runners in the race. It looked like it was going to rain again. King checked his shoelaces, high-fived Musa, and dashed out to the handoff line.

After King took the tasuki from Nico, Sakaki from Totai and the runner from Maebashi caught up to him in no time. They had been behind by four seconds at the Hiratsuka relay station, but they'd closed the gap in the blink of an eye.

King glanced back at the two competitors running right behind him. Maebashi already had big beads of sweat on his forehead. It was 35.6°F, and a gentle wind blew from the sea on their right. It was neither too hot nor too cold to be uncomfortable to run. *Maybe this guy's feeling sick*, King thought.

That meant his present enemy, of course, was Sakaki. He was running behind King on the left, cunningly using Maebashi as a shield from the wind. Sakaki was clearly taunting King with his look: *I can outpace the likes of you any time I want. So, what are you going to do?* It was a silent threat, disguised as a question, to make King move aside.

But King had no intention of backing down. He kept running in the middle of the road. Then Sakaki swerved around from the left and shot ahead without even pausing to line up next to him. *That jerk.* Not to be outdone, King ramped up his speed, too. He chased straight after Sakaki over the Shonan Bridge at the three-kilometer point. Maebashi couldn't keep up with King and Sakaki. The sound of his heavy panting grew more and more distant.

King forgot about Haiji's warning to preserve his energy. He was running too hard even to spare a glance at the vast ocean stretching out on his right as he crossed the broad, long bridge. The overcast sea was raging against the fresh water streaming into it from the Sagami River. Blind to these waves, King was also raging, possessed by the need to crush Sakaki. He completely forgot about the difference between their abilities.

No matter how much King pushed on, the distance between them kept growing. He desperately tried to hang on to Sakaki, and the effort made his breathing ragged. The gazes and the cheers from the roadside crowds ricocheted in his fuzzy brain, and none of it felt real. King kept sprinting, his glare pinned on Sakaki's back.

King was thrown into a blind panic. Everything weighed down on King: the peculiar condition of running in a race, Sakaki's declaration to lick him, and how he had done just that. The pressure plunged King into confusion, depriving him of the presence of mind to make the right calls.

Of course, Kiyose would never miss what was happening to King. At the five-kilometer point, the landlord's voice rang out behind King.

"King, take a deep breath. What's the big hurry? Hey, King!"

King came to himself and deliberately exhaled a big breath. His shoulders had been stiff as rocks, but now they started to ease down. He swung both elbows around to loosen up and to signal to the landlord that he'd relaxed.

"You better take deep breaths every five kilometers," said the landlord, sounding relieved. "You charged in like a mad bull—Haiji called me right away, you know."

One of the Kansei students stationed along the course had called Kiyose to share the latest update. When Kiyose heard that King was accelerating much faster than the set pace, seemingly blind to everything around him, he guessed how things stood. King shouldn't let Sakaki get to him. Kiyose had to help King regain his composure as quickly as possible to prevent him from sabotaging himself.

The landlord was allowed to speak to the runner for one minute every five kilometers, so he rattled off the rest of his message.

"Haiji says he wants you to tell him the history of Yugyo-ji when you boys meet at Otemachi. You hear me?"

Oh yeah, Yugyo Temple. Haiji gave me a heads-up about it, didn't he?

King swung his elbows around again to show that he was all right now. He dropped his pace and carefully gauged how tired he was. Sakaki was obscured from view by the staff car between them, and soon enough it was also out of sight. But King found his own pace and focused on going steady. He remembered whom he was really fighting against: not Sakaki, but his own easily provoked mind, which made him forget his own abilities.

King was a bit of a finicky coward, so his pride was easily wounded. He could never let his guard down around people for fear of getting stung. He couldn't allow his true timid self to be seen by anyone, so on the surface, he put on an act of being an outgoing, sociable guy.

As a result, he had a sizable number of friends he could party with, and he thought he got along pretty well with his housemates, too. But if someone asked him whom he could share his troubles with, he couldn't name anyone. Was there anyone who would have his back when he found himself in a tight spot? He wasn't so sure.

Kiyose would never hurt King's self-esteem. Had it been the twins or Yuki or Kakeru running the eighth leg, Kiyose would have cut to the chase and said, "You think you can make it through the Yugyo-ji hill, going at a pace like that?"

Kiyose's subtle tact used to annoy King. He couldn't bear to have Kiyose seeing right through him, but he was also tickled by the fact that someone cared about him that way. A mix of mortification and pleasure would wash over him, and his self-loathing mounted. He was afraid of expecting too much from Kiyose, of hoping that Kiyose might accept him for who he is—because it was obvious that Kiyose didn't see him as his "best friend."

When King started at Kansei, he'd stumbled across a faded floor plan tacked up in the corner of the noticeboard in front of the student affairs office. He went to look at Chikusei-so, enticed by the unbeatably cheap rent. When he found out that there were two other first-years living there, he decided to move in. *Might be fun to live in a run-down dorm*, he'd thought. *Something different.* The two first-years, of course, were Kiyose and Yuki.

Since all the rooms on the first floor were already taken, King moved into room 202. Rumor had it that they'd tried filling in the rooms from the ground floor first to keep the upper floorboards from falling through. One other tenant, a fourth-year, was on the second floor, in room 205, where Shindo lived now.

All the older students who used to live there—the fourth-year in 205; Nico in 104, same as now; the second-year who used to live in 103 before Kakeru—were easy to get along with. Soon, King was chatting often with

Kiyose and Yuki, too. Though he was relieved that he felt at home in Chikusei-so, King still couldn't shake the feeling of being left out.

As much as he wanted to, King just didn't have a knack for navigating relationships through tacit understanding—finding that sweet spot between being not too familiar and not too reserved. Wherever he was and whomever he was with, he always felt like he didn't quite fit in. He tried to be nice and friendly to everyone so that he could stay on good terms with them, but he couldn't really open up to anyone. He kept up appearances, concealing any signs of weakness. It was no wonder, then, that no one tried to break through his outer shell. To blot out the shame of feeling lonely, he would only amp up his outward friendliness.

Each of the Chikusei-so residents had someone he especially got along with. For example, there were Kiyose and Kakeru, Yuki and Nico, the twins and Prince, Musa and Shindo—friends who somehow gravitated toward each other, who often ended up hanging out together without having to ask or fix a time. They could sit in comfortable silence, each doing whatever he liked in the same room. King saw scenes like that countless times at Chikusei-so.

King himself had never had such a close friend in his life. He could have fun with anyone, but that was as far as it went.

He disliked himself. He knew that for a fact, but he still didn't know how to change the way he lived.

But when he was running, things were different.

In a relay marathon, every member of the team had to be present. If even one was missing, the race would fall apart. As a member of the Kansei team, King could truly feel that he was needed by everyone. He could hurl his diffidence and pride to the ground and simply join the group in supporting each other. What's more, everyone was alone when he ran, so King could be honest with himself, free from speculating about what others thought of him and dealing with the yoke of relationships.

When he ran, King didn't have to pretend to be in tune with everyone else. He could focus on reining in his tendency to worry about other people's opinions of him. He could distance himself from his obsession with finding a place where he belonged.

King turned left at the intersection at Hamasuka and headed north toward Fujisawa, away from the coastal road. The turn marked the ten-kilometer point. The landlord called to him again from the coach car.

"You're going at a good pace, nice and steady. Haiji was saying you've done well bouncing back. Right now, Totai is thirty seconds ahead of you. Just forget about him. You got to watch out for Teito; he's gaining on you from behind. But make sure to keep going at your current pace. Over and out."

King swung around his arms to show that he'd heard. He thought it must be on Kiyose's orders that the landlord dutifully talked to him every five kilometers. Through the landlord, Kiyose was telling him, "I'm watching over you. So don't worry, just run."

I'm no match for that guy, King thought. *He always sees right through me.*

When he passed the Fujisawa police station, it started raining. The spectators didn't even take out their umbrellas as they kept on cheering for the runners, waving their little flags. The sound of paper flags flapping and fluttering in the air with each wave of their hands filled the hush of the drizzle. Their rustling blended together and followed King's progress like undulating waves.

King looked at all the faces of people he'd never met before thronging the sidewalks. The wall of spectators would probably continue unbroken from here to Otemachi, their voices spurring the runners on.

King veered away from Fujisawa Station and proceeded farther northeast, where he would eventually hit National Route 1 extending across the inland area. At the fifteen-kilometer point, he took a water bottle from the Kansei student in a waterproof poncho. King felt damp from the inside out in the cold rain, but he still took a little gulp to calm himself down.

"Haiji's got a message for you: 'It's showtime. Are you ready to press the buzzer?'" the landlord said.

King tossed the bottle on the side of the road and swung around his arms to loosen up. After sixteen kilometers, the hill at Yugyo Temple was coming into view.

As a quiz fanatic, King had of course gathered some fun facts on the temple already.

Yugyo-ji was the head temple of the Jishu school of Buddhism. Its official name was Totaku-san Muryoko-in Shojoko-ji. Since the Holy Priest Donkai Shonin founded the temple in 1325 during the Kamakura period, Fujisawa had thrived as a temple town.

King was pleased that he remembered the provenance of the temple—and that he still had enough composure to recall it even in his present state. *Wait till I get there, Haiji. I'll give you a whole lecture about it at Otemachi.*

In the Edo period, people who paid a visit to the Benzaiten, one of the seven gods of fortune, in Enoshima would pass through Fujisawa-shuku, climb this very hill, and worship at Yugyo-ji as well. The road still held a faint impression of what it must have looked like back then. A majestic tree soared over the hill, catching the rain on its evergreen leaves as if to protect the runner below.

But seriously, this hill is a killer. Running on it is nothing like reading about it. Did folks back in Edo times really climb a hill this tough?

King's chin started jutting out from the strain. The hill wasn't even one kilometer in length. It didn't look that steep, either. If you were to drive over it in a car, you'd barely notice it was there. But for King, who'd been running for sixteen kilometers, it almost resembled a mountain.

His legs felt like lead. He couldn't help glancing down at his feet to check whether he was still running on asphalt and not wet mud. His reaction to Sakaki's provocation was taking a toll on him now. He had trouble adjusting his posture to suit the angle of the road. The sound of fluttering flags surged, rolling toward him from behind. It was probably the Teito runner closing in on him.

I won't let you. He didn't care how desperate or undignified he looked. He swung his elbows back and forth to propel himself forward, gasping for breath.

Haiji, you said you wondered whether this was all a dream. To tell you the truth, I wish it really was a dream.

At first, we started running 'cause you dragged us into it. I was only going with the flow—I was like, "Hakone Ekiden? I dunno, guess it sounds cool." I didn't want to be the only one left out. I didn't want to feel more out of place than I already was at Chikusei-so.

But now it's different. The Hakone Ekiden isn't just your dream anymore, Haiji. Now it's a dream for all ten of us. I've gotten so into running—it's deep, it's painful, but it's fun. Our team, the way we're working together toward the same goal, gives me a rush, just like racing to hit the buzzer in a quiz . . . and that's why I run.

I've never been able to share something like this with anyone before, something so intense and intimate. I'd never laughed with anyone or gotten angry together—I mean, not for real. And I probably won't have anything like this in the future, either. When I'm much older, I'll look back on this year with you guys and feel nostalgic, wistful.

You know what, Haiji? I want this to be a dream.

It's a dream so good I never want to wake up from it. I wish I could keep drifting in it forever.

"Rikudo University is destined to win at Hakone."

Fujioka spoke calmly. It was twenty minutes before King's arrival at Totsuka. Kakeru and Fujioka were sitting next to each other on the tarp at the back of the relay station.

"It's not just that we have top-notch runners. Rikudo has a large network of connections in junior and senior high schools across the country to discover the most promising talent. We have facilities as well as an excellent coach to give us the most effective training. And plenty of funds to maintain all of that. In every respect, Rikudo is the sovereign, and so it follows that we are meant to win. It's fate."

Fujioka wasn't boasting; he spoke falteringly, merely explaining how things were. Kakeru saw the truth in what he said. They were sitting in Rikudo territory now. No less than five students accompanied Fujioka, attending to his every need before the race. Those younger students were also the ones who secured this space for Rikudo in the packed relay station, like those people who go to the park extra early to save a good spot under the cherry blossoms for their hanami picnic.

The five attendants were meekly standing a little way off from the tarp to give Fujioka some space. Joji stood with them, perhaps shrinking before Fujioka's imposing dignity. Joji kept nervously stealing looks at Kakeru now and again, but he didn't come any closer.

The true leader of Rikudo, the champion of Hakone, was Fujioka. Even the spectators milling about the relay station gave him a wide berth in respectful awe. Like a giant warship floating in the vast ocean, serene and unshakable even on a stormy night, the Rikudo tarp square was the only space in the relay station that remained untouched by the commotion of the surrounding crowd.

"Doesn't it make you choke? When you're expected to win every time?" Kakeru asked.

"No, that doesn't bother me. You learn to live with it." Fujioka closed his eyes as though in meditation. "But . . . it *is* heavy. I've endured its weight over the past four years and fed on it to become a stronger runner." After a pause, he asked, "Since you were at Sendai Jōsei, you must've felt it, too. Haven't you, Kurahara?"

Kakeru shook his head. Sure, his school did win national championships from time to time, but that was nothing compared to a team that regularly won the Hakone Ekiden, both in terms of the level of running and the pressure from others. Fujioka held a certain position in the running world, which required him to carry an immense burden that Kakeru couldn't even begin to imagine.

"I must lead Rikudo to victory." Fujioka rose to his feet and took off his tracksuit. The younger students rushed forward at once to take it, with an almost reverent air.

Boso was just passing the twenty-kilometer point of the eighth leg, still in the lead. Rikudo was closing the distance but was still behind by a minute.

"At the same time, I'll overcome myself and you, Kurahara."

"Me too. I'll definitely beat you and myself."

Kakeru rose, too, and faced Fujioka head-on. A short puff of air escaped Fujioka. It might have been a laugh. He gave a slight nod, took a step toward the changeover line, and then turned back to Kakeru as though he had just made up his mind to say something.

"I told you Kiyose and I were on the same team in high school, didn't I?"

"Yes."

"Rikudo offered a place for him, too. I was looking forward to running with him at university. But he declined and took the general entrance exams to go to Kansei."

So that's what happened, Kakeru thought. Going to Rikudo on a track referral was a dream coveted by many student runners, but Kiyose had turned it down. Kakeru recalled what Kiyose had told him on the Tokaido train last night.

Haiji, you said I was driven by a "real, honest desire to run"—but that's actually what drives you. It drives you more than anyone else. Kakeru felt a lump in his throat, and he bit his lip.

"Kurahara," Fujioka said, "show me what it is that Kiyose chose for himself."

"I will," Kakeru promised.

At 11:13:45 a.m., Fujioka took the Rikudo tasuki and set off from the Totsuka relay station in second place. Rikudo was behind Boso by fifty-eight seconds. Everyone looked to him, and him alone, for Rikudo's comeback and triumph in the entire race.

The ninth leg of the Hakone Ekiden had begun.

Kakeru watched Fujioka go and realized that he was nervous.

Kakeru tried to channel his tenseness into pumping himself up for the race, but his fingertips kept trembling.

Joji finally came up to Kakeru again, portable TV in hand. "It's looking like King won't catch up to Sakaki. In fact, Teito might even outstrip him."

Don't worry, I'll outrun them right back, Kakeru tried to say, but the words got stuck. He exhaled a long, reedy breath, not to give away his anxiety in front of Joji.

"I'm going to call Haiji real quick," Kakeru said.

Joji thought he was worried about Haiji's leg. "Sure," he said, looking back down at the TV. Kakeru casually stepped away from him and called Kiyose's number.

The phone had barely rung when Kiyose picked up. "Hello, Kiyose speaking."

"Haiji." Kakeru's voice came out feeble and hoarse, so he cleared his throat.

"Well, this is new. Are you feeling shaky?" Kiyose teased. It helped Kakeru calm down somewhat.

"Uh, I just wondered how your leg's doing . . ."

"It's good. The painkiller's working well." Kiyose's voice was sure and steady, soothing to Kakeru's ears. "Did you see Fujioka at the relay station?"

"Yes. We talked. And I guess it did shake me up a little."

"Come on, Kakeru," Kiyose laughed. "I know Fujioka, too. And I can still say with absolute certainty that you're an incredible runner. You'll only keep getting better."

"Does that mean I can't beat Fujioka as I am now?" Anxiety still clung to him, and Kakeru couldn't help but ask.

"You know that time you didn't want to participate in those track meets and IC races? Remember what I said to you then?"

"You told me to be stronger."

"After that."

"Um . . ." *What was it?* Kakeru traced back in his memory, but Kiyose gave him the answer first.

"I said, 'I believe in you.' Do you remember now?"

That's right. I was getting cold feet before the Totai track meet. I was scared that Sakaki might beat me, now that he's in a track powerhouse. I thought people might talk behind my back, how I'm that kid who got violent. I worried that the Chikusei-so guys would find out and not like me anymore after all that bonding we did. I was scared of everything.

But Haiji reassured me. He told me that he believes in me. That's why I made up my mind to run at the track meets and started thinking about what it means to be strong.

"I remember," said Kakeru.

"To tell you the truth," Kiyose began gravely, "that was a lie."

"What?!" Kakeru's voice flipped, and Joji looked up in surprise.

"It was a lie when I said I believe in you," Kiyose repeated.

Kakeru felt like crying. "Come on, why tell me that now . . . ?"

"What choice did I have?" Kiyose sighed. "We'd only known each other for about a month. How could I have known whether you were worth believing in or not? But if I hadn't said something like that, it looked like you'd never run in official meets or races again. It was a last resort if ever there was one."

As he listened, Kakeru started to grasp what Kiyose was trying to tell him. "So, what about now?" It was all he could do to keep his voice from sounding shrill in fear and anticipation. *Say it. Please. Tell me you believe in me, for real this time. Tell me that Kakeru Kurahara is a stronger, faster runner than anyone, that there's no way I'd lose to Fujioka.*

"Now, after watching you run and being with you for the past year . . ." Kiyose's quiet voice slaked Kakeru's thirst like a deep, translucent lake. "A word like *believe* just doesn't cut it. It's not about believing or not believing in you. You're just—you. For me, Kakeru, you are and always will be the best runner."

A rush of delight swept over Kakeru. *That means the world to me. He's given me something irreplaceable, a light that will keep shining bright for as long as I live.*

"Haiji . . ."

Thank you. For chasing after me that night in spring. For guiding me to discover what it really means to run, for trusting me, for accepting me for who I am.

Kakeru tried to voice everything racing through his mind but couldn't. Mere words weren't enough to catch this flood of emotions.

In the silence that followed, Kiyose seemed to have picked up on Kakeru's thoughts. "It's too early to thank me," he said.

"I'll be there soon. Wait for me, okay?"

"Don't trip," said Kiyose. There was a smirk in his voice.

11:20 a.m. Kakeru finished the call and handed his phone to Joji, then took off his tracksuit and did some light stretches. The misty drizzle hung in the air like smoke, neither drifting nor falling. Meanwhile, more eighth-leg runners were arriving at the Totsuka relay station one after another, and the ninth-leg runners were setting off.

11:23 a.m. At the staff's announcement, Kakeru approached the handoff line. With their belongings in hand, Joji followed him with a tense expression.

"Joji, I like Hanako, too." Kakeru finally said it out loud, but it wasn't as if the world would change as a result. "But I think it'd be nice to see you two happy together."

At Kakeru's abrupt confession, Joji looked at him wide-eyed, but his face soon broke into a grin. "Don't beat me to the punch, Kakeru."

"I won't," Kakeru laughed with him. He nodded back at Joji's wave and was about to step out toward the line. Sakaki, who'd just finished his run, was swerving to the side.

"Just give up, Kurahara. Kansei is done," Sakaki murmured in his ear as he brushed past. It was probably his confidence talking; he'd just outrun four competitors, including King, and brought up the team's rank to tenth place. Sakaki's time was one hour, six minutes, thirty-eight seconds, and he was the fifth-fastest in the eighth leg.

Kakeru glanced in the direction of Fujisawa. Kofu Gakuin and Akebono hurtled into the relay zone. King was running behind them. Teito had just overtaken him. Even so, King was still running as hard as he could so as not to fall behind, heading straight for the relay station and Kakeru.

"No way we're done," Kakeru said firmly, looking into Sakaki's eyes. *Sakaki, I know you still have a grudge against me for shutting everything down, for being too selfish to think about the race or my teammates back then. It's no use apologizing to you now, and I don't want to, either. I just can't bring myself to think that I was really in the wrong.*

But now I've found a different way to move forward—a way to show how I feel without resorting to violence.

I want you to watch me do it, Kakeru wanted to say, but he also knew he didn't have the right to ask such a selfish favor from Sakaki. So Kakeru merely told him what he was determined to do.

"From now on, I'll keep going, no matter what." He slowly walked away from Sakaki and stood on the handover line. Teito passed the tasuki right next to him.

"King," Kakeru called, raising his right hand high in the air, as if he were holding up a light in the fog. King stretched out his hand, gripping the tasuki.

"Sorry, Kakeru," King panted, pressing it into Kakeru's hand. For a brief moment, Kakeru gently placed his other hand on King's, which was damp from sweat and rain. *No need for that, King.*

King had completed the 21.3-kilometer course of the eighth leg. He was exactly one minute behind Totai's Sakaki. King's time was tenth in the course, at one hour, seven minutes, forty-two seconds.

The Kansei team was now running in the fourteenth position in the race. Their actual rank, based on their total time, was sixteenth. The total time of the Totai team—which was in tenth place at present and therefore within the seed rights zone—was ahead of Kansei by two minutes, fifty-three seconds. Kansei had to close the gap to zero and come out on top, even if by a narrow margin.

11:24:29 a.m. Kakeru, gripping the tasuki of hope in his hands, shot out of the relay station.

Everyone—the crowds cheering from the sidewalks, the people watching the live coverage at home, the TV announcer, and the commentator Yanaka—was captivated by the struggle for the top place unfolding in the ninth leg.

Boso was in the lead, fifty-eight seconds ahead of Rikudo. Boso was desperate to keep it that way, and Rikudo was trying to snatch back its place on the throne, to demonstrate for all to see the strength of the true champion. Both teams had entered their captains for the ninth leg, also known as "the ace course of the return journey" or "the other second leg." It was a clash between two teams, each as determined to win as the other.

The captain of the Boso team, a fourth-year named Sawachi, wasn't about to let his guard down just because the team was in the lead. He ran the first kilometer at a fast pace of two minutes, forty-six seconds. Rikudo's Fujioka couldn't see Sawachi running ahead of him yet. He was also speeding, at two minutes, forty-eight seconds. Who would be the first to use up his energy and drop his pace? Or would they both keep sprinting at this speed? All eyes were on the battle of the captains.

"Even though they can't see each other on the road, they've both whizzed past the first kilometer at an aggressive pace, as if they'd promised each other beforehand," the broadcaster said, his excitement brimming over. "It looks like this is going to be one hell of a race, Yanaka."

"Sawachi and Fujioka are certainly showing how they're worthy of their title as captain. But as far as I can tell through the screen, it seems Fujioka can stretch even further. There could be a shift in the rankings around Yokohama Station."

Just then, the live footage from the second vehicle came in.

"Oh, what do we have here?" the broadcaster exclaimed. "There's Saikyo in fourth place, and Kikui, Manaka, and Kita-Kanto are gaining on him."

"Exactly," the reporter on the second vehicle replied. "These four are about to form a pack. They'll lock horns for fourth place! Both Manaka and Kita-Kanto ran the first kilometer at an incredible pace of two minutes, forty seconds. They're hot on the heels of Saikyo and Kikui."

"Which means," the main broadcaster in the studio with Yanaka said, "Boso and Rikudo are racing for the top as we speak. Daiwa is in third place, about five minutes behind Rikudo. And Saikyo, who passed on the tasuki in fourth place, one minute after Daiwa, is now in danger of getting swallowed up by Kikui, Manaka, and Kita-Kanto, who're coming up close behind him."

"We might see more dramatic upheavals now that we've entered the latter half of the return journey." Yanaka leaned forward, engrossed in the footage.

Next came the view from the third vehicle, which was trailing Dochido in eighth place.

"Vehicle number three here. We're already starting to see Yokohama University in ninth place catching up to Dochido! Yokohama's first kilometer was at two minutes, forty-three seconds. Totai, who'd passed the Totsuka relay station in tenth place, two seconds after Yokohama, is starting to lag behind."

"Whew, what a wild performance!" The main broadcaster wasn't just impressed; he was dumbfounded. The ninth leg was a long one, spanning twenty-three kilometers, but these runners were coming like a freight train at two minutes, forty seconds from the outset. It was a reckless run, as though they'd flung away any concept of pacing.

"What in the world is happening here, Yanaka?"

"Yokohama and Totai are on the borderline for the seed rights, so it's no wonder they're getting desperate. The first three kilometers of this course are downhill, so it's easier to accelerate, too. But after starting out so strong, some runners might struggle later on."

"In other words, we're starting to see some movements in the ranks, but it's also possible that some teams will face setbacks," the main announcer summarized. He peered at the monitor. "What's this? Snow? Looks like it's starting to snow again."

The lower-ranked teams, who fell beyond the range of the three broadcast cars, were followed by a bike, which could move around more freely. It was just when the first powdery flakes of snow were beginning to flutter that the footage from the bike came into the studio.

"Broadcast bike here," said the reporter. "We're trailing the Kansei team in thirteenth place right now, and just look at his speed! He's running one kilometer at two minutes, forty-two seconds!"

It's snowing, Kakeru thought dimly, noticing the tiny, ash-like specks dancing in his field of vision. *It was drizzling just a minute ago—when did it turn into snow? No wonder it's cold.*

Though it had been snowing on Mount Hakone, Kakeru hadn't expected it would snow again past Totsuka, where the land was flat. He wasn't wearing a long-sleeve shirt or arm warmers. *Maybe I should've put on something warmer.* The thought flitted through his head, but he forgot about it the next moment. His body began to burn up so much that it dispelled the bitter wind blowing against him.

He'd already outstripped Teito, who'd been seven seconds ahead of him at the relay station, in the first four hundred meters of the course. Right now, Kakeru was thirteenth. It was no use worrying over Kansei's time difference with Totai or their actual ranking. He would have to wait for more news. *Just keep running. Get to the Tsurumi relay station as fast as I can. That's all there is to it.*

Kakeru took advantage of the gentle downhill to hurtle through the first kilometer. He didn't have to check his watch. He could tell without looking that he was running better than ever before. His joints moved smoothly. Blood coursed through his veins, steadily pumping oxygen throughout his body. Though he didn't think he was putting that much force in his strides, his legs kicked the ground tirelessly, their steady rhythm carrying him along.

Kakeru felt like he was flying. But his mind was calm. Like a pool of water in a magic basin that could reflect the future, his mind lay tranquil and translucent, without a single ripple to disturb its luster.

What's up with me? Have I lost my drive? Kakeru suddenly felt uncertain. *What if my mind's tricking me into thinking I'm riding on the momentum, when I'm really going unbelievably slow?*

He checked his watch for the first time. Two kilometers in five minutes, thirty seconds. *Not bad. But you can't rule out that the watch might be broken. What then?*

His agitation shook his breathing a little. In that instant, the cheers from the crowds flooded his ears. An infinite wall of people extended behind the guardrails. Even the people sitting in the cars on the opposite lane—which had slowed down to a crawl because the drivers were watching the runners—were looking at Kakeru. Some of them even opened their car windows to encourage him.

He noticed that the broadcast bike was just ahead of him to the side, and the video camera was pointed directly at him. *They're watching me. That means I'm running at a good pace.* He finally felt confident that he wasn't just imagining things and regained his stability.

Just before the three-kilometer point came the first mound in the course. The path branched off toward the mountain, drew a gentle arc, and joined back with the main road. Kakeru's body adapted itself to the short hill effortlessly. The rhythm of his running dominated his entire being, catapulting him forward.

The view and the noise gradually faded from his awareness again. Everything around him looked flat, like a photo that was too much in focus, the outlines unnaturally sharp. Sounds echoed in the distance, as if he were in an indoor pool. His flushed skin felt like it was wrapped up in some cushioning that kept him apart from the outside world. He didn't feel the nip of the flurrying snow at all—he was gliding through a dream.

A pure, supreme concentration began to wrap Kakeru in a cocoon of strange serenity and numbness. But Kakeru himself hadn't yet noticed.

Naturally, Kiyose was the first to notice Kakeru's condition. Kiyose's eyes were fixed on the cell phone screen as he followed the TV coverage with Prince at the Tsurumi relay station.

The live footage from the broadcast bike was slightly shaky, but it captured Kakeru's powerful run. Kakeru was running in perfect form, without a hint of slanting or swaying. The strength and speed that exuded from his body made it clear to all who saw him that *this* was what running was all about.

"It's beautiful," Kiyose murmured. Prince glanced sideways at Kiyose, who looked entranced, as if he were mesmerized by a supernatural beast.

"Seeing him run like this makes me feel pathetic," Prince laughed feebly. "Like I'm powerless."

Kiyose knew exactly how Prince felt. There was virtually nothing one could do in the face of perfection. It was painful to be confronted with that fact—painful, yet also impossible not to stare at it, to yearn for it. The internal conflict that it provoked could only be described as feeling utterly futile.

"Just goes to show that it's hubris to think hard work will solve everything," Kiyose said to comfort and encourage Prince, as well as to persuade himself. "Track isn't very forgiving. Still, there's more than one destination to aim for."

Running on the same track didn't mean everyone would arrive at the same destination. All runners were looking for their own goal that awaited them somewhere. As they ran, they tried to figure out where they were supposed to be going and at times lost their way; when they strayed off course, they would start all over again.

If there had been only one answer, one destination to reach, Kiyose wouldn't have been so enamored of long-distance running. And he surely wouldn't have been able to keep this passion alive when he felt so powerless before Kakeru's run.

Every single runner—including Kakeru, who embodied the perfect run; Kiyose, who looked on at Kakeru with quiet delight, the will to fight burning in his eyes; and Prince, who ran to the very end, though he'd never be able to measure up to either of them—all stood on equal ground in the world of long-distance running.

"You're right." Prince nodded. He felt a certain sense of fulfillment that was close to resignation. For a while, they were quiet, following Kakeru on the screen. Their contemplative silence was broken when Kiyose's phone went off.

"Haiji my boy, why haven't you called me?" the landlord blurted out worriedly. "We're almost at the five-kilometer point, you know. What should I say to Kakeru?"

"Nothing. Please don't say anything to him."

"But he's not even reacting to the crowds' cheers. He looks dazed. He might be overwhelmed by the race."

"No, it's the other way around," Kiyose said. "Kakeru is completely absorbed in his run right now. We shouldn't distract him."

Just as a monk who has undergone extensive training sits in zazen meditation and attains nirvana or a shaman enters a trance by pounding the earth in repeated beats, through the familiar act of running, Kakeru was reaching toward another state of mind.

Kiyose could sense Kakeru trying to pull the thin thread inside him so taut it was on the verge of breaking. His whole being was engrossed in running, as he sought to add a tiny drop of something more to a vessel already bursting with nerves and excitement.

We shouldn't get in his way. No one should touch Kakeru. Not right now.

Kakeru was running past the eight-kilometer point. Under the gray sky, lonely specks of snow flurried incessantly past his line of sight.

The two-lane road drew a gentle curve. Along this suburban road were small, somewhat faded shops. Kakeru liked views like these. A run-of-the-mill town, so plain you could say it had seen better days. But in a place like this, he could glimpse the day-to-day lives of the locals. The slight undulations of the road bore traces of all the people who'd walked on it over many years.

At a pace just under three minutes per kilometer, Kakeru climbed up Gontazaka with ease. The evergreens on the side of the road bristled with black shadows.

Kakeru saw a footbridge ahead of him. A large banner for the Hakone Ekiden hung across it, swelling in the wind. Though both sides of the course were packed with spectators, there was no one standing on the bridge. The banner sailed solemnly over the road like a royal crown with no head to rest on.

From the top of Gontazaka, he had a clear view to the foot of the hill. He saw Akebono, Kofu Gakuin, and Totai descending the slope. Heat flared up in the core of his head. He was a predator fixing its eyes on the prey. He bounded toward them in one breath, stretching and contracting his supple muscles.

Gaining momentum from the downhill, Kakeru caught up to the pack and outstripped them. He had no intention of running alongside them and waiting to see how they responded. The most effective way to crush their willpower was to leave them behind in one swift move.

When he passed the runners, it *looked* like he was moving up in the ranks, but that was only in appearance. In terms of their actual total time, the Kansei team would still be behind Totai. But the trick was not to let his opponents realize that fact. Even if it was just a bluff, he had to make them feel they had no chance against his run.

Kakeru had accelerated to two minutes, forty seconds per kilometer going downhill, and when he reached the bottom, he readjusted his pace to two minutes, fifty-five seconds. Riding on the rhythm, his body could instinctively select the right pace without his having to think about it.

I've overtaken three runners, so now I'm tenth in the course, Kakeru thought. But Kansei's actual rank was still outside the seed rights' range. A little less than fifteen kilometers remained in the ninth leg. Even combined with the twenty-three kilometers of the tenth leg, Kansei had less than forty kilometers to the end of the race now. Could the team turn the tables within that distance?

It's not enough. Kakeru gritted his teeth in frustration. *If only we still had more distance left, if only I were allowed to keep running, I would have definitely outrun them all. I'd have outrun all the teams ahead of me and showed them the fastest time they've ever seen.*

Kakeru laughed at his own thoughts.

I feel like I always have this craving to run forever.

Snow flickered down. In the past, he'd run through snow by himself. Whether he was running on the sports field at school or jogging along the riverbank, Kakeru had always been alone. Of course, he'd had teammates, but he'd never gotten close enough to them to talk about track together.

Kakeru had rebelled against the coach, who emphasized speed and team solidarity. Kakeru preferred to focus on self-reflection and running at his own pace without any distractions. His speed was a cut above the rest, and his teammates kept their distance from him. *Kurahara's a weirdo*, they said. *Kurahara's just a born runner*, they said.

That's not true, Kakeru had wanted to shout back at them. *It's not like I have any special talent. I'm only faster 'cause I practice harder than anyone else. All I want to do is run.*

Why did the team have to do exactly what the coach told them and be on constant guard to maintain order within the club? Why did they have to jog for yet another hour when they were already exhausted from practice and their heart wasn't in it? *Running like that is pointless*, Kakeru had thought back then. *Can people really get faster with these insane training routines that they push on us—"anything is possible with hard work" and all that? I don't see that happening. Matter of fact, it doesn't look like anyone here's ever going to beat my time.*

Kakeru couldn't understand his teammates who obediently followed the "club activities" so as not to get scolded by the seniors or the coach. What Kakeru wanted was to be completely immersed in the act of running, to stay honest to himself and his own body.

When he was in high school, Kakeru had been lonely. He believed his approach to running was the right one, and he just couldn't accept that it could be otherwise. No matter what people said around him, he stuck to his own principles. But the more he ran, the more isolated he became. Speed won him praise, but at a price. It also robbed him of the joys of being with others.

The oval track, a never-ending loop. Kakeru hated being trapped there, but he couldn't escape from it, either. He'd gotten into the school on a sports referral. His tuition was waived. His parents expected so much from his promising career in track. If he were to escape, where could he have gone?

And more than anything, the act of running itself ensnared Kakeru and refused to let him go. Whatever praise he got was only temporary. The more he devoted himself to running, the deeper his isolation became. He knew all that, but he couldn't bring himself to quit.

The jealousy of his teammates, who tried to drag each other down; enforced practice and discipline—Kakeru had struggled against it all, but he had nowhere else to go. He'd kept running alone, though he couldn't figure out how far he had to go or where his goal was. He'd felt like he was suffocating in a prison cell.

Now things were different. Kakeru brushed his hand over the Kansei tasuki strung across his chest. He had changed in the past year. Now he knew that running didn't have to be isolating. Despite being a solitary act, running had the power to connect people, to make them bond in the truest sense of the word.

Before he met Kiyose, Kakeru hadn't realized that power lay hidden inside him. He'd been running all along without really knowing what long-distance running meant as a sport.

To run was to be strong. Strength wasn't speed; rather, it lay in the runner's capacity to connect with others while maintaining a sense of solitude.

It was Haiji who taught me that. Kiyose had led the Chikusei-so residents by example. They were a group of people with different interests and backgrounds, yet through the act of running, they experienced the rush and joy in connecting with each other, no matter how fleeting.

Haiji said the word believe *doesn't cut it. I'm with him.* A boundless confidence had welled up in Kakeru's heart, a belief so unquestioned that using any word to describe it might feel like a lie. *For the first time in my life, I learned how valuable it is to trust in someone, and rely on people other than myself.*

Running is like that, too. No need for reason or motive. It's as natural as breathing—it keeps me alive.

Running would no longer hurt Kakeru. It wouldn't exclude or isolate him. The thing that Kakeru had risked everything to seek didn't betray him. The run responded to Kakeru's commitment; it gave strength back to him. Like a close friend who would turn around and draw nearer if he called, running was right there by Kakeru's side. Not as an enemy that had to be wrestled down and conquered, but as a pillar of power that would always stay with him and hold him up.

"Look, Haiji."

Displayed on Prince's phone was the view in front of Yokohama Station. Rikudo's Fujioka had finally overtaken Boso's Sawachi.

"Fujioka's in the lead!" the broadcaster exclaimed. "Rikudo, the defending champion, is finally back at the top in the ninth leg!"

Despite having run nearly fifteen kilometers, Fujioka maintained a pace of three minutes per kilometer. Now that he was in the lead, he accelerated even faster.

Fujioka would likely leave Sawachi far behind and run the rest of the course unrivaled, up to the Tsurumi relay station. Rikudo must have seen this coming ever since the teams announced their course lineups.

Rikudo had kept Fujioka among the team's reserve runners when the lineup was first announced, paying close attention to Boso's strategy and to which day of the race their rival was putting in their best runners. Then, when Rikudo saw that Boso placed their strongest members on the lineup for day one, Rikudo entered Fujioka in the ninth leg, swapping on the morning of the race. In other words, Rikudo had chosen to follow Boso as a close second on the journey to Mount Hakone and then make a comeback on the return journey to seize the overall victory.

It was a strategy that Rikudo couldn't have pulled off without the team's large troop of quality runners. As the captain of the team and the key player in the comeback, the pressure weighing down on Fujioka must have been immense. Fujioka, however, was fulfilling his duty in perfect form. His run showed everyone watching how a champion should carry himself.

"Sawachi can't keep up," Kiyose observed. He intuited that it wasn't just Rikudo's victory that Fujioka was after. "Fujioka's going for a new course record."

"What?!" Prince did a double take. The course record for the ninth leg had been set five years ago by another Rikudo runner at one hour, nine minutes, two seconds. Fujioka's current time and the record time were displayed next to each other in the corner of the screen. His pace was almost on par with the record holder's.

From the outside, Fujioka looked as though he was pressing on with perfect composure. But a fervent fire was burning inside him. Prince was surprised. Fujioka betrayed none of his insatiable desire, his ambition not just to lead his team to victory but to seize the course title for himself. His sheer lust for running was even exhilarating to watch.

"Kakeru is the only one who can take on Fujioka. We need data to give him a push in the last part of the course. Keep a close eye on Fujioka's time, Prince." Kiyose took off his bench coat and handed it to Prince. "I'll go warm up."

Kakeru now had four kilometers to Yokohama Station. The road became wider, with two lanes on each side. The masses of onlookers also swelled in size, and some people were even getting pushed out into the road.

"Please stand back, it's dangerous! Don't hold up the flag at the runners!"

The security staff and police officers pressed back the surging crowd desperately, screeching their warnings at them. Though the scene was over in a split second, Kakeru kept seeing similar tussles so many times along the course that he found it funny.

To me, the Hakone Ekiden is a dead-serious, one-shot race, but to them, it's like a big New Year's festival.

Kakeru fought back a laugh. Many people cheered for them with all their heart. Some of them called out, "Kurahara!" as he ran past. Even though they were complete strangers to the runners, the people watching looked up the individual contestants and gave them strength. And then there were those who were more eager to get on TV than to watch the athletes run.

A man holding up a paper flag stepped out into the road, and Kakeru almost ran headfirst into it. The contestants were running faster than bicycles, so if they crashed into someone, both sides would get hurt. Raising a hand, Kakeru brushed aside the little flag in his way. He'd tried to do it gently not to be rude, but the paper nicked the back of his hand, and a thin red line oozed out of his skin.

He licked his blood. He felt neither pain nor irritation. He merely remembered that his hands were numb from the cold and that he'd forgotten to wear gloves.

Well, if they're here to enjoy themselves, that's fine by me, Kakeru thought. He didn't need them to understand what he was putting into his run, how much stamina and willpower he was using to pull through it. Only the runner could fully grasp the torture and the thrill of running.

But everyone could share in the excitement. Together, runners and spectators alike could savor the fervor and the roar of the crowd that continued all the way up to Otemachi.

He was alone, but not alone. The road went on like a flowing river.

At the thirteen-kilometer point, Kakeru spotted Saikyo and Kikui ahead of him. *I can catch them. Outstrip them. No sweat.* He gradually closed in on them, sure and steady.

Kakeru passed the Tobe police station at 13.7 kilometers. There wasn't a single gap in the wall of people along the course. The crowd only grew bigger. He crossed the intersection at Takashima at the 14-kilometer point, passed under the railroad bridge, and emerged at an even wider road with four lanes on each side. Above him loomed a complex tangle of expressway overpasses.

Masses of spectators were swarming in front of Yokohama Station. The sidewalks were jam-packed with people, and there were people standing in every available niche—on the slightly raised steps around the shrubbery, the slopes leading up to the office buildings, anywhere that afforded a bit of space. Their cheers bounced off the elevated concrete overhead, reverberating like a deep, furious roar, and the wide road underneath nearly shook from the impact.

Kakeru couldn't believe how many onlookers had gathered just to root for a bunch of people who ran. Even he was startled by the crowd's size and volume. The constant beating of the paper flags formed a writhing mass, resembling a forest on a stormy night.

Kakeru passed Saikyo and Kikui, two in a row. The crowd erupted at the hunt unfolding right before their eyes. For an instant, Kakeru's run made the spectators forget which runner or team they were rooting for. They'd just witnessed a run they couldn't help but admire: a run of unassailable beauty, and speed, and strength.

Around 15.2 kilometers in, a short-distance student in a Kansei tracksuit leaped into the road with a water bottle for Kakeru. For a while, Kakeru didn't notice he was running alongside him.

"Kurahara, Kurahara!" the student called out.

Kakeru looked sideways. It was only when he saw the bottle in the student's outstretched hand that he remembered it was time to hydrate. Since it was cold, with enough snow to make the ground wet, he didn't feel thirsty. But the student sprinted hard to keep up with Kakeru, still holding out the bottle. He took it.

"Fujioka might break the record!" the student told him in one breath.

I knew it, Kakeru thought. There was no time to ask for Fujioka's pace. He left the student behind and pressed on.

How fast did he run down this road? Will I be able to beat his time? No, I have to.

Kakeru was in the eighth position now. He couldn't see the runner in front of him, and there was no way of telling how many seconds separated them. Kakeru's opponent was not any runner he might see, but time itself. He had to haul on the formless strand of time, so that the Kansei team could rise higher, even by just a single place. He had to make a mark on the history of the Hakone Ekiden with the best run he could muster.

The wider view in the four-lane road affected his perception of speed. He felt like he wasn't moving forward regardless of how much he ran. *Be patient*, he told himself, taking a gulp of water. *I'm all right. I can go farther. I can run faster.* His whole body, right down to the last cell, was on fire. His muscles were screaming, as if something were tearing them apart. *Faster. Break the limits and go beyond.*

He threw away the bottle on the side of the road. Cool liquid slid down his throat.

"Ah . . ." A hoarse sound escaped him, but no one heard.

Deep inside him, something exploded with a sharp bang. The burst of power spread from a single point all through his body, down to his fingertips. Was it spreading, or converging? The rush of energy was so fast that he couldn't tell which way it flowed. It coursed through him and filled him to the brim.

All sound suddenly grew distant, and his brain became clear and sharp. It was as if he'd separated into two selves, one running on the ground, the other looking down at himself from above. Every speck of snow that fell around him appeared strangely vivid.

What is this? It was a stillness that bordered on frenzy. Silence cocooned him. He felt as if he were running through empty, moonlit streets. The path he was meant to take glowed faintly, giving off a pale, white light.

Kakeru felt so high that he thought he might never find his way back down. It was almost frightening. He was carried forward by a powerful wave toward a fixed star shining in the sky. *Please, someone pull me back. No, don't get in my way. This is good. I want to keep going. On and on, even farther. I don't care if I go up in flames. There it is, I can see the world beyond. Only a little more to go until I reach the thing that glitters.*

After finishing his warm-ups, Kiyose became absorbed in the live coverage on Prince's phone. The cameras switched from Kakeru, who was keeping up his phenomenal run, to Fujioka, who was coming to the end of the ninth leg.

"Fujioka of Rikudo University passes on the tasuki at exactly one hour, nine minutes!" the broadcaster exclaimed. "We have a new course record!"

At 12:22:45 p.m., the crowd at the Tsurumi relay station went wild over Fujioka's new record. Kiyose looked up. Fujioka had left the hand-off line and was coming into the waiting area of the relay station.

The younger students from Rikudo surrounded him, celebrating their rise to first place. The spectators showered him with praise for his achievement, journalists lined up for a quick interview, and Fujioka didn't seem to have time even to catch his breath.

Fujioka looked a little overwhelmed as he gazed at the buzzing crowd around him. His eyes came to rest on Kiyose, sitting at the back of the relay station. He slipped out of the ring of people and approached Kiyose.

"Prince, can you call the landlord and tell him Fujioka's time? So that he can let Kakeru know at the twenty-kilometer point," Kiyose instructed Prince in a low voice, then turned to Fujioka with a cordial smile. "Congratulations."

"Save it," Fujioka said. Though he'd just broken the record, he remained stone-faced, without a hint of triumph. "You think Kurahara will beat me, don't you?"

"We'll see." Kiyose's smile was also like armor, hiding his true thoughts.

There was another stir around the changeover line. Boso's Sawachi had just passed on the team's tasuki. Boso was now one minute, thirty-one seconds behind Rikudo. The other teams were still nowhere to be seen. Clearly, the battle for the championship was down to Rikudo and Boso. But now that they had only one leg remaining, the gap of a minute and a half that Fujioka had forged in the ninth leg was almost insurmountable. Judging by the credentials of the runners representing the two teams for the final stage of the race, Rikudo had by far the greater advantage.

"Looks like Rikudo is set to win," Kiyose said. "Your run was as strong and steady as it's ever been."

"Our team's in the lead. However . . ." Fujioka swallowed back the words. They heard the broadcaster from someone's radio nearby.

"Kansei's Kurahara is revving up again after twenty kilometers! Is there no limit to this runner's stamina?! We might just see another new record for this stage!"

For the first time, a faint smile crossed Fujioka's face. He looked like he'd taken a bite of something bitter but was forcing himself to call it sweet. "I wonder—how far do we have to go, Kiyose? Even when we think we've reached the goal, there's always something beyond it. It's still far away. The ultimate run that I'm after . . ."

Kiyose saw the dark glint of despair in Fujioka's eyes. He recognized the same shadow that dwelled in Kakeru's: the mark of the one who ran on a solitary path, always in pursuit of the ideal.

You're not the only one. Thanks to you, Kakeru's leveled up. You'll

keep pushing each other to reach for even greater heights—I'm sure of it.
Both of you will keep running until someday, you'll cross into a realm that
no one else has ever been able to set foot in.

Kiyose tried to voice his thoughts, but couldn't. He envied them: both Kakeru and Fujioka, those who were chosen by running. So he only said, "But you won't stop, will you? You can never stop running. Right?"

"Right." This time, Fujioka's face creased into a real smile. "I'll start over from scratch."

Kiyose watched in silence as Fujioka left the relay station with the younger students. Probably not a single person on his team realized that there was still an empty hole in Fujioka's heart, a hole that hadn't been filled even as he led his team to victory and set a new record.

It wasn't that Fujioka had lost. He just wanted more. This desire would spur him on to run again and make him even stronger.

"It never gets easy for us runners," Kiyose muttered, then walked back to Prince. "I see Kakeru got the memo."

"Yeah, the landlord just called me. He said Kakeru got fired up as soon as he heard Fujioka's time."

Kiyose peered at Prince's cell. Kakeru was on the screen. Two kilometers left to the relay station. Not a trace of pain marred his face, even after running more than twenty kilometers. His eyes were fixed straight ahead.

He'll be here soon. Kiyose lightly stroked his right leg over his track pants. His leg felt numb; the touch of his fingers gave only a vague, prickling sensation. But that also meant his pain was far-off. *I can run.*

Five minutes, eight seconds after Boso, Daiwa passed on the tasuki in third place; then there was a flurry of activity in the relay station as Kita-Kanto and Manaka arrived, one after the other.

"Runners for Yokohama and Dochido, please come up to the change-over line," the staff announced through a megaphone. "Next up, Kansei, please get ready."

Excited murmurs ran through the crowd. Kansei, having begun the return journey from Lake Ashi in eighteenth place, was now about to be the eighth runner to arrive at Tsurumi. Kansei had overtaken no less than ten teams over the course of four legs in the return journey—but what was the team's actual rank now? Had Kansei climbed up enough to be within reach of the seed rights?

All eyes were drawn to Kansei's last runner, Kiyose. He calmly proceeded to the changeover line, taking no notice of the looks and whispers of the people around him. Prince didn't care how people saw them either. He took Kiyose's bench coat and tracksuit and, finally, glanced at his right shin. He wasn't wearing a brace or any taping. It looked so vulnerable.

"Shouldn't you secure it somehow?" Prince asked hesitantly.

"It's fine. Can't be bothered," Kiyose replied casually. Prince could sense that he was determined not to make excuses on account of his injury. He decided to see Kiyose off with a smile.

"Haiji," he said, looking straight into Kiyose's eyes. "I had fun this past year."

"Me too." Kiyose gently grabbed Prince's shoulder and gave him a light shake.

Kiyose went to stand on the handoff line. Yokohama and Dochido passed their tasukis right next to him, but he didn't even see them.

His gaze was fixed on the access road leading to the relay station—the last hundred meters of the ninth leg. He was watching Kakeru sprinting toward him down the straight road.

From the night we met, I knew. I knew you were the one I'd always been waiting for—the thing I always wanted.

Kakeru embodied Kiyose's ideal run and brought it alive. He effortlessly materialized the very thing that Kiyose had pursued, struggled to attain, and finally failed to reach. Kiyose couldn't imagine a creature more beautiful than this.

You're like a meteor ripping through the sky. Your run is a cold silver stream rushing across the dark.

Ah, it glitters. The trail you leave is a pure streak of light.

At the twenty-kilometer point in the ninth leg, Kakeru learned about Fujioka's new record. As soon as Kakeru's ears caught the landlord's words, his body accelerated of its own accord. But Kakeru himself was still half immersed in the strange, lingering sensation of being cut off from his senses.

He'd experienced runner's high before. His mind and body would float in the air, and he'd feel like he could run forever. What he felt right now was slightly different. It was a quiet, more lucid kind of ecstasy.

He could still take in new information and break it down. Fujioka's time was one hour, nine minutes. *Whether I can beat him or not hangs on how much I can keep pushing it in the last kilometer.* That much he could see.

Most of his consciousness and sensations, however, seemed to stray free of the part of his brain that processed these thoughts. And before he knew it, the rest of him was carried away to a distant shore. His nerves were wide awake, but his consciousness drifted like wisps of cloud. He couldn't do anything about it. He felt as though he was in one of those oddly realistic dreams he had when he slipped in and out of sleep, swaying between its waves—like the time he thought he'd gotten out of bed and was all ready for school, but when his eyes snapped open, he was still lying in bed. As he ran, a similar sensation came over him.

He didn't feel sick, nor did this sensation get in the way of his run. In fact, the movements of his body were sharper than ever, immersed in the constant ebb and flow of lulling euphoria. The only thing that worried him was that he didn't know what came over him, what this trance was exactly.

I'll ask Haiji at Otemachi. I'll tell him what happened. Once Hakone is over.

Kakeru thought he was holding a steady pace, but he realized that his body had suddenly put on a spurt, and he hastily checked his surroundings. Apparently, he'd been spacing out again. He discovered that he had already entered the last kilometer. He could tell the distance from the placard held up on the side of the road. His body seemed to have registered the number and judged that it was time for the final push.

The smear of screaming people rushed into his eyes and ears like a torrent. He checked his watch. It was one hour, eight minutes, twenty-four seconds since he'd started running. *Will I make it? Can I break Fujioka's record? It's a close call.* He sped up by a notch. Pain pierced him. As if his body had just remembered, his pulse started throbbing wildly in his skull.

He veered into the access road bordered by a row of trees and entered the final stretch to the Tsurumi relay station. One hundred meters left. He could see the buzzing crowd, the handoff line. And Kiyose, who stood waiting for him there.

Kiyose stood motionless, staring straight at Kakeru. He was smiling in a way that seemed half-happy, half-sad.

Kakeru snatched the tasuki off his shoulder, as though he was struck into motion or pulled by strings. Ten meters left. To run, to pass on the tasuki—any other movement was excess. He stopped breathing. Didn't even blink. Poured all the oxygen and strength left in his body into the last few steps.

Kiyose drew back his left leg, his body slightly twisted toward Kakeru, and held out his right hand. Kakeru stretched out his hand as far as he could.

They didn't even feel the need to call each other's name. In that moment, with a single fleeting glance into each other's eyes, everything that was inside them passed between them. *Haiji, we've come a long way. We've finally made it, to this faraway place where words and flesh eventually lose all meaning.*

The black tasuki slipped out of Kakeru's hand.

Kakeru stopped once he crossed the changeover line and gazed after Kiyose sprinting away with the tasuki streaming behind him. He started breathing again, greedily gasping for breath, shoulders heaving.

His heart was pounding, wild and uncontrollable. The swirling snow turned into tiny drops of water as soon as it fell on Kakeru's skin.

"Kakeru, you did it! You did it!" Prince leaped on him, and at that same exact moment, he heard the broadcaster gush from Prince's phone, "Kakeru Kurahara of Kansei University comes in at one hour, eight minutes, fifty-nine seconds! He broke Fujioka's time by one second! It's another new record for course nine!"

Prince looked teary as he clung to Kakeru's neck, swept up in the moment. The staff told them to back away from the handoff line. Kakeru dragged Prince to the back of the relay station.

Kakeru was showered with applause and cheers from the crowd. The TV camera nearby was pointed right at him. Someone who looked like a journalist for a track magazine was hurrying toward him for an interview.

Kakeru looked down at his left wrist in a daze. The watch, which he'd forgotten to stop, was still dutifully counting the time. The thrill of the run lingered over him, leaving him fuzzy and slow to react.

As he took a few more steps, the exaltation began to subside. Like a glider landing smoothly on the ground, he came back to reality with a soft touch. *We have to hurry* was the first thing that crossed his mind when he snapped out of his trance.

"Prince, do you have our stuff packed?"

"Yeah, why?"

"Then let's go to Otemachi." Kakeru grabbed their duffel bag from the corner of the relay station and dashed off without a moment's delay. Prince hastily picked up the paper bag with their change of clothes.

"Kakeru, what about changing? Wipe your sweat, at least!" Prince called after him, pulling out a towel and a fresh tracksuit from the bag while trying to keep up. "Hey, slow down! Wait up!"

The people at the relay station gaped at them as they dashed off toward Tsurumi-Ichiba Station. The TV crew, who were hoping for an interview, looked at one another in bewilderment.

It was 12:33:28 p.m. when Kakeru set the new course record. It happened only ten minutes, forty-three seconds after Fujioka had set his own record. For the first time in the Hakone Ekiden's history, the record for the ninth leg, measuring twenty-three kilometers, broke through the wall of one hour, nine minutes, even if it was only by a single second.

The Kansei team was the eighth team to pass on their tasuki at Tsurumi. Totai arrived fifty-one seconds later in the eleventh position. But in terms of their actual time, Totai was still in tenth place overall. As for Kansei, the team had been sixteenth at the Totsuka relay station, but Kakeru's strong performance had pulled them up to twelfth place. The gap between Kansei and Totai in tenth place had narrowed, but the teams were still apart by one minute, two seconds.

Between the ninth and thirteenth teams at Tsurumi, the time difference was only one minute, eighteen seconds. In other words, these five teams—Saikyo, Totai, Akebono, Kansei, and Kofu Gakuin—were all vying for tenth place by a close margin. Any of them could make it into the top ten and seize the seed rights. Any of them could drop out.

The final outcome of the race depended on the twenty-three kilometers of the tenth leg. From here on, every second counted more than ever.

While they were waiting for the Keikyu express train on the platform at Tsurumi-Ichiba, Kakeru borrowed Prince's phone to call Yuki. Yuki picked up instantly and said, "We were watching. You killed it." After a beat, Kakeru realized he was talking about the course record. Kakeru's head was consumed with thoughts of Kiyose's run.

"Thank you. Where are you now?" Kakeru asked.

"We're all here at Otemachi, except for Joji and King."

"Me and Prince will catch the next train that comes. Could you make sure Haiji gets all the info he needs till I get there? And can you give the landlord a breakdown of the race and tell him the times?"

"Don't worry, we've got it covered. We have a secret weapon up our sleeve."

What weapon? Kakeru wondered, but the train was coming in, so he didn't get a chance to ask.

At 12:46 p.m., Kakeru and Prince got on the express train. They would switch to the Tokaido line at Kawasaki and head toward Tokyo Station. On the train, Kakeru quickly pulled on a tracksuit over his uniform, then flung on Kiyose's bench coat.

Prince looked up the train route on his phone and said, "If we run from the Keikyu Kawasaki Station to JR Kawasaki, we might be able to catch the limited express, Odoriko. What do you want to do?"

"Run, of course."

"Okay, then you take this." Prince handed the paper bag to Kakeru. Making Kakeru carry all their gear seemed like the only way Prince could hope to keep up with him.

12:43 p.m. Kiyose was running across the Rokugo Bridge at the three-kilometer point. He crossed over the Tama River and, with it, the prefectural border between Kanagawa and Tokyo.

When he reached the middle of the giant bridge, which extended over four hundred meters, Dochido came into view. Dochido had left the Tsurumi relay station about one minute, thirty seconds before Kansei. The fact that Kiyose had gained on the runner enough to catch sight of him already meant something was wrong. *He's probably sick. Could be a stomachache or something,* Kiyose thought. Fine snow was still falling, and the cold was bitter. Since there was no cover on the bridge, gusts of wind swept across it relentlessly. It was probably around 34°F at most.

Kiyose himself was going steady at three minutes, three seconds per kilometer. He didn't rush forward just because Dochido came into view. He knew that, running at his current pace, he should overtake Dochido around the five-kilometer point anyway. It was best to be patient. If he put too much strain on his leg early in the race, he might not even manage to finish the tenth course.

What Kiyose was battling against weren't other teams. His real opponents were time and the old injury in his own leg.

After the bridge, he stayed on the Dai-Ichi Keihin toward Tokyo.

He skirted the railroad tracks of the Keikyu Main Line, which lay on his left.

At the five-kilometer point, the landlord gave him an update from the coach car.

"We've now got the total times of all teams as of the end of the ninth leg. Rikudo's at the top, at nine hours, fifty-three minutes, fifty-one seconds. Boso is behind by one minute, thirty-one seconds."

Never mind them, Kiyose thought, waving his hand to brush them aside. *I don't care about the top teams right now. What I want to know is how much time we have to gain to cut into the top ten.*

"Ahem, skipping the middle . . . Kansei is now in twelfth place. Total time: ten hours, five minutes, twenty-eight seconds. Totai is in tenth place at ten hours, five minutes, twenty-five seconds. On a side note, Saikyo is in ninth place, three seconds ahead of Totai."

Kiyose rapidly calculated the time gap in his head. That meant he had to run the tenth leg at least one minute, two seconds faster than Totai.

Tough race, Kiyose thought. On the road, Totai was running behind him. There was no obvious target for Kiyose to aim for, no opponent to show him that if he passed that runner, he would be in tenth place. Instead, he had to keep closing the time gap without even seeing what kind of pace Totai was going at. And of course, allowing Totai to overtake him on the road was out of the question.

The coach's allotted one minute to speak was almost up. The landlord added quickly, "As for Totai, he was running at three minutes, five seconds per kilometer as of the three-kilometer point. Over and out."

He says it like he saw it happen with his own eyes, Kiyose thought, amused. The data must have come from Yuki, who'd been on the lookout for any information that might help Kiyose.

My pace is three minutes, three seconds per kilometer. Totai's is three minutes, five seconds. The tenth leg is twenty-three kilometers long, so the amount of time I can gain on him would be only forty-six seconds, if I just go by these numbers. We wouldn't be able to beat them then.

I have to speed up, Kiyose decided. *I should close the gap as much as I can before my leg starts to hurt.*

The railroad crossing near the Keikyu Kamata Station came into sight. It was the Keikyu Airport line that would join the Main Line.

It was just his luck that a train was approaching. The alarm started ringing. The crowd on the sidewalks looked from Kiyose to the crossing and back, shouting, "Hurry!" The barrier remained upright; in its place, police officers and staff rushed to control the traffic. They stopped the cars in the opposite lane with a red flag, but they were coordinating with one another by radio to keep the road open for the runners until the last possible second.

Kiyose couldn't let the crossing get in his way. It would ruin his momentum. He took it as a timely opportunity to accelerate. *Let me pass*, he implored the staff with a look, then dove across the flashing red lights. The people watching were almost screaming in frenzy as they cheered for him to make it through.

Kiyose crossed the track. A collective sigh of relief escaped the crowd. Riding on the momentum, he hurtled past the Dochido runner in one fell swoop. He remained calm, noting that his pace was now just under three minutes. And he hadn't felt any pain in his leg yet.

An endless stretch of spectators, cheering for the runners. *I'm here, running as the tenth member of Kansei, experiencing the same thrills as the rest of my team.*

The image of Kakeru's run in the ninth leg flashed in his mind. It had been just like Kakeru to overtake the other runners right in front of Yokohama Station, where the crowd was largest. There was something captivating about Kakeru's run: a special charisma. He not only had the speed to stun everyone who saw him, but he knew when and where to shine.

Kiyose was convinced that the Hakone Ekiden had made Kakeru an even stronger runner. He wasn't sure whether Kakeru himself was aware of this, but he had been in the zone while running the ninth leg. It was a singular condition of the body and mind, brought on by extreme concentration. They said top athletes who'd undergone intense training would sometimes get in the zone when they pushed themselves to the limit during a race or game.

Kiyose himself had never experienced the zone. He'd read a book about it. In the book, there were all kinds of renowned athletes talking about how it felt to get into the flow—not just track stars, but professional golfers, baseball players, speed skaters, figure skaters. At first Kiyose thought this "zone" might be the same thing as the runner's high, but as he read on, he noticed there were subtle differences between the two.

The runner's high can come about even when you're jogging. You can get there if you run for long enough, and certain stars align in your body and mind. And when you get used to runner's high, you can sense when it's coming. You can edge yourself toward that state of mind before you begin the race. Kiyose thought of it as a kind of habit—in the same way that you might have a tendency to dislocate your shoulder if you raised your arm in a certain angle, for example, or that you're more likely than not to have a nightmare, somehow, when you mix beer and wine. He suspected it was a reflex mechanism of the brain in response to certain routines the body went through. The zone, on the other hand, was supposed to come out of the blue. It was more vivid than the sensation of a runner's high. It happened instantaneously and only during races.

When Kiyose read that matadors, in the decisive moment before killing the bull, also experienced a strange rapture that lifted them above the folds of time, it all made sense to him. The runner's high and getting in the zone were similar phenomena with different triggers. The runner's high was set off by certain motions of the body, whereas the zone might come about by supreme psychological concentration.

Put another way, the zone seemed to be a condition that comes without any warning, plunging the athlete straight into a surreal, super-human state. Both the runner's high and the zone, in fact, were tricks of the mind, the work of opiate chemicals generated in the brain. But a runner who could focus on the race enough to get in the zone proved that he had the aptitude to become a first-rate athlete.

Just after passing Yokohama Station, Kakeru's run had become even sharper. Even on the tiny cell phone screen, Kiyose had seen it clearly. Kakeru seemed slightly perplexed by what was coming over him, but his running never slackened. He kept his form all the way until Kiyose took the tasuki from him at Tsurumi.

Kakeru would surely grow to be a runner loved by many, just as he had captivated Kiyose from the moment they crossed paths. Kakeru's running would continue to mesmerize everyone who saw him.

Kiyose felt fulfilled in a way he'd never felt before. He didn't mind the snow biting his face or the wet surface of the road.

12:50 p.m. The block around the *Yomiuri Shimbun* headquarters at Otemachi, Tokyo, was teeming with people. The familiar faces of the shopping arcade, who'd come out to cheer on the Kansei team, were busy trying to secure their spots by the course.

Nico, Yuki, Shindo, Musa, Jota, and Hanako sat on the side of the moat around the Imperial Palace, which faced Tokyo Station. Nira was with them, too, relishing the touch of Hanako's hands with a drowsy face as she stroked him between his ears.

Hanako's dad was staying at home to get everything set up for the after-party, so the plasterer had taken on the job of bringing Nira to Otemachi. Startled by the huge masses of people, the dog had hidden his tail between his legs as soon as he got out of the station wagon. Hanako, feeling sorry for him, invited him to come with them for the team meeting by the moat. He happily tagged along, as if to say, *I don't mind where I go as long as it's quieter than here.*

At the strategy meeting, on center stage was Yuki's "secret weapon": his laptop. He had entrusted it to Hanako, and she'd been carrying it around safely for the past two days.

"What are those stick figures supposed to be?" Jota asked, peering at the screen. "They're moving like a video game from thirty years ago."

A few stick figures were laboring across the screen from left to right.

"It's simulating the tenth leg right now," Yuki answered, typing away on the keyboard. "The black one is Haiji. The blue is Totai. The rest of the teams are pink."

"I coded the software," Nico added. "If you punch in the total time of each team so far, along with the predicted speed of each runner, it simulates how the race might play out."

"Impressive." Musa looked at the screen curiously. "Oh look, the Haiji stick passed one of the pinks."

"That must be Dochido," Yuki said.

"He already passed Dochido a couple minutes ago!" Jota exclaimed. "What kind of simulation lags behind real life? How's that gonna help?"

"Well, the laptop sure sounds like it's working hard, though," Shindo said, trying to calm Jota. He still had a mask on, and he sounded like he was talking through a stuffy nose. The silver body of the computer made a slight clattering noise as it toiled over the calculations.

"We're better off drawing on graph paper or something," Jota grumbled.

Hanako had to agree, so she nudged the conversation away from the laptop. "Joji and King are taking a while. Hope they make it in time before Haiji finishes."

"Kakeru and Prince should be okay." Jota was apparently too shy to look at Hanako properly, so he directed his answer at Nira, who was sprawled on the ground. "When I texted them, they said they'd get the Odoriko."

"Odoriko, as in *dancer*? Did you write to some cabaret boss by accident?" Nico said, puzzled.

"They must have meant the limited express—that Odoriko," Shindo said.

"Neither of them is used to texting, so that must have been all they could manage to type," said Musa, defending the absent pair.

"So, um, what about Joji?" Hanako pretended to look down at Nira, a faint blush spreading on her cheeks.

Guess she couldn't care less about King, everyone thought.

"King and Joji might be a little late," Jota replied, with a subtle emphasis on *King*. "They told us they're getting held back by traffic control."

Yuki looked up from his laptop. "The simulation is complete."

"Let's see."

"How'd it go?"

They all half-rose to get a better look at the screen.

"According to this," Yuki said gravely, "if Haiji runs at his usual pace, it'll be a bit difficult for him to overturn the time gap with Totai."

"Duh! We don't need a computer to tell us that!" Jota said. "What we need right now is a plan, right?"

"We should trust Haiji and wait," Yuki said coolly, shutting his laptop.

"So much for a secret weapon! It was useless!" Jota jeered.

Nico quickly wiped the simulation software from his head and turned his attention to the portable TV in Musa's hands. "Hey, Totai's pace is falling." The screen showed the runner around the nine-kilometer point, and he was clutching his side with the occasional wince. "Call the landlord."

Kiyose heard about Totai at the ten-kilometer point. He was running neck and neck with the Yokohama runner just past the Keikyu Omorikaigan Station.

It's good news that Totai's slowing down, but there's just one problem. My leg's starting to act up again.

Every time his right foot struck the ground, a dull, tingling pain shot up his shin. Still, Kiyose held his pace of three minutes, four seconds. He passed underneath an elevated railroad that stretched along the right side of the course; a train rattled past as he pressed on.

The streetscape leading to Shinagawa Station seemed to be smeared in gray—probably a combination of the heavy snow clouds looming low overhead and the soaring concrete beams of the elevated railroad. The sight made Kiyose feel hemmed in. He caught a glimpse of a small shopping arcade, bustling with shoppers eager to snag the first deals of the New Year. Though the town looked out onto Tokyo Bay, their view of the sky was obscured by the elevated railroad. Yet the townspeople seemed to be leading a vibrant life in their own community, likely having put down roots over generations.

Kiyose thought back to the sky in his hometown in Shimane Prefecture. What took him by surprise when he first came to Tokyo was how many days the sun shone. But at night, he could make out only a few stars. Shimane was often cloudy during the daytime—the skies in his memory were mostly a gray blur—but when night fell, the clouds lifted somehow, and the sky was filled with glittering stars.

Kiyose felt a similarity between the feel of the neighborhood he was running through and the town he came from. How the people didn't let themselves get shut in by the gray and went about their lives with their feet planted firmly on the ground.

The senior high school Kiyose had attended was the top school in the prefecture for track and field. Fujioka had enrolled in the school from outside Shimane, and he lived in the students' dorm. Kiyose remembered the paths he and Fujioka used to jog on together and the almost-sweet scent of summer rice fields. At night, countless fireflies would surround them, flickering their delicate yellow-green lights. He recalled how Fujioka, creeped out by the swarm, had said, "Isn't this a bit overkill?"

Kiyose had been lucky to have a strong teammate to run with. He did disagree with his father's coaching methods at times, but Fujioka would comfort him, or they'd grumble over it together, and soon enough, Kiyose would forget what had even frustrated him. At least, until the leg issues started.

In the autumn of his first year at senior high, his shin began to hurt after any strenuous run. He tried massages and acupuncture, but the pain lingered and eventually became chronic. The doctor, whom he went to see without telling his father, informed him that he was on the verge of getting a stress fracture. The best way to heal would be to take a temporary break from running.

But Kiyose couldn't stop running, not when his time was getting better. Accustomed to the grind of an intense running routine, he was obsessed with keeping up with the workload. He also couldn't let himself show any sign of weakness to his father.

Perhaps because he was running in a way that minimized the strain on his shin, he then suffered an avulsion fracture in his kneecap. A small fragment of bone jammed in his joint, and it had to be removed by surgery. He spent his entire summer holiday in his second year of senior high focusing on rehab. Even when he managed to start running again, his speed seemed to stagnate.

It's over, Kiyose had thought. He used to believe that he was born to run, and while he'd poured everything into the sport, his body had betrayed him. His father told him to be patient, but a deep despair curdled in Kiyose's heart. His injury was fatal for a track athlete. He knew that better than anyone.

He was among the best runners in senior high, but that was as far as he could go. If he tried to stretch further, he would do irreversible damage to his right leg, and he'd never be able to compete again. Still, he clung to what little hope there was and kept up the practice.

Kiyose felt like a freakish plant trapped inside a dark box. Even though it was clear that his leaves would bump against the lid, that he was bound to rot from his roots, he couldn't help trying to slither out his tendrils to unfurl his leaves, greedily hanging on to life. His body had reached its limits, but he couldn't stop himself from running.

He thought he'd die if he stopped. His spirit would die, and his body, too, would waste away in time. If he allowed that to happen, he could never forgive himself. Somewhere in the back of his mind, he knew it was pointless, but he wanted to keep running races for as long as he could. That was the only way he knew to keep his soul alive.

Fujioka supported Kiyose and told him that once he finished growing, his injury might heal completely. He invited Kiyose to keep running together, to take the opportunity Rikudo had offered him.

Kiyose reflected. He mulled over distance running as a sport and about the act of running itself. And after much consideration, he chose Kansei. He'd decided that being a part of a team clearly set up for success wasn't for him. But he never could extinguish his burning desire to keep running. What he needed was to be in a place where he would be surrounded by people who had nothing to do with running and to confront the question anew.

He had to ask himself, *Why do I run?*

Kansei didn't have the right facilities for runners, and he often regretted his choice. He even thought of quitting, but he stopped himself every time. As he spent more time at Chikusei-so, he gradually came to understand why.

Whether you ran or not, there would always be pain. But there was also just as much joy. Everyone has their own problems to grapple with, and even when they know they're fighting a losing battle, they still strive against the obstacles.

By distancing himself a little from track, Kiyose realized this mundane truth. If pain was inevitable no matter what path he chose, then why not stand his ground and seek what his soul truly desired?

Despite the ticking time bomb that was his right leg, Kiyose kept running. As he ran, he waited for an opportunity. And at long last, in his fourth year of waiting, he met Kakeru. Ten people assembled at Chikusei-so, and together, they were now taking on the Hakone Ekiden.

Mount Hakone wasn't a mirage. The Hakone Ekiden wasn't just a dream. It was a very real race, charged with the pain and the pleasures of running. The Hakone Ekiden awaited the dedicated students of the sport. It had awaited Kiyose, who kept running through all his struggles. Its gates were always open for those who sought the race.

Ever since Kiyose went to Kansei, his father had practically disowned him, barely speaking a word to him even when he went home for the holidays. But on New Year's Day, he gave Kiyose a call. "We bought a new TV, so I'll watch the race with your mother," his father had said. "It looks like you've found yourself a good team."

That's right—we make the best team. I'll show you what hope looks like, now that I've finally found it. All ten of us will show you what it means to run with every fiber of our bodies, each in our own way. Just watch.

When Kiyose learned that his injury meant he wouldn't be able to run the way he used to, he felt betrayed. He'd devoted his whole life to running, and this is what he got in return. But he'd been wrong. Running had come back to him, reborn in a form that was much more beautiful.

Now Kiyose was glad. His heart swelled with happiness. He wanted to cry, to scream at the top of his voice.

Even if I can never run again, this is enough for me. Running gave me something better than I ever dared to hope for. And I'm content with that.

On the gentle climb up Yatsuyama Bridge at the thirteen-kilometer point, Kiyose threw off the Yokohama runner. Numerous railroad tracks stretched under the overpass to convene in a giant terminal. The road curved to the right, descending toward Shinagawa Station.

The snow had stopped falling.

1:14 p.m. Kakeru dashed out of Tokyo Station toward the Marunouchi district. He had a duffel bag slung across his chest and a paper bag in his left hand. His eyes were glued to the cell phone in his right hand. He'd snatched the phone away from Prince to watch the TV coverage. The screen showed Kiyose, who'd just passed the Yokohama runner and risen to sixth place.

"Kansei's captain, Haiji Kiyose, is still going strong," the broadcaster commented.

"No," Kakeru muttered. *His leg hurts. The cold and the pressure of the race are pushing him to the limit. But he's still running like nothing's wrong.*

"Keep going straight, Kakeru," Prince wheezed from behind. He'd gotten a text from Yuki before Kakeru stole his phone. "Everyone's by the moat. Let's head there instead of Otemachi."

Their group, dressed in Kansei tracksuits and bench coats, were standing in front of the outer garden of the Imperial Palace. Nira jumped up when he noticed Kakeru and Prince approaching. Hanako held the dog's leash tight so he wouldn't spring out into the road. Joji and King didn't seem to have arrived yet.

"Hey, way to go, Kakeru! Congrats!" Jota called out.

"Kinda feels like I haven't seen you in years," Nico said with a big grin.

"The announcer was saying something funny about your run, Kakeru— um, what was it . . ." Shindo got stuck mid-sentence and blinked a few times, his eyes a little glazed from the fever. His cold was still giving him brain fog. Musa jumped in to pick up where he left off.

"The 'black bullet,' that's what he said. 'Kakeru Kurahara of Kansei University is flying like a black bullet!'"

Kakeru blushed. "Why're you all hanging out here?" he asked.

"We were having a team meeting," Hanako said. She was about to fill him in on their failed secret weapon, but Yuki started walking off before she could get a word in.

"It's packed near the finish line," Yuki explained. "So we were taking cover here—but we better head back soon."

They all walked along the moat toward Otemachi. The cacophony of the cheer squads drifted past them, carried by the wind. Since the squads were singing their respective school anthems all at once, the result was complete chaos.

The tenth leg diverged from the route of the first leg near Tokyo Station. In the first leg, the course went straight along the moat to Tamachi, while the tenth leg turned right at Babasaki Gate, veering to the east of Tokyo Station. The route cut through Nihonbashi and proceeded toward Otemachi, directly facing the Imperial Palace. Kakeru and the others were taking the moat-side road to Otemachi, so they would come up just behind the finish line.

As they approached the *Yomiuri Shimbun* building, the crowd grew bigger and bigger, the din rising with them. Their enthusiasm even warmed the wind whipping through the skyscrapers.

"Can't believe I set off from here just yesterday." Prince looked all around him. "I feel like it's been a hundred years." People stood by their office windows, looking out at the street below. Prince was surprised they were working over New Year's, but upon closer inspection, he noticed many of them were holding beer cans. They must have shown up at their offices just to get front-row seats to the final moments of the race.

The staff saw that they were the Kansei team and loosened the rope barrier to let them through. They stepped over the rope into the space around the finish line.

"Wow . . ." they couldn't help but murmur. On both sides of the wide road, there were four or five rows of people crammed together. Everyone in attendance, both the spectators flapping their little flags and the cheer squads from each university, waited for the runners in bright-eyed anticipation. The sea of people stretched on endlessly, even beyond the railroad bridge of Tokyo Station.

"That's a *lot* of people," Jota said, his mouth hanging open. "The crowd never looked this massive back when I used to watch the race on TV."

Kakeru nodded. "It's mind-blowing when you see it in person."

"I think there must be as many people here as there are in my home-town." Musa shook his head slowly, wavering between bewilderment and wonder.

"More than my entire village, that's for sure." Shindo tottered a little, his head spinning.

The main broadcaster and Yanaka, the commentator, had moved from the TV studio and were now sitting in front of microphones on the rooftop of the *Yomiuri Shimbun* building. The crowd could hear two sets of voices like an echo: one coming down from the roof, picked up by their mics, and the other sounding from the TV.

"The current temperature at Otemachi, Tokyo, is 32.7°F. The snow has stopped, but the wind is blowing hard. In about ten minutes, we should see the first runners making their way here through these gusts of wind."

Though cordoned off from the public, the space behind the finish line was still teeming with staff and participants. Kakeru and the others found a recess in the wall of a building, and they huddled there to wait. Nira was trembling in Hanako's arms. The poor dog had his tail tucked between his legs, and his ears lay flat on his head.

Nira wasn't a small dog. Kakeru thought Hanako might get tired from holding him for so long. He was about to tell her he could take the dog when he remembered he was holding the paper bag. He put it down on the ground and straightened up again to offer help. But by then, Jota had caught wind of Hanako's situation.

"Here, let me," said Jota, taking Nira from Hanako. "He's pretty heavy. You're strong, Hana."

"Carrying veggies all the time keeps me fit." Hanako laughed a little sheepishly. Kakeru didn't know what to do with his hands now and stuck them in his pockets. Nico and Yuki smirked, Shindo and Musa pretended not to notice, and Prince was poring over a manga he'd pulled out from the duffel bag.

"Oh, I'm reading that one, too," Hanako said to Prince. "It's really good, right?"

Now was his chance. Kakeru sidled up to Jota and whispered, "Joji said he's going to ask Hanako out. He says you're not allowed to beat him to the punch."

"Seriously?" Jota yelped. Nira's ear twitched. "Then I'm gonna do it, too!"

They're acting like they're on the playground, Kakeru thought, but he burst out laughing when he saw Jota getting pumped up. "Maybe I will, too," Kakeru said.

"Huh? What's that supposed to mean? Wait, so you actually do like—"

Nico called Kakeru over, so he left Jota blabbering.

"What do you think of Haiji's run?" Nico asked, holding up the tiny phone screen to Kakeru. "Doesn't he look like his leg's hurting?"

The times of the runners as of the fifteen-kilometer point were listed on the screen. The first-year from Rikudo was far ahead of the rest, going at a pace that could set a new course record. His run was charged with vigor. He seemed determined to avenge Fujioka's regret. It seemed impossible for Boso to catch up. Unless something drastic occurred, it was already a given that Rikudo would seize the victory.

Kiyose's pace as he passed the fifteen-kilometer point was second-fastest after Rikudo's. But because Kakeru had been watching Kiyose run from up close over the past year, he could tell that something was wrong. There was a faint tinge of pain on Kiyose's face.

"Haiji got a painkiller shot from a doctor this morning," Kakeru said.

"I knew it," Nico muttered, scratching his head.

"I guess it's no use asking the landlord to tell him not to be reckless," Yuki sighed.

"And Totai's pace?" Kakeru asked.

"He's the third-fastest now. He lost his groove in the middle, but he got back into it," Yuki replied.

"Guess the guy's just as desperate as the rest of us," Nico said.

"Haiji's gonna be fine," Kakeru said firmly.

"What makes you so sure?" Yuki asked.

"He promised me he would be."

Yuki looked at Kakeru with pity in his eyes. "You never learn, do you, Kakeru?"

I don't care. Kakeru gazed out at the road, in the direction Kiyose would be coming. *Haiji can trick me a hundred times. If he says he'll run, I'll wait for him. I'll believe his every word, till I see him break out into the best run of his life. I'll wait for him however long it takes.*

Once Kiyose passed Shinagawa Station, he started seeing more and more skyscrapers. He turned left at the Shiba Go-chome intersection, which marked the 16.6-kilometer point, leaving Dai-Ichi Keihin and entering Hibiya Avenue. Each lane of the road widened, and his surroundings turned increasingly into a metropolis.

High-rise buildings lined the street on both sides. But running down the road made Kiyose notice that there was also a surprising number of trees around it. He passed Zojo Temple in Shiba. The path in front of its imposing gate was also full of people cheering him on.

The road itself was empty because of the traffic control, and Kiyose had the whole expanse to himself. By this time, he felt searing pain shoot up his right leg every time his foot hit the ground. But he had to press on. He wondered how many seconds he'd managed to gain on Totai. There was always the possibility that the gap might be growing, too. Dropping his speed wasn't an option for him at this point.

Kiyose was desperate. Though he was the one in pursuit of Totai, he felt like something was chasing him down. Surely not even a zebra fleeing from a cheetah would gallop so hard. Like a frantic beast, he pushed down his pain and accelerated further.

A car came into view ahead of him. It was the coach vehicle trailing Manaka. The driver noticed Kiyose rapidly drawing closer and swerved aside to the next lane. Locking eyes on the runner's back, now helplessly exposed, Kiyose charged forward to his right.

Manaka didn't back down. He dug in and held on tight. They went neck and neck for about two hundred meters. The sound of their ragged breathing beat on their eardrums, impossible to tell apart. Kiyose sensed his opponent's eyes on the left side of his face, but Kiyose didn't even spare him a glance. He fixed his eyes on the road straight ahead.

They passed by Hibiya Park, and the view opened up on their left. They had emerged at the moat of the Imperial Palace. Next came the right turn at the intersection in front of Babasaki Gate.

This is it. A lightning bolt of intuition jolted Kiyose's entire body. Using his position on the inner side of the corner to his advantage, Kiyose threw off Manaka. It was a move he could have made only after years of competing in races, whetting his mind and body to the breaking point.

His body bent to his will, and he sprang forward, faster, faster. He could sense Manaka falling away, as if sinking into water. Kiyose bit back a groan. His right leg grated under the strain of accelerating. The pain was so staggering he could have sworn it was gripping his very nerves with bare hands.

His leg was throbbing like a massive toothache. The pain pulsed all the way up through his waist to his skull, so piercing it made him want to laugh. Bones and teeth were both chunks of calcium, after all—not much difference. If he hadn't laughed, he would've broken down.

Kiyose passed under the railroad bridge and emerged at the Yaesu side of Tokyo Station. Though he didn't feel the slightest bit cold, his breath still came out white.

At the twenty-kilometer point, the landlord's loudspeaker screeched. "Mayday, mayday," the landlord murmured in a mic check. Kiyose smiled wryly—*Who even says that anymore?*—but strained his ears for the news to come. The crowd was howling like a thunderstorm, almost drowning out everything else.

"Here's Yuki's forecast. At this rate, you'll finish six seconds short of Totai."

Damn. It's still not enough? Kiyose clenched his teeth.

No, it's not the end yet. Three more kilometers to go. Don't give up. Run. Run like you mean it. If I give up now, this time I'll really lose it for good. Now that I finally got it back, I can't let something this precious slip out of my grasp again.

I'll never let it go. Whatever I do, I'll get there.

He turned left onto Chuo Avenue. It was a glitzy street lined with office buildings and department stores. Two kilometers left. His leg throbbed. The tasuki felt heavy. It actually did weigh down on him. The cloth had soaked up rain, snow, and ten runners' worth of sweat since yesterday, and it hung heavy on his shoulder like something much more than a strip of fabric.

One kilometer to go. Kiyose crossed Nihonbashi Bridge under the overpass of the Metropolitan Expressway. The river flowed calmly toward the sea in the shadow of the roads.

He turned left after the bridge. The deep rumble of the crowd and the booms of the cheer squads swept over him. The last eight hundred meters were a straight line. He passed under the overpasses for the expressway and the railroad one more time.

A strong gust of wind whipped past him through the buildings.

Kiyose saw what he had been pursuing all this time. Down the road, under a banner that read "The Tokyo-Hakone Round-Trip College Ekiden Race," the residents of Chikusei-so were standing together. They were all calling to Kiyose.

The finish line. *I've finally come this far.*

Kiyose ramped up his speed again. Fifty meters left. *Will I make it? If only time would stand still, just for me. I want to outrun time itself.* He ran like he was cutting through air. It was now or never. He leaned forward a little and struck the ground with a final burst of energy.

A dry crack came from his shin. In that split second, the din of the crowd seemed to vanish, and he heard the small but strangely clear snap of his own bone tearing apart.

Pain turned into thick sweat gushing out of every pore of his body. His body started tilting sideways, but he stood his ground and pushed on. He saw Kakeru standing near the finish, his face twisted like he was fighting back tears. He looked furious even as he choked back a desperate scream.

Don't be silly, Kakeru. I'm all right.

I'll get there, I promise. I can feel it in the rush of wind. I'm running. The run I've always dreamed of. It's incredible. I couldn't be happier.

Kiyose suddenly looked up at the sky. Heavy clouds stretched over the tall buildings. But his eyes didn't miss it.

A soft beam of sunlight streamed through a break in the clouds—a faint, white glow amid the gray.

Behind the finish line, the interview of the winning team, Rikudo, was underway. Dressed in matching purple tracksuits, the club members were going wild, celebrating their victory.

Amid the commotion, Fujioka stood with his usual serene composure. Kakeru, jostled by the other athletes and staff rushing to and fro, caught sight of Fujioka. Fujioka noticed him, too. In the few seconds in which they locked eyes, they commended each other's run with tacit recognition.

"We made it!" someone exclaimed and leaped onto Kakeru's back. It was Joji. Apparently, he and King had sprinted over from Tokyo Station. King was out of breath.

"So what's the news?" Joji asked.

"Boso just finished second. In the end, Rikudo won by four minutes, forty-one seconds," Kakeru said.

"Still leaning back on their throne, huh," Joji groaned. But a second later, he perked up and chirped, "Oh well, we'll drag them down someday."

Joji's words were filled with confidence. And it didn't even occur to Kakeru to doubt him. Now he felt that if they put their minds to it, they could really make it happen.

Ten runners taking on Hakone. It had seemed like an impossible dream; people had laughed at them, but they had done it.

1:41 p.m. Daiwa finished in third place. The Chikusei-so residents couldn't see where Kiyose was now; the TV had switched to the interview with Rikudo.

"Maybe it's time to get closer to the finish line?" Musa suggested hesitantly.

"Isn't it too early?" Nico said, but he started moving.

"What happened to Totai?" Yuki muttered under his breath.

"I don't know," Kakeru replied, dropping his voice, too. He thought anxiety and anticipation would crush his lungs. With the rest of the Chikusei-so team, Kakeru edged his way toward the finish line.

"Here comes another runner on the final stretch!" The broadcaster's voice echoed between the buildings. "It's Kita-Kanto University. Closely followed by another one coming into view from under the overpass—"

"*Haiji!*" Kakeru yelled.

"Oh! There he is!" Joji shouted.

"Haiji, run! Don't kill yourself but run as hard as you can!" King cried, jumping up and down with Joji. They all called out to Haiji, waving at him with outstretched arms.

"It's Kansei University! Would you believe it, the fifth runner to appear at Otemachi is Kansei!" The announcer was shouting himself hoarse in excitement. "Kansei, the underdog team of only ten members, is here in fifth place in their first-ever Hakone Ekiden! They were last in the first leg, and though they climbed steadily up the ranks, they hit an unexpected wall in the fifth leg. They started the return journey this morning in eighteenth place!"

"No one asked you for a full recap," Prince said, as Shindo fidgeted awkwardly.

"But from there, Kansei rose again, and what great strides they've made!" The announcer's voice was trembling with emotion now. "Iwakura was second-fastest in the sixth leg, and in the ninth leg, Kurahara smashed the course record. And now, in the tenth leg, their anchor, Kiyose, is also putting up a strong fight. He's seconds away from crossing the finish line! What do you think, Yanaka—this team really worked together to get through the race, didn't they?"

"Yes," Yanaka answered in a gruff voice. "The story of this small brave team will be passed down for as long as the Hakone Ekiden lives on. Kansei's presence made this year's race all the more absorbing and inspiring."

At Yanaka's words, the crowd's cheering surged. From the sidewalks, from the windows of the office buildings, from every direction came clamor and applause for the Kansei team. Jota's shoulders quivered, and he looked down at his feet. Shindo quietly closed his eyes.

As they were showered with acclaim, Kakeru's eyes were fixed on Kiyose advancing toward them. He could tell Kiyose was biting back the pain. But Kiyose didn't ease his pace. He was trying to close the time gap with Totai, even by a millisecond.

You've done enough. No need to hurt yourself more than you already have, Kakeru wanted to tell him, but he forced himself to swallow back the words. Kiyose was running with everything in his soul and body. His fierce will was almost tangible, lashing out at the air around him. His body seemed to flash in a burst of energy as he leaned in for the final dash.

It happened in that moment.

Kakeru didn't hear or see anything wrong, but he sensed it. *Haiji*, he tried to scream, but he couldn't find his voice.

Kiyose lurched, but immediately straightened up again. He didn't lose any speed. His run grew even more powerful, his eyes locked on the goal.

Please stop, you're going to break down. You'll never be able to run again. Kakeru glanced around at the others in a panic. *Did no one else notice? How? What should I do?* He wanted to jump out over the line and cling to Kiyose. He had to make Kiyose stop running, even if that meant dragging him down, or else there would be no way back.

Kakeru turned back to Kiyose and took a step forward. They locked eyes. A smile crept onto Kiyose's sweat-stained face. It was the face of a man who had thrown everything away and seized everything in return.

This is a race, Kiyose was telling him through his entire being. His right leg must feel as if it were shattering into pieces, yet Kiyose was as resolute as ever. *The small team of ten missed the seed rights by a narrow margin, but they fought hard*—none of them wanted to hear those superficial consolations. *We run. We run till the very end, fighting*

for every second. We charge on and seize our own victory, just for our-
selves. Isn't that what we're here for? Kiyose's eyes spoke passionately
to Kakeru.

Kakeru was rooted to the spot. He couldn't stop Kiyose. He couldn't
tell him not to run. No one could rein in the soul who longs to run,
who has chosen to run.

Kakeru saw Kiyose glancing up at the sky, and a clear, transcendent
expression came into his face, as though he'd just discovered something
priceless, something beautiful.

Haiji, you told me you wanted to find out. You wanted to know what it
really means to run. That's where everything started. I think I know how
to answer that question now.

I don't know what it really means. But I do know both happiness and
anguish are there. Everything about me and you, everything we care about,
is packed into our life of running.

Kakeru felt certain. *I want to run for as long as I live.*

When there comes a time when his body can't run anymore, his
soul wouldn't stop running until he took his last breath. Running itself
gave Kakeru everything. Everything vital to him on the face of this
earth: joy, pain, thrill, envy, respect, anger, and hope. Through running,
Kakeru gained everything.

On January 3, at 1:44:32 p.m., Kiyose crossed the finish line at
Otemachi. He was panting heavily, his knees crumpling under him as
Kakeru darted forward to hold him up.

All the Chikusei-so members rushed forward and flung their arms
around Kiyose. They raved and howled like beasts. Kiyose thrust his
right arm high in the air in the middle of the circle. He gripped the
black tasuki in his fist.

After a long journey of 216.4 kilometers, the tasuki of the Kansei
University Track and Field Club had returned to Otemachi once again.

As the whole team went wild, Kakeru put a hand on Kiyose's shoulder. Kiyose was drenched in clammy sweat.

"Haiji, quick, let's get you some help."

"No, I'm fine." Kiyose looked up and quickly cut him off. "I want to stay here for now. What about Totai?"

Kakeru and Kiyose looked toward the course. Totai's anchor was just sprinting down the last twenty meters with all his strength.

Still huddled together, the Chikusei-so residents stopped breathing. The Totai team was next to them, calling to the runner frantically, "Hurry, hurry!" Sakaki was there, too. Kakeru no longer felt any anger or concern at the sight of him. Every one of Kakeru's senses felt numb. He couldn't even will the runner to slow down.

The only thing he was aware of was the word that kept ringing somewhere in his head: *Please. Please. Please.* He wasn't sure anymore whom he was begging or what he was praying for.

Totai crossed the line. The crowd held its breath, and a momentary hush fell over the block.

"What's their time?!" Yuki shouted impatiently. A moment later, the announcer shrieked from the top of the *Yomiuri* building, "We have the total times. Tokyo Taiiku comes two seconds behind Kansei!"

This time, they couldn't even utter a sound. Kakeru, Kiyose, Nico, Yuki, Musa, Shindo, King, Jota, Joji, and Prince—they all pulled each other into a tight, silent embrace.

"Kansei University, running in Hakone for the first time in history, has now seized the seed rights!" the broadcaster announced, his voice turning shrill. "Kansei's total time was eleven hours, seventeen minutes, thirty-one seconds, placing tenth. Tokyo Taiiku came in eleventh, narrowly missing the mark by two seconds."

King trembled as he choked back a sob. Shindo and Musa were by his side, gently wrapping their arms around him. Yuki handed his glasses to Nico and wiped his eyes with the back of his hand. Joji and Prince double high-fived. Next to them, Jota hugged Nira close, burying his chin in the dog's back. Nira's fur was wet with the tears streaming down Jota's face.

Kakeru and Kiyose, who had been standing side by side, stock-still, now looked at each other. At the same exact moment, they let out a roar from the pit of their stomachs. Like wolves howling, their scream was contagious, and the Chikusei-so residents drew together again, whooping and hollering.

As they exploded in wild delight, a panoply of cameras turned to them: two for TV and at least five for print media. "Congratulations on winning seed rights!" an interviewer exclaimed, thrusting a mic at them. The landlord and Hanako, who had been watching the scene unfold nearby, now walked over to the group.

Kakeru and the others finally let go of each other and looked around, blinking. The landlord had gotten caught by an interviewer, instead of the group, who could barely talk. Hanako handed Kiyose an ice bag.

"Thanks," said Kiyose.

"Your time was one hour, eleven minutes, four seconds. The second-fastest in the course," Hanako told him. "The Kansei team completed the return journey in five hours, thirty-four minutes, thirty-two seconds." She was smiling through her tears.

"Haiji," Kakeru murmured in a daze as the reality of their achievement sunk in. "We really did it."

"Yeah." Kiyose sounded stunned, too. "We ran the whole Hakone Ekiden."

Kakeru and Kiyose held each other tight for a brief moment. Kiyose threw Kakeru a mischievous look.

"Told you everyone at Aotake's got what it takes. Believe me now?"

"I always did!" Kakeru said loudly. "A lot more than just 'believe.'"

Kiyose laughed like he was on top of the world. Then he looked around at everyone and said, "Now do you see the summit?"

Epilogue

Somewhere in the distance, flowers were blooming. Their sweet scent mingled in the twilight air.

It seemed like only yesterday that he had come here with the Chikusei-so residents. Kakeru Kurahara looked at the Odakyu train rattling across the iron bridge over Tamagawa. It was spring again.

Lights were already glowing in the train windows. The river, starting to take on the colors of the night, flowed as serene as before. The bank was deserted. Kakeru gradually slowed down his jogging. As he took a few steps down the slope of the embankment, the soft grass hugged his well-worn shoes.

He sat down on the grass and gazed at the river for a while, its surface reflecting the neon lights on the other side.

"Kakeru." He turned around at the voice. On the road at the top of the embankment stood a new freshman who was set to join the track club this spring. When Kakeru nodded to him, he came down with a skip in his step and sat next to him.

"Have you been jogging this whole time?" asked Kakeru. "Don't get too excited."

"No, I went to get some groceries from the shopping arcade earlier," the rookie replied, looking a little nervous. "Joji's the one getting too excited. He bought a whole lot of meat and veggies—he wants tonight to be a party."

I bet he's thinking yakiniku, Kakeru thought. Come to think of it, Jota had gone to the clubhouse earlier that day to borrow a big griddle from the cafeteria lady. The twins had probably settled on a barbecue because they were craving meat, but they also couldn't pass up a chance to shop at Yaokatsu.

"It's too bad they're knocking it down," the first-year said. "I wish I could've lived in Chikusei-so, too."

"You'd have kicked a hole through the floor."

"Did that actually happen?"

"Yup."

"That's crazy," he laughed.

"Is everyone there already?" Kakeru asked.

The freshman's face grew serious. "Yes," he said. "That's partly why I came out for a jog. I was surrounded by senpais I've never met, and I didn't know what to do." He sat up straight. "Kiyose-senpai—what's he like?"

"Haiji? Why do you ask?"

"Joji told me that you could've gone to a much stronger corporate team if you wanted to. But you chose the new team because Kiyose-senpai is the coach there."

"I'm just not cut out for big teams, that's all."

"Really?" The student didn't seem convinced. "To be honest, today got me pretty hyped. I didn't think I'd get to meet Kiyose-senpai. I made up my mind to go to Kansei and join the track team when I watched you guys compete in the Hakone Ekiden, the year when Kiyose-senpai was the anchor."

Kakeru plucked a tuft of grass and tossed it gently on the breeze. "It's getting chilly. Let's head back."

When Kakeru got up and started jogging, the freshman hastily followed suit. Kakeru subtly adjusted his pace to match the student's.

"So, about what Haiji's like . . ." Kakeru said.

"Yes?"

"He's a liar."

"What?"

"He's really good at lying, so be careful he doesn't trick you."

"Okay . . ." the freshman said, sounding unsure about what to make of that.

A thin smile played on Kakeru's lips.

Haiji said he was going to be fine. But he lied. He must have known he'd never run again. Still, he stuck to his lie till the very end. To keep his promise to me. To turn our dream into reality—the dream we all chased after together.

I've never been told a single lie so bold, and cruel, and beautiful.

They jogged across the field and down the narrow alleyways winding through the neighborhood. The chimney of the bathhouse, Tsuru no Yu, rose above the low rooftops of the houses. The thin veil of dusk fell upon the streets. The scent of someone's dinner wafted out from a window facing the street, blending into the spring air and melting away.

"Wonder if people who're good at lying make good coaches," the first-year murmured, tilting his head. "When you first ran in Hakone, Kiyose-senpai was practically the coach, wasn't he? And now he's coaching a corporate team."

"Hmm, who knows?" Kakeru never thought about whether Kiyose was a natural at coaching. Kiyose was just Kiyose. He was always cool and collected, ready to consider things from each runner's perspective, and more earnest than anyone else when it came to the pursuit of running. Kiyose was a steady, unwavering pillar, always there for those who were drawn to the run.

"All I know is, Haiji taught me everything," Kakeru said. "Except for one thing."

"What's that?"

What it means to run.

That was the only thing Kiyose never taught him. Maybe he simply couldn't.

Kakeru ran, still searching for the answer. He would keep on running. There were times when he'd thought he'd scaled the highest summit. But the sense of achievement was gone in a moment, and the answer still eluded him.

"You'll figure it out soon enough," Kakeru said quietly to the first-year jogging next to him. "As long as you keep running, you'll see it someday."

When they turned a corner, the hedges around Chikusei-so came into view. They heard a babble of voices. Nira, whose walks had gotten shorter these days, was chiming in with barks. The freshman disappeared through a gap in the hedges, and Kakeru followed him.

All the familiar faces were gathered in the yard outside Chikusei-so.

Nico and Yuki were laughing together. Prince's silhouette passed from one window to the next as he went around turning the lights on. Musa and Shindo were carrying the grilled meat to the table. King was letting Nira lick some sake and getting scolded by the landlord. Hanako and the twins were putting their heads together in animated conversation.

Am I dreaming? Kakeru wondered. *Maybe it's come back—that one year that felt too good to be true.*

When Kakeru stepped into the yard, the gravel crunching under his feet, Kiyose looked up from the griddle and smiled. He walked over to Kakeru, a slight limp in his right leg, and offered him a cup of sake.

"Welcome back, Kakeru."

"Good to be home." Kakeru took the cup.

It was Kakeru's last night at Chikusei-so. He would move out tomorrow.

Even if he felt the urge to come back someday, there would be nowhere to return to. Tomorrow, Chikusei-so was going to be demolished, and a new dorm for the track and field club would take its place. But he didn't feel lonely. Kakeru now knew that when something was torn down, it didn't mean everything was lost. Just like race records, which were broken and wiped clean, only to live on in memory.

The windows of Chikusei-so were aglow with light. Kakeru held out his cup, gazing at the soft lights floating in the sake.

"Do you remember, Haiji?"

Instead of asking about what, Kiyose just laughed quietly.

An especially loud whoop went up in a corner of the yard. A small out-of-season firework was set off, and the smell of damp gunpowder rose to the sky. Kakeru and Kiyose stood side by side, following the white trail of smoke with their eyes.

A burst of light illuminated everyone in the yard in vivid colors.

Kakeru had spent an intense year—the most rewarding of his life—with people who had become indispensable to him. A time like that might never come again. But still.

—Do you like to run, Kakeru?

One spring night four years ago, Kiyose had posed that question to Kakeru. His face was so sincere, it was as if he was asking about the essence of life itself.

—I want to find out. What it really means to run.

Me too, Haiji. I want to know, too. After all these years of running, I still haven't figured it out. Now I run to ask that question. And I'll never stop looking for the answer.

I want to find out.

So let's go. Let's run, wherever it takes us.

The light of conviction always shone inside the heart. The path was clear and bright: a narrow line stretching on through the dark.

"Come on, hurry up, Kakeru."

Friends were calling. Kakeru took a step forward toward the circle of people gathered around the grill, Kiyose close by his side.

ACKNOWLEDGMENTS

I am indebted to many people who helped me with my interviews and research (the titles and positions given here are those they held at the time). I remain deeply grateful to them. Any details that deviate from fact in this novel, whether intentional or otherwise, are of course my own responsibility.

Shinya Tadakuma, Coach of the Daito Bunka University Track and Field Club

Everyone in the Daito Bunka University Track and Field Club

Yoshiyuki Aoba, Captain of the Daito Bunka University Track and Field Club

Michihiko Narita, Ekiden Coach of the Hosei University Track and Field Club

Everyone in the Hosei University Track and Field Club

Haruo Kariya, Former Captain of the Hosei University Track and Field Club

Kenji Kubo, Koji Yamazaki, and Satoshi Iijima of the Nissan Motor Track and Field Team

Toshikatsu Kojima, Fumikazu Enomoto, Takeo Ueno, and
Toshiko Suzuki

Yutaka Hirose of the Inter-University Athletic Union of Kanto

Masako Narita

Norio Tanaka

REFERENCES

Hakone ekiden kōshiki gaido bukku (The Hakone Ekiden Official Guide Book). Rikujyō-kyōgi-sha.

Kōdansha MOOK—shasin de miru hakone ekiden 80 nen (Kodansha MOOK: 80 Years of the Hakone Ekiden in Pictures). Rikujyō-kyōgi-sha.

Hakone ekiden—atsuki omoi wo mune ni tasuki ga tsunaida 80 nenkan (The Hakone Ekiden: A History of Passion Passed Down Through the Tasuki Over 80 Years). Bēsubōru-magajin-sha.

A NOTE FROM THE TRANSLATOR

Kakeru's journey to become a stronger runner is a journey of self-expression. As he hones his body to run faster and to unleash his full potential, he also discovers how vital it is for him to grapple with language. Once he realizes that words are what he lacks, he tries to find the right words to capture—or attempt to capture—the fleeting, nebulous stuff of life, such as sensations, emotions, thoughts, and memories. (Perhaps this is partly why Miura deploys so many similes about that liminal space between waking and sleeping when describing Kakeru's feelings.) By gradually acquiring language, he is able to connect with people around him, meditate on the act of running on a deeper level, and better understand himself. Running itself seems to be a form of expression for Kakeru: the very first time he felt pure joy in running as a child, he was sprinting across a fresh field of snow, his steps leaving a trail of patterns behind him, like words on a blank page.

Translation is also a hunt for words, an endeavor to convey something as elusive as the experience of reading a story in another language. Like a very sedentary ekiden, the translator takes the tasuki—the spirit of the book—from the author and, after many months of living with the characters, passes it on to the editor. After several turns of passing it back and forth, the tasuki then travels via everyone who is involved in turning a manuscript into a book on the shelves and eventually reaches the next reader, forming new connections.

Miura's writing has a warmth and an openness, though it's hard to put a finger on what exactly gives it that feeling. Her all-embracing love for human beings and their everyday lives, in all their messy glory, seems to seep through her words and touch us, too. Her characters come alive on the page, each possessing their own past and future. As readers, we are pulled into that embrace, and, like the spectators of the Hakone Ekiden, we feel absorbed in the Chikusei-so team's endeavor as if we were running alongside them ourselves.

My general stance in translating this novel was to prioritize the momentum of the story, the feel of each character (and their relationships, with all the banter), and the authenticity of the language revolving around running. At the same time, I wanted to retain as many Japanese terms as possible, and in a way that allows curious readers to look things up. After all, it's perfectly natural to come across unfamiliar words or concepts while reading any book, no matter the language it was originally written in. Luckily, it's easier than ever to find out what an engawa or a kamaboko looks like, or what a higurashi sounds like. Of course, there are many English videos and articles about the real-life Hakone Ekiden as well, packed with as much human drama as the story of the Chikusei-so team.

While *Run with the Wind* is already a familiar title to fans of the anime adaptation, also available in English, the Japanese title is *Kaze ga tsuyoku fuiteiru*, or "the wind is blowing hard." As Miura writes in an essay, the title came to her when she heard an announcer say a similar phrase on a Hakone Ekiden broadcast.* Charged with the sense of dynamic movement (accentuated by the present imperfect), the title calls to mind the feel of wind on your skin mid-run, and how the Chikusei-so team overcomes adverse winds to scale their heights.

---

* Shion Miura, *Manā wa iranai: shōsetsu no kakikata kōza* (No Need for Manners: A Guide to Writing Novels), Shueisha, 2020.

Chikusei-so (竹青荘), which the residents fondly call Aotake (アオタケ or 青竹), is written with the kanji for *bamboo* (竹) and *blue* (青). The name conjures up an image of supple strength and youthful radiance. Bamboo is commonly regarded as a symbol of resilience: its green leaves endure through the winter (in Japanese, 青 can refer to blue or green depending on the context), and even when it bows under the weight of snow or strong winds, bamboo doesn't break. Bearing this old-fashioned, faintly nostalgic name, the dorm sets the perfect scene for a novel like this one, which anyone who knows Japanese would call a seishun (青春) story—in other words, a story of the dazzling springtime (春) of life, with all its youthful passions and pains. Bamboo grows strong, shooting up toward the blue sky.

The Chikusei-so residents follow their dream without holding anything back. Their bond, bound by the tasuki, forms the core of this novel. In words and in actions, Kiyose shows Kakeru that he is no longer alone: he is a member of the team, one of "us." The recurring friction between Kakeru and Sakaki, his teammate from senior high school, throws the special nature of this friendship into relief. Sakaki taunts Kakeru by asking him whether he is having fun running alongside his new "friends." Kakeru bristles at Sakaki's use of the word *nakama*, "friends," since the relationships between his high school teammates were a far cry from such friendship. As fans of manga such as *One Piece* and *Naruto* may already know, the word *nakama* has slightly different connotations than *friend* in English. Being a nakama is not just about mutual affection, but about joining hands and supporting each other toward a shared goal, often as part of a close team. (*Nakama* is sometimes rendered as *comrade* in English, though it has too much of an Orwellian ring to my ears.) Knowing these nuances could enhance the way Kiyose's words hit home: when a prying journalist interrogates Kakeru about his troubled past, Kiyose says in his defense, "He's a gifted athlete. More than that, he's a true friend we can trust." The word Kiyose uses here is *nakama*. For the first time, Kakeru has found his home base, a team who believes in him and waits for him at the finish line: Haiji, Nico, Yuki, Musa, Shindo, Jota, Joji, Prince, and King—every one of them indispensable. Instead of running away from something, Kakeru has found people he can run toward.

Throughout the book, Kakeru and Kiyose act as a guiding light for each other. The prologue begins with Kiyose absentmindedly looking for a shooting star in the night sky. Soon, a runner hurtles across his path and leaves a trail of light gleaming through the dark alleys: "Like the beacon cast by a lighthouse across a dark, raging ocean, the beam of light would unfailingly illuminate the path he was to take." This is not the only scene in which Kakeru's run is described as a streak of light, and the silver lines on the Kansei uniform evoke a shooting star. The same imagery returns at the end of the epilogue: "The light of conviction always shone inside the heart. The path was clear and bright: a narrow line stretching on through the dark." These sentences follow immediately after Kakeru's thoughts, but there is no pronoun to indicate whose heart it is, or who is seeing this path in the darkness. (Pronouns can be omitted in Japanese much more naturally than in English, the subject/object implied by context.) I made a conscious choice to keep it ambiguous in English, in order to harken back to Kiyose's discovery in the prologue, as well as to let the text suggest that it is both Kakeru and Kiyose who kindle that light in each other.

One conspicuous addition to the English edition is the epigraph of the song about Mount Hakone. The editor Alexa Frank and I decided to include my translation of it because Kiyose takes a line from the song—"*Mount Hakone is the most savage in the world*"—and uses it as a rallying cry. (The song's original title, by the way, is "Hakone hachiri," so strictly speaking, the distance of the journey is eight Japanese ri, not leagues—but *league* has a folkloric ring.) Not every Japanese reader would know the full verse either, but the epigraph sets the stage for the Chikusei-so team's reckless quest. The mountain itself comes to resemble a savage beast that can devour those who challenge it; it is also where the runners become fierce hunters.

Miura first had the idea for a Hakone Ekiden story right after the publication of her debut novel. She spent years researching the sport and the race, conducting numerous interviews, and developing the structure of the novel. The passionate voice of her words in this book makes the reader want to start moving, and I hope this translation carries that vitality forward.

Here ends Shion Miura's
Run with the Wind.

The first edition of this book was printed
and bound at Lakeside Book Company
in Harrisonburg, Virginia, in September 2024.

A NOTE ON THE TYPE

Released by the Compugraphic Corporation in 1979, Garth
Graphic was named after Compugraphic co-founder Bill
Garth. The font was originally based on the 1960s font
"Matt Antique" by John Matt, before being subsequently
reworked by Compugraphic staff designers Renee LeWinter
and Constance Blanchard. With its cupped serifs and cal-
ligraphic curves, Garth Graphic has a distinct pen and ink
sensibility. However, its precision makes it a reliable and
sturdy choice for printed matter.

HARPERVIA

An imprint dedicated to publishing international voices,
offering readers a chance to encounter other lives and other
points of view via the language of the imagination.